DREAM PALACE

DREAM PALACE

Amanda Moores

Carroll & Graf Publishers, Inc.
New York

First Carroll & Graf edition 1994

Carroll & Graf Publishers, Inc.
260 Fifth Avenue
New York, NY 10001

Library of Congress Cataloging-in-Publication Data is available.

Manufactured in the United States of America

For my father, Richard Moores,
and Joseph Helguera

I would build that dome in air,
that sunny dome! those caves of ice!
And all who heard should see them there.
And all should cry, Beware! Beware!
His flashing eyes, his floating hair!
Weave a circle around him thrice.
And close your eyes with holy dread.
For he on honey-dew hath fed,
And drunk the milk of Paradise.

—Samuel Taylor Coleridge, *Kubla Khan*

The eye, my dear, the wicked eye, has such a strict alliance with the heart, and both have such an enmity to the understanding. What an unequal union, the mind and body!

—Samuel Richardson, *Clarissa*

DREAM PALACE

PART I

ONE

The first time I saw Jim Wellman was the night he saved my life: December 18, 1970. I was fifteen years old.

That evening after supper, a soft winter evening when the fallen snow was only a shade lighter than the sky, my mother and I drove out in the country to buy our Christmas tree at Cantrell's nursery. Cantrell's sold the best trees in central Indiana, my father had always said, but we had never gone there while he was alive.

Long before we arrived, we could see the glow of their lights in the distance, rising in turquoise waves against the sky. We parked beside a gold El Camino with a broken taillight and oversized rear wheels. There were no other cars in the lot.

Under the flickering Christmas bulbs strung along the top of the cyclone fence, everything was blue: the blue-black earth clotted with blue-white snow in the cornfield behind the parking lot, the dozens of dark-blue trees, the gray-blue wisp of smoke hanging motionless above the tiny wooden shack—even the shack itself looked like a square of blue velvet. The air was heavy with the scent of cut pine.

A brown-haired boy of about thirteen came out of the shack. His cheeks had reddened from the jawbone upward, and his eyes and the downy groove of flesh beneath his nose glistened from the cold. He was wearing a nylon windbreaker under an army jacket.

"I was just going to lock up, ma'am," he said to my mother,

his breath rising in quick puffs. "I don't know why, but it's real dead tonight. What kind of tree you looking for?"

"The best one," I said. "The strongest and most beautiful one of all."

The boy turned to me and smiled. "We got a lot of good ones—that's for sure." He followed us without speaking down a long row of trees, occasionally stopping to pull a fallen tree upright and shake the snow from its branches.

By itself, near the end of the row, stood a tall balsam. I squeezed my mother's arm. "How about this one, Mom?"

"I think so. It's lovely."

"You got that right, ma'am. There's nothing wrong with this tree," the boy said, dragging it through the powdery snow that glittered pale sapphire beneath the lights. "A lot of folks looked at it, but it was just too big for them."

He laid the tree down just outside the shack. "To me, there's only one tree that makes a prettier Christmas tree than a balsam—a blue spruce is your perfect tree. But it's bad luck to kill them. My dad says God don't want to see them killed for His son's birthday. That'll be fifteen dollars even."

"I think your father's right," Mother said. "Maybe it's wrong to kill any tree."

"No, ma'am, not any tree." He laughed. "I'm not trying to talk myself out of business. This tree is meant for you."

"Yes, I believe it is," she said, opening her purse.

He stamped his feet and rubbed his arms before he leaned down to pick up the tree. "I'll get her in the Dart for you, ma'am."

The boy switched off the lights along the fence when my mother pulled out of the parking lot. As we reached the end of Cantrell's drive, he roared past us in his El Camino and down the highway.

"It's funny," I said, "but when I was a little girl, I always thought it was snowing the night Jesus was born. It must be from that paperweight I used to have, but I still see snowflakes on the Wise Men's beards when I think about Christmas, like that's part of the miracle—snow in the desert."

My mother smiled. "You know, it's such a pretty night, I think we'll take a longer way home." She drove across the highway and turned into a narrow two-lane road.

"Mom, remember last summer when you let me drive a couple of times? You said—"

"I'm not going to let you drive now, Laurie, so kindly forget it."

"Please, Mom. That boy at Cantrell's is not even as old as I am, and he was driving a *truck*. I'd go really slow, and there's no snow on the road or anything."

"Absolutely not."

"All right. I just thought it would be an early Christmas present, that's all." I turned on the car radio. We passed drifted signposts and mailboxes and a couple of farmhouses set back from the road, their windows warm rectangles of light.

"Anyway, we sure found a beautiful tree, didn't we? Won't Grace love it?" I said.

"I'm sure she will, especially if we have it all decorated before Uncle Leland brings her back." My sister Grace, eight years old, was visiting our cousins in Indianapolis for a few days.

"Maybe this could be your second favorite—I mean, next to your candle tree."

"Maybe."

Before my mother and father were married, she told him once that she had always wanted to see a Christmas tree lighted like her great-grandmother's trees; and their first Christmas together, when they were renting an old frame house in Indianapolis, my father had surprised her with a tree ablaze with white candles. He had filled every pot and pan and bowl in the house with water and placed them around the tree.

"That was the loveliest sight I've ever seen," Mother said. "I'll never forget it as long as I live."

"Whenever Dad told the story, he always said that the water looked so beautiful."

"Oh, honey, it was. The light from the candles made tiny moons in the pans—little pools of light—and your father was standing beside me surrounded by all those shining pools, and I couldn't say anything—not even thank you—and then he kissed me." That was where the story had always ended before, but this time she went on: "And we lay down right there, Laurie, right under the tree next to all those pots and pans, and we didn't dare close our eyes. . . ." Her voice trailed off and she stared out at the road.

Elvis's "Blue Christmas" came on the radio and I sang along.

Before the song was over, she pulled the car over to the side of the road, turned off the engine, and handed me the keys.

I drove slowly down the dark road, the steering wheel still cold in my grip, remembering the summer afternoons when Grace and I had packed picnic lunches and ridden our bicycles out from town and onto a road like this one, the sunlight on our legs, our faces wet in the oven-hot wind, past patches of Queen Anne's lace and flurries of pale yellow butterflies in the long grass. Now, except for the golden glow of our headlights on the snow by the roadside and the illuminated blur of the asphalt ahead, everything was black.

"Switch the station. Okay, Mom?"

I didn't see the ice until I was too close to do anything except keep going, and then we were spinning around in a circle and my mother was screaming "Turn into it!" But it was already too late. The car was out of control, fishtailing to the other side of the road, pushing through the hardened strip of plowed snow on the shoulder, and then bumping backward down the slight incline until it stopped, lights on, the engine still running.

Mother turned off the radio and lit a cigarette, the collar of her nurse's uniform gleaming white in the sudden glare of the match. "I can't believe this! I don't know what I was thinking, letting you drive. I really don't know."

"Oh, God, Mom—I'm sorry."

"I know you're sorry, Laurie, but right now we have to think. Let me move over there."

The temperature had dropped at least ten degrees since we left Cantrell's, and the sky was clear; and as I walked around the car to the other side, the cold air burned my face and neck. The moment I got into the car, my mother put her foot down on the accelerator and the back wheels made a sound like howling.

"Just what I was afraid of—I can't move it! Damn it, Laurie, I don't know what to do."

"I'm so sorry."

She moved close to me, pressing her cheek against mine. "Oh, honey, come on now, don't cry."

"I should never have kept asking you—you didn't want me to. I'm never going to drive again."

"Oh, don't say that—it's a special night, honey. And surely someone will come along soon. It's not that late."

She turned off the engine and we waited, listening to the silence.

She had wiped the windshield clear with her mitten several times, but each time it had misted over again after a few minutes, streaked with tiny beads of water that glittered like strands of jewels in the pale light. I kept looking over at my mother smoking in the dark beside me and through her window at a clump of tall, dead milkweed stalks outside. I could hear ice cracking in the branches of trees somewhere behind us.

Through the misty glass, the approaching car at first resembled a black heart floating slowly closer, its broad flanks pierced by two silver shafts of light. The car came to a stop at the curve in the road and a tall man got out, the exhaust billowing around him as if he were standing on clouds. As he walked toward us, I knew what my mother was thinking—a young woman had been raped and strangled by a stranger when her car had run out of gas near Posey a few months earlier. My mother rolled down the window a couple of inches.

"Are you all right in there?" the man asked, leaning down. "Nobody hurt, I hope?"

"No," my mother said in a strained voice. "We're just a little cold."

"Looks like you ladies could use some help."

"Yes, I'm afraid we could."

"How long have you been here?"

"I don't really know—a while."

"I can believe that. Nobody uses this road anymore. Where were you headed?"

"Back to Catalpa."

"I'm going there myself." He smiled gently. "Look, ma'am, I know if my mom got stuck somewhere out in the country like this, she'd be a little scared too, but believe me, I'm going to get you both home safe and sound."

"Oh, thank you. You're very kind."

"By the way, I'm Jim Wellman. Catalpa's my home, too."

"Well, I'm very glad to meet you, Jim Wellman." My mother unrolled the window the rest of the way down and he shook her mittened hand. "I'm Marian Longstreet, and this is my daughter, Laurel."

"Hi," I said. My mouth was so cold that my lips stuck to my teeth as I smiled back at him.

"Hi, Laurel." He looked again at my mother. His face was oddly familiar, and then I knew where I had seen it before: it was the face of Zephyr blowing pink roses over the emerging Venus in Botticelli's painting—the same straight, slightly up-turned nose, the same pensive, blue-white eyes; only Jim's hair was dark, densely dark like trees at night in the summer, and his lashes were inky and long.

"Now don't worry, Mrs. Longstreet. I'll get you out."

"Thank you."

"But you'll have to let me in the car first."

My mother laughed. "Oh, of course." She unlocked the door and he got into the car.

"Boy, it sure smells like Christmas in here. Did you get your tree out at Cantrell's?"

"Yes," she said. "We found a beautiful tree."

"A beautiful tree for two beautiful ladies. Well, let's try it." He hit the gas hard and the back wheels threw up a short spray of ice, spinning against the frozen ground.

"She's in there pretty good. We're going to have to get out and push." He leaned forward so that he could see me past my mother. "How about it? You feeling strong tonight, little girl?"

"Yes."

"Good. Mrs. Longstreet, you don't mind if I have a smoke first, do you?"

"Of course not. I think I'll have one myself."

I had been sneaking cigarettes from her purse since the summer and she must have known, because she shook one loose from her pack of Silva Thins and offered it to me.

Even commingled with the odors of tobacco and pine, I could distinguish Jim's scent, sweet and fresh like bread and butter; and as we smoked, I couldn't stop looking at his fingers, tanned and immaculate, resting on the steering wheel.

"Are you ready?"

"Yes," I said.

"Mrs. Longstreet, you sit here, and when I yell to you, you do what I tell you. Eventually, you're going to drive it straight that way and then back onto the road. Just go with it and don't stop until I say so. Okay?"

My mother nodded.

"All right," Jim said. "Let's get to gettin'."

I stood a few feet from him, ankle deep in the snow, but I wasn't cold. Whenever Jim called out to my mother to give the car gas, we would push and rock the car forward for a few inches, the tires spewing dirty snow on us, until he told her to stop.

"Take a break."

"I think we're pretty close," I said, but my voice sounded so thin and strange and breathless that I wished I hadn't spoken.

"Real close." He reached inside his unbuttoned shearling coat and pulled out his box of Winstons. "But you sure picked a cold night for a driving lesson."

"How did—"

"How did I know?" He smiled. "Come over here and put your hands around this match for me."

He leaned down to my cupped hands, the flame of the match glowing through my pink wool gloves like a golden-pink rose. Now his face reminded me of an angel's—not an angel who sings hymns and hallelujahs in heaven, but one of the warring angels—beautiful and intolerant and loyal and angry, like Saint Michael.

"Hey, you look pretty out here in the night, little girl. You really do."

"Oh, no, I don't. I look terrible."

"You're crazy. With those big brown eyes, and that long silky hair? Just like a little model." He threw his cigarette into the snow.

Suddenly, the silver light of the stars seemed to scatter as a freezing gust of wind struck at the trees, the cars, the snow, and the road. It blew strands of Jim's dark hair across his forehead and threw me against the trunk of the car. Then the wind died away, and except for the sounds of the two idling cars and a distant train, it was quiet again.

"Jesus, where do you think that came from?"

"Nowhere," I said.

"It sure did. Out of nowhere." He kicked at the hard snow with his boot. "Don't worry about this. We've just about got it. Everything in this world is just a matter of timing and touch."

"Everything?"

"Everything. How about you just sit up here on the bumper,

Laurel. Give us a little traction. There, just like that." He braced himself against the left rear fender, close to me. "All right, Mrs. Longstreet, this is it!"

"Okay!"

When she accelerated, Jim drew his breath in sharply and pushed hard and the car began to ease away under its own power. I hopped down and stood beside him.

"Keep going! Keep going, Mrs. Longstreet!" The car moved across the snow and up to where the shoulder and road became level.

Jim reached into his coat for a cigarette and smiled. "What did I tell you?"

Jim's black car stayed a short distance ahead of us as we drove home. Its rear window had fogged over, but I stared at the spot where I knew the back of his head would be. I imagined Jim in our living room, laughing as he reached up to attach my great-grandmother's carved German angel to the top of our Christmas tree; and later I would sit beside him in front of the fire, gazing into his snow-blue eyes, and my mother would go up to bed and leave us alone, and I wouldn't be afraid, and we would lie down right there, together under the tree.

"I'm glad it was Jim who found us," I said.

"Yes, I'm very grateful to him."

"I'm so sorry, Mom. I don't want to drive again. I mean it— never."

"Well, I don't know about that, but I do know you're not driving again until you have your beginner's permit and it's a little nicer outside. That boy up there may have saved our lives tonight. There's a good chance no one else would have come along."

"I know. How old do you think he is?"

"Too old for you."

"But how old do you think?"

"Oh, I'm not sure. I think he seems older than he really is. I'd say he's in his early twenties."

"Don't you think he's the handsomest man you've ever seen, Mom?"

"Well, he certainly is handsome." She rapped the steering wheel sharply with her hand. "Laurie, I just thought of something. I'll bet that house on Pennsylvania Avenue is his parents' house. You know which one I mean, with the slate roof and stained glass windows."

"And all the big trees in front?"

"Yes, that one. Remember I showed you an article in the paper about it? Ulysses S. Grant spent the night in that house on his way to Washington."

"But why do you think it's Jim's house?"

"Because the woman who owns it is named Wellman, the same as an author I like who writes about the Civil War. I'll bet you, Laurie, that's his house."

"Mom, that's where the snake lady lives!" I remembered her, tall, her yellow hair pulled back in a tight ponytail, standing on the steps in her pale green dress, and the boys in the grass holding out their bare arms to her, the snakes dangling limply from their hands.

"What are you talking about, Laurie? What do you mean— the snake lady?"

"Well, when I was about ten, the boys in the neighborhood called her that because she had a lot of garter snakes in her yard. She paid them a dollar for every one they killed. They would hit the snakes' heads against the sidewalk."

"God, that's terrible!"

"It didn't kill the snakes, Mom—it just knocked them out. And after she paid the boys, they would throw the snakes back in her yard. Craig Spencer told me that I should always walk on the other side of the street because the yard was full of crazy snakes."

"Well, I guess it was. That's an awful story, Laurie."

"I know. Maybe that woman just lived there. Maybe she wasn't Jim's mother at all."

"I'm sure she wasn't."

"Mom, don't you think we should invite Jim in? For tea or a drink or something? I mean, to thank him. Don't you think we should?"

"Of course I do," she said, smiling at me. "I was just thinking the same thing."

We never had a chance to ask him. When we reached the intersection of Route 23 and Tecumseh Avenue, he honked his horn twice, and waving to us through his unrolled window, drove off toward Hillwood.

TWO

For the rest of that winter and spring, I walked by the Wellman house nearly every day after school, but I never saw Jim. On quiet nights before bed, I told my sister everything I could remember about how he had saved Mother and me, and sometimes on weekends she and I would walk by his house together.

One May afternoon I stayed after class to paint backdrops for our sophomore production of *The Crucible*. On my way home, I saw a faint blue light in one of the downstairs windows of the Wellman house.

Almost as if I were being pulled by the house itself, I found myself moving through the beige-green grass and dead weeds in the yard and beneath the branches of the black locust and blue spruce trees that half smothered the front of the house.

The sky, patched with plum and greenish gold, seemed immeasurably far above me. I was standing about two yards from the window. The dark trees were still, as if their leaves were made of bronze. Not even the stiff brown geranium husks stirred in the window box. I moved closer and looked into the room.

In the middle of a long table stood an enormous pewter vase filled with withered white gladioli that appeared pale blue in the light from the television set. The vase was surrounded by dirty glasses and cups, their rims stained and clouded with lipstick, a few large ashtrays overflowing with cigarette butts, and stacks of books and unopened mail. Beyond the table, near the charcoal-colored wall, I could see a dove-gray sweater draped over the back of a blue velvet chaise longue. A crystal chandelier hung above the table, its prisms, ambered with smoke and grime, glowing dully in the slanted rays of the early evening sun.

As I turned to leave, a sudden shaft of light fell across the wooden floor, and the snake lady walked into the room. She set the drink she was carrying on the table and lit a cigarette. I knew instantly that she was Jim's mother—her deepset blue eyes were shaped exactly like his—and my heart began to pound as if I were seeing Jim himself. Mrs. Wellman kicked off her high wedgie shoes and stood barefooted in front of the television set, cool and beautiful in her white slip, her flesh tinged the yellow of ivory or ancient marble; and in the flickering light from the screen her lipstick was the color of old blood.

It was a hot, blue-and-gold day in late July, and the sun, slipping in and out of immense white columns of clouds, threw odd-shaped shadows and bright shimmering light on the cement deck where Grace and I lay belly down, wet and shivering, our arms pressed closely against our sides. Above our heads I could hear the plastic pennants at the top of the diving tower flapping wildly on their guy wires.

When I was very young, my father would swim with me out near the diving tower to what I called "the deep deep." The water there, unlike the sparkling turquoise of the rest of the pool, was opaque, dark blue, and mysterious. At the count of three, we would take a deep breath and go underwater, my father holding me tightly in his arms, spinning us around and around; and when I opened my eyes, stinging in the chlorinated water, I could see his blurred face surrounded by white bubbles, heavy white bubbles that seemed to be pulling him down, down to the bottom.

My mother usually waited for us by the side of the pool, dipping her feet in the water, her chocolate-colored swimsuit making her seem even tanner than she actually was. But some-times when my father brought me back from the deep deep, she would be swimming in one of the practice lanes, and he always stopped, holding me against his chest, and watched her—the graceful, effortlessly rhythmic strokes, the rapt, serious expres-sion on her face; and when she had finished swimming and was walking back through the shallow water, he would smile, his eyes never leaving her.

Grace, as usual, was already asleep. The hypnotic drumming sound of the pennants made me feel sleepy, too, and I turned onto my side and looked up at the grassy incline leading to the pool that was known in my family simply as "the hill." It was the last day of the county fair, and from the hill you could see the highest rides on the midway, the Sky Diver and the double Ferris wheel, rolling above the dark, misty trees in the park.

Half closing my eyes, I could make out several families sitting on towels near the beige brick refreshment stand. I turned over to my other side, leaving behind a steaming, misshapen shadow of myself the color of sand, the sun on my eyelashes edging my field of vision with tiny irregular shapes as iridescent as insect wings, and then, not more than fifteen feet away from me, I saw Jim Wellman.

Arms above his head, he was leaning against the cyclone fence that encircled the pool, staring out at the glittering water, his eyes appearing almost white against the deep tan of his face. He was wearing faded blue jeans and he had a white towel around his bare, muscular shoulders. A brown-haired girl with big sunglasses was standing beside him, combing her hair with a pink rattail comb. Her pale pink sleeveless blouse, worn unbuttoned over her black tank suit, was spotted with water. Her shoulders were burned a deep rose.

"Grace," I whispered, "Grace." She didn't stir.

A curly haired man walked over to Jim and the girl and started talking to Jim through the fence. I couldn't hear what they were saying, but they were both laughing. The girl moved a few feet away from Jim, still combing her hair, and he released his grip on the fence and reached for her. He pulled her close to him, and I could see her breasts moving rapidly up and down as she breathed, standing next to him, smiling up at him. I couldn't stand to see her smiling, and I closed my eyes, feeling the blood pulsing through my body. When I opened them again, the curly haired man was gone and Jim and his girlfriend were walking down the sidewalk toward the fair.

The next morning I bought a pale pink sleeveless blouse at Pretty Miss, and for the rest of that summer I combed my hair with a rattail comb.

*   *   *

Late one afternoon the following October, when our house was
permeated with the autumn smells of apples and marigolds and
burning leaves, I was lying on my bed talking to Grace when
the telephone rang. Paula Lake spoke quickly, softly running her
words together, her voice strained and sweet.

"Oh, Laurie—I'm so glad you're there! I need to know if there
is *any* way you could baby-sit tonight. I wouldn't ask you with
so little notice if it weren't important."

"I'd like to, Mrs. Lake, but I can't. I have a big French test
tomorrow, and—"

"You could study over here. The boys will be good, and they've
already promised me they will go to bed for you without any
trouble."

"Oh, it's not that. They're never any trouble, Mrs. Lake. But
I really have to—"

"I'll be happy to pay you twice what I usually do."

"Thank you, but I honestly can't."

"Honey, it's just that he's leaving tomorrow for California to
go to diving school, and I won't see him again for six months."

"Diving school?"

"Yes, he's going to be a deep-sea diver."

I laughed. "Jack? A deep-sea diver?"

"No, not Jack. I'm not seeing Jack anymore. It's Jim who's
going away. Jim Wellman."

I sat up in bed. "Jim *who*?"

"Jim Wellman. Do you know him? Oh, Laurie, he has the
biggest baby-blue eyes you ever saw—he really does—and I just
have to see him tonight. I want to give him his going-away
present."

Grace was frowning and waving her hands at me. "Who is it,
Laurie?" she whispered. "Is it *your* Jim?"

I shook my head and closed my eyes. "Oh, what did you get
him?" I asked, trying to sound nonchalant.

"I bought him a religious medal." She laughed. "You know
I'm not religious, Laurie, but I couldn't resist. I wanted to get
him a Saint Christopher's medal but the saleswoman told me
Saint Erasmus was what I wanted. He's the patron saint of sailors. I'm going to make him promise me he'll wear it every time
he goes diving."

A warm wave of nausea made me so dizzy I fell back onto
the bed.

"Are you sure you can't come tonight? It would only be for a couple of hours, and I would consider it a real favor."

"Then of course I will."

"You will? Oh, that's wonderful! Thank you, honey! Do you think you could be here in half an hour? Would that be too soon?"

"No, that's fine."

"I'll see you in a half hour, then. And thanks again, Laurie. You saved my life."

Through the sheer white curtains of Paula Lake's front window I could see Jim Wellman standing, hands on hips, in the driveway, staring down at his idling motorcycle. The sound of the engine was so low and loud that everything, even Jeremy's small hand grasping my skirt, seemed to be vibrating.

Jim let the motorcycle run until I thought I could hear my own heartbeat over the noise; and then he turned off the engine, lit a cigarette, and stood as motionless as a statue in the fading afternoon light, head held high, only his eyes moving slowly over the front of the house.

"Who is it, Laurie?" Paul, who was only three years old, asked. "I want to see, too."

I picked him up and held him so close that I could feel his little heart pounding—almost as fast as my own. Jeremy pressed the side of his face against my thigh.

"Who is it, Laurie? I can't see."

"It's your mother's friend—Jim."

"It's Jim! It's Jim!" they both shouted.

"Sssssh," I whispered.

"Let Jim in," Paul said. "He's our friend. Come on, Laurie!"

"I'll do it," Jeremy said. He let go of my skirt and reached up for the doorknob.

The faint, bitter odor of burning leaves filled the hallway. I ducked behind the open door and wiped Mrs. Lake's Palomino Pink from my mouth with the back of my hand, afraid he might recognize the color and know I was wearing her lipstick.

"He's throwing away his cigarette," Jeremy said, and then Jim Wellman was standing in the doorway, looking past me into the hall.

"Hi," he said, brushing his hair back with his hand.

I couldn't speak.

"Hey, boys. How you doing?"

"Hi, Jim," they said together softly, strangely shy.

He patted Jeremy's head. "Is your momma upstairs?"

"Yes," Jeremy said.

"Paula!" Jim started up the bare wooden stairs, taking two steps at a time.

"I'm not ready," she called down.

"Well, I am!" They both laughed.

He turned at the landing and disappeared from view. It was too quiet at the top of the stairs and I knew they were kissing. The gold-flecked air whirred around me, and the floor seemed to move beneath my feet. I leaned against the newel post and closed my eyes. *You look pretty out here in the night, little girl. You really do.* I heard Mrs. Lake laugh and the sound of their footsteps as they walked down the hallway to her bedroom.

"Laurie!" Paul was tugging at my skirt. "What's wrong, Laurie?"

"Nothing, honey."

"Come on, Laurie, let's play," Jeremy said.

"Yes!" Paul said, clapping his hands. "Come on!"

I followed them into the living room.

"Lie down, Laurie," Jeremy said, pointing to the tobacco-colored corduroy sofa. "Please."

"Why do you want me to lie down?"

"So we can tie you up."

"Well, all right, but I don't see any ropes."

"They're invisible ropes."

"Yeah, 'visible," Paul said.

"Okay. But do my legs first. And be very quiet." I lit one of Mrs. Lake's Salems. Through the picture window the chrome tailpipe of Jim's motorcycle gleamed like a mirror above the gravel in the driveway.

"Laurie, could you come up here for a minute?"

"Time out, guys. Your mother's calling me," I said, standing up.

"You can't go!" Jeremy said. "You're tied up!"

"I know. That's why I'm taking little steps." I hobbled into the foyer and climbed the stairs to the landing. Mrs. Lake was standing in the upstairs hallway, leaning over the banister. She was still wearing her jade-green kimono, and her short brown hair was tousled and damp.

"I'm sorry, Laurie." She scrunched up her button nose. "It's taking me a little longer than I expected to get ready, so could you please make sure and keep the boys downstairs?"

She looked younger than I had ever seen her. Her large dark eyes were even wider than usual, with a strange, soft, drowned expression in them.

"Yes—of course." My voice sounded unusually high-pitched, girlish, and I wondered if he could hear me.

"Thank you, dear. Oh, there's angel food cake—and cigarettes on the coffee table, if you want any."

"I already smoked one. I hoped you wouldn't mind."

"You know I don't ever mind, honey. I have a carton."

"I ran out," I said, so that if Jim was listening he wouldn't think that I couldn't smoke at home. "Thank you."

"No, Laurie," Mrs. Lake said in a lower voice, "thank *you.*" The floor creaked beneath her bare feet as she walked back to her bedroom.

I went into the living room and sat down on the sofa. The boys complained that they were hot, and I helped them take off their white terry-cloth bathrobes.

"You guys sure do have cute pajamas."

"Mom made them," Paul said, climbing onto my lap.

"Well, I wish I had something like that for sleeping."

"Maybe my mom could make you some, too," Jeremy said.

Paul got down from my lap, and, standing in front of me, spread his legs apart and held his arms out from his sides.

"You look like a star in the Milky Way," I said. "A little yellow star."

"I can do a star dance," Paul said, extending his arms and twirling around the room.

"And Jeremy, you would look like a blue star if you held your arms out, too."

"No, mine's a moon suit. I'm doing a moon dance." He began to dance around his younger brother, holding his arms up to form an awkward crescent shape that made him scuttle sideways.

"Jeremy's a blue moon," I said, and they laughed.

"Dance with us," Paul said.

"Okay, but I don't have to move very much because I'm the sun."

They began to circle me, moving rhythmically as if they heard music.

"Here we are," I said. "The sun, the moon, and a star, dancing to the music of the spheres."

As we danced, the Lakes' pregnant black cat rubbed her head against my legs and then weaved in and out between them, mewing to be fed.

"Look!" Paul said. "Zorro's dancing, too!"

We danced until Jeremy had a stitch in his side; then we went into the kitchen and I fed the cat and smoked a cigarette while the boys ate angel food cake with their fingers.

Then they wanted to play hide-and-seek, and we all agreed that I should be "it" because I could count the highest. I could hear Jim and Mrs. Lake upstairs talking, and I went into the living room and turned on the television set.

"No, Laurie, don't turn it on—it won't be scary. It's not even dark yet," Jeremy said. "Please?"

I flipped off the set and went over the rules of the game with them; then they ran away and I returned to the kitchen to count to one hundred. I covered my ears as I called the numbers out so that I wouldn't hear the sounds upstairs.

"Ninety-eight, ninety-nine, one hundred! Here I come, ready or not!"

But I didn't look for them right away. I pushed up the sleeve of my cardigan sweater and kissed myself deep in the crook of my arm, pretending, as I had pretended many times over the last ten months, that I was kissing Jim Wellman. I heard footsteps in the upstairs hallway and then the door of the linen closet being opened. I pulled down my sleeve and waited. The house was silent.

I smoked a cigarette in the living room before I searched the screened-in porch. "I have looked everywhere!" I said in a loud voice. "I just don't know where else they could be!"

There was no laughter, no scuffling noises—only silence. And then I heard a sound. At first, I thought it was the soughing of the wind in the oak tree outside the window; but as I went into the dining room, the sound became louder, and I realized that it was the upstairs shower. I walked into the bathroom and sat down on the black plush-covered toilet seat, my shoulder brushing against the black plastic curtain. The sound was directly above me now, and when I heard Jim's voice, the words indistinguishable, I put my face in my hands and started to cry.

"Surprise!" The shower curtain jerked forward. The two boys

were sitting in the bathtub. Paul started crying, too, and I picked him up and sat him on my lap. Jeremy got out of the tub by himself.

"Oh, no, sweetie—don't you cry. I didn't mean to make you cry." I wiped Paul's cheeks with a ball of pink toilet paper and then I wiped my own.

Jeremy stood beside me, stroking a thin frond of the palm that fanned up and out of a lacquered black pot next to the bathtub. "But why are you crying, Laurie?"

"Oh, because—because you boys hid so well. I was afraid I couldn't find you at all, and I thought, what will I tell their mother? That I lost her boys in their own home?"

They were laughing now, and Jeremy stopped stroking the plant and began stroking my hair.

"But, boys, I have to ask you a favor. Please don't tell your mother I was crying. She might think I'm a *baby*."

"We won't," Jeremy said solemnly.

"We won't," Paul echoed.

"It's a deal, then," I said, shaking their small hands.

I left the boys lying on their stomachs in front of the fireplace drawing crayon pictures of Jim's motorcycle and went into the bathroom. I studied my face in the mirror. My eyelids were pink and slightly swollen from crying, so I splashed cold water on my face and patted it dry with a towel. When I was brushing my hair I thought I heard someone coming down the stairs. I held my breath and listened, the hairbrush still against my temple. Then the vibrating noise started outside again, and I hurried into the living room. Mrs. Lake was kneeling beside the boys, holding their drawings in her hands. She was wearing the cream-colored suede boots that Mr. Lake had bought her when he was on sabbatical in Italy.

"Oh, I like the flames coming out the back," she was saying to Jeremy. She had to speak loudly to be heard above the roar of the motorcycle.

"Aren't they good?" I said.

"They really are." She turned, her long silver and amethyst earrings dangling against her flushed cheeks. "I love your outfit, Laurie. You look so pretty in that shade of blue. You didn't break a date to sit for me tonight, did you?"

"No, I didn't."

"I'm glad."

"We had angel food," Paul said.

"Well, did you now?"

"Laurie didn't feel good, so we got her cake. We shared it," Jeremy said.

"Oh, honey, aren't you feeling well?"

"I'm all right. It's just cramps."

"Oh—okay. Well, there's aspirin in the bathroom if you need any, and I hope you feel—"

"Paula!" Jim yelled from the front yard. "Come on! Let's get to gettin'!"

"I'd better go. He's starving. We'll be at the Hunt Room if you need me for anything." She tied the belt of her bulky Peruvian sweater and bent down and kissed the boys. "Mommy has to go now, darlings. Be good for Laurie."

"We will," Jeremy said.

"I know you will, and, honey—thank you," she said, kissing me with the same soft, wet mouth that had kissed Jim Wellman.

I waited until I could no longer hear his motorcycle before I took the boys upstairs. They followed me into their mother's bedroom. Mrs. Lake was a careless housekeeper, so I was surprised at how meticulously the king-size bed was made, the corners squared, the white wool blanket smooth and tight. I sat down on the edge of the bed, the blanket taut beneath my legs, and I knew that Jim had made the bed.

"Turn the light on," Paul said. "Please."

"No," I whispered, "it isn't dark yet, not deep dark. It's twilight—see how everything is blue?"

"Yes!" And then both of them were on the bed with me. "It's blue! It's blue!"

"Boys," I said in a loud whisper, "listen. If we lie here very quietly, so quietly we can't even hear ourselves breathe, we can watch everything get bluer and bluer, and then—"

"And then it's dark," Paul said.

"Deep, deep dark." Jeremy patted me on the back.

"That's right, that's exactly right. But we have to be very quiet, boys."

We lay on the bed in silence. Glass wind chimes rang softly on the porch below us. My eyes adjusted to the darkening light, and I picked up the gold Saint Erasmus medal glimmering on the nightstand beside me. It felt warm in my hands and against my lips when I kissed it, and it left a taste on my mouth like salt.

In the dream my mother was calling my name, and when I opened my eyes, I thought for a few moments that I was in my room at home. I heard her coming up the stairs, and I got up from the bed.

"Laurie, honey?" she said as I walked into the hallway. "It's so late. I want you to go home now and get some sleep. I'll stay until Paula gets back."

"I'll stay, Mom. She'll be here soon."

"Honey, it's after midnight."

"Please."

"This is a school night, Laurie, and there's no telling when she'll be in."

"But, Mom—"

"Now don't argue with me. If we're going to get you into the University, you have to keep up your grades."

"My grades *are* good, Mom."

"I know, but they have to stay that way."

"Well, then, will you help me carry the boys to their room? They fell asleep in here on Mrs. Lake's bed."

My mother watched me walk the short block home from the Lake's front porch. In the misty, cold air, the tears felt hot on my cheeks.

I climbed the stairs carefully so that I wouldn't awaken Grace, but she wasn't asleep: she was standing barefooted in the hallway. In her pale nightgown she looked like a cherubic ghost, backlit by the light that seeped around the edges of the door to her room.

"Hurry, Laurie," she said, taking my hand. "I only fell asleep once."

She wanted me to tell her everything, but I didn't. I didn't tell her about Jim and Mrs. Lake kissing at the top of the stairs or about them taking a shower together.

"You mean you didn't say *anything* to him?" she asked.

"I just couldn't."

"And he *really* didn't know who you were?"

"No—he really didn't."

She sat straight up in bed, frowning. Tears shone like tiny diamonds in the corners of her dark, wide-opened eyes.

"Mrs. Lake is too old for him!"

"I know. She's ten years older than he is, at least. She's almost forty."

"And she's married!"

"She's separated—you know that."

"Well, she's still an old lady," Grace said more softly, and she was warm in my arms as I hugged her.

"Don't worry, Laurie—someday you'll be older, too."

I eased her back to her pillow. "Don't you worry—it doesn't matter that much," I said, straightening her blanket. "It doesn't."

I heard my mother unlocking the front door and I jumped up. "And don't you tell Mom about any of this. Promise?"

"I promise."

"Good." I kissed her on the cheek.

"I hate him, Laurie."

"Sssh—you go to sleep. It's late."

"Don't you hate him, too?"

"Yes," I whispered. "I hate him, too."

THREE

I didn't see Jim Wellman until five years later, on a warm winter night that seemed more like March than December. At seven-thirty in the evening, Jenny Caneer, my best friend in college, and I were standing in front of a gray, shingle-sided house on Duncan Road. Each of us was carrying a large cut-glass bowl of clam dip and a bag of potato chips. Up and down the street, Christmas bulbs blinked along the eaves and around the windows of the small square houses, bathing in bright prismatic color the hobby-shop wooden Santas and reindeer and créches staked down in the treeless yards.

Jenny rang the doorbell. Water dripped down steadily around us from the icicles that hung all along the gutters of the porch roof. Driven by a strong southerly wind, huge sfumato clouds swept across the moon, obscuring it for a moment, then revealing it, and then obscuring it again. Between the clouds a few stars glittered in the indigo blue sky.

"That's Orion," I said.

"Where? Oh, I thought that was the Big Dipper." Jenny rang the doorbell again.

"No, that's Orion. See the three stars—that's his belt. There's the Seven Sisters—the Pleiades—and over there," I said, pointing to the west, "I think that's part of Cygnus, the swan."

"How do you know all of them?"

"I don't know all of them, but my father did. I was so disappointed the first time he showed them to me. I thought they

24

would really look like pictures in the sky—like those dot-to-dot drawings we used to do when we were little. Remember?"

"Sure. I thought the exact same thing. You know, one time someone wanted to take a pen and draw lines between my freckles to see if they made a picture of anything."

"Who wanted to do that?"

"Well—Keith did." Keith was Jenny's boyfriend. They had been going together since ninth grade.

I reached over and lightly brushed a few wisps of red hair from the corner of her mouth.

"Did you let him?"

"Of course not! And even if they did make a picture, it probably would have been of a fat pig."

"Oh, come on, Jen—you look great. You've lost a lot of weight."

"Some."

"Isn't Keith coming to the party at all?"

"He said there was no way in hell he was going."

"Did you tell him Glenn said this isn't just a Christmas party— it's to celebrate Michelle's one-woman show?"

"I told him everything, Laurie. I really wanted him to see me all dressed up for once."

"I know, Jen, but no one gets dressed up anymore."

"Tell me about it." She rang the doorbell a third time. "Oh, what's keeping him?"

Glenn, Jenny's elder brother, opened the door. He wore a bright red, brass-buttoned vest over his green T-shirt. A sprig of mistletoe was Scotch-taped to the top of his head, his matted, brick-red hair lying flat around it.

"So you two made it," he said, closing the door behind us.

"We're not early, are we?" Jenny asked.

"No way. We've been partying down all afternoon." He held out his arms. "Give me your coats."

I looked over his shoulder into the small, crowded living room. Everyone at the party seemed to be at least five years older than Jenny and me. They were all casually dressed, even Michelle, Glenn's live-in-girlfriend, who had on white painter's pants and an old, aqua blue tropical shirt patterned with yellow palm trees and magenta fish. Jenny and I looked at each other. Beneath my raincoat I was wearing a low-backed, mauve satin dress my mother had made for me.

"I think I'll just keep my coat on for a while, Glenn," I said. "I'm a little cold." I took off the pearl and opal earrings that my father had given my mother on their wedding day and put them in the pocket of my coat.

"Cold! You kidding me, Laurie? It's like spring outside, and it must be at least a hundred in here. We can't shut these damn radiators off, and they keep cranking out the heat. Michelle's sinuses are a mess." He rubbed his small, bloodshot eyes. "And so are mine."

Jenny looked down at her new green suede pumps. "I think I'll keep my coat on, too."

Glenn shrugged. "Suit yourselves."

"Come on, Laurie," Jenny said, walking away. "Let's take these bowls to the kitchen."

Michelle was kneeling in front of a wooden speaker cabinet that was blaring out "Sympathy for the Devil." Eyes closed, her elbows propped on top of the cabinet and her chin in her hands, she sang along with the music. The music was so loud that some of the people in the living room seemed to be pantomiming speech, their voices inaudible, while others were almost screaming. I glanced at Michelle's framed photographs of blurred, amorphous shapes lining the walls: "Autumn Scherzo," "Paean to Siddhartha," "Holocaust Number Two."

In the kitchen three men in bell-bottom blue jeans and plaid flannel shirts were smoking a joint and throwing darts at a poster of Farrah Fawcett thumbtacked to the wall next to the refrigerator. They had stuck darts in her eyes and chest.

Jenny and I unwrapped our clam dip, set the bowls on platters that she took down from a cabinet above the sink, and surrounded them with potato chips.

"Hey, jailbait," one of the men said, staring at me, "why don't you come over here and take Farrah's place?"

They all laughed.

"We're both twenty-one," Jenny said, her face flushed, and they laughed again.

Michelle staggered into the kitchen.

"We brought clam dip," Jenny said to her.

Michelle fell into one of the red director's chairs near the table, knocking over an empty wineglass with her right arm; the glass smashed on the floor.

"Are you all right, Michelle?" Jenny asked.

Michelle folded her arms on the table, looked up at us for a moment wrinkling her small thin nose, and then dropped her face into her arms. Strands of her long dark hair fell into one of the bowls of clam dip.

The men laughed. "She's down for the count," one of them said.

"I'm going to find Glenn," Jenny said.

Glenn lifted Michelle up in the chair. "Hey, babe, you all right?" He shoved the bowls of clam dip towards Jenny. "Get this shit out of here!"

Jenny and I carried our platters into the dining room and stood beside a small circular oak table, unsure of where to put them.

"Gross," Jenny said, looking at a bowl of onion dip with a cigarette in it. She finally set down her platter between a mutilated ham on a blue carnival glass plate and a brown plastic bowl of deviled eggs. A fat bayberry-scented candle had fallen into the bowl of eggs and lay upside down in a pool of congealed green wax. The white paper tablecloth was soaked with red wine.

"What you got there?" The man had a long, oily nose and his dark brown, shiny hair was tied in a ponytail that hung halfway down his back.

"Clam dip," I said, putting my platter down next to a large untouched fruitcake.

He thrust a potato chip deep into my bowl, and, as he lifted it, a gob of dip spilled onto his linty, black corduroy Western shirt. He shoved the chip in his mouth.

"Not bad, but I like bearded clam better." He licked his thin lips and smiled. His teeth were caked with dip.

Jenny and I exchanged glances.

"You two been to Michelle's show at the Civic Center yet?"

"Not yet," I said.

"Yeah, me neither. Are you college girls, or you out in the real world?"

"We're students," I said. "Well, we were, but we graduated last week."

"Where from? Up at the college here?"

"Yes. Allison University."

"So what's your name?"

"Laurie. This is Jenny."

"Gary Lynch. I thought about going to the big U once myself,

but then I got a good gig making PA cabinets, so I didn't."
He scooped more dip out of the bowl. "So what'd you study
over there?"

"We both majored in painting," Jenny said.

"Oh, yeah?" He turned to me again. "Hey, you ever paint any
nude models?"

"Sometimes."

"No shit. Hell, maybe I should go back and study art my
ownself." He laughed. "So what're you girls going to do now
you're out of school?"

"Laurie's been saving money to go to New York. I guess I'll
be staying here in town for a while."

"New York?" he said. "I been there, and it's all a big nothing.
Dog shit everywhere and drinks cost a fucking fortune. And everybody makes such a deal of that crappy park, like those were
the only damn trees in the world. What do you want to live in
New York for?"

"Because it's the place to be for an artist, and Laurie *is* an
artist."

"So are you, Jenny."

"No, I just put paint on canvas. It's not the same thing."

"Yeah, well, you girls want a beer or something?"

"No, thanks."

"Oh, come on, it's a party. They might still have some champagne left."

"Beer is fine," Jenny said.

"Don't move. I'll be right back."

As soon as he walked away, Jenny grabbed my arm.

"Let's go into the other room."

We had made our way to the only empty space left in the living
room and were standing next to a scrawny Christmas tree strung
with pulsing red lights. Fallen needles lay in flat piles on the
floor beneath the tree.

"I'm so sorry, Laurie. I can't believe I practically had to beg
Glenn to invite us. I'm going upstairs and call Keith. I'll see if
he can come and pick us up."

"Are you sure you want to leave?"

"Yeah, I'm sure. I'll be right back."

"Put on the Eagles!" a thin girl with braids and a muddy
complexion yelled. " 'Hotel California'!"

In a corner on the other side of the tree, an obese woman wearing red crushed velvet bell-bottoms was lying on a black imitation leather beanbag chair, drinking champagne. Beside her a skinny, curly-haired man ran his hand slowly up and down inside one of her pant legs. The woman's eyes were glazed, gazing at nothing, as she stroked the man's head with her free hand.

Glenn walked over and kissed me hard on the mouth. "The mistletoe comes in handy," he said, moving on.

Now the skinny man was clutching one of the woman's huge breasts. I looked away and saw Gary making his way through the crowd.

"Here you go." He handed me a bottle of Budweiser. "Sorry it's warm."

"Thank you." I took a sip and set the bottle down on the windowsill.

"Hey, why don't you take off your coat? Stay awhile."

"I will in a minute. I'm still cold."

"No way you could be cold, babe. I'm sweating like a pig." He waved at the people in the corner. "Hey, Big Pat, how's it going?"

Big Pat looked over, raised her fist, palm inward, and slowly extended her middle finger.

"I guess I can see how it's going," Gary said, laughing. "Big Patty's a great girl." He leaned so close to me that I could smell his sour breath. "Hey, do you know why fucking a fat girl is like riding a moped?"

I didn't answer.

"Because they're both fun until your friends find out about it." He stepped back, nearly falling into the Christmas tree. "Don't you get it?"

"Get what?" Jenny asked, coming up to us. She glanced at the couple in the corner and rolled her eyes at me.

"Nothing important," I said.

"Keith can't get here for an hour," she said. "I'm sorry."

"That's all right. I can just call my mom."

"But Keith can give you a ride. Really, he doesn't mind."

"I know, but I don't think I can wait that long. I'm not feeling so great."

"I had it all wrong about the party. I'm sorry."

"Hey, don't worry about it. Everything's fine." I put my lips close to her ear. "It's just that I think my period started," I whispered, "and I don't have anything with me."

"Well, I'm sure Michelle does."

"No, that's okay, Jen. I think I'd better just go on home. You understand, don't you?"

"Sure, I understand." She looked down at her green suede pumps. "You can use the phone upstairs, but be real quiet—there are a couple of little babies asleep on the bed."

"I will."

"Oh, and Laurie, while you're up there, take a look at the spare bedroom and see what Michelle's done with it. You'll really appreciate it."

"Okay."

"Hey, you're not thinking of splitting yet, are you?" Gary said. "Come on, babe. It's not even eight."

"She's just going upstairs to use the bathroom. Right, Laurie?"

"Right," I said.

A poster of mad King Ludwig's castle was Scotch-taped to the door of the spare bedroom. The slender spires seemed to rise weightlessly above the tall firs and blue-green mists of Bavaria. I opened the door and flipped on a light switch.

Leafless white-painted branches interlaced with strings of tiny white lights leaned shoulder high against the four white walls. Standing on the pale beige carpet, I felt as if I were in the middle of an ice-covered pond with snowy birches grown up all around it; as if the tiny lights were stars, bright among the branches.

The room was warm—even warmer than downstairs, but it was a gentle warmth—moist and soft and balmy—and as I stood in the center of the room surrounded by the white branches, I imagined that the glittering lights were tropical blossoms, and the muffled noise of the party below was the sea breaking on a moonlit shore.

I took the earrings from my coat pocket: they glowed softly in the silvery light, like the water in the pots and pans around my mother's candle tree. I put on the earrings, then I slowly slipped my coat from my shoulders down to my elbows, and the air felt cool on my skin. I heard the door open and close but I didn't turn around.

"It's beautiful, Jenny," I said. "Almost magical—like a dream palace."

"Well, I don't know what Jenny thinks, but those sure are the right words. You're definitely beautiful, and I'm going to see what I can do about the magic part."

There was no mistaking his voice. I turned around. Jim's hair was longer now, and he had on a bone-colored duster like one I had seen Clint Eastwood wear in a Western movie. His eyes were the same—almost impossibly blue. He was holding a glass of champagne in his hand.

"I finally found you," he said. "I was afraid you'd already left the party."

"You were looking for me?"

"Absolutely. Anybody in their right mind would have been tracking you down. I saw you the second you walked into the party—if you want to call this a party. Hey, don't even think about putting that coat back on, little girl—it'd be a crime."

"But I feel stupid in this dress. Glenn said it was a special party, and I thought—"

"Well, it wasn't special but it is now. Here, give me your coat. There. Now you look like a real princess."

He folded my raincoat over his left arm. "I'm Jim Wellman—and you are?"

"Laurie. Longstreet."

"Well, pleased to meet you, Laurie Longstreet. Here, I brought you something." He held out the glass of champagne, mirrored and shimmering like mercury; and as I reached to take the glass, our arms and hands were outlined in silver.

"It's the last good champagne in the house. It's not the best, but it's a hell of a lot better than the swill they're uncorking down there now."

"Thank you," I said, taking a small sip.

"So, Laurie Longstreet, you from Indy?"

"No, I grew up here."

He shook his head, smiling. "Well, that's the best damned kept secret in Catalpa. I sure didn't realize there were any princesses in this podunk town."

"I know you—I mean, we've met before, but you probably don't remember it."

"I don't think so. Believe me, I would remember it."

"But we have. You're a deep-sea diver, aren't you?"

"Yeah, I am." He shook his head again. "There's just no way I would ever forget meeting you. I couldn't have been that drunk."

"Oh, I don't think you were drunk that night."

"Then I'd have to have been crazy—and, princess, I know I'm not crazy."

"Being a deep-sea diver must be dangerous."

"Hey, I'll tell you what's dangerous."

"What?"

"You are, little girl, with those big, brown eyes of yours. Dangerous—no other word for them."

"No, seriously."

"Okay, yeah, diving can be dangerous. That's why they pay you the big bucks. I've lost a few buddies over the years, but I've been crazy about diving ever since I saw *Sea Hunt* on TV." Jim folded his arms, slightly shaking his head. "Hell, my friend Bobby bought it just a few months ago when we were out in the North Sea. Evidently he didn't get a perfect seal on his helmet because of his beard. Now Caldwell Diving—that's the company I work for—has a rule we all have to be clean shaven."

"I'm sorry about your friend, Jim."

"Yeah, it's a pretty stupid way to die."

"I just can't imagine what it's like to be that far underwater."

"Well, it's pitch black, and you're usually high the whole time you're down there, so you have to concentrate real hard on every little thing you do."

"You mean you get high before you dive?"

He laughed. "No way, little girl. You're high on nitrogen. It's called 'rapture of the deep.'"

"It sounds beautiful."

"It's not beautiful, believe me. Sometimes a guy gets so confused he thinks he's *as*cending when he's really *de*scending. You know, he's actually going down deeper, and he just keeps going until he's dead."

"God, that's terrible!"

"Yeah. It doesn't happen real often, but it does happen." He smiled. "So let's talk about that time we met before. When did you say it was?"

I took another sip of champagne. "We met when you saved my life."

"Oh, I did, did I?"

"Yes, and my mother's, too. But you probably don't remember—it was six years ago. Six years almost to the night."

"No kidding?" He gave a short laugh. "Now exactly where did this mission of mercy take place?"

"Out in the country somewhere, near Cantrell's nursery. You had an old black car."

"Old black car? An old Cadillac?"

"I don't know. It looked old. I mean, it was shiny, but it looked old."

"Six years ago, huh? Then it had to have been that 1949 Caddy. I only had that car for a couple of months. Made some good money when I sold it, but I should have held on to it—ran like a champ." His voice trailed off, and he looked over at the sparkling white branches. "I sold it to get that damned Porsche, which was nothing but trouble from day one." He looked back at me. "So what happened then?"

"Well, our car had gone off the road. I was driving, and I didn't even have a beginner's permit. And then you came along and we pushed the car together. It took a pretty long time and you were smoking Winston cigarettes."

"Still do," he said, tapping the front pocket of his blue oxford-cloth shirt.

"I didn't think you'd remember."

"Now hold on here a minute, princess. It was snowing that night, right?"

"No, but it was awfully cold. You said we would have frozen to death if you hadn't found us."

He laughed. "Oh, I said that, did I?"

"Yes, you did—and it was true."

"Well, you know what this means, don't you, Laurie Longstreet?"

"No."

"In China or Japan or someplace like that, they say if you save someone's life, then that person owes you a life in return."

"Oh, that's what they say, is it?" I said.

"That's what they say."

"Who's 'they'?"

"Well, me. I say it."

"So you're saying I'm indebted to you."

"For a lifetime," he said, putting his hand over mine. "We only have one glass, but let's drink to that night. To the beginning of the end." He guided the glass to my lips, and a cold trickle of champagne ran down the side of my mouth and onto my chin. He wiped it off with his fingertips.

"The end?" I said, laughing.

"The end of us not being together. Hell it took six years for us to meet up again, and Laurie, I'm not letting you go easy." Taking the glass from my hand, he turned the stem between his thumb and forefinger until the smear of my Palomino Pink lipstick was in front of him; then he raised the glass to his lips and sipped.

"You know, Jim, I saw you again after that night—at Paula Lake's house. I was baby-sitting her two little boys."

"No kidding! When was that?"

"Just before you got into diving school in California."

"Got in? Anybody with the dough can get in. It's what you do with your training when you get out that makes you a diver."

"Well, anyway, you came over on your motorcycle."

"Jesus, that's right. That's when I had the Norton. How do you remember all these things?"

"I remember everything. You took her to the Hunt Room for dinner, and she gave you a Saint Erasmus medal as a going-away present."

"Yeah, I still wear it every time I go diving. Paula's a special lady—she really is. God, I haven't seen Paula in years, not since she got divorced and married that English prof. But I can't believe I met you that night."

"Well, we didn't exactly meet. All you said was 'hi' to me and then you went upstairs."

"I guess I'll have to plead insanity after all." He gently rubbed the side of the cool champagne glass against my hot cheek. "Why didn't you say something to me?"

"I wanted to but I just couldn't."

"Why not?"

"Because I was shy then. I was only sixteen."

"Yeah, and you were probably just as pretty as you are now. The boys must have been lined up clear around the block back then, and I'll bet they still are." He took the glass away from my cheek and ran his index finger around the rim: it made a soft, bell-like tone. "Well, you're not shy of old Jim now, are you?"

"No."

"Good." He downed the rest of the champagne and set the

empty glass on the floor. "You know what I think we should do, Miss Longstreet?"

"No, Mr. Wellman. What do you think we should do?"

"I think we should get out of here pronto. First, let's get you back into this." He helped me into my raincoat and buttoned it.

"Hold out your arms, Laurel." My father's breath like smoke in the cold foyer. "Now the other one." The black velvet collar soft on my neck and his cheek smelling of lime and pipe tobacco rough against mine. "That's a good girl."

"I almost hate to leave here, Jim. It's like a dream."

"Yeah, I know." He opened the door. "Hey, here you go, princess," he said, tapping the poster of Ludwig's castle with his finger. "There's your palace." He moved closer to me, and I could smell his warm, bread-and-butter breath.

"Where are we going, Jim?"

"Back to the scene of the crime. Let's you and the kid here take a drive out in the country. I want to find that place where all of this started. Only this time there's going to be a different ending. I can promise you that."

FOUR

"That's mine over there," Jim said, pointing to a small gold-colored car down the street. He took my hand as we walked across the soggy yard. Small pools of melted ice gleamed silver in the dead grass, reflecting the moon and stars in the cloudless sky.

"It's beautiful, Jim. What kind of car is it?"

"It's a Beemer—three point oh CS—prettiest BMW ever made. I love all that glass."

I looked up at him. He was shaking his head slowly from side to side.

"What's wrong?" I asked.

"Nothing's wrong. Everything's great. I was just thinking if I hadn't gone to this party tonight, I wouldn't have met you."

"It was perfect timing," I said, smiling. "You know everything in this world is just a matter of timing and touch."

"Yeah, that's right!" He let go of my hand and put his arm around my shoulders. "You really do remember everything, don't you?"

He helped me into the car, and as I slid into the seat, the wet oak leaves caked on the soles of my shoes fell in fragments onto the floor mat. Jim walked around to his side of the car and got in.

"I'm really sorry. My shoes are dirty."

"Hey, don't worry about it, little girl. She's due for a good cleaning, anyway." He drew me to him and kissed me on the mouth. I didn't close my eyes. In the faint light inside the car, his eyelids, closed and still, were as translucent as alabaster. My heart was beating like a bird's wings against my ribs, faster and faster, the blood pounding through my body. When Jim opened his eyes and saw me staring at him, he smiled.

"You have a boyfriend, little Laurie?"

Leaning into the curves on the Triumph past the blurred cornfields, my hands gripping Tommy's hipbones, his rippling white T-shirt smelling sweetly of fabric softener and new sweat, I felt at once both safe and reckless, like that time Uncle Leland let me touch the Luger pistol he had brought back from World War II. And Tommy standing on our front porch after church in his seersucker suit, tie loosened, his thick blond hair casting a stainlike shadow over his forehead. Suddenly I couldn't remember his face.

"No," I said. "Not anymore."

He turned the key in the ignition. "You do now, Laurie," he said. "You have me."

We turned onto Pennsylvania Avenue. Through the misted windows of the houses, the jeweled glow of Christmas trees seemed to float out into the warm night air like neon after a rain. Jim took my hand.

"How old are you?" I asked.

He put my hand to his lips and kissed it. "I just turned thirty."

"When's your birthday?"

"November twenty-second."

"The day Kennedy was shot?"

"Yeah. So when's yours?"

"October fifteenth."

"And you're how old? Fifteen? Sixteen?"

"No, I'm twenty-one!"

"I know, I know. I'm just kidding you." He smiled. "You don't look twenty-one."

I laughed. "Oh, thanks a lot, Jim."

"Well, you don't. You're beautiful, though."

"I'm glad you think so."

"It's not a matter of thinking. It's a fact—just like the Earth is round and the sun is a star." He slowed the car. "See this place coming up on the left? That's where I grew up."

A single amber light on the second floor flickered through the bare branches of the locust trees.

"I still stay at my mom's when I'm in town. I'm usually only here for a couple of months at a time, so it's not really worth getting an apartment."

"I knew this was your house, Jim."

"How did you know?"

"General Grant spent the night there once, didn't he?"

"Yeah. My great-great uncle used to own a weekly newspaper here in Catalpa. I guess they were pretty good buddies. You must have read that article in the *Chronicle*, right?"

"No, my mother told me about it."

He switched off the ignition and put his arms around me, hugging me close, and his hair smelled like rain and his breath was warm on my face.

"Don't worry," he said. "We're not going inside. But I do want you to meet my mom sometime." He kissed my cheek. "Sometime soon."

"I'd like that very much."

I remembered Mrs. Wellman in her white slip standing bare-foot in the blue light from the television set, her flesh as pale as an Ingres odalisque.

"You know, Jim, after that night—the night you saved my mom and me—I used to walk by this house almost every day after school, hoping that I would see you again."

"You did?"

"Yes." I could feel my cheeks burning. "I should never have told you that. It was my secret. How do you like that for playing hard to get?" I laughed a small, stupid laugh. "God, I always promised myself that if we were ever to meet again, I'd never, never tell you about what a crush I had on you."

He laughed, and then he was kissing my neck.

"This isn't a crush, Laurie, because I feel it, too. And, Jesus, don't ever think I'd like you to play hard to get. I've been out with so many women who play games. I'm sick to death of it. You don't know how touched I am that you told me this. It's incredible—like you were a little guardian angel in my life and I didn't even know it. No wonder I feel like we've always been together—because in a way we have, you walking by here for six years."

"Well, it wasn't six years. I stopped doing it after the night I baby-sat at Mrs. Lake's house."

He stopped kissing my neck and looked into my eyes. "How come?"

"Because I just couldn't. I don't want to tell you. I should never have brought any of this up in the first place."

"You can tell me anything in the world. It's secrets that make people close. You know that? So why wouldn't you go by my house anymore?" He stroked my temple with his thumb. "Come on, princess, tell me."

I looked down at my lap. In the semidarkness of the car, the satin of my dress glimmered a soft gray violet.

"Because, Jim, I could hear you and Mrs. Lake upstairs."

"God." He closed his eyes for a moment. "I never loved her."

"You don't have to—"

"I know I don't have to, but I want to. Paula's real sweet, but—well—it was absolutely nothing. I never felt anything for her like I feel right now—nothing even close. You have to understand that."

Before I could say anything else, he was kissing me hard on the lips.

"Don't you ever close your eyes, little girl?"

"I'm sorry. I guess I just can't believe this is real."

Jim put the car into gear. "Oh, it's real all right, baby. It's as real as it gets."

Jim drove down Sycamore Avenue to avoid the campus-town traffic, past the bright lights and black asphalt of the fast food places and used car lots, past Carter's Rib House, with its long brown-and-orange-striped canopy running up to the door, and then, under the viaduct, into Catalpa's business district. The sprawling old red brick railroad station looked deserted as we drove by; in the distance the six-story art deco Municipal Building loomed over everything else downtown.

At all the major intersections, fat tinsel snowflakes hung on wires above the street, shimmering in the warm December wind. We passed Buell's Department Store and General Meade Park, where the big bay windows of the two Victorian funeral homes on the far side cast soft golden light into the darkness. Then we passed the old square building, faced with white marble and flanked by Corinthian columns, where my father had his law office.

I squeezed Jim's hand. "That's where my father used to practice law. He died from a heart attack when I was eight."

"My dad's dead, too. I guess we have that in common."

"Oh, I'm sorry."

"Don't be. I mean, he's still alive, but he's dead to me."

I didn't know what to say.

"The last time I talked to my dad I was eighteen. I hadn't seen him for ten years, and so one time when I was in Chicago I decided to give him a call at Victor Machine—he was some kind of big-shot executive over there. Anyway, I just called him and said, 'Look, Dad—I know you're remarried and have a new family and everything, but we're both grown men, so why don't we get together for a drink or something?'"

"What did he say?"

"Nothing. He just hung up on me."

"God, Jim."

"That's just the way it goes sometimes." He gently stroked my left ear. "You know, Laurie, you're the only person I've ever told about that phone call in my whole life."

"Really?"

"Yes, really."

"He could have had a drink with you. After all, you're still his son."

"Yeah, well, that's what I thought, too. Your father was Joseph Longstreet, right?"

"Yes, he was."

"I thought he might be when you said your name but I wasn't sure. Well, my old man wasn't like yours, Laurie. I didn't know your dad personally, but he helped out an old friend of mine, Phil, who didn't have a dime, and your dad took the case for nothing—got him off completely, too. Phil said your old man was really smart—that he had a lot of class."

"You would have liked him, Jim."

"Well, I sure like his daughter."

At the next stoplight Jim pulled me close to him and kissed me, again and again, his hands cupping my face, even after the light had turned green and the honking cars behind us had driven around.

❖   ❖   ❖

We reached the edge of town. The prairie lay before us like a thin black line against the sky. A few raindrops splattered on the windshield.

"So, Laurie, what did you study in college?"

"How did you know I went to college?"

"I can tell. Come on, what'd you study?"

"Art. I majored in painting."

"Yeah? What do you paint?"

"Oh, lots of things: portraits of famous people from old photographs, and Valentine boxes—you know, silk hearts and lace. But lately I've gone back to painting flowers."

"Like—what do you call them?—still lifes?"

"Well, yes, but they're not what most people think of as still lifes. Mine are more like flowers that you dream than real ones. I mean, I'm interested in the effects of light on the colors and— it's kind of hard to explain, but—"

"Hey, you ever been to New Orleans?"

"No, I haven't."

"Well, New Orleans has some really beautiful flowers. I spend five, six months a year down there."

"You do?"

"Sure. That's where Caldwell Diving is located."

"I've always wanted to go to Mardi Gras."

"You'd love it. The weather is great and people are all dressed up in wild costumes. My best friend, Billy Kane—do you know him?—he's from around here."

I shook my head.

"Well, he's a diver too, and he lives down there all year. Anyway, last Mardi Gras night he got himself some Elvis suit with the big belt and everything. You should have seen him." He laughed. "It's ten days of nonstop partying."

"I didn't realize Mardi Gras lasted ten days."

"Yeah, and every night the parades get bigger and better. There's Momus and Proteus and Rex—I don't remember all their names—and then Comus, the best one, on Mardi Gras night—Fat Tuesday. Trust me, you've never seen anything like it. Some of those floats are fifty feet long."

"Oh, I'd love to see them."

He smiled at me. "Don't worry, Laurie. You will."

❊ ❊ ❊

For miles I waited for the glow in the sky from Cantrell's lights, but there was only darkness. Jim turned into the long driveway.

"You know, the night you saved us everything was blue," I said. " 'Blue Christmas' was even playing on the radio. Nothing looks blue now."

"Yeah, it looks like they've gone out of business. You want to get out, anyway?"

"Yes."

Jim left the engine running. The headlights illuminated a few coppery, desiccated Scotch pines lying on the bare ground beyond the cyclone fence. The door of the little shack had been boarded shut, its single window broken out and covered with a piece of torn plastic that moved in the damp wind.

"Does this place make you sad?" Jim asked. He was leaning against the cyclone fence, his fingers grasping the smooth wire.

"No, Jim," I said. "Nothing could make me sad now."

He was looking past the shack at a broken cornstalk, pale in the field on the other side of the fence. His jaw muscles flexed back and forth and he took a few breaths. The air was heavy with the scent of black earth.

"What are you thinking about?" He didn't answer me. "Is anything wrong, Jim?"

He turned around, his lips curved slightly in a nervous smile.

"I knew it," I said. "I should never have told you about walking by your house. It was too soon."

"No, Laurie, it's nothing you said. It's me. I just can't believe I could feel this way so fast. Like lightning."

"I know."

Jim took out his pack of Winstons and lit one, shielding the match with his hands. *His face leaning down to my trembling hands, the flame of the match glowing through my gloves like a golden-pink rose. "You look pretty out here in the night, little girl. You really do."*

"I don't believe it," he said. "I've only known you a couple of hours—God, not even that long!—and I feel as high as a kite just being with you." He shook his head. "It's crazy."

"But I feel that way, too. That's not bad, is it?"

"No, it's great as long as I don't make any mistakes with you. I don't want to be thinking I'm lifting us up—lifting you up— you know, making you happy—and then it turns out that all the time I'm really dragging you down deeper and deeper."

"But it won't happen." I laughed. "God, for a minute when you wouldn't answer me, I was afraid that this all might be a big joke to you."

He put his arms around me and pulled me close. "No, Laurie. The way I feel is no joke." He looked up at the sky, which had suddenly filled with low gray clouds. "Uh-oh. I'm sorry, but I think we'd better turn around and get back to town pronto."

"But why? I thought you wanted to find the place where we met that night."

"I do, but some other time. We're going to have one hell of a storm real soon. Trust me. Weather's one thing you figure out real fast on the water. Besides, we've already found the place— the only place that really counts." He touched my chest and then his own with his open hand. "It's right here."

As Jim turned onto the highway, six or seven connected streaks of lightning, like gigantic silver veins, broke out of the smoke-colored clouds, and sheets of rain, blown almost horizontal by the wind, swept against the car with a loud hissing sound.

"God, Jim, this is a hard rain."

"Yeah, well, this is the Midwest. You know how crazy it gets here sometimes." He wiped off the inside of the windshield with the sleeve of his duster. "Jesus, she's really coming down."

When the lightning flashed again, I could see a windbreak of poplars bending nearly to the ground in a field on my side of the highway. I looked down at my hands. My fingernails had imprinted tiny half-moons in the soft flesh of my palms.

"Hey, little girl, how close are we?"

"I don't know."

"We're this close, aren't we?" he said, placing his middle finger over his index finger. "Now you do it. There you go. We're like that. Are you afraid of thunderstorms?"

"Not usually, but I am tonight."

"Don't worry. I'll get us home. Everything's going to be fine. Light me a cigarette, will you? I'd appreciate it."

In the light from the match I could see Jim's face, calm and yet somehow exultant, his eyes fixed on the road ahead, both hands relaxed on the steering wheel—he enjoyed driving in this storm. I leaned back in my seat, suddenly tired, and closed my eyes.

*   *   *

The rain had stopped. My mouth was dry. I opened my eyes. Low on the horizon hung massive milky-orange clouds slashed with ribbons of black sky—long black ribbons spattered with stars, their faint rays nearly lost in the darkness. The lights of Catalpa glowed in the distance.

"Welcome back to the world, Sleeping Beauty."

"We made it!"

"Of course we made it."

"How long was I asleep?"

"Half hour, maybe forty minutes. I had to drive real slow."

"Forty minutes! I never fall asleep like that."

"Well, you did tonight. It was like someone knocked you out. One minute you were talking to me, and the next thing I know you're dead to the world."

"It must have been the excitement," I said. "Thank you for getting us back to town."

"No big deal. The worst that could have happened was a wet distributor cap. It isn't like that night with you and your mom."

"You're the best driver in the world," I said.

He laughed.

"All right, then, you have the best car in the world."

"I don't know about that, but it's a pretty tough little car. No doubt about it. Those Krauts sure know how to build them."

"I think it's the nicest car I've ever been in."

"Yeah, it's a shame I have to sell it this week, but I'm really going to need a truck in Florida."

It took me a moment to catch my breath. "You mean you're going away?"

"Got to. See, I have a sailboat down in the Keys—the *Brigand.* For a Midwest boy, I caught the bug pretty bad living on the water and all. Half the guys at Caldwell sign on for double shifts just to make the payments on some little boat or another. Anyway, it's going to take a lot of work to make the *Brigand* ship-shape. That's why I'm buying a truck—so I can haul the stuff I need."

"How long do you think you'll be gone?"

"I don't know—long as it takes. A few months, maybe."

"A few months," I repeated.

"You shouldn't own a wooden boat unless you live on her— I've learned that much." He lifted my chin with his thumb and index finger so that I faced him. "Hey, what's all this? What happened to that world-class smile?"

"I just can't believe you're going away."

"But you'll be seeing me soon."

"I don't call a few months 'soon,' Jim."

"How about a few days, then?"

"But I thought—"

"You thought wrong. I couldn't leave you for a few months. Tell you what: I'm going down there in a couple of days, and after I've made the *Brigand* at least halfway livable, I'll send you a plane ticket. I'll bet you look like a million bucks with a tan."

"You really want me to come?"

"If you don't, I'll just have to drive back up here and get you. Do you think your mother will mind if you come down?"

"I'm twenty-one. I can make my own decisions now."

"Great. That's what I like to hear. But I want you do one thing for me first."

"What?"

Very softly, close to my lips, he said, "Bring your birth certificate, Laurie. So we can make it right."

Then he was kissing me, and this time I closed my eyes.

We were married ten days later by a justice of the peace in Key Largo, Florida. That was a year ago.

PART II

FIVE

Thirty miles outside New Orleans we saw the first dead dog on the highway. Jim was humming a song and beating time with his free hand on the dashboard, and I was trying to guess the title. We had been playing the game for over an hour.

"Don't look," he said.

The dog was lying on its side in the tan grass of the median, its entrails smeared purple and red across our lane.

"You always look when I tell you not to look."

"I'm sorry."

"Hey, it's just a dead dog. Don't get bent out of shape over it. He probably never knew what hit him."

I stared out the truck window. Louisiana reminded me of the drawings in a book about dinosaurs I had read when I was a little girl. Gray Spanish moss hung from the branches of the tall, narrow trees, dipping into the bayous. A green coating that resembled cold grease covered the brown water, and the moist air smelled of eucalyptus. The sky was almost white.

"Hey, more road pizza."

There was a black heap in the middle of the highway, with red tread marks trailing from it.

"I said don't look and I meant it!" He started to squeeze my left thigh and I looked at him.

"Jim."

He smiled and patted the seat beside him. "Come over here

49

and sit by me, little girl. That's better. You excited about going to New Orleans?"

"Yes."

"Well, we'll be there soon. Before we go over to Billy Kane's place, though, I want to show you this house I almost bought once. You'll like it. It's pink, your favorite color."

"Pink?"

"Yeah, but it needs a lot of work."

The pink house was just off the highway, square and stark against the sky. All of its windows were broken, and pieces of red tile from the roof lay in the dead weeds of the front yard. Ragged palm trees, overgrown with vines, flanked the brick wall leading to the porch.

Jim pushed against the heavy wooden door. "Shit, still stuck."

"Are you sure we should be here, Jim? Maybe we're trespassing."

"Don't be such a chickenshit. Come on."

I followed him over to one of the windows.

"Now be real careful climbing through here," he said, bending down. "There's glass everywhere."

Even though I carefully raised the skirt of my navy blue dress, the hem became frosted with gray cobwebs on my way inside. I brushed them off and looked down at the parquet floor. There were wide gaps in the intricate patterns, and small shards of wood were strewn around the room like shattered teeth.

"Oh, Jim, this floor must have been beautiful once. Look at these fleur-de-lis."

"Yeah, they're ebony." He picked up a fragment of wood and crumbled it between his fingers. "I bet I could get somebody to restore this floor. Hell, I could do it myself. You know, this house might be a great investment, honey. And I could get it real cheap. It's been for sale a couple of years."

"Is this the house you flew your mother down to look at?"

"Yeah. Jesus, was that ever a mistake. She damn near drove me out of my mind. Listen, I'm going upstairs. I want to check out how much damage has been done since I was here before."

I stood in the middle of the ruined floor, staring past the tangled grapevines growing through the broken windows. Outside, twin pools of clouded rainwater stood on a flagstone under

a rusted gutter spout: tan-gray water flecked with green algae—
the color of Midwestern rivers—the color of my father's eyes.

*Mother sitting across from us in my father's old leather
office chair, the January light dying on the snow-covered
sycamore trees outside, their bark mottled tan, ivory, and
gray-green, like the patterns in a paint-by-number picture.
Jim getting up from beside me on the love seat. "Before I
go any further, Marian, I want to apologize. I know Laurie
and I haven't been very good house guests, but I'm the man
here, so I take full responsibility for that." My grandmother's watercolor of three tulips in a black lacquer vase over
the mantel. French tulips, the blue-violet of veins. Jim taking
the folded sheet of ruled yellow paper from his shirt pocket,
unfolding it, smoothing it flat with the palm of his hand.
"Please, Marian, before you say anything, I want you to
look over this list. These are all the things I've promised
Laurie I'm going to change about myself. Everything will
be different from now on. Trust me."*

"Hey, Laurie, come up here! There's something you'd like
to see."

I walked into the hall, my feet crunching fallen plaster and
smashed ceramic tiles. Through the years, the winding wooden
stairway had twisted out of plumb in the damp air, and the
ceiling by the wall had flowered white and fallen away.

"What is it?"

"It's a painting or something. Come on up."

I slowly climbed the stairs, clutching the rotted banister.

Jim was standing in a large room staring at a mural on the
ceiling.

The only section of the mural left fairly intact consisted of two
cherubs, each carrying a basket of flowers in one hand and strew-
ing white petals across the rosy sky with the other. Rainwater
had seeped through the upper part of their faces, leaching all
the color from their eyes.

"The whole ceiling is in pretty bad shape. Do you think you
could restore something like that, Laurie? You know, match up
what's missing?"

"Maybe. Probably. But they don't have any eyes."

"What?"

"Those cherubs don't have any eyes."

He laughed. "I swear, you're the strangest little girl. Those are just water stains." He kissed me softly on the cheek. "I can see by your face that you think I'm going to buy this place. It's true, I could make it perfect—just the way it was when it was first built—maybe even better. But I'm not going to buy it."

"You're not?"

"No, I remember what I promised you and your mom. I'm not buying or selling anything without talking it over with you, and believe me, you can take that to the bank." He kissed me on the cheek again. "Hey, how close are we? Me and you?"

"Close," I said.

He crossed his middle finger over his index finger; then he picked up my right hand, placed my middle finger over my index finger, and smiled. "That's right, close," he whispered, kissing my fingers.

"Things really are going to be better in New Orleans, aren't they, Jim?"

"Absolutely. And right now I'm going to start showing you just how good they can be."

Jim scraped an area free of broken glass with the side of his boot; then he slipped my raincoat off my shoulders and spread it out on the dusty floor. "Sit down."

"Here? Why?"

"Don't say anything—just sit down. Please, baby."

I sat down on my coat, and he gently pushed me back until I was lying down, my hair flowing over the top of my coat onto the floor.

"Here, you need a pillow," he said, taking off his black cotton sweater. He folded the sweater and put it under my head. And then he was kissing my cheeks, my lips, my closed eyes. Quickly he unbuttoned the front of my dress and, without unfastening my bra, he pushed it up and began kissing my breasts.

"Oh, Laurie, I want to be inside of you. That's the only time I feel that things are right in the world."

"But, Jim, we can't here."

"Yes, here. I want to show you how much I love you."

"But we can't take off our clothes. Someone might come in."

"No one's going to come in. Besides, who said anything about taking off our clothes?" He pushed my dress up to my waist. "Except these. I'm afraid these have to come off," he said, pulling my stockings and panties down to my knees. The incredible, familiar feeling came over me, the crazy, feverish feeling I could never get used to, never get enough of, even after a year of marriage, every time, any time Jim wanted me. His mouth was soft against my stomach.

"Sssh. Just let me. Let me do what you love most. Kiss you all over your sweet little body."

"Oh? But Jim—"

"Oh? But nothing—you just lie still and look up at those angels, because I promise you, little girl, pretty soon you're going to think you're in heaven."

The whooshing of cars on the highway was like the sound of waves breaking and dying away on a beach.

From the bridge crossing the Mississippi, New Orleans spread out in a crescent before us, smothered by a pearl-colored mist that stretched raggedly over the river. Jim pointed out the *Delta Queen* as she paddled past the freighters and fishing boats moored along the piers and down the brown water toward the Gulf of Mexico.

"So what do you think? Pretty, huh?"

"It's fantastic!"

"Well, you either love it or hate it. Sometimes both, like me. The Velvet Rut. That's what they call New Orleans—the Velvet Rut. The Big Easy."

"Why do they call it that?"

"You'll find out. Wait until you've lived here through the summer."

As we left the bridge, the setting sun illuminated the city with warm light. The fronts of the hotels and restaurants were bathed in a rich gold, and the red flowers around the necks of the horses in Jackson Square glowed like tiny globes of fire.

"See those paintings, see right up all along that fence there? Guys do some little fountain in a courtyard or a cafe in the Quarter or whatever and bring it to Jackson Square, sell it to the tourists. See them? Artists, at least compared to those lushes that go around the bars and draw your portrait for ten bucks. They're all over the place and some of them are pretty good."

The narrow pastel houses of the French Quarter passed before us, packed close together behind small fenced-in yards. Orange light poured through the filigreed wrought iron of the balconies, casting lacelike patterns on the sidewalks.

"Some of these houses are so little, Jim."

"Well, they're bigger than they look. They go way back—one room after another. They're called shotguns."

"Shotguns?"

"Yeah. If you stood in the front room and fired a shotgun, the pellets would go clean out the back of the house. Kane lives in a shotgun and it's right up here on Esplanade."

We pulled up to a pale blue house. A huge dog that must have been at least half rottweiler was sitting on the porch.

"Wait in the truck. I'll go see if Kane's home."

When Jim ran up the steps, the dog barked furiously, baring its teeth. He held out his hand and the dog sniffed it.

"You remember me, don't you, Marie?" Jim said, ringing the doorbell. He rang the doorbell several times, shifting his weight from foot to foot.

"I'll bet he's at Dauphine's," he said. "It's just down the street."

Dauphine's was so dark that at first I couldn't see the face of the man standing at the bar.

"Jimbo! You two just get in?"

"Yeah, I figured you'd be here. How you doin', man?" They slapped each other on the back.

"I'm Billy Kane," the man said. "And you must be Laurie." His green eyes appraised me. "Well, kid, you look great. You always did know how to pick them, Jimbo."

"Yeah, but this time it's different, Kane. This time it's for keeps."

"I tell you, man, I couldn't believe it when I called your house and your mom told me you got married down in Florida. At first I thought she was putting me on because she said you'd only known each other a few days or something. But then I thought, no, that's just like Jimbo. Ever since he was a little kid, Laurie, when he wanted something, he'd just go after it. I only wish I could have stood up for you, old buddy."

"Well, I wasn't about to let this little girl get away from me," Jim said, rubbing the back of my neck. "It was pretty spur of the moment."

"I know, that's what your mom said. So how is your mom, anyway? Beautiful as ever?"

"Yeah, I guess. But she's still a pig."

"Oh, please call me Dolores." Propped up on pillows in her bed upstairs, she extended her hand to me, cool and limp. "I am so sorry the house is in such a state. If only you had called me earlier, Jimmy, I would have had Helena come in." Winter sun filtered through the closed window blinds, bathing her in pale greenish light. "Jimmy thinks I'm a little messy." "A little messy? Jesus, Mother, look at this place! Laurie, do you know who did all the housecleaning around here when I was a kid? Just take a guess, take a wild guess." "Now, Jimmy don't be angry with me." "Damn it, Mom, I told you I was bringing over the love of my life for you to meet. When have I ever said that before? Huh? Jesus Christ, just this once you could have cleaned up!"

Jim picked up his pack of Winstons from the bar and lit one. "So where's Toni? She still work at that import place?"

"Yeah, she's still at Jade Moon. She ought to be home around six."

"Hey, man, I almost forgot. We're not the only newlyweds here. How long have you two been married? A month now?"

"Five weeks. I finally got her to sign one of those prenuptial agreements."

"That was smart," Jim said, nodding his head.

"I don't know. Toni's still mad about it. Turns out she'd already been married for a couple of months to some rich old fart in Aspen who made her do the same damn thing. God, she's a wild one."

"No shit."

Billy laughed. "The other night we went out drinking at Moran's, and we got into it real deep. She was making so much noise, they were going to throw us out of the place."

"She's a lush," Jim said.

"Nah, she's French. You know, I didn't think we were ever going to tie the knot. We were supposed to three different times, and every time we went on a bender, and—well, it's a long story. Let me buy you guys a drink."

The bartender, a buxom, green-eyed woman in her thirties, looked up from washing a glass. Her frosted hair and the cross hanging from her neck gleamed silver in the lights behind the bar. Above her head, a brass ceiling fan faintly stirred the humid air.

"What can I get you all?"

"We'll each have a glass of red wine," Jim said.

"It's like drinking garnets or rubies." Mrs. Wellman slowly rotated the stem of the wineglass between her fingers, slashes of blood-colored light darting across her face. "Everyone has always been drawn to Jimmy, ever since he was a little boy. He's a man's man and a lady's man, too. A born leader. Some people may not like him, but that's because they're jealous. They don't understand him—they don't know what he's really like. When Jimmy told me about how you two met, I thought it was about the most romantic thing I'd ever heard, and I'm so happy he's finally going to settle down." The corners of her mouth, stained from the wine, curved upwards, transforming her smile into a clownish grin. "Jimmy needs you so much, dear. He told me you were the other half of himself he had always been searching for—the gentler half."

"Put them on my tab, Sheila."

"Good God, Kane, you still have a charge here?"

"Yeah; Toni does, too." Billy laughed. "Last night she got really pissed off about how she couldn't stand being so dependent on me. Then she had Sheila here start a tab for her under her maiden name. Jesus, the whole bar heard her. And you know who's going to wind up paying it, anyway."

"Why should you?" Jim said. "She makes good money at Jade Moon, doesn't she?"

"Sometimes. It depends on what she sells. She's on commission. Hell, I don't know if she's even got a job anymore." Billy winked at me. He had big white teeth, and he tilted his head slightly to one side when he smiled. The soft bar lights gave a golden cast to his pale skin and his light brown hair was combed back in a D.A. He reminded me of Steve McQueen.

"So what's going on with you two lovebirds? Your mom said you were living in Largo on your boat."

"Yeah, the *Brigand.* She sure was a pretty ketch. Beautiful lines, but a hell of a lot of upkeep. Ask this little girl here. See, we were only together a few days before I had to hightail it down to Largo to deal with the *Brigand.* I flew Laurie down a few days later. You should have seen her, Kane, when she got off the plane. She was all dressed up, her hair curled and everything, like we were going to stay in a hotel. But the next morning I had her stripping varnish off the brightwork."

"Boy, Laurie, I'll bet you never figured on being such a sailor before you met up with the skipper here," Billy said.

"No. It was kind of a surprise."

"The whole boat had to be sanded and painted inside and out, Kane—and there was some dry rot, too. We worked every day from the crack of dawn until it got dark. It took us five months to make her perfect."

"Jesus," Billy said.

"Yeah, and we lived on her the whole time. I was waiting for an IRS check from Uncle Sam for six K, and for a while there things got pretty tight. I had Laurie get a job waitressing at this Polynesian place, but I still had to sell the boat."

"You sold her? How much you get?"

"I only got nine grand for her."

"Only nine thousand! How big was she again?"

"Thirty-four foot."

"Boy, that guy got a sweet deal."

"No shit. But talk about great deals, Kane. Guess what I got then? A fifty-two-foot Chris-Craft! The *Sheherazade.* She needs a lot of work, but hell, she sleeps ten. And I got her for only five thousand! You can't even buy a fucking car for that."

"Five thousand dollars for a fifty-foot boat! Come on, man."

"Swear to God. Tell him, Laurie."

"It's true," I said.

"Yeah. Listen to this, Kane. You won't believe it. She was in the slip right next to the *Brigand*—deserted. So I asked Mark—he's the asshole kid who owns the boatyard—what the deal was, and he tells me that this rich Arab owned her—a big oil-money guy. Anyway, a few years back this Arab is having lunch on board with his wife, and suddenly he blows up from a heart attack. The wife is so whacked-out that she just locks up the boat and lets it sit there in the water for four years—doesn't even pay the boat yard bills. I get Mark to give me a verbal agreement that he'll sell her to me for what the wife owes him. See, Mark thinks he's ripping me off because the diesel engines are all froze up, but I burned his ass good. Right, Laurie? Oh, man, you should have seen the bastard's face when he heard those engines fire up."

"Jesus, Jimbo!"

"Don't get me wrong, Kane—I'll probably have to sink at least ten grand into her. But the important thing is the superstructure is fine. Mostly what I'll have to do is cosmetic. You should see her, man. Mahogany blinds, stainless-steel galley, two heads, veneered mahogany walls inside. Like I told Laurie at the time— this is a real fine investment. Fix her up and sell her for a fucking fortune." He stabbed out his cigarette. "That's why I got to get some good deep work real soon—dive a couple months in the North Sea so I can start whipping the *Sheherazade* into shape."

"Well, things are pretty slow right now, Jimbo. I heard nothing's going to break in the North Sea or Bahrain for at least a few months." Billy looked down at his red cowboy boots, shaking his head.

A small, black-haired man came out of the men's rest room, wiping his nose with the back of his hand. He was wearing a black T-shirt with SAN DIEGO printed across the front in bright yellow letters.

"How you doing, Ray?" Jim said.

The man nodded at Jim without looking at him and sat down at the bar.

"I like your boots, Billy," I said. "Are they snakeskin?"

"No, lizard. I got them in Texas. Hand tooled." He smiled and winked at me again.

"*Midnight Cowboy*," I said.

"Guess that makes you Ratso, huh, Ray?" Jim said, punching the black-haired man's shoulder.

"You're a real funny guy, Wellman," Ray said. His voice seemed incongruously low for such a small man.

"Laurie, meet Ray," Billy said. "He's a diver, too."

"Kind of," Jim said in a soft voice.

Ray's hand was clammy when I shook it. His eyes never left his glass on the bar.

"Listen," Billy said. "I think to celebrate you guys getting into town we should do some shots. Then we'll all go out to dinner as soon as Toni gets home. Hey, Sheila, break out the J.D. and have one yourself."

Sheila lined up five shots of Jack Daniel's on the bar.

"I think I'll just sip mine," I said.

"No way, kid," Billy said. "They may call it Tennessee sippin' whiskey, but nobody sips nothin' down here."

I tipped the shot down, burning my tongue, my throat, and then my stomach.

"Just like the big kids," Jim said.

"You hear about Trulock yet?" Billy asked.

"What about him?"

"It sucks, Jimbo. He found out he's got osteogenic sarcoma. Legs."

"What's that?" I asked.

"Bone cancer," Ray said, without turning his head.

"Shit," Jim said. "So what's he going to do? Quit diving?"

"He can't. They just bought a new house and Jeannie is going to have another kid. Caldwell said he can dive if he wants to, but there's no way they'll be responsible."

"Bullshit," Ray said. "I don't mean the bone cancer, but about Caldwell letting him dive. They'll never let him dive!"

"I feel sorry for the poor bastard," Billy said. "He was making more money than he ever had in his whole fucking life, and he just got back together with Jeannie. I don't know, Jimbo. It's tough. Real tough."

"Yeah. Hey, you been out at all, Ray?"

"Once. Few days in the Gulf. Shitty barge. The three twenty."

"Dredge work, huh?"

"Yeah."

"Christ." Taking a long drag from his cigarette, Jim stared past the hanging blue hydrangea plants in the front window.

"So, Laurie, I hear you're a college grad," Billy said, smiling. "Got that old pigskin. That's great."

"Yeah, she got her B.F.A.," Jim said. "But it don't mean diddley without a J-O-B."

"Jimmy's the only one in our family for four generations who didn't go to college. I've always thought it was a terrible shame. Why, his great-grandmother was one of the very first women to graduate from the university here. He's so bright, but he can be so stubborn sometimes." She picked

up a large framed photograph from the nightstand and handed it to me. A younger, crew-cut Jim wearing a military uniform looked out at me with pale, impassive eyes. "This was taken when Jimmy had just turned fourteen. I thought military school would be good for him—growing up without a father—but he simply hated it. He finally made it impossible for them to keep him there. I'm afraid he can have quite a temper at times. But look at him, Laurie. Isn't he darling?"

"You guys ready for another one?" Billy said. "Sheila, bring us three more reds."

Jim put his arm around my shoulder. "Isn't she adorable, Kane?"

"Sure. Wish I'd found her first."

"Those big brown eyes and that cute little nose. She's something, huh?"

"Absolutely, Jimbo. Too bad she doesn't have a twin."

"Isn't he darling?" "Just darling." I pointed to a hand-colored studio photograph in a small oval silver frame of a blond baby girl wearing a pink party dress. "Is that you when you were a little girl?" "Oh, my God, no. That's my Emily, Jimmy's little sister. Her heart—she was born with a heart defect. Hasn't he told you? James Senior and I went back and forth to the hospital week after week. Now there's an operation, of course, nearly always successful, but . . . She was with us two wonderful years. He really never told you? Mr. Wellman was crushed, utterly crushed." I kept my eyes on the photograph, on the baby's yellow tinted hair, on her happy blue eyes. "No, I'm so sorry."

Sheila set down our drinks.

"Hey, guess who I saw coming out of the Toulouse Theatre the other day," Billy said.

"Who?"

"Mrs. Beausoleil and her daughter."

"Did they remember you?"

"Of course they remembered me—especially Teresa."

"You know, Kane, Mrs. Beausoleil called me up in the middle of the night once. She was drunk and crying."

"What'd she have to say?"

"I don't know. She was as high as a kite, and I was half asleep. I couldn't understand her."

"Who is Mrs. Beausoleil, Jim?"

"Just a rich bitch. Don't worry about it, little girl." Jim stood up. "I'll be right back. I got to make a phone call."

After Jim left, I moved over to the stool next to Billy.

"Really, Billy, who is Mrs. Beausoleil? Did Jim date her?"

"I wouldn't say he exactly dated her. We met her a couple of years ago at the Napoleon House. She was having lunch with her daughter, and they came over to our table."

"Was she pretty?"

"Yeah, she was—well, she was older, but yeah, they were both pretty, her and Teresa. Classy-looking. Hell, Teresa was a debutante. Her coming-out party was that night. There were servants all over, getting the house ready, so we had to be real careful. That was a beautiful fucking house. Hey, sometime you ought to ask Jim if he still likes lace curtains."

"Lace curtains?"

Billy leaned his head closer to mine. "Yeah. Mrs. Beausoleil was naked and wrapped herself up in her curtains. Jim did it, too."

"He did?"

"Cross my heart. Teresa and I saw it. We were in her mother's bed at the time."

I hadn't seen Jim come back to the bar. He put his hands on Billy's shoulders.

"All right, Kane. No war stories."

"Sure, man. Listen, why don't we go see if Toni's home yet? Sheila, be a doll and put these in to-go cups."

"Can you do that?" I asked.

Billy laughed. "Sure. You can take booze anywhere you want here, long as it's in a plastic cup."

"Really?"

"Hell, yes—even in a car if you're not driving. Welcome to New Orleans, kid."

"The Velvet Rut," I said.

"Hey, this one learns fast! You got that right—the Velvet Rut."

SIX

Billy's living room was painted an off-white. All of the furniture except the television set was from the fifties. A grimy oil painting of a Paris bistro hung on the wall above the fireplace, and the small oriental rug in the far corner of the room was pocked with cigarette burns.

I sat down next to Jim on the orange vinyl sofa. He pulled me closer to him and crossed his feet on top of the brass replica of an antique diving helmet in the middle of the coffee table. Ray flopped into a brown corduroy chair, a flat silver canister under his arm.

Outside, Marie barked sharply and scratched at the front door.

"Oh, Christ," Billy said. "I'd better go get her or she'll drive us all crazy."

"When did you get contact lenses?" Jim asked, watching Ray blink.

"Couple of weeks ago. Why?"

"I just wondered if they helped you get girls. You must be quite a cocksman now."

"Hey, Kane, you want to see this flick, or what?" Ray yelled.

"Sure." Billy came back into the living room, followed by Marie.

"What kind of movie is it, Billy?" I asked.

"Well, have you ever seen *Lassie*?"

"Yes."

"It's kind of like that," he said, patting the dog's head. "Right, Marie?" She licked his hand and went into the dining room.

"Hey, you didn't answer me, Ray. Do you think those contacts have helped you with the girls?"

"Go to hell, Wellman. Just go to hell."

Billy laughed. "We're working on it. Right, Laurie?"

"Right. Could you please tell me where the bathroom is?"

"Straight back. Come on. I'll show you."

There was no furniture in the dining room. An old Stratocaster guitar stood in one corner, and a boxer's heavy bag and a small crystal chandelier hung from the ceiling. Black footprints ran in a crazy pattern up and down one wall.

"Ain't that something? Toni had a party the other night. Some of her coon-ass Cajun friends came up from Lafayette, and it got pretty wild. One guy was swinging on that chandelier. Lucky it didn't come out of the ceiling."

"Hey, Kane, how about that wine?" Jim yelled.

"Coming right up."

I followed Billy into the kitchen. Shelves of spices, herbs, and oils were mounted on the back wall; strings of dried apples, peppers, and onions hung from the ceiling; and two pine racks stocked with bottles of wine were stacked on top of the schoolroom-green cabinets. Greasy newspapers and scarlet translucent shells filled the garbage can.

Billy pointed to a peach-colored door to the right of the stove. "The bathroom's in there, Laurie. Watch out for the bird."

My shoulder brushed against a large brass bird cage in the bathroom. A pale blue parakeet was sitting on the perch, picking out yellow seeds from a hot pepper pod with his beak. Strands of bright multicolored plastic beads were threaded in and out through the bars. The bird stared at me without blinking, the luxuriant creamy feathers radiating from around his eyes like a rococo motif in white plaster.

When I came out of the bathroom, Billy was opening a bottle of red wine over the sink, a cigarette dangling from his pursed lips. He took the cigarette from his mouth and set it on the edge of the counter.

"Did you meet Cupid?"

"So that's his name. He's beautiful."

Billy went into the bathroom and came out with Cupid perched on his finger.

"Here," he said, putting the bird on my shoulder. "He loves pretty girls."

Cupid flew away.

"Don't worry. Toni lets him fly around free in here most of the time."

"Hurry up, you guys! We're starting the show!" Jim yelled.

"We're coming! Sorry I don't have any popcorn!" Billy picked up four wineglasses. "Laurie, grab that bottle, will you?"

Carrying the opened wine bottle, I followed Billy into the living room.

"All right, folks, it's show time!" Billy said, turning off the lights.

"What's this movie about?" I whispered to Jim.

"You'll see."

On the screen, a woman with hair resembling cotton candy stared into the camera. She was sitting on a bed that was covered with a rumpled green spread. Behind her, drawn curtains in a gold-and-orange floral pattern were tacked to the wall. Ray lit a joint.

The woman took off her robe, and she was wearing a garter belt, stockings, bra, and panties—all black. Even her brown eyes were outlined in black. She smiled and stuck a big wet tongue out and slowly licked her pink lips. Jim and Billy laughed. The image suddenly started fluttering, as if the cameraman had lost his balance. Billy and Jim laughed harder. The camera moved back, revealing two dogs lying on the bed. They were playing, nipping at each other, their tails beating slowly against the mattress. The smaller dog looked as if he were part collie; the other one was a German shepherd.

The woman began touching the smaller dog's genitals. I kept expecting Jim to say, "Don't look," but he didn't. The German shepherd rolled over and fell asleep. The dog the woman was fondling kept trying to move away from her. I started to get up from the sofa, but Jim put his arms around me, laughing.

"You aren't going anywhere, little girl. You told me you liked animal movies."

The woman bent down, her face over the dog's stomach, and opened her mouth.

"Please, Jim!"

"Oh, let her go, Jimbo."

I ran into the bathroom. A door slammed and I heard a woman's voice. The projector stopped. I cracked the bathroom door so that I could hear better.

"That fucking dog has an IQ that is higher than all three of you put together!"

"Not me! I'm as high as a dog!" Billy said.

"You know what I mean!"

"Relax, Toni, we were just having a little fun."

"Jim, your idea of fun is probably to pull the wings from the flies."

"Honey, how many drinks have *you* had?"

"Go to hell, Billy. Where is your wife? I want to meet her."

"In the bathroom," Jim said. "She didn't like the entertainment."

"Well, she is the only one with any brains. You bring that shit in here, Ray?"

I heard footsteps and Marie's claws clicking on the hard-wood floor.

"Hello, *bébé*, hello, Marie. *Comment ça va?*"

I opened the bathroom door wider. Toni was in the kitchen, petting Marie. She was a couple of inches taller than me—maybe five-seven—with short dark brown hair and almond-shaped gray eyes that didn't seem to have any whites. There was a small beauty mark above her upper lip and another one near her right temple.

She looked up as I walked into the kitchen.

"So you are Laurie," she said, smiling. Her teeth were ridged and spaced slightly apart like a little girl's. "You are beautiful." She kissed me quickly on the mouth. "I am so glad you have come."

"Thank you. I am, too."

"Can you believe these divers? They are such trash."

Cupid flew around the kitchen and then landed on her shoulder.

"Cupid, my poor *bébé*. Give me a kiss." She pushed out her puckered lips and the bird pecked her mouth lightly. "I thought Billy would at least take out the garbage. We had crawfish the other night. Here, let me give you a glass of wine." She bumped into the side of the kitchen counter. "I am always doing that, chérie. I have bruises and I have no idea where I get them."

"From being a lush." Jim was standing in the doorway to the dining room, a big grin on his face.

Toni didn't say anything as she poured the wine. She lit a

cigarette and walked into the bedroom, with Cupid still on her shoulder.

"Come with me while I change. I want to show you my Degas prints."

A large, unmade brass bed stood in the middle of the tiny room. Above the bed were three Degas prints of ballet dancers framed in silver leaf. Cupid flew off Toni's shoulder and perched on one of the knobs of the headboard.

"Do you like these mats I made for them?"

"They're very nice."

Toni stepped out of her taupe skirt and unbuttoned her cream-colored silk blouse. I saw something dark above her left shoulder blade: it was a small candy-pink tattoo of a butterfly. She slipped on one of Billy's dress shirts and it came down almost to her knees. Then she sat on the edge of the bed and unzipped her high-heeled leather boots.

"The goddamned rain is ruining these. The heel is about to come off, and I can't afford new ones."

"I know what you mean."

"Can you believe that disgusting little imbecile, Ray? I don't understand why Billy hangs around with him. Billy likes everyone, though."

"He seems pretty easygoing," I said.

Toni stepped out of her panty hose. "Why does Ray hate Jim? Do you know?"

"No."

"Maybe he gave Jim some shit about the jewelry when they were in diving school and Jim made him regret it."

"I don't understand. What about Jim and jewelry?"

"He never told you? Billy says that is how Jim got the money for diving school. He stole some watches and rings from his uncle's store and sold them." She reached out and patted my arm. "It doesn't matter, chérie. Come sit by me."

I sat down beside her on the bed and lit a cigarette. She moved closer to me and brushed a wisp of cobweb from the hem of my skirt.

"Do you know Connie? Billy's old girlfriend? No? Well, she is short and blond—not naturally, of course, but men cannot tell. They do not care, anyway." She took a drag. "I am so goddamned mad and I cannot forget it. Billy is still sleeping with her, and we haven't been married even six weeks! Yes. And two nights ago she came into Dauphine's. Billy wasn't there, and she walked up to me and said that I should keep him from calling her and coming over. Can you believe such a thing? That bitch. I hate her."

"What did you say?"

"I told her that until Billy slept with her in my house, I considered him my husband. And I told him if he didn't stop, he would live to be sorry and so would she."

Toni crushed out her cigarette in a swan-shaped ashtray. "I will tell you one thing, chérie. In the morning when Billy makes love to me, he stares into my eyes—and the last look in his eyes is so beautiful that I know he is mine. *Totalement.* Do you understand, Laurie? He bites back his lower lip and he looks so—*je ne sais pas quoi*—determined. Yes, that is it—determined. It is this face that makes me stay with him—why I married him. It is absurd to have a marriage with someone because of how his face is for a few moments of a day, isn't it?" She took a long drink from her glass of wine. "Never trust a man who won't make love to you in the day or with the lights on at night. Those men are afraid."

"Afraid of what?"

"Afraid that you will see that he is *yours*. That kind of fear is sick in a man, chérie. It is unnatural—like a woman who kills her children."

"I don't know, Toni. I don't know if that's exactly true."

"Don't smile at me, Laurie. I am right."

"Girls, what're you doing in there? Don't you want to get something to eat? It's all right. Ray split. Toni?" When Billy opened the door, I could hear Jim punching the heavy bag in the dining room.

"I am almost ready," Toni said, standing up to close the door. She tucked her blue jeans into her boots. "We're going to Gerrard's for dinner—to celebrate you coming to New Orleans. They have delicious escargot, and I know the girl who plays the piano there. You like escargot, don't you?"

"I don't know. I've never had it."

"Well, you will love it. Tell me, is it true how you met Jim? Did he truly save your life? Or is that only more diver bullshit?"

"No, he really did. And I've been afraid to drive ever since that night. But Jim said I have to get my license—that it's easier down here."

"Nothing's easier down here, chérie. It just seems that way."

"Come on, girls, let's go!" Jim yelled, pounding on the door.

"We are coming." Toni leaned closer to me. "What a patient man he is," she whispered. "But do me a favor, chérie. If Jim wants to save my life someday, please tell him not to bother." She burst out laughing. The inside of her mouth was bright red—like the mouth of a wild animal. "All right, Cupid," she said. "Back in the cage."

SEVEN

After Escargot and wine at Gerrard's, we had walked all over the Quarter, stopping at Pat O'Brien's, the Chart Room, and the Old Absinthe House. Jim, Billy, and I were sitting at the bar in a place called Funky Butt's. Toni was still at the Old Absinthe House, talking to some waiters she knew. It was four o'clock in the morning.

"Kane, you want to go with me Monday and get your physical?" Jim asked.

"Already had mine. I tell you, I got to get some work soon my ownself. I am *broke*. I went through a lot of money, and I got no idea what I did with it."

"Probably up your nose or on that Jag." They both laughed.

"It got smacked twice last Mardi Gras. Two fucking times in the same day. Can you believe that? I still haven't got the body work done."

"That ain't nothing," Jim said. "When we got back to Catalpa, I bought me a little sixty-nine Vette. Paid five thousand cash. Beautiful car. Anyway, I'd been out at Jeff Barnett's—you know where that is—out near Posey—and—"

"God, I haven't seen Jeff since high school. What's he up to these days? Still farming?"

"Yeah, he's got over eight hundred acres now. So anyway, me and him were drinking Wild Turkey all afternoon, and on the way back into town—you know the curve near that new subdivision? Manchester Fields? Well, I was coming around that curve

like I was Mario Andretti, and I wound up taking out about forty
feet of split-rail fence. No shit—I'm lucky I wasn't killed. I tell
you what, though—seeing those big chunks of fiberglass all over
the road sobered me right up. I could have ripped the whole
ass-end off that Vette with my bare hands. Hell, Laurie could
have done it. Then I drove it all the way to my mom's house
and covered it up with a tarp. I just couldn't stand to look at it."

"Did you total it?"

"Almost—but I had her completely rebuilt, and now she looks
perfect. Cost me a fortune. I'm going to get rid of it, though.
You know, once the frame gets fucked up like that, the car's
never the same."

"Don't I know it. Talk about cars, Jimbo, you know that beat-
up brown Duster Connie had? Well, I bought it to teach Toni
how to drive. I paid Connie for it in checks, and Toni got hold
of them and went wild. Made me make Connie buy it back. She
accused me of still seeing her."

"Are you?"

Billy laughed.

"I love that little bitch," a young man said from a table behind
us. His voice was raspy but high pitched, like a teenager's. I
didn't turn around, but I could tell that he was talking to a girl.
I stared at my untouched White Russian on the bar in front
of me.

"I love her," the young man said. "I do. I really do, and you
know how pretty she is. She's so goddamn pretty, and now all
of those boys are hanging around. I tell you, it drives me out of
my mind. I swear I can't take it. I'm going to slit my throat."

"Don't talk that way. You don't mean it—it will just take time,"
the girl said.

"I hate that little bitch. I do."

"No, you don't. You don't hate her. You're just hurt right now.
She *is* awfully young."

"But she is so goddamn pretty, and all of those boys sniffing
around like dogs. I can't take it. I've got to do something."

I heard the girl leave the table, her high heels tapping on the
stone floor, and Billy and Jim laughed. Then I heard the boy
again. He was sobbing, and the sound made my throat ache.

"God, I love that little girl so much. So much."

I turned around on my stool, pretending that I wanted to get
something out of my coat. The boy's head was down on the

table. He had very short hair, small ears, narrow shoulders, and thin arms. Suddenly, the boy raised his head, as if he sensed I was watching him. He stared straight at me, his pencil-thin brows arched above puffy eyes. I looked down at his neck. There was no Adam's apple.

"Fuck you lookin' at?" the woman said, picking up her leather jacket from the back of her chair.

"Fooled you, huh?" Jim said, laughing. "Down here you got to learn to tell the boys from the girls." He leaned over and kissed me on the cheek. Th ewoman walked out of the bar.

The bar door swung open again and Toni walked in.

"So you are still here. My friends said surely you boys would have taken Laurie home by now, but I knew it was not true."

"Another five minutes, you would have missed us, babe," Billy said. "I was starting to worry about you."

"I told you to never worry about me."

"But you know I do. This is New Orleans, not Aspen."

"So?"

Jim stared down at me.

"I don't believe it. Laurie's got tears in her eyes. Get this, Kane. This little girl here told me once that she cried about some neighbors burning worms off their trees. She felt sorry for the bagworms."

"I *was* a little girl then."

Toni brushed my hair back from my shoulders.

"I can see why someone might feel that way when they were small—someone sensitive," she said, glaring at them.

Jim and Billy laughed until they were gasping for breath. Whenever one of them stopped, the other would start again. Toni looked at me and rolled her eyes. Billy put his arm around her. She took it off, and Billy asked the bartender for the tab.

"Kane, did you see Laurie's face when she found out it was a girl? I'd give a hundred dollars to see that again."

"It's still sad," I said. "Sad and lonely. Loneliness is loneliness. Love is love."

"Spare us, huh, kid?" Jim said.

Toni took my arm as we left Funky Butt's. "You should never let them do that to you. It is not at all funny."

I was having difficulty walking straight, and so was Toni. I took deep breaths and looked up at the white starless sky. The air smelled faintly of cinnamon and smoke. There was no one else on the street except two men kissing against a parked car.

"These divers are such macho shits. You were right what you said in the bar," Toni whispered to me. "Love is love."

"I caught Toni the other day drinking my English Leather," Billy said. "She read on the label that it was twenty-five percent alcohol." Jim doubled over with laughter.

"Get fucked, both of you!" Toni shouted.

"Toni, you're beautiful when you're mad. Ah, Kane, I tell you—French girls."

"Yeah, French girls are the wildest. French girls and nurses."

"Go to hell," she said.

I couldn't feel my legs beneath me. My head was spinning and my mouth was dry. Jim was walking next to me now and Toni was walking in front of us with Billy.

"You hate me because I am Catholic!" Toni yelled. "Why don't you admit it? Just once!"

Billy laughed. "I didn't even know you were Catholic."

The soft glow of the gaslights became yellow streaks rushing by me. The earth was moving too quickly under my feet; no matter how fast I walked, I couldn't keep up with it.

"I am so tired," I said.

Jim put his arm around me and kissed my cheek. "We're almost home, baby. Come here. I want to show you something. Look up there." He pointed to a high stone wall between two red, shuttered houses. Under the gas lamp, emeralds, sapphires, amethysts, and topazes glittered along the top of the wall.

"You want me to set you up there with all those pretty jewels?"

"They're beautiful," I said, shifting my weight and almost falling over. I squinted so that I could see the wall more clearly. Jagged bottle fragments had been stuck in the mortar on top of the wall so that their edges pointed upwards.

"You don't want to get up on that wall, little girl—it would cut you to pieces," Jim said, hugging me. Across the street, Billy was kissing Toni.

Jim and I slept on a mattress in a corner of the dining room. I awakened about six o'clock and ran to the bathroom. After I had finished vomiting, I rested my head against the cold porcelain rim of the toilet. Cupid fluttered around in his cage.

I tiptoed, shivering, back to bed and pulled the sheets up around me. Jim turned over and looked at me through half-closed eyes.

"Hey, Sleeping Beauty, I thought I told you to open a window before we went to bed."

"I thought I did."

"Well, you didn't! Get up and open one, for Christ's sake. Girl, don't you know you can die from these heaters?"

"I'm sorry."

"People are always dying from them."

"It's stuck."

"Shit." He threw back the sheets. "I'll do it."

The morning light tinted his skin the yellows and pinks of a tea rose.

"I'm not kidding you, sister. You watch that business with the heaters."

He rolled over, his back to me. I stared up at the black footprints on the wall.

When I finally fell asleep again, I dreamed of the pink house. I was standing in the living room, ankle deep in dirty, broken glass. Rosy angel wings trembled in the ruined windows.

"It's the cracked salt that makes it good. That and the Pommery. The salt's got to be the right size, same size as the seeds in the mustard. Then you've really got something. You use the meat juices for the sauce but you add pearl onions and the liquid they're bottled in, and here's the secret, Kane: you throw in two spoons of Worcestershire sauce and two spoons of Coca-Cola."

"This is your gourmet recipe, Jim?" Toni said. "But of course, it is too perfect. The secret is Coca-Cola."

"Hey, you got to admit it's good, honey. You said so yourself." Billy slid the last slice of London broil off the platter and let the sauce dribble onto his plate.

"Of course, it is delicious, and as behind so many of the delightful things in this world, there is always the unimaginable secret. Thank you, Laurie, so much. This is living, you cooking dinner for us. How appropriate that we eat it in the living room." She was smiling.

"Thank you for helping me rearrange all our boxes in the dining room," I said.

"It was my pleasure. What could be better than an afternoon

helping you follow orders?" She rolled her eyes at Jim. "He's such a sergeant, this one."

"I wanted to do it," I said. "Really."

"You know what would be real good right about now, Kane?" Jim looked steadily across the table at me. "Coconut cake, you know, from that little place you got around here."

"Ideal Pie and Cake?"

"They grate the coconut over the cake right after you buy it so it'll be fresh."

"That's them, Jimbo."

Jim glanced down at his watch. "What time you got?"

"Five twenty-two."

"At least this fucking thing works. That's more than I can say about some people. All right, you're through eating, Laurie. You're just playing with that salad. How about you run down there while the boys here have a little after-dinner brandy?" Jim held out a twenty dollar bill.

"Okay, only I don't really know my way around very well." I stood up.

Toni began stacking dirty plates. "It is so simple, chérie. You go out the front door and go left. Ideal Pie and Cake is five blocks away. I will make the coffee."

He stood with his back against the plate glass window of an empty store a few doors down from the bakery, his face and upper body indistinct in the shadow cast by the awning above him. I hadn't noticed him when I walked by earlier.

"You know what time it is, ma'am?"

"No, I'm afraid I don't."

He pulled me hard by the sleeve and I could feel his breath on my neck. "Time to give up the money, honey." With his free hand he pressed something sharp and cold against my ribs. "Don't say shit or I'll cut you. Believe it. I don't play."

Now I could see his face, the skin coffee colored and smooth, his eyes cloudy, his lips pulled taut over his teeth. "Give it up, bitch, and the box too. Don't look at me!" I let my fingers go limp and he took the cake box out of my hand. "How about the money? You going to get it out of your pocket or you want me to fish for it?"

"Here." I held up the wadded bills in my fist. "It's all I have."

He let go of my sleeve. "Now get the fuck out of here. Get!"

I backed away, my eyes downcast.

"Turn around. Keep walking and don't look back."

It had been dark enough under the awning that at first, as I walked away, I was startled by the early evening light, and by the noise and movement around me. A man in a rumpled gray suit, flush faced and balding, pushed his way out of the grocery across the street with a bag under his arm. Fifty feet away a woman was walking her dog, a buff-colored Pomeranian, on a silver leash. I could hear Dixieland coming from somewhere nearby and laughter. Cars paused at the intersection and moved on. I turned around and looked back under the awning. There was nobody there. I ran until I was out of breath, about three and a half blocks down the street.

Jim jumped up when I came into the room. "What is it? What happened?" He was holding my arms and I could hear Cupid chirping but the sound seemed far away. The words were clear in my mind but when I started speaking everything came out wrong. "Jesus!" Jim was saying. "Slow down. You're not making sense. Who robbed you?"

"He took the cake. He took the money." I could talk all right now but I was crying. Billy was putting on his jacket.

"Take deep breaths, chérie."

"What'd he look like? What was he wearing? Tell me, Laurie. Was he black? White? Tell me right now!"

"He had an Afro, a short one, and light skin, and he had a knife, Jim. I think he had a knife."

"He's going to wish he'd kept it out of sight. He's going to wish a lot of things." Jim took the truck keys out of his pocket. "Let's roll, Kane. Bastard's still got the cake!"

Marie was barking. I sat up in Toni's bed. The door opened a crack then Jim stuck his head in. "Honey?" He turned on the small bedside lamp, closing the door softly behind him. "We got him, honey," he whispered. "And we got your cake." He put the cake box beside me and then he sat down on the edge of the bed. "Lie back, baby. There." He was stroking my hair.

"How in the world did you ever find him?"

"Nothing to it. He was sitting on a bench on North Rampart Street, probably waiting for a bus; had the cake next to him. We jumped out of the truck and got a hold of him before he even knew we were there."

"Didn't he try to get away? Did he pull—"

"Forget all about the knife. When we got him settled down he told us he'd just been pretending about the knife. Took a key and held the tip on you like a knife, and I believe him because we searched him all over."

He stroked my hair straight back and kissed my forehead. "It's over, Laurie. Everything's all right. I know he scared you but it's over. Look up here. Look at me."

He held me by my shoulders and studied my face in the lamplight. "You never have to worry about shit like that as long as I'm around. Never. Nobody's going to hurt you. You're mine. I just won't have it."

Looking into his eyes, I felt a warming calm sweep over me, safe now in his arms, inside the circle of his protection.

"I would lay down my life for you. Really, my life. Do you understand what I'm telling you?" His eyes were bright like jewels. "Never forget."

He hugged me close against his chest, the buttons on his shirt pressing into my cheek, and he kissed me hard all along my neck.

"All better? Here." He let go of me and put the cake box on his lap. He untied the bow of red and white string, pulled the box open and took a small piece out of the cake with his fingers, flakes of coconut falling onto the sheets.

"Open your mouth." He pushed the cake into my mouth and then he kissed my lips.

"If we'd gotten married here these are the guys I'd have had make the cake. We should've had a cake. We should have had a real wedding, you know that?" He held another piece up to my mouth but it broke apart in his hand and the frosting fell down my shirt.

"I'll get it," he said and then he lifted my shirt and was kissing my breasts. I lay back and Jim set the cake box on the floor.

"You love me don't you, Jim?" I held my arms open to him.

"Oh, I love you all right, sugar." He was pulling off his shoes. "I love you to death."

Afterward, while he was still inside me, we looked into each other's eyes and kissed and I could feel my tears spill over and down my face and into my mouth, salty-sweet, and as he kissed me, into his.

He pulled away. "Oh, sweetheart, don't cry." He wiped my tears with the palm of his hand. "There's nothing to worry about. Don't be sad, baby."

"I'm not sad. I just—"

"Don't worry. Everything's all right."

"I hope so. I want—"

He didn't let me finish. He was kissing me again and again, lower and lower. I looked down at his hand on my breast, the knuckles cut and purple, and I brought it my mouth. For a moment he looked up at me, his eyes the limitless blue of a winter sky, and then he was kissing my thighs, and I thrust my fingers into his hair and held him there.

"Laurie." Jim was standing by the bed in his jeans lighting a cigarette. "Hurry up and get dressed. I don't know about you, but I could use a couple drinks."

EIGHT

"Good morning, Laurie."

"Good morning, Billy." I walked into the kitchen. He was wearing blue-and-white striped pajama bottoms. There was a pink V-shaped scar about an inch long just under his left collarbone.

"How about some coffee?" he asked.

"Yes. Well, maybe not. I don't feel too great."

"I'm not surprised, after the robbery and all that hoo-rah. How are you holding up?"

"Oh, I'll be all right."

He laughed. "I'm not hitting on all six cylinders my ownself. But you wait and see. Toni will feel fine. I hope we didn't keep you guys up last night."

"No. I was dead to the world."

"How about a Pepsi? It's good for hangovers."

"Wonderful."

"Jimbo went to check out an apartment."

"I know. He left a note on the bed."

"I swear, I don't see how he gets up so early after carrying on like we did last night."

"God, neither do I. I feel like hell."

"I wouldn't be up at all except that Cupid got loose and I was trying to get him back before Toni wakes up. Shit, she's going to kill me."

"Oh, no, the poor thing. What happened?"

78

"Toni forgot to shut Cupid's cage last night, and he flew out the door when Jimbo left this morning. Jim said it happened in a flash. He came back and told me. Man, I sure don't usually get up this early." Billy pressed his fingertips against his temples. "Not if I can help it."

"Maybe Cupid will come back," I said.

"Nah, he won't be back." Billy handed me a Pepsi in a Pat O'Brien's Hurricane glass. "Why would he come back to live in a cage?"

"I don't know," I said. "Maybe because there's nowhere else to go."

"Well, I hope you're right, but I sure as hell wouldn't bet on it. Oh, did we get you up, honey?"

Toni was standing in the doorway of the kitchen, rubbing her eyes. She was wearing an oversized burgundy brocade bathrobe that must have been Billy's.

"How do you feel, Laurie? I hope you will forgive New Orleans for your terrible reception yesterday."

"Sure. I guess nothing really bad happened."

"No. Not so bad."

"I made some coffee, honey. I have to get dressed and get out of here."

"Why? Where are you going?" A night's sleep seemed to have drained her. Her skin was tinted an ivory shade, like fading gardenias, and her lips were red and puffy.

"I'm going to Caldwell to work out at the gym."

"Oh, come on, Billy."

"I got to. I didn't work out yesterday."

"Kung Fu himself," she said.

Billy started to say something, but Toni walked past him and into the bathroom.

"Where is the bird? Where is Cupid?"

"Now, sugar, don't be upset. It was an accident. He got out this morning when Jimbo left."

"What!"

"He flew away. He's gone. I'm sorry, babe."

"Oh, Christ!"

"I'm sorry," I said.

"Why should you be sorry?"

"I'll get you another one," Billy said. "I'll get you one today."

"No, I don't want another one. When are you coming back?"

"Couple hours," Billy said, walking toward the bedroom.

"So you showered and shaved just to go to the gym?"

"Stop it, Toni. I didn't shower."

"Stop what?" She yawned, staring at me. "You are pale, chérie, You must have slept badly."

"I drank too much."

"Do you want a drink?"

"God, no."

Toni walked over to the cabinets above the sink and took out a bottle of vodka. "Billy, did you drink all of the orange juice?" she called.

"There's grapefruit juice in the fridge."

Toni poured herself a tall vodka and grapefruit juice and sat down next to me at the table, leaning on her elbows. Her robe opened and I could see the butterfly tattoo.

Billy came into the kitchen. He was wearing pressed blue jeans and a gray V-neck sweater without a shirt.

"Well, don't you look nice to go visit the boys."

"Knock it off, will you?" He winked at me.

"Take that cage with you. Throw it away."

"You really don't want another bird?"

"No."

"Well, let's keep it for a little while, honey. I mean just in case you change your mind." He turned to me. "Tell Jimbo I'll be back later unless I get tied up."

"I will," I said.

Toni started to laugh and then Billy laughed, too. He ruffled her hair and then kissed the top of her head.

"Don't you even think about telling Laurie that story."

"I am going to."

"Tell me what?"

"Wait until he has gone and I will tell you." She took a sip of her drink.

"Honey, you didn't put booze in that, did you?"

"What if I did?"

"Damn it, Toni!"

"If you have to leave, why don't you just get the hell out?"

"I'll see you, Laurie."

He walked into the dining room, punching the heavy bag as he passed, then through the living room, and out the front door.

"He is going to see her," Toni said.

"You don't know that, do you? Isn't he going to the gym?"

"That's what he says, but I don't believe him." She took another sip of her drink.

"What were you two laughing about?"

"Oh, well, before we were married, Billy had one of those bondage magazines. I don't know where he got it—probably from Ray, that little *crétin.* Anyhow, Billy had all these big ideas, but I told him I would tie him up instead. So I undressed him and tied him up tight." She laughed. "He thought I was going to do all sorts of wonderful things to him."

"What did you do?"

"I went down to Que Sera's and had a few drinks. I only intended to have one, but I ran into some people from Paris."

"You mean you left him there?"

"It was supposed to be a joke, but I forgot the time. He was tied to the bed for about three hours."

"Wasn't he mad?" I asked, laughing.

"He was not very happy then, but he got over it. Now, whenever one of us says that we are tied up, we both think it is very funny." She downed the rest of her drink.

"God, I don't know how you can stand to drink that first thing in the morning," I said.

"People always have a hard time understanding what other people can stand. *Par example,* I don't understand why you stay with Jim. The only thing I can think of is he must be excellent in bed. It is in his eyes. He could take you around the world without leaving the room, *n'est pas?*" She reached across the table for her Gauloises, shook out the last cigarette, and then crumpled the light-blue package into a ball. "So, chérie?"

"But it's more than that, Toni. In my life—in my entire life— there has never been anything stronger. I've never known anything more beautiful than the way I feel when Jim makes love to me. It is beyond making love—way beyond sex."

"Beyond sex?" She laughed. "But what do you mean?"

"It's hard to explain, but whenever we make love, when Jim is inside of me, I see dreams. Even with my eyes open I see them. Fragments of dreams, really. Like mosaics."

Toni lighted her cigarette and inhaled deeply.

"A lover who can make you dream with your eyes open? Come on, chérie."

"It's true."

"Jim must have been your only lover, then. Your first and only. Am I not right?"

"No, he wasn't my first lover."

"Of course. Pardon me, chérie," she said, smiling.

"He wasn't. I went with one boy, Tommy Dietrich, for about a year."

"And how was it?"

"Terrible." I picked up the crumpled cigarette package from the table. "Neither of us knew what to do, I can barely remember it."

"Then there has really never been anyone but Jim."

"No."

Toni smiled again. "So please tell me. You have my complete attention. What can only Jim make you dream?"

An incandescent moon stringing bright beads of light on a lake, the flickering opal of a dragonfly's wing, a drowned cathedral, its great doors dimmed bronze, ancient hiero-glyphs of gray-green lichen on stone, pale fish darting in deep green water, long, black velvet ribbons of thorns, and always a rose, a blooming, burning rose. . . .

"Oh, I don't know, Toni," I said. "Lots of things."

It seemed to take forever to shower and dress. I swallowed three aspirins, stared into the bathroom mirror, and tried to put on makeup. As I dried my hands, I could hear Jim's voice.

"It really isn't bad, Toni. It could be real nice. I'm taking her over there right now."

"Where did you say it was?"

"Up on Prytania Street—across from Commander's Palace."

"Is that by the cemetery?"

"Real near. Oh, honey, there you are. You all set to go? I was just telling Toni that I found us an apartment."

"Already?"

"Yup. You know how the kid here likes to get things done."

Toni was still sitting at the table, peeling off the rind of a navel orange in one piece.

"I can't wait for you to see this place, Laurie. It's a really old house in the middle of the Garden District. The landlady is coming over to show it to you. Her name is Mrs. Morisot."

"An Impressionist landlord," Toni said. "You are lucky. Ours is a Primitive."

"So, Mrs. Wellman, you ready to see your new apartment?"

"Yes. I mean, I'm ready to consider it."

"Be sure and take your coat. It's damp outside. Tell Billy we'll all meet later to celebrate getting the apartment—if we take it."

Toni bit into an orange section and juice misted into the air. A cigarette was burning next to her in the swan-shaped ashtray.

"I will see you later, but I am not celebrating. I cannot do it."

"We'll see," Jim said.

She smiled but without looking at us. Her eyes went cold.

"Toni, I'm sorry about the bird," Jim said.

"It doesn't matter."

I looked out the truck window at the houses on St. Charles Avenue—huge, sprawling pink and white and peach houses with galleries and shutters and yellow-green lawns.

"Wait until you see this part of town in the spring," Jim said. "There'll be flowers all the way up and down St. Charles." He patted my leg. "You like it here, don't you?"

"Yes."

"And you like old Jim, don't you?"

"Yes."

"That's good." He took his hand off my leg. "All right, now, I want you to get this story right, so listen up. I told Mrs. Morisot that you were a graphic designer, free-lance, and that you make over three-fifty a week."

"You *what*?"

"Look, I want her to think we're both employed. You got that?"

"But it isn't true."

"Oh, I see, you can lie about anything in the world to me, but when you're supposed to tell a little fib for a good reason, then you can't do that, right?"

"I don't want to lie. Not about anything."

He reached over and pinched the inside of my thigh so hard that I screamed. The truck swerved.

"God damn you! That hurt!"

"Now, what are you going to tell her? That you are a graphic designer, a free-lance designer making decent bucks, right?"

"Yes," I said, rubbing my leg.

"I didn't hear you."

"Yes," I said again.

"Oh, oh, here we go. You haven't cried since last night. It's a new record."

"Why do you want us to fight?"

"Nobody's fighting. I'm just telling you what you're going to say."

"I can't believe you're being so mean."

"No one is being mean. Everything will be fine between us if you just do what I say. I'm not asking you to tell a big lie. I don't understand what you're getting so upset about."

"Because you pinched my leg. You know I hate it and you still do it."

"Well, there are plenty of things I hate that you still do, little girl. But we don't have time for any of that crap right now, so clean up your face. We're almost there."

I looked out the window again at the passing houses. The paint was peeling off some of them, and the lawns were brown. We drove past a cemetery. Jim pointed across the street at a large Victorian mansion painted a bright blue green.

"That's Commander's Palace. Pretty, huh?"

I wiped my cheeks and took a deep breath.

"Commander's is one of the best restaurants in New Orleans," Jim said. "A long time ago it was a whorehouse. We'll go there for dinner sometime. Would you like that?"

"I guess so."

"Hey, what are you going to do? Sulk?"

"I'm not sulking."

"Is that why your lower lip is sticking out about a mile?"

"It isn't sticking out."

He put his hand against my cheek and gently stroked my temple with his fingertips.

"I know—I know it's not," he said softly. "I'm sorry I pinched you—but don't you see, little girl? I just have to get you settled in a nice place before I take off—a place of our own. Red over at Caldwell says I'd better get a beeper fast. Work's going to break any day now."

"Do you think so?"

"Absolutely." With his thumb, Jim wiped away a tear from the corner of my eye. "Laurie, I don't think you really understand what it's like down there on a dive. You can't be distracted, you can't be worried at all. I don't mean about bills or money or things like that. I mean worrying about the person you're in love with—because if you do, you can wind up dead. I've seen it happen way too many times. That's why the last thing I need right now is to have you staying over at Kane's house. Especially after the robbery. I'm sorry, okay? I really am. I guess I'm a little on edge with my physical coming up."

"Why? Don't you feel well?"

"Yeah, I feel all right. But I always feel better after my long-bone X rays check out. Jesus, look what happened to Trulock. Poor bastard's a dead man."

We parked in front of a two-story cream-colored house with black-shuttered windows and black cast ironwork across the porch and balconies. A rusted iron fence ran along the yard, dipping at irregular intervals into the long brownish-green grass. Jim put his arm around me as we walked up the steep steps to the porch.

"The whole place needs to be renovated," he whispered.

On the porch, partially hidden by a mass of dead vines that hung from the roof, stood a frail woman of about fifty-five wearing a silver fox coat. Her skin was very white under her makeup. She had dyed ash-blond hair, a slightly hooked nose, and extraordinarily beautiful legs.

"Mrs. Wellman, I'm so pleased to meet you," she said, taking off a gray leather glove and extending her right hand. Her fingers were ice cold.

"We'd better go on inside. It's so chilly. It is, however, highly unusual, Mrs. Wellman, for it to be so chilly this time of year. I'm afraid it will be a cold Mardi Gras, don't you think?"

"I'm afraid so, Mrs. Morisot." Jim said. "But it's been a bad winter everywhere." He held the heavy front door of the apartment house open for us and we entered a long, narrow hallway.

"What an odd hall," I said.

"Oh, yes, it's very characteristic of this particular style of architecture. You see, this house and the one next to it are both examples of Blakeley's Blunders. Really, that's what they're called. Blakeley was the architect who designed them. They just weren't practical as houses, but they do divide up into nice apartments. Lovely apartments." She leaned over to unlock the door. The smell of her hair reminded me of dead flowers. She looked up at Jim and smiled.

"Could you please get this door for me. Mr. Wellman? I'm afraid I'm not very good at this."

Jim reached around her shoulder and turned the key.

"Ladies first," he said, opening the door.

The living room was painted Wedgwood blue, with off-white molding and a big, dingy white ceiling. Two narrow windows about eight feet high overlooked the front porch, but the view was obscured by canvas shades and tattered lace curtains that hung several feet above the sills. The only furniture in the room was a scratchy-looking maroon sofa.

"Those windows are simply elegant," Mrs. Morisot said. "But for some inexplicable reason, the previous tenants used them as an entranceway. Can you imagine?"

"Well, I can in a way," Jim said, smiling at Mrs. Morisot. "They are sort of convenient."

"Yes, I suppose you're right, Mr. Wellman. I think this is the most charming fireplace—original, of course, though why anybody painted over this marble I can't begin to understand." Mrs. Morisot scraped off a few flecks of white enamel with a long fingernail.

"Shouldn't be too much trouble to take it back down to the stone," Jim said.

"I'd be more than happy to pay you for the trouble, Mr. Wellman. Follow me to the kitchen, if you please."

An imitation Tiffany lampshade hung by a brass-plated chain from the ceiling above where there must have once been a table, casting a weak circle of light on the green and yellow, diamond-patterned linoleum that covered the floor. The wall over the stove was scorched, and tawny clumps of rice clung to the prongs of the front burners. Mrs. Morisot caught my eye as I looked again at the misshapen grape clusters on the lampshade.

"I just had these cabinets put in last year," she said, pointing above the stove at two wood-grained Formica boxes with clumsy, antiqued handles.

"I thought they looked new," Jim said.

"The bathroom, I'm afraid, is a bit small." Mrs. Morisot held open a door and turned on the switch above a bare bulb that hung on a wire from the ceiling. The floor was filthy and covered with black hairs.

Jim came up behind me and gripped my arm. "It's plenty big enough for us, isn't it, honey?"

"I'll have Charlotte come over tomorrow," Mrs. Morisot said, smiling at Jim. "She's the girl who works for me."

"That is very kind of you," he said, "but Laurie can handle it."

The large, off-white bedroom was completely empty.

"Mrs. Morisot, do you mind if I talk this over with my wife?"

"Not at all, Mr. Wellman. I'll be outside in the hallway."

After she had closed the door behind her, Jim took my face in his hands.

"Well, what do you think? Before you say anything, you have to try and visualize how nice it will look when it's all fixed up. Mrs. Morisot says there are some things in the garage we can use until we can get our own furniture."

"I don't know, Jim."

"Listen, this place is only a hundred and ninety bucks a month. That's fucking cheap for New Orleans. And you couldn't ask for a better neighborhood. You'd be right by the streetcar if you needed to get somewhere."

"But I don't really like first-floor apartments."

"Yeah, but honey, look how pretty it is from the window."

I walked over to the window and looked out across the dank side yard. Patches of jade-green ferns swayed in the shadows near the house, and a few short, moss-covered trees spread their branches over the dense snarl of Virginia creeper that blanketed the ground. My breath made a misty circle on the glass. I wiped away the circle and turned around. Jim was staring at me.

"If you don't want this place, fine. Sure, I'll be worrying my ass off about you down in the bell, but so what? Just don't be bitching at me if we have to move across the river because you're such a fucking chicken that you never got your driver's license. Well, what do you say? Do you want it?"

"I guess maybe it'll be nice."

"All right!" he said, hugging me. "Let's go tell Mrs. Morisot the good news."

"I'll be there in a minute. I have to use the bathroom."

"Okay, but don't be long."

I threw up as quietly as I could, trying not to look at the hairs on the floor. There was nothing in my stomach except the Pepsi I had drunk at Billy's house.

Jim and Mrs. Morisot were standing by the front door, talking.

"Honey, we're going to meet Mrs. Morisot at her house." He put his arm around me and kissed the top of my head.

"You look ill, Mrs. Wellman."

"I'm just a little tired."

"Well, I'm sure you'll feel much better once you're all settled." She put on her gray leather gloves. "I'll see you both at my house, then. You do know where it is, Mr. Wellman?"

"Yes. And thank you so much for showing us the apartment."

"Tea? Or would you rather have port?"

"No, tea is fine, thanks," Jim said.

We were sitting at a long mahogany table in Mrs. Morisot's dining room. In the center of the table was a tall silver candelabrum with twelve pale blue candles that had never been lighted. A fire was smoldering in the brick fireplace.

Mrs. Morisot sat down beside Jim and placed a copy of the lease on the table in front of him.

"Please read this, Mr. Wellman. I think you will find the terms and conditions identical to those we agreed upon earlier." She put on her glasses and peered around the candelabrum at me. "Do you like New Orleans, Mrs. Wellman?"

"Oh, yes."

"Where are you staying now?"

"We're staying with friends in the French Quarter."

She made a face. "I haven't gone past Canal Street in twenty years. I find the quarter distasteful, overrun with the wrong element."

"I know, but that's the real New Orleans, isn't it? The Vieux Carré."

Jim glared at me.

"I think it's prettier uptown, though, and I hope it's safer," I said quickly. "This is uptown, isn't it?"

Mrs. Morisot laughed. Her laugh was like a little girl's.

"Of course this is uptown," Jim said. "The Quarter is downtown." Shaking his head, he looked back down at the lease.

"Your husband tells me you're a graphic designer. That must be very interesting."

"Yes, it is."

"And you make between three and four hundred dollars a week. Is that correct?"

"Yes." I stared into my teacup.

She turned to Jim, smiling. "And your income is forty-five to fifty thousand dollars a year, I believe."

"That's right."

"I spoke with the diving company that you work for, Mr. Wellman. Caldwell Diving, isn't it? Yes, Caldwell. Well, I am happy to say that they gave you a glowing reference."

Mrs. Morisot picked up a gold fountain pen from the table and handed it to Jim.

"So if you'll just sign the lease form, Mr. Wellman, our little business will be completed." She stared at the back of his head as he signed his name.

"Mrs. Wellman, you must be proud to have a hero for a husband."

"Pardon me?"

"Well, it seems your husband is a real hero. At least that is the impression I received from a Mr. Ted Trulock. He gave you quite a reference, young man. He told me that you saved his life once, and in his book, that's as dependable as you can be." She looked at Jim, beaming. "And I must say, I am very much inclined to agree with him."

She signed her name to the lease, folded it into thirds, and put it inside a white business envelope.

"A hero," she said, still beaming.

"Hardly a hero." Jim looked down at the table, smiling and shaking his head.

"You're too modest, Mr. Wellman. After that kind of reference, I could hardly turn you down for the apartment. I would have hated to do that, considering how well you liked it from the second you saw it, and I admire men who make quick decisions. Still, if you had had a bad reference . . . Now in the old days, I would rent a place to a man on the strength of his handshake and the expression in his eyes, but no more." She shook her head sadly and stood up. "Please remember what I said about looking in the garage for some things you can use. I hope you will find what you need."

"Thank you. That's very nice of you," Jim said, standing up.

"Not at all. And you did notice the clause about not using the driveway and no pets, didn't you?"

"Yes. We don't have any pets."

"Wonderful. Mrs. Wellman, it was nice meeting you, and I do hope that you're feeling better soon. You don't look at all well."

"She'll be fine. A lot of it is just the excitement and settling in," Jim said, patting me on the back. "Laurie always wanted to live in New Orleans."

"Oh, really? Well, I already have your check Mr. Wellman, so I believe that's everything. Oh, except for the key." she said with a laugh, pulling a key ring from her sweater pocket. She handed the ring to Jim. "Could you get the key for me, please? Thank you very much."

It was cold in the truck, a damp cold that seemed to go right through my body.

"Jim did you tell Mrs. Morisot we would take the apartment before you talked to me?" I couldn't keep my voice from trembling.

"I took you to see the place first, didn't I? Before I signed the lease."

"But you had already given her the check!"

"All right, what if I did? If you weren't so damned stupid, you would know that sometimes you have to make a decision right on the spot. Especially in a neighborhood like this one. But you wouldn't know anything about that. You've never made a decision, let alone a quick one, in your whole fucking life! Christ, if it had been you down there in the Persian Gulf, Trulock would have been dead! Just like you and your mom if I hadn't come along."

"But you promised that I would always be included in all the decisions that affect us."

"I think you had just better drop it."

"I don't want to drop it. It's important right from the start that we decide things together, Jim. You said so back in Indiana. You wrote it down on your list,"

"Look, I did what I had to do. Now we have a place, don't we?"

"Yes, but—"

"I don't want to hear any more about it. We're not in Indiana now, sister, and I'm not going to spend another fucking second begging your forgiveness. If you had an ounce of brains, you wouldn't want to continue this conversation. Know what I mean?"

I sat as far away from him as I could, hugging my shoulders. The traffic light switched to red, and Jim slammed to a stop. We were in front of a white, three-story house with high, narrow windows. On either side of the walk leading to the house were circular clumps of new green spears, like the peony bushes in my mother's front yard in early spring. . . .

"Earth to Laurel. Come in, please."

"What?"

"What were you thinking about?"

"Nothing."

"It had to be something."

"I was thinking about peonies."

"Peonies! What about them?"

"Well, you know how they look when they're in full bloom? Those tall bushes and the flowers so huge you need two hands to hold one? But then it rains, and the bushes are bent way over, beaten down almost to the ground, and there are pink and white petals scattered everywhere. Just one rain. It doesn't even have to be a hard rain."

"Oh, that's *real* interesting."

"You asked me what I was thinking about, and I told you."

"Well, it wasn't worth hearing." He shook out a cigarette and lighted it. "What do you say you and the kid here go get an oyster po'boy at Parasol's? Put something solid in that old tummy of yours."

Toni was sitting on the couch, cutting a wedge of Camembert on a plate in her lap. Billy was walking around the room reading a newspaper, an unlighted joint in his mouth.

"I take it the bird didn't come back," Jim said.

"Nah, he's gone for good. Flew the coop," Billy said. He took the joint from his mouth and put it behind his ear.

"Well, old Jim got him a place. And it's going to be real nice when we get it fixed up."

"Great. You like it, Laurie?" Billy said, tossing the newspaper on the couch.

"I think it will be all right, especially in the spring."

"Laurie can't wait to see the flowers on St. Charles. We had an interesting talk about peonies."

Jim leaned down next to Toni and opened his mouth. She looked at him for a moment and then put a piece of cheese on his tongue. Her face was expressionless.

"What are you guys doing tonight?" Jim asked.

"I was thinking about taking Toni to a Clint Eastwood movie, but I'm not sure she'd understand it. Toni thinks a forty-four Magnum is a big bottle of vintage champagne."

"Actually," Toni said, "I thought it was some kind of sports car one of you two fools would be buying about now. The time is right—you are both almost broke."

"Maybe we should celebrate tonight, Jimbo. I mean, you guys getting the new place and everything."

"Sounds good to me, but I don't know about Laurie. We went to Parasol's for a po'boy, and she puked out in back as soon as she ate hers."

"Maybe it's just all of the excitement and settling in," I said, glaring at Jim.

He bent over to pick up the newspaper from the sofa. "Don't get smart. Remember what I said about not being in Indiana," he whispered.

Toni got up from the sofa and stood behind me. She gently rubbed my shoulders.

"Go lie down in my room, chérie."

"I think I will. Let me know if you're going anywhere."

"Yes, boss," Jim said, laughing. "You don't mind if I go out and get some smokes, do you, boss?"

I had been lying down for about five minutes, staring at the Degas ballerinas, when there was a knock at the door.

"It's me. Billy." He cracked the door and peeked in. "I thought you might need some of this." He held out a bottle of Pepto Bismol. I propped myself up on my elbow and he sat down on the bed.

"Billy, I didn't really throw up in back of Parasol's. I just thought I was going to, and Jim took off in the truck. He said he didn't want to stand around and watch."

"Open up," Billy said, putting a spoon in my mouth. "Well, he came back for you. I guess that's something."

"I guess. I know he's a little worried, but—Billy, do you ever get worried before your physical?"

"Sure. Everybody does. But then I figure if it turns out I got the Big C, what can I do about it? Diving is always a gamble. Hell, every diver in New Orleans is betting he can save enough money to start up some kind of business before he gets killed out on a dive or comes down with bone cancer. You can't dive for that many years, anyway. Thirty-five is real old for divers."

"God, I didn't know it was that dangerous," I said.

"Yeah, but I tell you, that doesn't bother Jimbo. He sees himself as pretty much untouchable. That's the way top divers have to think. Don't get me wrong. They're still real careful down there, but they're untouchable. You know what I mean?"

"I think I do. So Jim's a good diver, then?"

"More than good. He's a first-rate diver overall, but where he really shines is when something intense has gone wrong and there's no one else who can do the job—or wants to. That's when he really likes to dive—when he really comes to life."

"That sounds like him."

"You should see him, Laurie—he's like a big cat or something, staring down at the water, real stiff and peaceful. But all the time he's thinking, planning every little step he's going to make. And then he goes down and just does it—whatever it takes. It can get crazy down there, too. I thought skydiving was intense, but it's nothing compared to an hour of deep work."

"I'm glad he's a good diver."

"The best. That's why I became a diver—because of Jimbo. Did he ever tell you about the time out in the North Sea when Kevin Wright got killed?"

"No. He never mentions diving to me. What happened?"

Billy picked up a pack of Marlboros lying on top of the small walnut nightstand. He offered me one but I shook my head.

"Well, I don't know exactly what happened because I was out on a different barge, but somehow on a dive Kevin died and Jimbo brought his body back to the SAT unit, you know, the bell. He told the guys topside what had happened, but they wanted him to stay down there a couple more days and finish the job."

"You mean with the body still in there?"

"Yeah. It was a priority job and it takes money to send the unit down or haul it up and you've got to pay a guy for time spent even when he's just decompressing—the deeper you are, the longer it takes. Hell, you spend most of your time getting down to the job site or coming back up on these repair details, anyway. I guess they figured as long as they were paying him, might as well get the job done. But asking a guy to sleep with a dead friend on board is asking a lot."

"God—"

"But Jimbo did it. He didn't have to. He could have raised

hell, but he didn't. That's just the way he is. He believes if you're going to do a job, do it right. Plenty of guys at Caldwell owe him their lives."

"Really?"

"Sure. Ted Trulock and Kenny Perkins's brother. Hell, so does Kenny Perkins, in a way."

"Well, he saved my life, too," I said. "I guess he told you how we met."

"Yeah. It's pretty weird him stopping to help you and your mom like that and then, what?—five years later or something— you meet him again at a party?"

"It is strange, isn't it?"

"He's really crazy about you, Laurie. Hell, he told me that every time he called me. Now how long was it you stayed down in Florida?"

"About six months. Then we sold the boat and moved back to Catalpa."

"Yeah, Jimbo said you guys had a pretty tough time—living at your mom's and everything. I guess that's always hard."

"It was hard," I said softly. "I think it was the hardest eight months of my life."

"I'll bet. Still, you two getting hitched is the best thing that ever happened to him. You know what he told me once? He said the way he sees it, you're actually the one who saved his life, not the other way around."

"Really?"

"Yeah, really. Hey, there's a smile. Maybe later you'll feel like going out."

"Maybe."

"Good. Toni wants to go to the Dream Palace."

"The Dream Palace?" *Champagne mirrored and shimmering like mercury, our arms glowing in the silvery light. Slender spires above the blue-green mists, pierced by thousands of stars. "There's your palace."*

"Yeah, it's a bar, but I think they serve food out in the court-yard. I've never been there, but Toni likes it."

"Oh, I'd love to go. Where is it?"

"I'm not sure. I think it's somewhere out on Constantinople. Well, I hope you feel better." He got up from the bed and walked to the door.

"Billy?"

He turned around.

"I really feel bad about Toni's bird."

"Yeah. She doesn't want another one."

"Maybe she'll change her mind."

"No chance. She won't change her mind. Remember who we're talking about."

He closed the door softly behind him.

NINE

"We're walking in circles, Toni," Jim said. "I thought you said you knew where it was."

"I do. I am just trying to remember should we turn left or right."

"Well, I've seen that yellow house over there at least three times," Billy said.

"The hell with it, then! We'll go somewhere else. I know I am able to find it, though. But men aren't patient, *n'est-ce pas*, Laurie?"

"Let's just go to Dauphine's," Jim said, cupping his hand over the match while he lit a cigarette.

"But we're probably really close."

"Look, Laurie, we've been walking around for an hour."

"It hasn't been an hour," Toni said.

"Well, in this cold it sure as hell feels like it. We're going to Dauphine's."

Toni dropped behind Billy and walked next to me.

"We will go to the Dream Palace sometime, chérie. Just you and me."

At Dauphine's Billy and Jim ordered Myers and orange juice and Toni and I had White Russians.

"Sheila, put these on my tab," Billy said. "And could you give me some quarters for the jukebox."

"I hope you are not going to sing along tonight," Toni said. "Last week he sang 'Betty Sue' in here."

" 'Peggy Sue,' and you loved it. Everybody loved it."

"Kane, I swear I don't know why you're a diver," Jim said. "Seems like all you ever really wanted to be was a rock-and-roll star."

"You know me: Mr. Johnny B. Bad. Hey, Jimbo, what ever happened to that old Woodie you had? Remember when we took it up to Baton Rouge?"

"The Willys? Long gone, pal. Sold it."

"What a surprise," Toni said.

Jim turned to Billy and started talking about the *Sheherazade*.

"Do you like working at the Jade Moon?" I asked Toni.

"It's all right. They gave me a few days off. Anyhow, I still have a job. I had quite an argument with the owner—or so I've been told."

"You've been told?"

She smiled at me. "Well, I certainly don't remember." She held her drink against her lips. "I wish I were back in Aspen. For the sunsets, you understand. I was so happy there for a while."

"Colorado must be really pretty."

"Beautiful."

"Prettier than France?"

"No."

Jim drained his drink and stood up.

"I got the pictures over at your place," he said to Billy. "Be right back." He dropped a twenty dollar bill on the bar. "I'll get this next round, Sheila. And have one yourself."

"Thanks, Jim." She stared at him as he walked to the door.

"Just look. Don't touch," Toni said.

"That's all I ever do."

"I'm going to play the jukebox," Billy said, standing up.

Toni set down her glass and motioned to Sheila. "A glass of burgundy for me, please, and another White Russian for my friend."

"I don't care for one," I said.

"Go ahead, Sheila. She'll change her mind."

Buddy Holly's "That'll Be the Day" came over the jukebox. Billy was standing in the middle of the floor, arms outstretched, singing.

"Don't look at him, Laurie. You will only encourage him."

When the record ended, there was scattered applause. Billy

strolled back to the bar, bowing from side to side, and sat down beside Toni.

"You sounded pretty good," I said.

"Thanks. Hey, Toni, I meant to tell you. I ran into Matthew over by Crazy Shirley's and he sends his best. He was in really high spirits. Said he'd been taking photographs of Donnie."

"Who's Donnie?"

Billy smiled at me. "Donnie the leather dwarf. He's part of the local color. And his boyfriend is even funnier. He's about six feet six and wears one of those leather flying helmets and a white silk scarf like a World War One ace. So does Donnie. And they both wear dog collars—Snoopy and the Red Baron, or some shit. Sheila, when you get a chance, another Myers and OJ."

"Chérie, have you ever noticed what homophobes these divers are?"

"Homophobe? What's that supposed to mean?" Billy asked.

"It means that you and your diver friends are always talking about 'fags' and 'gays,' and yet you spend months together on a boat with no women around." She turned again to me. "So tell me, chérie, what kind of conversation were you and Jim having about peonies today? I find it unbelievable that he was talking about flowers."

"Oh. Well, he wasn't really. I was just thinking out loud, I guess. I was telling him about how peony bushes bend over after a rain. You know, they always look so strong, but they aren't—"

"Oh, Christ, Laurie. Not again." Jim was suddenly behind me.

"Well, Toni asked me about—"

"Yes, I asked her, Jim. I find the subject fascinating."

"See, Jim?" I said, smiling. "Some people don't think it's stupid." I gulped down the rest of my drink. My hands were shaking.

"Are you going to be Toni's protégée? Take smart-ass lessons?"

"Please, Jim."

"Oh, I don't think she needs any lessons," Toni said. "She is bright. I'm sure if she had the right kind of environment, it would surface. You know, like freedom from fear."

Jim's jaw was flexing back and forth. For a moment, I thought he was going to hit her.

"Hey, Jimbo, lighten up," Billy said, putting his arm around Jim's shoulder.

"Sorry, Toni. Guess I have a lot of things on my mind."

"Save it. For Laurel."

"No, I mean it. I'm sorry. You know I'm crazy about you, don't you, kid?"

Toni stared at him for a few seconds before she smiled. "All right, but spare me the charm."

Jim and Billy began poring over the photographs that Jim had brought back to the bar.

"This is your Vette, huh? Is this before or after, Jimbo?"

"What do you think, Einstein?"

Toni leaned over and told me to meet her in the rest room. She was staring at herself in the mirror when I came in.

"So why didn't you say something, chérie?"

"I was trying to."

"Not for me. For you. Stand up for you." She took a sip of wine and set the glass down on the rim of the basin. "He hits you, doesn't he?"

"What?"

"You know," she said, putting her fists up like a boxer.

"No."

"Tell me the truth. I know he does. He must. Billy told me about Stacy, Jim's old girlfriend."

"No."

"Tell me."

"All right, yes. Yes, he has." I started sobbing. "But he's never going to again, Toni. Never."

"Sssssssh!"

I lowered my voice. "Never."

My mother's head bowed over Jim's list, silver-gray smoke spiraling from the long ash of her cigarette. Jim taking the cigarette from her fingers and putting it out in the Mexican ashtray on the end table. "Thank you." "So, Marian, what do you think?" "Well, I think it sounds pretty good, if you can really do it." "Oh, I can do it all right. I can do anything if I put my mind to it." Mother biting back her lower lip, the worn rose lipstick pale under the pressure of her teeth. "But, Jim, there is something that bothers me. Why did you leave the first one on your list blank?" "Well, it's kind of personal, but Laurie and I talked it over, and she knows what it is." The paper dropping onto her lap. "Oh,

*I don't know. I just don't. If only Joe were here. He'd know
what to do."*

Toni put her arms around me. "You must stop crying. What
I am trying to say is that we have to stick together. Trust each
other. It is important, chérie. Those two jerks always stick together, and we have to do the same thing."

"He begged me to come down here, Toni. He said that we
would start over in New Orleans and forget the past. But it's
so hard."

"I know," she said, holding me closer.

"Please, please promise me you won't tell Jim or Billy that I
told you this. I swore to Jim I would never tell anyone, and if
he ever found out—"

"I give you my word. Let me dry your eyes." She dabbed the
corners of my eyes with a folded sheet of toilet paper. "There.
Maybe, chérie, maybe New Orleans will be everything you
want."

She hugged me for a moment and then picked up her glass.
"You go back first. Don't worry. I will never say anything to
them."

Jim watched me walk over to the bar.

"It's about time."

"Sorry."

"What were the two of you doing in there?"

"Nothing."

"What do you think we were doing in there?" Toni said.

"Search me." He gave me a strange look. "You know, you
should let Toni cut your hair. She's an ace at it. She cuts Billy's
hair and she's going to cut mine."

"Cut whose hair?" Toni said, sitting down next to Billy.

"Laurie's," Jim said.

"Do you want it cut?"

"No. I'm trying to grow it long."

"It is long, chérie."

"Well, I mean longer."

"I think you would look cuter if you had it cut. Don't you,
Toni?"

"Laurel would look pretty any way she wore her hair."

"See," I said, smiling at Jim.

"See what? You'd look a lot better with your hair cut."

Sheila set another round of drinks in front of us. "Why?" she asked. "What's wrong with her hair?"

"It's old-fashioned, for one thing. No one wears long hair hanging down now."

"It's not hanging down," I said.

"And I'm telling you that you look like a farm girl. A little Midwestern farm girl."

"I'm not a farm girl."

"No, I forgot. Your daddy was a hot-shot lawyer. Some law-yer—he represented every two-bit loser in town."

"If you mean his *pro-bono* work, he—"

"Pro-bonehead work is more like it. When he kicked off he didn't leave your mom with a pot to piss in."

The open office door, the dusty light through the yellowed wooden blinds falling in stripes across my father's face, the papers scattered on his desk, the pale leather soles of his shoes, and, in the shadeless window facing the park, the pink crab-apple blossoms pressing against the black-lettered glass: Joseph W. Longstreet, Atty. at Law. Mother grasping my shoulders: "Laurel! Please look at me! Wait in the car with your sister!"

"Why don't you leave her alone?" Toni said.

"Why don't you keep your nose the hell out of this?"

"Jim! Please!" I looked in the mirror behind the bar. My hair was just long enough to cover my breasts. I grasped a strand of it, knocking over Jim's glass. Red wine spilled over the photo-graph on top of the pile.

"God damn you!" Jim yelled, gathering up the photographs. "Just look at this picture of the galley. It's ruined!"

"Oh, God, and you only have thirty more," Toni said.

"I'm really sorry, Jim."

"Oh, you're sorry! If you weren't so goddamned clumsy, it wouldn't have happened. A clumsy, fucking farm girl."

"Damn it, Jim, stop it!" I shouted, standing up.

Billy held my left arm. "Come on, Laurie—stay. Jimbo doesn't mean it."

"Let her go, Kane," Jim said.

I ran, my heart pounding, until I reached Billy's house. The front door was unlocked.

I caught my hipbone on a corner of the sofa on my way to the bathroom. I locked the bathroom door and stared at my face in the mirror. Mascara was smeared under my eyes, and a beige-colored moustache had dried above my upper lip from my last White Russian. I tried to remember whether my mascara was supposed to be waterproof, but I couldn't. I was shaking and laughing and crying all at the same time.

I lit a cigarette and rested it on the sink; then I opened the medicine cabinet door and took out a pair of scissors. A pamphlet fell to the floor: *Know your Parakeet.*

"Farm girl! I'll show you who looks like a fucking farm girl." The first snip was loud. A piece of hair about eight inches long fell to the floor. I could hear the doorknob twisting back and forth.

"Laurie! Laurie, let me in!"

I didn't answer. I kept cutting the rest of my hair to shoulder length.

"Open up, God damn it!"

The door burst open. Jim stood in the doorway, his shirt wet with sweat.

"What in the hell?" He looked at my face and then at the floor. "Oh, so you want to be a martyr? A little fucking martyr? Well, I'll help you. You want a haircut? I'll give you a haircut!" He snatched the scissors from my hand.

"No! Jim, no!"

He held his forearm so tightly around my neck that I could hardly breathe; then he grasped a clump of hair and hacked at it until it fell to the floor. He poked my neck with the point of the scissors. I screamed.

"Hold still, God damn it! You're just making it worse on yourself by moving around."

"Stop it, Jim!"

"Shut the fuck up!" He threw the scissors down and pushed me in front of the mirror. "I'm finished. Why don't you take a look?"

My hair in back was still more or less shoulder length, but he had chopped the hair by my left ear into short, jagged patches.

"Now, guess where we're going? That's right. Back to Dauphine's so you can show off your new hairdo."

I broke away from him. He lunged toward me, and I knocked

over the bird cage. Feathers and birdseed and bright plastic beads scattered over the floor.

"God, you pig! Look what you've done!"

"Just leave me alone!"

"No! We're going back to the bar. You know how much I love to show off my wife."

"You're drunk!"

He laughed. "Oh, and you aren't?"

He dragged me out of the bathroom, one arm around my neck. The kitchen spun around, the overhead light stinging my eyes. Marie barked at Jim, her white teeth bared.

"It's all right, girl," he said. "It's all right." She wagged her tail. "Now, come on!"

He pulled me through the dining room and living room and onto the porch. I sat down. My heart was beating so fast that it made a rushing sound, like a television set with the volume up on a vacant channel. He picked me up and carried me over his shoulder down the front steps. I slid off his shoulder onto the wet grass by the walk.

"Get up!"

I couldn't.

"Get up!"

"Please don't take me in there! Please!"

At first, all I could see were the lights of the jukebox and pinball machine and the shining silver pour caps on the liquor bottles. Jim tightened his grip on my shoulders.

"Look, everybody! Laurie's got herself a really nice haircut. Very sharp, wouldn't you say, Toni? Very French."

"Jesus." Toni stood up.

"Well, Toni, what do you think? You usually aren't at a loss for words. Isn't it original, one side shorter than the other? Chic, huh?"

"She's still pretty," Billy said.

I heard the rushing sound again, and I felt Jim let go of my shoulders. Then there was a much smaller and lighter arm around me.

"I can fix it," Toni said. "Come on. Let's go back to the house."

"Thank you," I said, putting my head on her shoulder as we walked out of the bar.

*   *   *

"No, I'm not too drunk to do this! I know what I am doing. Believe me, please. I'm not going to screw it up." She snipped a small piece of hair and then lit a cigarette. "Damn him. If he hadn't chopped off that one big piece, I would not need to cut the rest so close."

"I know," I said, looking down at the floor. "I'm the one who knocked over the bird cage. I'm sorry. I'm sorry about the bird, too."

Toni took a long drag from her cigarette and then rested it on the edge of the bathroom sink. "Don't worry about it. Don't worry about anything. Just sit still. We have to get this done before he comes back here."

"Well, what do you think?" Toni asked, giving me a hand mirror. "See? Who is too drunk to cut hair?"

"Oh, Toni, you did a wonderful job. Thank you so much."

"You do look glamorous, chérie."

"I just can't believe I did anything that stupid!"

"So what? It looks fine now. I cannot believe him. He is a son of a bitch, that one is."

I didn't say anything.

"But not always. That is the tricky part, eh? Your Jim has the most beautiful eyes I have ever seen."

"I'm a fool, aren't I?"

"Yes. But that is all right, chérie. At least you are a fool for love. These divers are the real fools: they are fools for money. Someone once said to me one should only be a fool for art, a fool for love, or a fool for God."

"Who told you that?"

"My father's mistress."

"Well, I still feel like an idiot for cutting my hair just because of what he said to me. Have you ever done anything that stupid because of a man?"

Toni took a drag from her cigarette, closing her eyes when she inhaled. She pulled down the front of her sweater. It took me a moment to realize that she was pointing to the butterfly tattoo.

"All right, Toni, I'm ready to see this masterpiece of yours," Jim said.

"Oh, Christ, let her sleep!" she said in a loud whisper.

I lay still with my eyes closed, listening.

"Hey, how come you always sound more French when you're drunk?"

"Good question, Jimbo."

"*Vas t'enculer!* There's some French for you! I am going to bed now, and I cannot tell you both how lovely you have made my evening. And I believe I can speak for Laurel, too."

I heard the dining room door close. Jim and Billy laughed.

"Jesus, Kane, look at her. Isn't Laurie beautiful?"

"She sure is. You're a lucky guy, Jimbo."

"Kiss Laurie good night," Jim whispered.

"Kiss her?"

"Yeah. Why not?"

"You want me to kiss her?"

"Sure. She likes you."

"She'll wake up, and with my luck Toni will come in here with my gun."

"Go ahead. Laurie won't care."

I remembered a night long ago when my parents came into my room, whispering, to kiss me good night—the smell of rain and pipe tobacco when my father's coat brushed my cheek, my mother's cool, soft fingers as she smoothed my hair. . . .

Billy smelled like baby lotion. He kissed me lightly between my lips and nose.

"See you in the morning," Jim said.

"Okay. Hey, Jimbo, if I was you, I wouldn't fuck this one up. I'd be real careful."

"Don't worry about it. I'm not going to lose Laurie. I'd never lose her."

"I'm glad to hear you say that. Well, good night. We'll try and keep it down."

I could hear Jim undressing. After a few minutes, he knelt down on the mattress.

"Honey, you asleep?"

I turned and stretched and then slowly opened my eyes.

"God, you look great! Toni did a perfect job!"

"Do you really like it?"

"I love it."

"What time is it?"

"Late."

"Day?"

"Almost. Listen, I'm sorry about playing that joke on you. I know it doesn't help much, but I did apologize to everyone at Dauphine's. I told them you're the greatest little girl in the world, and you are, too."

He slipped in bed next to me and started kissing my neck.

"Don't, Jim."

"God damn it, you're my wife!" He threw back the sheet and stood up. "I'm sick of walking on pins and needles around you, trying not to get mad."

"I really thought things were going to be different in New Orleans."

"They are."

"How? You said after we got out of my mother's house, things would be better—that you'd change. I believed you. I thought we'd be close—really close—and it's still like living with a stranger. And I'm afraid again, Jim—even more afraid."

"I'll tell you one more time, and you damn well better remember it. You're not in Indiana now. Mommie is far away. You try to leave, and I swear to God I'll drag you back and you'll be sorry. You just aren't going to walk out on me. I'll find you no matter where you go. You got that, sister?" He tightened the grip on my arm. "Do you?"

"Yes."

"Good," he said, releasing my arm. "The only way I see out for you, little girl, is to sneak off while I'm gone on a dive. That would be just your style—take the shortcut when nobody was looking. And who knows? If you're real lucky, I might not find you."

"But you promised me I could leave if things didn't work out. Remember? You said that if I came down here with you—"

"I lied."

"You what?"

"I lied. I never lied to you before—not about anything I've done—but I had to use everything I could to keep you. And baby, if things don't work out, I'm not going to let you go. So I guess you had better work real hard on making them work out." He stood over me, swaying, his undershorts very white in the blue light. "Now I'm going to brush my teeth."

I closed my eyes to the sound of running water in the bathroom and the rhythmic squeaking of the Kanes' bed.

"I just got too drunk," Jim's voice said softly beside me. "This

is no good, us getting drunk. Maybe it's being here at Billy's—
I get a little wild around him. Anyway, this is our last night, and
then we'll be safe in our own place. Oh, that reminds me. I have
to call Mrs. Morisot when I get up."

"Why?" I was wide awake now.

"Because she'll pay for the paint. Get rid of that blue. I
hate it."

"I like it. It's pretty."

"Well, we're painting it white, so we better get some sleep."
He kissed me on the cheek. "I love you, little girl. I really do."

TEN

Standing on the stepladder Jim had brought from the garage, I slowly spread paint up and down the wall, trying to recall every detail I could of my grandmother's bedroom in her house on the lake in Michigan. I remembered lying on her big bed and looking across at the matching bed where my grandfather slept. The chenille bedspreads hung to the floor, pale and clean and smooth. "Sea foam green," my grandmother said—it was her favorite color. The twin yellow clocks on the nightstand and dresser; and on my grandfather's side of the nightstand, paperback mysteries and a glass tobacco jar filled with coins. . . .

"God damn it, listen up!" Jim was shaking me.

"What's the matter?"

"Do you read lips? Watch my mouth: more paint."

"You want more paint?"

"Hey, you catch on real fast. Another gallon should do it. Now, here's what you do. Take a right at Commander's Palace and go past the cemetery. The hardware store is across from the Little Home Restaurant. You can get us some sandwiches at the same time. And don't give me that look, Laurie. It's high noon and we're in the Garden District. That's why we moved up here. You'll be fine."

Outside, the trees and the tall, narrow houses seemed to float in the mist. I crossed the street and walked beside the whitewashed wall of Lafayette Cemetery. It started to drizzle.

108

I stopped in front of the wrought-iron gate. The peaked white tombs were raised above the ground; and high above them all, wings outspread, stood Saint Michael.

I pushed open the gate. My footprints in the dead grass filled instantly with water as I walked.

Saint Michael, in breastplate and pauldron, was smiling down at me, his elegant feet straddling the sloped sides of the vault roof. He brandished his sword above his head, muscles flexed, and in his left hand he held a pair of scales. Standing on tiptoe, the rain prickling my eyes, I touched his left foot. It was surprisingly warm.

I started back toward the street. Something cold wrapped itself around my bare ankle. I kept walking, too terrified to look down, until I reached the gate. A thick satin ribbon oozed rivulets of red dye into my tennis shoe and trailed off into the muddy grass behind me. The white carnations that the ribbon had bound were lying in a puddle about fifteen feet away. I tried shaking the ribbon loose; then I tried scraping it with the side of my other foot. Finally, I reached down and pulled it off with my fingers.

Carrying the can of paint and a warm bag of hamburgers and french fries, I walked down the brick path to the back of the house. Mrs. Morisot had said that there were some potted plants on the patio we could have for the apartment, and Jim wanted me to look at them.

All of the plants were dead except for a few fat gray-green cacti. I started to walk away, and then I heard a soft whimpering sound. At first, I thought that it was the torn patio awning flapping in the wind. Then I heard it again—like a baby crying. It seemed to be coming from beneath the house.

I set my bags under a broken granite bench and got down on my knees. Part of the foundation of the house had caved in, leaving irregular gaps in the stonework.

"Come on," I said coaxingly. "Come on out."

The whimpering became louder. I crawled underneath the house.

"Please come here. I won't hurt you. Come here."

I saw two glowing eyes a few feet from me; then they disappeared. I squeezed back out.

I was brushing myself off when a small red foxlike mongrel

emerged from under the house, shaking muddy water on me and wagging her tail.

For some reason, I couldn't stop crying. I fed the dog my hamburger and french fries. She was shivering, and I picked her up. Fleas crawled all over her stomach.

"Laurie, where the hell you been? We got work to do." Jim was standing in front of me, a cigarette dangling from his mouth. His clothes were splotched with paint, and there was a semicircular smear of white under his right eye. "This morning I told Billy maybe we'd all go to the Momus Parade tonight, but nobody's going anywhere till we're done painting."

"I know," I said, "but, Jim, look at this little dog."

"Look at yourself. You're filthy."

"But isn't she sweet?" I put my face against the dog's head, and she sniffed my ear. "She's so skinny I can feel her ribs."

"Where'd you find her?"

"Underneath the house."

"She's probably covered with fleas. They thrive under these old houses."

The dog stared up at Jim, her watery eyes clotted at the corners with black mucus. Jim put his hands on his hips and looked around the patio.

"Shit. So this is it for the plants?"

"Just the cactus."

"Fuck the cactus." He threw his cigarette against the side of the house. "Well, let's get back to work. There's a pay phone in front of that hardware store. You better call the Humane Society and have them come get her." He scratched the dog's head and she licked his hand. "Sorry, girl, but you'll get a good home."

"Oh, Jim, what if she doesn't?"

The torn awning smacking above us sounded like the beating of wings. I closed my eyes. Saint Michael folded his wings around me and the little dog, lifting us far up into the sky. Jim's flannel shirt was pressing against my cheek. His breath was warm on my neck as he kissed it.

"You want to keep her, don't you?"

"Yes."

He looked up at the thickening clouds, his eyes as blue as the unlighted candles on Mrs. Morisot's table.

"It's going to pour like hell any minute. Bring her inside, and I'll give her a bath when we're done painting."

"You mean I can have her?"

"Yeah, but remember, you've got to house-train her. She's your dog."

"Oh, thank you!"

"So what're you going to call her?"

"I'm going to name her Echo."

"Echo. I like that."

I hugged him around the neck. "Thank you, Jim. Thank you so much." I felt his hand between my legs, rubbing me through my jeans.

"You can thank me inside," he said.

"Remember what I told you, Laurie? Ten days of partying, and we're smack in the middle of it. Hey, Kane, don't bogart that booze-olay."

"It is Beaujolais, *crétin!*" Toni said.

Jim laughed. "I make zee leetle joke, Frenchie."

As we passed the locked gate of the cemetery, I could hear band music. Tiny drops of water blew in the wind, but it was no longer raining. Billy gave Jim the bottle of wine. Echo was whimpering, and I put her down beside the gate, where she sat sniffing at the scents of wet earth, popcorn, cotton candy, beer, and grease that the wind wafted toward us. Jim tilted the wine bottle to his lips and then handed it to Toni. Toni pushed up her red satin half mask as she drank.

"Come here, girl. Come here, Echo," Jim called, clapping his hands. The dog jumped away from the sound and squeezed through the narrow space under the gate.

"God damn her! That little bitch!"

"Need some help, buddy?" Billy asked.

Jim didn't answer. He climbed over the top of the gate, jumped down, and disappeared into the darkness.

A man and two women dressed in evening clothes were leaving Commander's Palace across the street, sinister in their black masks. Warm light spread onto the sidewalk from the gaslights inside the restaurant's windows. In the distance I heard Jim calling for Echo.

"Jimbo's sure pissed," Billy said. "Hey, babe, pass Laurie the wine."

I took a big gulp of red wine, looking up at Saint Michael.

His body glistened in the cold mist as if it were beaded with sweat. I heard Echo yelping.

"Don't let him." I whispered to Saint Michael. "Please don't let him."

The gate clanked, and then I heard a thud and Jim stood in front of me with Echo panting in his arms.

"You didn't—"

"Didn't what?" he said, his chest heaving up and down. "Didn't what?"

"Hit her. You didn't hit her, did you?"

"Now, what do you think?" He cradled Echo tightly against his chest. "I'm going to take her home, Kane. You guys go on to the parade. Be sure and get a good spot so Laurie can see."

"Will do."

I watched Jim cross the street. He stopped under a street lamp and, bending over, kissed Echo on top of the head. Arm in arm, Toni, Billy, and I walked toward the music and the crowd.

The dark sky was marbled with fluorescent streaks of orange; strings of plastic beads, caught on the branches of the trees, sparkled in the eerie light. In front of us were two men wearing oversized diapers, with small gauzy wings fixed to their backs and golden bows slung over their shoulders. Beside them, a short, fat man was dressed as a ham sandwich, his head covered with a tight green and red cap that resembled a Spanish olive. Nearly everyone was drinking from plastic cups. An old woman poured beer along the curb for a large black dog. His pink tongue flicked in and out over the foamy puddle, lapping it up.

"I'm glad Echo's safe at home," I said.

"Yes, if she is safe." I could tell from Toni's eyes that Jim was coming up behind us. His arms encircled my waist.

"Excited, baby?"

"Yes!"

"Just you stick with old Jim here. You'll have some fun."

Row after row of skeletons marched past, the orange flames and oily wisps of black smoke from their flambeaux rising above the crowd. The skeletons were followed by a papier-mâché float of Poseidon about twenty feet high and fifty feet long. Masked women wearing mermaid costumes in aqua and cool greens stood in a line along the sea god's tail, throwing handfuls of bright beads into the crowd.

"Come on, Laurie!" Billy said. "Don't be shy. Get those arms up. They always throw them to pretty girls."

Jim raised my arms over my head, and a string of purple beads hooked around my wrist. He hugged me.

"Cold?"

"Not now."

"Hey, Kane, give Laurie some more wine. I don't want her to get cold."

There was a metallic tinkling in the street; costumed children rushed toward the sound, making whirlpools of color in the crowd.

"When you hear those doubloons hit, look down," Jim said. "And if you see one, put your foot over it."

Toni grabbed my arm. "Look, chérie."

"Cool," Billy said.

The float was a lurid reconstruction of Botticelli's "Birth of Venus." A girl wearing a knee-length blond wig and a flesh-colored bodysuit waved and threw beads as she perched, feet together, on a pedestal within an immense nacreous pink papier-mâché shell.

The flatbed of the next float was garlanded with thousands of silver and gold paper roses. Overhead, swinging stiffly in the wind, were gargantuan figures of Apollo and Daphne portraying the exact moment of Daphne's metamorphosis into a tree. Daphne's pink mouth was open in a rigid scream, and her body turned away from Apollo's touch, her fingers already spreading into branches and her legs twisting thickly into a tree trunk. Daphne's gilded leaves and Apollo's sandals reflected the golden, flickering flames of the flambeaux. Masked men dressed as woodland nymphs clung to green vines made of rope and paper leaves, their white legs dangling off the sides of the float.

"What are they supposed to be?" Billy asked.

"I don't know," Jim said, lighting a cigarette. "Gods or something."

"Hey, Toni, look! It's Calvert Earlewine!" Billy pointed to a paunchy, bald drunk about fifty years old who was leaning against a street lamp twenty feet from where we were standing with an empty plastic cup in his hand.

"Vas t'enculer!"

"Who's Calvert Earlewine?" I whispered to Jim.

"Billy's just kidding around. That's the name of Toni's first husband." He was smiling.

"Idiot! Calvert might have had nothing on top, but at least he was not empty in here!" Toni tapped her temple with her forefinger.

Two tall black boys wearing sunglasses marched by carrying a red-and-white satin banner: *Children of the Innocent Blood.* They were followed by a drum-and-bugle corps of black children, some of them quite young, wearing white felt uniforms with red satin sashes. Those not playing instruments twirled wooden rifles in frenzied syncopation, their shining faces strangely solemn in the torchlight.

There were more flambeaux and floats crowded with gods, goddesses, satyrs, centaurs, harlequins, and Arabian dancers in pastel silks, kings and queens wearing dark satins and powdered wigs, saints on ponies, skeletons, knights, hangmen, and animals. A white-bearded man in black face pushed a wheeled brown bin ahead of him with NUTZ scrawled in red letters across its front. The hundreds of peanut shells sewn to his black coat and trousers swung out momentarily right or left as he threw paper bags of roasted peanuts to onlookers on either side of the street. High-kicking uniformed school bands from nearby bayou towns marched in ordered rows. Shriners in red felt fezzes and clown makeup wobbled through synchronized stunts on tiny, sputtering motorbikes.

And then it was over, the music dying away down the street, laughing knots of painted faces swirling past us as we stood in the damp grass. My eyes burned from not blinking. I closed them and turned my face toward the sky, feeling the mist caress my cheeks.

"Hey," Jim said. "You guys coming in for a nightcap?"

"I guess so. What do you say, babe?"

Without answering, Toni walked inside. Billy laughed, shook his head, and followed her.

I stood alone on the front walk. Raindrops glistened on the iron fence, and the dark branches above me spread like a web against the gray-white clouds. There had never been any time since I had been in New Orleans, day or night, when the humidity was low enough that I could see the literal color of anything. Now I felt as if I were gazing through wet gauze. Every object had a ghost image, like a badly tuned-in television set. A watery phantasm of columns oscillated behind the columns on the front porch where Jim was standing.

"What the hell are you doing, Laurie? You're mooning around down there like a moron."

I hurried up the steps, across the porch and into the long dim hallway. Toni and Billy were waiting in front of our door.

"It is not like the apartment on North Rampart. Yours was on the second floor for one thing and then there was all that fruit-wood paneling," Toni said.

"Yeah, but it was down a skinny hall and the door was on the left like this place. Everything all right, Jimbo?"

Something moved at the base of the stairs at the far end of the hallway.

"Echo! Get over here, God damn it!" Jim yelled.

The dog ran toward us but then turned and raced back down the hallway. She stopped abruptly, cocking her head at the sound of footsteps in the hall upstairs.

A man and a woman walked down the stairs. They were both about my height and in their late twenties. The woman had light brown hair and a round, pretty face. Her floor-length kaftan was tight in the sleeves and flattened her large breasts. The man had wavy black hair with a pronounced widow's peak. He smelled of old sweat, patchouli oil, and beer.

"So she's *your* dog. She's so cute!" The woman yawned without covering her mouth. "You just moved into the first apartment, didn't you?"

"Yeah. How in the hell did she get out?" Jim asked. "I put her in the house."

"You left your window open. I'm Pat Crawley," the man said. When he shook Jim's hand, I saw his dirty long underwear beneath the rolled-up cuff of his green flannel shirt. "This is Sarah Glass. We live up in fourteen."

"Jim Wellman. My wife, Laurie, and Billy and Toni Kane. I guess you met Echo."

"Oh, what a cute name." Sarah yawned again and looked down at Echo lying on the bottom stair. "I hate to tell you this, but Mrs. Morisot doesn't allow pets."

"Well, we have Echo now and we're keeping her," Jim said.

"Then you'd better get her house-trained fast," Pat said, chewing on the mustache hairs that grew over his upper lip. "Mrs. Morisot is hard core. She's a drunken bitch, too."

"Pat!"

"Well, she is. She always smells like bourbon."

"Or mothballs," Sarah said.

"See, we kind of manage this place, Jim. You know, maintain it. I got all the keys, so if you ever want to go snooping around to find some stuff for your apartment—"

"Thanks. Might take you up on that. Mrs. Morisot give you cheap rent?"

"No rent."

"Best kind," Jim said.

"He doesn't do much," Sarah said. Pat glared at her, and I realized that he was drunk. Sarah seemed straight—straight and tired.

"You'd better not let Echo go up these stairs," Sarah said. "She went to the bathroom in the hall. I think she's got worms."

"Oh, I'm sorry," I said. "God, I'm really sorry."

"It's all right. It wasn't any trouble."

"Not for Sarah," Pat said. "I told her I wouldn't touch that shit, but she's used to it at Audubon Daycare."

"Stop it," she said softly.

"You guys smoke?" Billy pulled a joint from his wallet.

"She doesn't, but I do," Pat said.

Billy lit the joint, took a quick drag, and passed it to Pat.

"So, Sarah, you work at Audubon Daycare," Billy said, exhaling smoke. "You ever know a girl named Kim Kincaid? Tall. Blond. She used to work there."

"I don't think so. No."

"How do you like it?" Jim asked.

"Early hours, but I love the children."

"They don't pay shit," Pat said.

"They don't pay much, but I like it." She gave Pat a cold look. "It's a job."

"So you manage this place, huh?" Jim shook his head at the joint Pat held out to him. Toni took it from Pat's fingers.

"I vacuum the carpet." Pat smiled, his eyes dark, glittering slits.

"Sleep until noon. Get up to water the plastic flowers," Toni said, and Pat stopped smiling.

"Well, we really have to get to bed," Sarah said. "Anytime you need anyone to baby-sit Echo, we're upstairs. Just let me know."

"Thank you," I said, yawning.

"Listen, you guys want to come in for a nightcap?" Jim asked.

"Oh, we can't. It's late, and I have to get up early." Sarah rubbed Pat's shoulders.

"I understand," Jim said, smiling.

"I'm going with them," Pat said, moving away from Sarah. "Don't wait up."

"Good night, then," Sarah said. "Glad to have met all of you." She turned and started up the stairs.

I picked up Echo and followed Jim and Pat down the hall to our apartment door.

"You got any tools, man?" Jim asked Pat. "The heater in the apartment isn't on. I got to light the damned thing."

"I've got some in my car," Pat said. "I'll go get them."

"Look, Toni," I heard Billy whisper behind me. "I told you— it was a long time ago."

Lying on the sofa in the living room, I watched Jim unscrew the heater vent from the kitchen floor. Pat squatted beside him, drinking brandy and handing him tools. Billy leaned against the arm of the sofa, rolling a joint on a copy of *Yachting* magazine, and Toni sat on the floor playing tug-of-war with Echo and a strand of Mardi Gras beads. Suddenly the strand broke, sprinkling magenta and black beads across the floor. Jim looked up, frowning.

"Relax, Jim," Toni said. "I'll clean them up."

"Get that lazy butt to help you."

"Jim!"

"Help her, Laurie."

"All right, I will."

"Goddamn right." He handed Pat a wrench and stood up. "I think it'll work now."

"Jim, maybe you shouldn't light the heater," I said. "It might blow up."

"No one's going to get blown up. You'd better watch out or we'll make you light it. You know what we need, Pat? A stick or something so we can get the match way down there."

"I got a yardstick out in the car," Pat said.

"Go get it."

"Sure, man."

"What kind of car you got?"

"Old VW bug."

Jim didn't say anything, and after a long moment, Pat went out the door. I turned away from the light, pressing my face into the stiff maroon fabric covering the arm of the sofa, and closed my eyes.

When I awakened, the heat was on and everyone was in the kitchen. The air was dense with smoke, and a charred yardstick lay on the kitchen floor.

"So Sleeping Beauty's finally up," Jim said, as I walked to the bathroom.

When I came out, I saw my hand mirror on the countertop with a few white lines of powder and a razor blade on it.

"You guys make a lot of money, then," Pat said.

Billy shrugged. "We do all right when there's work. Here, let Laurie do a line."

"Is it cocaine?"

"No, Laurie, it's Sani-Flush," Jim said. "Don't be stupid."

"Where did you get it?"

"From Pat. We chipped in and bought a gram." Billy's eyes were bright pink and drooping.

"I don't want any."

"Come on, honey."

"I'll do hers if she doesn't want it," Pat offered.

"No, she's going to do it. I have my own reasons for wanting her to wake up." Jim moved his eyebrows up and down like Groucho Marx and Billy and Pat laughed.

"Why? Isn't it a little late to make her start painting again?" Toni said.

"I think I'll just go back to bed."

"No, you're not. This is our housewarming, and you're staying up."

"Let her get some sleep, Jimbo. We're going to cut out pretty soon."

"Good night, everyone," I said.

I went into the bedroom and shut the door. The room was freezing. I put on the white flannel nightgown with the pink rosebud pattern that my mother had given me for Christmas when I was in the sixth grade. Jim hated the nightgown, but he let me wear it when the weather was really cold. I got into bed and pulled the blanket up to my chin. The door clicked open and Jim was looking down at me.

"All right, sister, where are they?"

"Where are what?"

"The pictures of the boat. You know, the ones you ruined."

"I don't know."

"Well, you better find them."

"I'm telling you, Jim, I don't know where they are."

"Then start looking—and watch that tone of voice with me."

He walked over to the bed with his hand clenched. I jumped up, but it made me so dizzy that I almost fell down.

"You're learning." He walked out of the room without closing the door.

Then I remembered that the photographs were on the mantel where Jim had laid them. I put on my bathrobe. I couldn't look at Toni as I passed her on the way to the living room. I handed the packet of photographs to Jim and went back to the bedroom. I lay down again and stared at the ceiling. It seemed as far above me as the ceiling of a church. In the corners, long gray cobwebs swayed back and forth. . . .

"Baby? You still awake?" Jim was standing in the doorway. "Echo wants to sleep in here with you if it's okay?"

"It's okay."

"But don't let her get on the mattress. She's still got fleas." He opened the door and Echo shot into the room.

"I'll leave the door cracked a little so it'll get warm in here. Good night, girls." He made a clicking noise with his teeth. "Don't let the bedbugs bite."

I had to move Echo off the bed three times before she curled up in a corner between two boxes. I took off my bathrobe, folded it, and put it under her; then I loosened her new flea collar a notch, kissed her on the nose, and went back to bed.

"I'm glad we burned that fucking yardstick," I heard Jim say. "It really brought something back to me."

"What was it, Jimbo?"

"Oh, it's not that interesting."

"That's never stopped you before," Toni said.

"Go on, man," Pat said. "We want to hear about it."

"Well, I guess I was about—oh, maybe three or four. I was real young, anyway. My mom was out of town, so it was just me and my dad. He took me down to the basement where he had his tools. It was a Saturday, but he said I couldn't go outside because he had something for me to do. He handed me a one-by-two and a little coping saw and a yardstick. Said he wanted me to cut the piece of wood fifteen inches long. *Exactly* fifteen inches. And not to come upstairs until I had done it."

"Can I have one of your Winstons?" Pat asked.

"Yeah. Anyway, I wanted the cut to be perfect. I wanted to show the old man that I didn't care if I couldn't go outside as long as I got this right. Well, to make a long story short, I finally figured out how to do it without fucking up. I put the yardstick on top of the piece of wood and cut right through the both of them at exactly fifteen inches."

"How did you know it was fifteen inches if you were only four?" Pat asked.

"Because he showed me where fifteen was on the yardstick, that's how."

"So you cut through his yardstick," Billy said. "Was he pissed?"

"You know, it's funny. Real funny! The bastard. He knew the whole time I was cutting that piece of wood—working on it all goddamned day—he knew all along that I was cutting a paddle for him to beat me with. Afterwards, after he beat the shit out of me for fucking up his yardstick, I threw the paddle in the fireplace, but he said that I could never get rid of his hand. I did, though. The son of a bitch cut out three years later." Jim's laugh was strange. "Well, enough about that. So, Pat, you're not working now?"

"Nah."

"How about driving my car down here from Indiana? For money, I mean. Here's a picture of it. Ever see one of these before?"

"Just a minute," Pat said. "I got to piss like a racehorse."

I heard the bedroom door open again.

"Honey, where's that ashtray of yours?"

"What ashtray?"

"You know, the one your mother gave you."

"You mean my rose dish? That's not an ashtray."

"Well, whatever."

"I think it's still out in the truck," I said.

"Oh, okay. Go back to sleep now, baby. We'll try to keep it down." He closed the door softly behind him.

Somewhere on the back of the truck, under a heavy canvas tarp, was a Four Roses carton that Jim had marked "Laurel's Stuff;" and inside the carton, nestled like a jewel in a small white box lined with cotton, was the rose-patterned dish my mother had bought for me at Woolworth's on that Saturday morning when my father died.

"Laurel! Please look at me! Wait in the car with your sister!" Mother pulling me through the open door, her gloved hand stroking my cheek, brushing smooth against my ear, and then crying in the dark hallway and down the walk and in the front seat of the car as I turned my rose dish over and over in my hands. Grace's fat fingers clutching the side of her bassinet in the backseat, and through the rear window the ambulance wailing far down the street, coming closer, closer.

I turned my pillow over to the cool side and tried to make my mind go blank. At first, all I could see were tiny black patterns, twirling and popping like pinwheels; then everything became white—pure white—as white as the snow in my mother's front yard. . . .

"I never made a snow angel before, Laurie—not even when I was a little kid. But I'll make one for you." Snowflakes on his eyelashes and our breath in clouds. . . .

ELEVEN

"What in the hell were you thinking, Laurie? I thought I told you to tie her up! Didn't I tell you to tie her up?"

"I did, but she was barking and crying so much, I couldn't stand it anymore. It was so sad. She just wanted to be free, and I was afraid Mrs. Morisot—"

"Oh, you couldn't stand it, huh? Well, I sure hope you can stand it when we find Echo smeared all over St. Charles Avenue."

"Don't say that, Jim! Please don't say that! I'm sorry. I really am. God, I'm so sorry." Tears were streaming down my cheeks.

"Oh, that's it! That's always your answer for everything. Don't *do* anything, just start crying. Well, it's a pretty fucking stupid answer if you ask me."

"I know it's all my fault. I won't let her run free again if she'll only come back. She has to come back. She has to!"

"She doesn't have to do anything if she's bleeding to death out there somewhere. Christ, Laurie, you make me sick."

"Damn it, Jim! Please, please don't do this. You promised me—and you promised my mother—you wrote out that stupid list about all the things you were going to change in yourself, like not losing your temper. But it didn't mean anything. It's killing me and you know it and you don't care. What about what you did to my hair?" I started crying harder.

Jim snuffed out his cigarette in my rose dish and sat down

beside me on the sofa. His face had entirely changed, his eyes gentle and luminous now.

"Your hair looks beautiful," he said softly, taking my hand. "You have such a beautiful face. I know I had no right to cut your hair—no right at all. But you're even prettier now." He wiped the tears from my cheeks with the back of his hand.

"Look at me, little girl. Now put those arms around old Jim's neck. Come on. There you go." He kissed me on the lips, but I couldn't move, I couldn't kiss him back. "Honey, I know I haven't been good to you lately, but I've had so much on my mind. I've been worried sick about Trulock and getting you settled in—and Christ, with all the bills we got now, I don't know when I'm going to get some work. Hell, you heard what Kane said. I'm not trying to make excuses, Laurie. There's no excuse for taking my problems out on you. I can see that now."

"I don't understand you, Jim. I don't understand why you want to hurt me so much."

His cheek was warm against mine. "Oh, Jesus, I don't know. I honestly don't know why I am like I am."

"You said things would be different, Jim, and I believed you—"

"I know. I *do* know. And they will be different. Honest."

"I don't think they will ever be different again. Why do you want to hurt me when you know how much I loved you?"

"Don't say *loved*. You still love me. I never mean to hurt you. Not ever. You're just upset because of the dog."

"It's not because Echo's gone—that only makes it worse. It makes me feel even more empty."

"But you *do* love me. I know you do, baby. You love me, and more than anything in the world I love you. And I'll prove it to you—I'll bring her back safe and sound. You'll see." He gave me another long kiss on the lips and then stood up. "If it's the last thing I do, I'll bring her back to you. I promise. You believe old Jim, don't you?"

"I want to."

"Then do. All right?" His lower lip was trembling.

"All right," I said.

"And once she's home and safe, we're getting back to business. I'm going to show you how much I love you, Laurie. I'm going to kiss every inch of that beautiful little body of yours. You can believe that, too."

"Please find her, Jim. Please."

"Don't worry. I'm not coming back without her." He kissed me on the forehead and put on his suede jacket. "But once she's home again, honey, you've got to keep her tied up. I know she wants to be free, but she doesn't know what's good for her." He walked over to the window and opened it. "It's like I keep telling you, Laurie—it's a big bad world out there, and there ain't no Santa Claus."

"Jimmy was very young when he stopped believing in Santa Claus, Laurie. I remember it so well because it was the first Christmas after his father left us. I think I overdid the Santa Claus business that year, you know, talking on and on about his coming down the chimney and the reindeer and everything. And that Christmas Eve, after we had set out graham crackers and a glass of milk for Santa, Jimmy asked me to sit down with him and have a serious talk. He wanted to know if I would be terribly disappointed if it turned out that there was no such person as Santa Claus after all. I remember laughing and reassuring him that there definitely was such a person. I suppose I wanted him to cling to that dream for as long as possible. Well, that night a friend stopped by the house, and I'm afraid we had a little more eggnog than was strictly good for us. Anyway, I fell asleep without putting out the presents or filling Jimmy's stocking or anything. And I didn't awaken until the next morning when Jimmy was standing beside my bed stroking my hair. He told me not to worry—that everything was all right—Santa had come in the night, even though he didn't leave us any gifts. He took my hand and led me into the living room to show me that Santa had drunk the milk and eaten all the crackers. Isn't that precious, Laurie? He wanted me to hold on to that dream, too."

It was almost midnight when I heard Jim tap on the window, and I jumped up from the sofa to let him in.

"Look who I brought home, Mom."

"Oh, you found her!"

"Yeah, but stay calm, Laurie. She's cut pretty bad."

There was blood all over one side of Jim's white shirt, and

Echo, mud-soaked and bleeding from her left foot, was lying with half-closed eyes in his arms.

"Oh, my God, she's hurt! And it's all my fault!"

"It's nobody's fault, honey. Clear off the kitchen table. We're going to have to work fast."

He carried Echo into the kitchen. "Get a towel."

I spread a towel out on the table. Jim took off his bloody shirt and started ripping the clean side into even strips about two inches wide.

"You know where I found her? In the cemetery."

"But I looked for her in the cemetery."

"Well, in a minute you can look in the phone book for an all-night vet. But right now I need you to hold her still while I bandage her leg. I think they can save it."

He bent over the dog, his muscles taut and golden in the pale light.

Dr. Cheryl Fontenot's office was out on Carrolton, past Tulane and Audubon Park, a small shotgun painted lavender with plum-colored shutters. Dr. Fontenot answered the door herself. She was a slender dark-haired woman in her late thirties with very white, nearly poreless skin.

"My receptionist left early tonight," she said, studying Jim from behind large horn-rimmed glasses. "Bring her right in." She held open the door to the waiting room.

"I'm Jim Wellman, my wife, Laurie, and this, of course, is Echo."

"I'm very pleased to meet you all. Now, what do we have here?"

"I think she was hit by a car," Jim said. "I bandaged her the best I could."

She examined the bandaged leg closely. "Well, you certainly did an excellent job, Mr. Wellman. Where did you learn to do that? I'm curious."

"I'm a deep-sea diver, so—"

"For Caldwell?"

"Yes."

"That's awfully dangerous work. You must worry about him all the time, Mrs. Wellman. I had a second cousin who was with Caldwell. He was killed in seventy-six. Perhaps you knew him. Bobby Angell?"

"Bobby! Hell, yes, I knew Bobby Angell. Good diver. Jesus, did he ever get a bad break."

"Yes, he certainly did. And Caldwell didn't do much for his family, either. They fought that suit every step of the way."

"Well, it's tough to beat the big boys—they call the shots—and Caldwell Diving is definitely one big boy."

She smiled. "I suppose so. Well, now, let's see what we can do for Echo. You've already done the most difficult part, Mr. Wellman, although I don't believe I have ever seen a bandage with buttons on it before." They both laughed. "Why don't you have a seat in here, Mrs. Wellman? And, Jim, I need you in the other room to help me."

I sat down on one of the small peach-colored vinyl chairs. A framed print of four dogs playing poker hung on the wall in front of me. The German shepherd held all the aces.

"Be sure she doesn't lick the ointment, Jim, and see that you reapply it every six hours or so. And don't let her bite at the wound when you change the bandage."

"We won't," Jim said.

I stood up and Dr. Fontenot put Echo in my arms.

"She's going to heal just fine, Mrs. Wellman."

"Thank you, Doctor," I said. "Thank you so much."

"Well, you really should thank your husband here," she said, taking Jim's hand. "That was a pretty nasty wound. Echo could have bled to death. Jim probably saved her life." She was still holding Jim's hand. "If you ever decide to give up diving, I'm always looking for a good assistant—they never stay here long. Your husband has a real gift for the healing arts, Mrs. Wellman. And as far as I know, no one has ever been killed working in a veterinarian's office."

Jim wrapped Echo in a white towel and laid her gently at the foot of our bed. "The poor little thing's exhausted."

"Thank you for finding her."

"No, I should be thanking you." He began kissing my hand.

"Me?"

"Sure. Thank you for being so sweet and so pretty."

"Did you think Dr. Fontenot was pretty?"

"What?"

"Dr. Fontenot. Do you think she's pretty?"

"Here," he said, patting the bed. "Sit down. I want to tell you something once and for all." He knelt down in front of me, and resting his elbows on my thighs, he pressed my hands together with his own as if we were praying.

"Look, Laurie, I've been out with a lot of women. I'm not saying that to brag—I'm not particularly proud of it—but it's a fact. And I'm telling you right now, Laurie Anne Wellman, the second I saw you at the stupid Christmas party, it felt like I had never been with any other woman in my whole life before. I'll never forget when you turned around and smiled at me, all dressed up like some kind of little princess. It was like my life began that night."

"Do you really mean that?"

"Hell, yes, I mean it. If I see a woman somewhere—any woman—I don't know whether she's pretty or not. Her face is blank to me, like she doesn't have a face at all. I can't explain it, but that's the truth. No one really exists in this world for me but you. So, to answer your question, yeah, Laurie, I guess Dr. Fontenot's pretty—but so what?"

"But you're—you're—"

"What darling? You can talk to old Jim here. I'm what?"

"You're so—you frighten me, Jim."

"I know, I know I do—and I hate myself for it. When I look at you sometimes and I see the fear on your face and I know it's there because of me, it makes me crazy. I can see I have my work cut out for me—proving to you how much I love you. Showing you how much I do."

"I don't know," I said, touching my cropped hair. "I don't know about anything anymore."

He stood up. "Listen," he said, smiling. "Let me shampoo your hair for you. I'll give you a bath—the royal treatment. What do you say?"

"But I've already taken a shower. I took one while you were gone."

"So? Come on, I'll wash you hair for you—give you a beauty bath. Hell, honey, your nerves are all shot from worrying about Echo. But we got her back, didn't we? Please let me. All you have to do is lie back and let me treat you like the little princess you are. Please? It's real important to me."

"Oh, Jim, if only you were always like this."

"Well, I'm going to be like this from now on. And you can

take that to the bank. I'm not worrying about anything except taking care of you. Now lift those sweet little arms up for me so I can take off your sweater. That's my girl." He slipped the sweater over my head.

Slowly and gently he undressed me, and then he carried me in his arms into the bathroom.

Jim lighted a candle and tilted it downward, dripping hot wax into my rose dish. He set the candle upright in the little pool of melted wax.

"Don't worry, honey, I'm not ruining your dish. When this wax gets cold, I can cut it right out with a blade." He rolled his shirtsleeves up above his elbows. "Come on, now—just lie back," he whispered. "I'm going to get you a glass of wine." He turned off the light as he left the bathroom.

I closed my eyes, took a deep breath, and went under the water. I thought of my father's pale blurred face in the deep deep of Crystal Lake pool. I lifted my head from the water and opened my eyes. The candle flame was flickering wildly in the draft from the open door, casting dark jagged shadows on the walls and ceiling.

Jim came into the bathroom, carrying two glasses of white wine. He set them down next to the candle.

"You look just like a mermaid lying there." He lathered the bar of Dove between his wet hands. "Now give old Jim one of those little tootsies." Slowly, carefully, he washed each of my feet. It tickled and I laughed.

"Come on, now, this is serious," he said, laughing too. "Stop fooling around."

I reached up and grasped his collar. "Suppose I want to fool around," I said. "Why don't you come in here with me?"

That night we fell asleep holding hands.

Jim was making a snow angel in my mother's front yard, his arms moving slowly up and down in an arc, his legs opening and closing in unison. "I never made a snow angel before, Laurie—not even as a kid. But I'll make one for you." And then we weren't in my mother's front yard anymore but underneath the house where I had found Echo. The snow grew darker now and Jim moved his arms and

*legs faster and faster and brown clouds of dust rose around
him until his body had disappeared under the thickening
clouds, and all I could see were his pale, unblinking eyes.
"Oh, please make it be snow again, Jim. Please make it be
snow!" And instantly the dark clouds became ice, glittering
in the light beneath the house. "Oh, thank you!" I said.
"Thank you!" I scooped up the ice crystals and held them
against my mouth. Blood. I tasted blood. Blood was streaming from my lips and down my arms, and I saw then that
I was clutching shards of broken glass in my hands.*

I awakened, my hands clenched, the fingernails pressing into
my palms. I turned toward Jim. He was awake, his eyes ice blue
in the early light, staring at the ceiling.

"God, Jim, I had the worst nightmare. I dreamed—"

"Yeah? Well I had a nightmare, too—except mine's still
going on."

I reached over to take his hand, but he moved away from me.

"What do you mean? What are you talking about?"

"You'll find out in the morning."

"Find out what? What's wrong?"

"Never mind. Just go back to sleep. You'll need it. You're
going to have a hard day tomorrow."

TWELVE

J im and I were sitting on the sofa, drinking the bitter chic-
ory coffee that he had brought from the French Market.
   "Laurie, you really are going to have to quit this lying."
I didn't say anything. I felt as if the breath had been knocked
out of me.

"Hear me, girl? Look at me when I'm talking to you. I said
you're really going to have to quit this lying."

"I don't know what you mean."

"Oh, don't give me that shit, little lady. Think hard. You know
exactly what I mean."

"But Jim, what about last night? You—"

"That was last night and this is today."

"But you said you would never be like this again. And after
you gave me that bath—"

"No bath will ever get you clean, Laurie. And you want to
know why? Because you're a dirty little lying bitch. That's why.
A dirty little liar."

"Please don't do this to me, Jim. I don't know what you're
talking about, but you're acting crazy." He clamped my mouth
between his thumb and index finger and pressed so hard that
my lips protruded grotesquely out from my teeth, making it impossible to speak.

"Don't you ever, ever say that to me again! You're the one
who's crazy! Do you hear me? Do you?"

I nodded.

He took his hand away from my mouth.

"Good."

"I can't believe this, Jim. You're scaring me again."

" 'I can't believe this, Jim. You're scaring me again,' " he re-peated, mimicking my voice. "Well, believe it! Maybe that's the only way you'll stop this lying. Hell, you grew up with a whole pack of liars. Your mom saying, 'Oh, Jim, I'm so glad you two are working things out,' and then turning right around and telling you behind my back, 'Maybe you shouldn't go down there with him.' "

"That's not how it was and you know it. She was just worried. All she said was that she didn't know—"

"I don't give a damn what she said, Laurie. She's a liar and you're a liar. Hell, little Gracie's going to be a liar, too, if she isn't already. All that lying is probably what killed your old man."

"My family is not a pack of liars. What about you? All the things you said last night were just lies."

"Last night I was telling you the truth, which is more than I can say for you, sister."

"Well, at least I never stole jewelry," I sobbed. I was sorry the moment I heard myself say it.

"That was real fucking smart." He closed his hand over mine and squeezed. "Who the hell told you that? Let me guess. Yeah, I stole jewelry. From my Uncle Jerry's store out at Elm Hill Mall. I stole some shit to get money for diving school because I knew nobody was going to lend me a fucking cent. But since we're talking about honesty here, maybe Toni didn't tell you that after I got some good deep work, I went back to my uncle and looked him square in the eye and told him what I'd done. And then I paid him retail for every fucking thing I took and then some. You hear me? I looked him in the eye and told him everything I'd done. You don't know what I'm talking about, do you?"

"You mean about your uncle?"

He squeezed my hand harder. "I'm talking about you telling Toni that I hit you. You did, didn't you? I can tell by your lying face. And after you promised me you would never tell anybody. You remember that?"

I stared at the waving shadows of branches on the wall across from me. "I remember."

"Well, see that you do. Do you have any idea how that makes

me feel? My wife telling her drunken friend our private business? And if you ask Toni anything about this, or tell anybody else our business, you're going to be sorry. Real sorry. That's a promise, not a threat. So let's just drop it." He lit a cigarette and blew out a thin stream of gray-blue smoke. "Now, have you thought about getting a job yet?"

"But we just got here. We're not even moved in."

" 'We're not even moved in,' " he mimicked. "Well, we'd be be moved in, smartass, if you'd finish unpacking the boxes."

I moved down from him on the sofa.

"The reason I'm talking about this right now is because I'll be going offshore any day. Probably just some Gulf work in Texas, but I don't know what you'll do for money while I'm gone."

"You really think you'll be leaving soon?"

"Yeah, but don't get too excited about it, little girl. I'll only be gone for a couple of days. I got to get over to Caldwell's right now and try and hustle up some work."

Jim stood up. He was wearing my favorite shirt, a pale blue broadcloth that matched the color of his eyes. The veins protruded from his arms as he tucked the tail of his shirt inside his pants.

"Pat's going to fly to Indiana and drive the Vette down here for me. When I pay him off, we'll be completely broke."

"Broke?"

"Only for a little while. After we sell—"

"You didn't tell me you were selling the Corvette."

"What? You mean I have to talk over selling things with you?"

"Well, money decisions. You said in your list—"

"Well, I'm saying now that I don't have any money, and the only decision here is whether you want to get a job this morning or this afternoon." He crushed out his cigarette in my rose dish. "God, girl. I thought you'd be happy about me selling the car."

"We wouldn't need the money if you hadn't—"

"What? Cracked it up! Go ahead and say it. I know that's what you're thinking." He got up and began pacing back and forth on the bare wood floor, the boards creaking under his weight. "Look, even if we had the money, what would you do all day if you didn't work?"

"I'd paint."

"Paint?" He laughed. "You wouldn't paint a goddamned thing. When I first met you, you were always talking about what an artist you are, but so far I haven't seen you paint a fucking thing. You want to know what you'd be doing without a job? You'd be getting yourself in trouble. That's what you'd be doing. You and that crazy Toni. Trouble with a capital T. I've been through all this before with Kane. His girl and mine got together, and there was nothing but trouble. Connie and Stacy. Yeah, Connie and Stacy, boozing it up with a bunch of their car show clients on that fucking steamboat. And that damn Stacy. She wrecked my car, a little sixty-six Mustang I had, and I had to pay for her dental bills. Doctor bills. Eating reds with Connie and drinking, and she said someone slipped her a Mickey at the bar. Shit! She slipped herself a Mickey!"

"I wouldn't get into any trouble. If I could just wait a little while before I start working—if I could just paint again, I'd feel—"

"I don't have time to argue with you. I've got to get over to Caldwell's. And I want you to ask for a job at Rosario's. Today. *Capisce?* Kane says it's nice, and it's close."

"But I don't even know where it is."

"Well, here's what you do." His voice was suddenly softer. "You know where St. Charles is, don't you? Just walk up St. Charles past Louisiana and that bar Que Sera. Keep going for a few blocks and turn left on Bordeaux, and you'll see the Cache-Cache Club. It's connected to Rosario's. Don't try and get a job at the club, though. I don't want you waitressing around a lot of drunks. And you don't need streetcar fare. I want you to walk it so you can find your way around. Here's a key I had made for you. Don't lose it."

"I won't."

"Famous last words of Laurel Wellman. Oh, I ran into Sarah just now, and she said there's some old dog shit upstairs in the hall. She was late for work and didn't have time to clean it up. One of these days I'm going to have to teach that dog a lesson once and for all."

I waited until I heard the flat sound of the truck door closing, and then I called my mother collect. I let the phone ring eight times before I hung up.

I stared across the street at the two doors. One of them had a frosted glass pane on which three capital C's were intertwined in an art-nouveau monogram. Rosario's was written in gold cursive script on the clear glass of the other door.

A man hosing down the sidewalk smiled at me as I crossed the street. He was a big, soft, sandy-haired man with cow eyes, meaty lips, and large white squared-off teeth.

"Pretty as a picture, you are. You light up my day like the sun does the side of this building," he said in a deep drawl.

"Thank you." I looked down at the two glossy-leaved camellia shrubs in lavender-blue urns near the door of the Cache-Cache Club. The urns were chained to the front of the building.

"And shy, too. The loveliest combination," he said. "Still chilly out. Isn't this the chilliest Mardi Gras season you can remember?"

"This is my first one."

"Where you from up north, darlin'?"

"Indiana."

"Indianapolis is a nice place. I've had me some wild times in Naptown. Yes, ma'am. So you're looking for a job? If you are, I know some lucky stars will have to be thanked. Buddy's my name. I know they need someone at Rosario's. And if you work there, I'll come over every day for lunch. I'll ask for you, and the sun will come out from behind the clouds like it did just now when you crossed the street. Every day I'll get to see you. And you blush, too. Old Buddy can make even the boldest blush."

"Do you work at Rosario's?"

"No, darlin', I work next door at the Cache-Cache Club. I own it, but I work my butt off, if you'll pardon me. I'm always there. Every day I wash off this walk. Even in the winter. I like to take care of things. Make them nice. Clean and beautiful. And I never ask anyone to do anything that I wouldn't do myself. Now, when are you going to tell me your name? As soon as you do, I'll know it's the prettiest name in the world."

"It's Laurel," I said, laughing.

"I knew it! The most beautiful name in the world." He took my hand and kissed it. "Please forgive me, but you are irresistible and I am such a flirt. But always a gentleman. Do they call you Laurie?"

"Yes."

"Well, then, Laurie, what do you say we go get you a job? You did want a job?"

I nodded.

"After you, darlin'." He held the glass door open for me and then took my hand and pulled me inside. His hand was so big and warm that I immediately felt at ease.

"Later I'll show you my courtyard. A garden for love."

The restaurant was walled in mirrors. It was empty except for two pretty waitresses dressed in black slacks and white blouses who were polishing the mirrored tops of the white tables. Tall ficus trees in chrome pots were scattered among the tables. The checkered floor of black and white marble tiles reminded me of a Vermeer painting.

"Hey, Buddy!" one of the waitresses, a doll-like woman with short auburn hair, called from across the room. "We're not even open yet, and you've already found someone new." She had an English accent.

"Sorry, Molly, but this time it's love. Tell Joey I've brought someone he'll be interested in."

"For you, pet, anything."

"Don't you worry, babycakes," Buddy said, patting my hand. "Once he sets eyes on you—"

A man walked through the swinging doors of the kitchen. He was young—not more than twenty or twenty-one—with a faint moustache. His black eyes sparkled as he tugged at the white cuffs protruding from the sleeves of his perfectly tailored navy blue suit.

"Joey, this is Laurel. What's your last name, honey?"

"Wellman."

"Wellman. She's looking for a job."

"Pleased to meet you. I'm Joseph Salerno." As he bent forward to shake my hand, I could smell the clean spice scent of his after-shave lotion.

"When can you start?"

"Anytime."

"Tuesday night? A girl quit, and I haven't replaced her yet. Maybe you could hostess just that one night, and then we'll put you on lunches waitressing. How does that sound?" He smiled and then immediately looked serious again, as if afraid that he had revealed his true age.

"It sounds great," I said.

"Oh, one more thing. Experience. You do have experience?"

"Yes. Both as a hostess and a waitress. I was a hostess at

Simpson's Restaurant in Catalpa, Indiana, when I was in college, and I waitressed at a Polynesian restaurant in Key Largo—the El Tiki—and—"

"Fantastic. Come in about four on Tuesday. You can fill out an application then."

"I will. Thank you. Oh, Mr. Salerno, could you tell me how much I'll be making?"

"Of course. We'll give you three-fifty an hour for hostessing and minimum plus tips as a waitress."

"Don't worry, darlin'," Buddy said. "The girls do just fine here."

"Thank you, Mr. Salerno. I'm looking forward to working for you."

"Thank *you*, Laurel. You really are helping us out of a bind."

"She's a beauty, isn't she, Joey?"

"Sure is. It'll be good to have you aboard, Laurel." He turned and walked toward the kitchen, his expensive black shoes clicking lightly on the marble floor.

"See, darlin', didn't I tell you? Can't have too many pretty waitresses. They would have hired you even if they didn't need anyone."

"I forgot to ask him what I should wear."

"Well, you'll want to wear something a little dressy to hostess in—you know, a cocktail dress or something. And when you waitress, just wear a white blouse and black skirt. You have a black skirt, don't you, darlin'?"

"Yes."

"Good. Now I'm going to show you around, and I'll start by introducing you to the best oyster shucker in Louisiana. Sweetheart, you like oysters?"

"Yes."

He took my hand again and we walked to the back of the room. A black man wearing a tuxedo shirt and trousers was cutting lemons into quarters at the oyster bar. Behind him was a terra-cotta wine rack that ran from the floor to the ceiling. A white wooden ladder was propped against the rack.

"Laurie, this is Felix, Felix Sylvester, the handsomest nigger in New Orleans. I'll bet you've never seen a blue-eyed nigger before, have you? Not up north. Come here, Felix. Let me tell you something."

Felix leaned over the bar.

"Love you," Buddy said, kissing Felix on the cheek. "Love the King of Spades. Blue-eyed king. This is Laurel. Isn't she a lovely creature?"

"Yes," Felix said, smiling a slow, enigmatic smile. "It's a pleasure to meet you." He wiped his beautiful hands on a white cloth wrapped around his waist like an apron and shook my hand.

"Isn't he the handsomest oyster shucker you've ever seen? And blue-eyed niggers, they bring you luck. Did you know that, doll? They're rare."

"Maybe bad luck, Buddy. Maybe I bring bad luck."

"I don't think so. You're lucky, all right."

Felix shook his head back and forth, smiling his strange smile.

"I'm having a little poker game on Saturday," Buddy said.

"Can't make it. Company coming."

"Oh, Sugarbread back in town?"

"Yes, sir." Felix said. "Laurie, would you care for an oyster?"

"Go on, Felix. Shuck her a sweet one. Isn't she as pretty as a picture? Look at her. Like a little Bambi deer. Have you ever seen lashes like that before?"

"No, Buddy. I can't say I have." Felix slipped on a gray rubber glove and palmed a medium-sized oyster. He forced open the shell with a flat-bladed knife and detached the oyster in a single graceful movement. He set the oyster, a tiny fork, and a silver cup of red cocktail sauce in front of me.

"Hey, look at that. First oyster and you get a pearl." Felix plucked a dull gray pearl from the shell.

"I don't believe it!"

"Not worth anything, but they're lucky," Felix said, handing me the little pearl.

I dipped the oyster in the cocktail sauce and swallowed it. Felix leaned over the marble bar, watching me.

"How was it?"

"Delicious—the best I've ever tasted."

"Anytime you want an oyster, you just let me know. I'll pick you out a good one."

"A gorgeous creature like this can turn your head around," Buddy said. "Even when you've been a bachelor your whole life like me. I swear, I just might change my mind about getting married."

"Looks like she already turned your head and broke your

heart. I keep telling you, Buddy, you've got to look for the gold,"
Felix said, glancing at my left hand.

"Well, she's still a gorgeous creature. I think I'm in love."

Felix laughed and looked at me. I looked away.

"Shy, too," Buddy said. "The sweetest thing in a woman. Now,
I know he doesn't agree because I've met his women. They are
not exactly shy, are they, Felix?"

"Not exactly, Buddy." Felix held a small gold lighter up to the
slender brown cigarette in his mouth.

"We have to be going next door now," Buddy said. "I want
to show Laurie my baby." He put a five dollar bill on the bar.

"I don't want it, Buddy."

"I don't want it either," Buddy said, picking up my hand again.
His fingers felt damp and puffy.

"Good-bye, Felix," I said. "And thanks."

Felix nodded without looking at me. Buddy pulled me through
a frosted glass door that led to the courtyard. A blue canopy
stretched above a horseshoe-shaped bar inlaid with ink-blue-and-
white Portuguese tiles. Near the bar, tables were stacked neatly
on tables, with white chairs aligned in short columns on top. The
courtyard spread beyond the canopy; in the middle of the courtyard was a leaf-choked fountain with a cement cherub. Tree
branches shadowed the high stone wall that enclosed the courtyard; vines curled down the face of the wall, nearly touching the
slate floor.

"There's my baby," Buddy said, gesturing with his free hand.
"I don't put the tables and chairs out until it gets a little warmer.
People love to sit out here and take in the night jasmine and
oleander. Birds singing. That's a Japanese fig tree and a flowering
almond. This one is a Chinese cherry, and that's a *magnolia
grandiflora* next to it."

"It's beautiful, Buddy."

"Isn't it? Even when it's smothering hot and they could be in
the air-conditioning, people want to come out here. Couples
mostly. I keep it nice. They appreciate it."

"I'd love to see it in bloom."

"You will, darlin'. Look at these little tables. They're from
Italy. And the heart shapes in the backs of the chairs? I paint
them every three months. See that little angel on the fountain?
How that one wing is broken? Damn nigger kid working in the
kitchen next door broke it. He shouldn't have been out here in

the first place. It doesn't look right, and I can't get it fixed. People don't know how to do that kind of work anymore, darlin'." He sighed wistfully.

"I know, but I think it looks more rustic this way."

"Maybe so. Couples throw so much money in that fountain making wishes, I can play poker once a week. The water breeds mosquitoes, though. Come on. I'll show you the inside and get Brent to make you a drink. I'm not about to let the love of my life die from catching a cold out in my courtyard."

Buddy led me across the courtyard to another frosted glass door opposite the oyster bar.

"After you, darlin'," he said, holding the door open for me. "Welcome to the Cache-Cache Club."

Inside it was cool and dark. Huge, ornate brass fans whirred over our heads. Warhol silkscreens of purple and magenta flowers hung on the raspberry-colored walls, and lavender love seats flanked the small glass-and-chrome tables.

Behind the bar, a slim young man with a cocky smile and a shock of platinum hair over his eyes was wiping a highball glass with a clean rag. He was wearing a long vinyl apron with the Union Jack emblazoned on it, and his shirt sleeves were rolled up past his elbows. I sat down next to Buddy at the bar.

"Now you'll have to watch Brent. He can't pass up a beautiful woman. And he almost always forgets to tell them he's married and his wife is having a baby. Don't listen to him, no matter what he tells you."

"Buddy, you're always trying to ruin my reputation," Brent said, glancing at my breasts.

"She's married, too. It's a tragedy. I finally found the woman of my dreams and lost her, all within an hour."

"Life in the big city," Brent said. "The sink's clogged again."

"Well, get the lady a drink, and I'll see what I can do. It's the second time this week."

"Hey, the boss was looking for you. I think he's still in his office. I saw his car when I was bringing in the wine."

Buddy stopped smiling and got up from the barstool.

"Fix her something special, Brent. She's a brave baby. A brave baby. I tell you. She's going to be working next door for Joey starting Tuesday night."

"When you come back, I need at least one more case of Heineken."

Buddy didn't seem to hear him. Suddenly he looked much older. I realized that he must have been smiling the entire time I had been with him.

"See you later, darlin'," he said, without looking at me.

"I'll surprise you," Brent said. "Make you something cold."

"Thank you. What did he mean about being brave?"

He laughed. I didn't like his laugh.

"Because it's Fat Tuesday, doll. You must be crazy starting over there Mardi Gras night. It's a madhouse. People have dinner at two in the morning."

"Oh. Is Buddy your boss?"

"He tell you he owned the club?"

"Yes."

His laughter rang out in the empty bar.

"Doesn't he?"

"Nah. Oh, a little piece of it. The boss let him buy a very small percentage just to keep him happy. Three percent or something. Buddy manages the place more than anything." He shoved a big buttermilk-colored ice cream drink in front of me. An eight-inch-long banana stuck out of it.

"That big enough for you, doll? It looks about your size."

"I don't think I'm much in the mood for a drink."

"What? Too early?"

"Yes."

"Never too early in New Orleans. Come on, doll. You'll like it. You'll want more. Take a sip. Cross my apron, you'll like it," he said, genuflecting. "Here. I'll help you." He reached over, pulled out the banana, and laid it on the bar in front of me. Melted ice cream beaded up under the banana and made little milky pools on the glossy wood. I raised the glass to my lips.

"It's good."

"My specialty. Banana Banshee. But you're supposed to eat the banana. The whole thing." He leaned against a mirror behind the bar and looked at his wristwatch; then he pulled out a Kool cigarette and lit it. I took another sip of the drink.

"Some girls prefer a big old Dirty Banana. That's when you use dark crème de cacao instead of white. Girls like you seem to prefer these." He held out a clean towel. "Look in the mirror. You have a cream moustache." He laughed his ugly laugh again. "I'll bet you've had a lot of those, darlin'."

I wiped the tacky froth from my upper lip with the back of my hand and stood up.

"Well, aren't you an odd one?" he said as I walked to the front door. "Aren't you even going to say good-bye?"

The frosted door shut behind me, and I was standing outside next to the two camellia shrubs in the chained blue urns.

THIRTEEN

I closed the door of the women's rest room at Dauphine's and faced Toni. She was swirling the liquor around in her glass.

"How could you, Toni?"

"How could I what?"

"Tell Jim that I said he hit me. You promised me you wouldn't."

"*Sucure!*"

"What?"

"Look, did he tell you not to ask me about it?"

"Yes, and for Christ's sake, don't—"

"He is a liar! I never told him anything."

"You didn't?"

"No, and if I had, you would know it. From me, not Jim."

"God, I can't believe that I fell for it."

"Well, the important thing is not to fall for it again. If he asks you whether you said anything to me, you look him right in the eye and tell him no. And from now on, just believe that I would never betray you. You do know that, don't you?"

"Yes."

"I can't believe that bastard. He must make you crazy."

"I never told anyone this before, Toni, but after he started hitting me I wanted to die. I wanted to be dead and I tried to, but all that blood made me sick."

I pushed up my shirtsleeve and held out my wrist to her. She took my hand and pressed it against her face. Her skin was cool.

"I thought so, chérie. But I will tell you something. I would never respect anyone who hadn't wanted to be dead sometime."

Drinks were set in front of our stools, and Sheila was pouring one for herself at Billy's insistence. When I sat down, I didn't look at Toni's face. Jim was talking about Stacy, and how he used to sit for hours poring over her portfolio.

"I couldn't believe how different Stacy could look. In real life, she was red on the head like a dick on a dog, but they put a black wig on her and you couldn't believe it was the same girl. Like night and day."

"Is she still modeling?" I asked, even though I knew she wasn't.

"What? Oh, no, she gave it up a couple of years ago."

"Why? Wasn't the money good enough?"

"Better than any job you ever fucking had. She just got sick of fags poking at her and sticking her with pins and pulling her hair, so she got out."

"She and Connie are both working over at Maison Blanche selling cosmetics," Billy said.

Toni looked at him. "How the hell do you know where she works?"

"Let me get this straight," I said, picking up my drink. "Stacy was a successful model making loads of money in a glamorous career. But she became disillusioned and yearned to enter the exciting, challenging world of cosmetic sales in a department store. It makes sense to me."

"Gee, and I didn't even see Toni's lips move." Jim leaned closer. "You're really pushing it, aren't you?" he whispered in my ear. "And you'll be sorry. I won't forget."

As Jim gathered his diving gear, I followed him back and forth from the bedroom to the living room, making a list of things he wanted me to do while he was offshore.

"Be sure and pay First Federal on that car loan. It's already late. And Sears and Mastercharge. Send them each a hundred dollars."

"How much do we owe Mastercharge?"

"I don't know. Call them up and ask. I think about fifteen."

"Hundred?"

"Yeah. Are you getting all of this down?" He took the list from my hand, read it over, and handed it back to me.

"But I can't sign those checks for you," I said. "My name isn't on any of your accounts."

"Just sign them. Oh, and call Pontchartrain Bank and see if I have any money left over there." He sat down on the sofa and stretched his arms above his head. "Glad to get rid of old Jim?"

"I just can't believe you're going so soon."

"It's always that way. When your beeper goes off and they say go, you go—unless you want to be blackballed. Now, sit down here by me. I want to talk to you about a couple of things. First of all, I don't want you going down to the Quarter while I'm at Brownsville-fucking-Texas. You know how dangerous it is, and you're liable to get in trouble again. If you want to see Toni, you have her come uptown. You got that?"

I nodded.

"Okay. Now, I've got a real important question to ask you, and I want an honest answer." He picked up his diving helmet and began turning it over and over in his hands. "I can't be worrying about this while I'm diving—it's probably just some bullshit salvage job, but I've got to concentrate on my work. You understand?"

"Yes." I looked down at the mesh bag on the floor in front of the sofa. Through the mesh, I could see the crinkled envelope in which he kept the photographs of his boats and cars.

"All right, then. Last night at Dauphine's when you and Toni were in the ladies' room, did you mention what we discussed yesterday? Don't be afraid to tell me, honey. I only want the truth."

"No."

"You didn't?"

"You said I should forget about it, didn't you?"

"That doesn't mean you did. You didn't mention it to her at all?"

"No."

"Then you wouldn't mind swearing to it, would you?"

"Why can't you just believe me?"

"Laurie, please. I've got to know. Swear to it, and we won't ever talk about this again."

"All right. I swear it."

"No, I want you to swear on something. Swear on your mother's health."

"I swear on my mother's health that it's the truth. There. Are you happy?"

"Yes. Now I can feel safe." He kissed me hard on the lips. "I love you, little girl."

A car horn blared in front of the house.

"That's Kane. Now remember, Laurie—if there's an emergency, call Caldwell. They know how to get a hold of me."

Billy walked in, wearing his cowboy boots. He gave me a sleepy smile.

"How you doing, kid?"

"Okay. How's Toni this morning?"

"You know Toni—cast-iron stomach. But God, that bourbon put her in a mood last night."

"Always does," Jim said, slipping his Saint Erasmus medal over his head. He rebuttoned the top button of his shirt.

"Well, you guys were smart leaving when you did. I finally went home, too, but Toni closed the place down. Hey, Jimbo, what did you say to piss her off so bad? She sure was on your case."

"I didn't even talk to her last night."

"You must have said something."

"I swear to God, Kane. I didn't say boo to her."

"If you say so. You all set to go? I'll carry the bag."

"I'll talk to you later, Laurie," Jim said, picking up his diving helmet from the sofa.

"When will you be back?"

"Before you can leave town." His eyes were like blue stones.

"See ya, kid," Billy said.

Across the street, Buddy was standing near the chained shrubs, hosing down the sidewalk. A sudden gust of cold wind blew his hair and fluttered his maroon corduroy shirt.

A champagne-colored Mercedes SLC with white leather interior was parked in front of the Cache-Cache Club. There were three *C*'s on the license plate.

Buddy turned off the hose. "Hey, darlin', what're you doing way over there?"

"Hi, Buddy," I said, crossing the street. "Is that your car? It sure is nice."

"Nah. That's Rosario's car. I have a Buick Riviera. Sky blue. Well, just look at you! You're pale as a little ghost. Let me feel your hand. I knew it! You're freezing. Did you come for lunch, babycakes?"

"No, I just wanted to pick up a menu before I start waitressing. I thought I would memorize what we serve for lunch."

"Well, come on inside," he said, opening the door to Rosario's. "You left the other day in such a hurry, I didn't have a chance to say a proper good-bye. That Brent didn't say anything to upset you, did he?"

"Oh, no."

"Well, that's good." Buddy reached behind the hostess station and handed me a forest green menu. The auburn-haired waitress I had seen the other day was brushing crumbs from the seat of a chair. She looked even more like a doll than I had remembered. Her short, boyish hair glistened like plastic, and four thin lower eyelashes were painted beneath her own.

"Molly, I want you to meet Laurie," Buddy said.

"Hello, Laurie." She offered me a delicate hand. "So you're Buddy's new love. He's thrown us all over for you. I really don't think I can go on."

"But I won't forget you, Molly."

"Too bad." She laughed. "I rather hoped you would."

"Now, you can't mean that. Laurie and I are going to have lunch in the courtyard. Do you think you could order us a little something and bring it out there?" Her white blouse opened as he hugged her, exposing deep cleavage and several gold chains around her neck.

"Oh, all right, Buddy. But only because Laurie is with you. Joseph said you're going to start Tuesday."

"Yes. I didn't realize it was Mardi Gras night."

"It's going to be wild, isn't it, Buddy?"

"You bet it is, but she's a brave baby. What's good for lunch, Molly?"

"Oh, I don't care for any lunch, thank you."

"Sure you do. You're too skinny as it is. I ought to make you drink a milk shake. Have Brent make us a couple of milk shakes."

"No, Buddy. Really. I'm not hungry."

"All right, Molly, we'll just have a couple of shrimp cocktails, then, and bring me an order of fries. You'll eat some shrimp, won't you, darlin'?"

"French fries! Are you off your diet again?" Molly said, shaking her finger at him.

"Never you mind. I'm still a growing boy. We'll be next door."

"It's freezing out there, Buddy," Molly said.

"Don't worry. I'm not going to let this little one freeze. I've got a heater for the courtyard."

Felix was behind the oyster bar, shucking oysters and dropping them into a plastic container near his elbow.

"How you doing, lady? Ready for the big night?" His voice was like velvet.

"She'll be just fine," Buddy said, hugging me. "How about some oysters, darlin'? Felix, we'll have a dozen when you get a chance."

"Sure, Buddy. Just let me finish these for the kitchen. I'll bring them out to you in the courtyard. I'll open up only the best ones because Laurie knows the difference."

There was one table with chairs around it near the door of the Cache-Cache Club. The other tables and chairs were still stacked under the blue canopy. Buddy plugged the heater into a covered socket.

"Warm enough, or should I turn it higher?"

"No, this is fine. Buddy, I didn't mean to invite myself to lunch."

"Of course not, precious. I asked you. How long have you been married. Wait. Let me guess. A year?"

"How did you know?"

He shrugged his shoulders. "Happy? Are you happy, little baby? Does he treat you good?"

"Yes. Yes, he does."

He stopped smiling. "Does he? Does he treat you like a queen?"

"He does, Buddy."

"He'd better. The best—you deserve the best, little baby. All women deserve the best."

Felix set a silver tray with a circle of oysters on it in front of us and walked back inside. Buddy didn't say anything until Felix had shut the door behind him.

"What's wrong, babycakes? Did I say something wrong? I did. I have a big mouth. The girls always say so. Here, have one of these little oysters. This one has your name written on it. Maybe you'll find another pearl and forgive Buddy for having such a big mouth."

When we walked by the oyster bar, Buddy slapped a five dollar bill on the marble top, but Felix didn't look up.

The kitchen was big and hot. Copper pots hung down from hooks on the eggnog-colored walls. I could smell black-raspberry jam cakes baking, shrimp sauteed in butter and garlic, strawberries, rancid wine, and detergent.

Behind the red heat lamps, a middle-aged black man wearing light yellow trousers and a starched, candy-striped shirt was fanning himself with a paper fan on which Jesus held outstretched arms over laughing, golden-haired children.

A tanned, good-looking man with dark curly hair was standing near the dish-washing machine, eating a piece of pecan pie that he held in the palm of his hand. He was wearing faded jeans and a work shirt. He looked about forty-five.

"Gabriel, this is Laurie," Buddy said to the black man in the candy-striped shirt. "She's starting Tuesday."

"Pleased to meet you," I said.

Gabriel mumbled something unintelligible.

"Don't let him bother you, honey," Buddy said. "His bite isn't as bad as his bark. He's been pulling doubles since Chef Ritchie quit. Right, Gabe?"

"Don't tell Vita I didn't make a wish," the dark-haired man said, still chewing. He had a loud, cocky voice, and he spoke with a slight accent that wasn't Southern.

"I wouldn't do that to you," Gabriel said.

Buddy started rubbing the back of my neck, and I didn't like it. He probably thought that I had come by just to see him.

"You're tense, babycakes." He began rubbing my shoulders.

Gabriel looked at him in disgust, and the dark-haired man shook his head and smiled without opening his mouth.

"So you're going to be working here?" he said. "Well, it could be worse. You could be next door in the club working under Buddy." He laughed. "Buddy," he said. "Buddy boy."

Buddy took his hands off my shoulders. He didn't seem to like the dark-haired man.

"Vita! Vita!" the dark-haired man called. "Where the hell is Vita?"

The stainless steel door to the big walk-in refrigerator opened, and a short, fat mulatto woman emerged from a curtain of ragged mist. She wore long golden earrings shaped like leaves, a polyester aquamarine shirt, and very bright purple stretch pants. Golden skin. Golden eyes flecked green near the pupils. Smoky-golden hair. She could have been twenty-nine or fifty-nine.

"Vita, this is the best damn piece of pecan pie I've ever eaten," the dark-haired man said. "You have to give me a whole pie for my dinner. I've got to get home and get some sleep."

"Well, you can't have a pie. I don't even got pie enough for lunch, and you should have thought about going to sleep two days ago. You just go on home and get out of my hair."

"I'm going," he said. "Vita, you're always so rough on me. This is Carnival. I say the hell with lunch and you come on back with me and bake me my own pie." He slapped her on the behind.

Vita's eyes slanted downward when she smiled, and a dimple appeared on the right side of her face. A gold cap gleamed on her right front tooth. The gold had been cut into the shape of a cross, exposing the white enamel beneath.

The dark-haired man kissed Vita on the cheek. She pushed him away, and he laughed.

"You need a shave. Now you get on home and take a bath and go to bed. You act younger than my littlest."

"I *am* younger."

Vita made a shooing gesture with her hands.

"I don't want to get Vita mad. She might decide to work a spell on me." He laughed again.

"I should," she said.

"I wish she would," Gabriel said, but the dark-haired man was too far away to hear him.

"See you later, Gabe. Buddy boy." As the dark-haired man walked past me toward the back door, I smelled bourbon.

Gabriel shook his head back and forth. "Oh, boy, glad to see you go. Don't you think I got nothing better to do than fix you something to eat and shoot the breeze?"

"So you are Laurel," Vita said, staring at me, her hands on her hips. "The one that Buddy saw crossing the street?"

"Yes."

"Laurel. Like the tree? It's a pretty name. Pretty girl. Buddy was right. I thought maybe he dreamed you up."

"She ain't no dream," Gabriel said.

"Shut up, Gabe."

"Vita makes all the salads and desserts here," Buddy said.

"That's right, sometimes everything else, too. I hope you like working here, honey. Shame you starting Tuesday. You'll miss Comus. The parade Comus. I have a son named Comus."

"You do?" Buddy said. "I didn't know that."

"There's a lot you don't know, Buddy. But don't you worry, baby. You'll do just fine. The best people will all be working Tuesday, and they'll help you out."

"I sure didn't know you had a son named Comus," Buddy said.

"Second to the oldest. I conceived him after Comus Parade. That night."

"Come on, Vita. How do you know if you conceived him that night."

"I know, Buddy." She wiped her hands on her apron. The green flecks swam in her eyes, and she blinked slowly, so slowly it was mesmerizing. She reminded me of a pear, a beautiful golden pear.

Buddy reached for a piece of the pecan pie, and she slapped his hand.

"You're on a diet, and—"

"All right, Vita. Baby, I have to go back next door and get to work on the courtyard. But you're welcome to come."

"Oh, no. I need to go home and let Echo out."

"Echo your dog?" Vita asked.

"Yes."

She handed me a warm wedge of pecan pie covered with tinfoil.

"Take it with you, baby. Give a bite to the dog. Dogs love sweets."

"What are you giving her that for, if you're going to be short for lunch?"

"Ain't he ornery for a man of the cloth? You mind your own business, Gabe."

"Then why didn't you give *him* some more pie?" Gabriel asked in a softer tone.

"Because *he* is going to sleep it off as soon as he gets home, and he never wishes on it, anyway. I can't stand a man who don't know the right way to eat pie. Or worse, one who knows and won't do it. Like him."

"Vita always makes us wish on the first bite," Buddy said. "You put that bite aside and eat the rest of the piece."

"That's right. Then you make the wish again before you eat that bite you held back on. But you give that piece to your dog." She smiled, showing the white cross on her capped tooth. "Go ahead, girl, and take it."

"Ain't she a special baby, Vita?"

"She is. But she's married, so you leave her be. You don't want to go getting her in any trouble."

"Don't worry. I'm an art lover."

"Art lover," she said, rolling her eyes back.

"Come on, baby. I'll walk you to the back door."

"Leave the door open," Vita said. "The air is getting awful thick in here."

"Does he always act this way?"

"He does."

"That's not true, Vita. Tell her the truth or she'll get the wrong idea. This one's special."

She seemed to look right through me and I could hear the big exhaust fan blowing and Gabriel's soft bass singing somewhere behind me.

"He thinks you special," Vita said.

"Thank you," he said, kissing her golden cheek. "Come on, sugar."

"Good-bye, Gabriel," I called. He said something I couldn't hear.

"Good-bye, Vita. Thank you for the pie."

"You welcome, baby. Remember to eat it right."

"I will. I always eat pie that way."

"You do?"

"Yes, my father told me about it a long time ago."

"You two should get along just fine, then," Buddy said.

FOURTEEN

I sat down in Que Sera's at a corner table behind half-opened French doors. The waitress placed a cut-glass vase of blood-red carnations on the white tablecloth. I ordered a Coke and glanced around the room. I couldn't shake the feeling that Jim might walk in at any moment—that he hadn't really left town.

Four expensively dressed young women were sitting at the only other occupied table. A blond man wearing tennis clothes leaned over the table, talking. Every once in a while the women would laugh. I wished that I were with them, listening to the blond man and laughing, too.

"Now when I clap my hands, you will awaken and remember nothing," Toni said, clapping her hands.

"Toni! Excuse me. I guess I was daydreaming."

"Oh, so that's what it was." She looked across the room at the blond man and the four women. "I thought you were playing tennis in that charming new way that is all the rage in Paris," she said in an exaggerated French accent. "Everybody is doing it sitting down." When she kissed my cheek, I smelled licorice.

"Thank you for coming, Toni. I didn't mean to sound so worried on the phone."

"You didn't sound worried. chérie."

"Well, I am—a little. Jim left in such a hurry, and I don't have much money. I can't even buy you a drink."

"That's okay. I have some money—not that Billy exactly left

me a fortune. Do you realize that if anything happened to those two idiots, we would have to pay all their debts, all their bills?"

"I know."

"They do not even have life insurance. Billy said it was too expensive, and for once he was telling me the truth. I asked an insurance man who comes into the Jade Moon, and he told me the premiums for divers are even higher than for race drivers. Can you believe that? But Billy said not to worry—Caldwell would take care of me."

"That's what Jim told me, too."

"Well, it's bullshit, Laurie. Caldwell has so many lawyers, and they only pay if they have to." She picked up my glass and sipped from it. "*Quelle horreur*, it is Coca-Cola! Where is the waitress?"

"I don't know. She was waiting on that other table."

"Christ, I could have stayed home if I wanted to make my own drinks," she said, pushing back her chair.

From the corner of my eye, I could see the blond man watching Toni walk to the bar. The four women stood up, laughing and holding their purses. One of the women, her light brown hair in a page boy, threw her arms around the blond man's neck and kissed him on both cheeks. Over her head, he continued to watch Toni. I felt a sudden inexplicable tinge of jealousy.

"*Pour vous,*" Toni said, setting a drink in front of me.

"Thank you." I took a sip. "Toni—"

"Relax, chérie. A little rum cannot hurt anything. And we are celebrating. Here is to the boys being gone." She clinked her glass against mine and sipped her milky-looking drink.

"Pernod?"

"And water. You should try it sometime." She moved closer to me. "Do you see that beautiful man at the other table?" she whispered. "He is really something."

"Yes, he is."

"He is a rich boy."

"Come on, Toni. How do you know he is rich?"

"Believe me, I do know. There are signs. *Par exemple*, look at his tennis shoes. The rich always wear fine shoes. More than anything else they love comfort."

"I don't know, Toni—"

"They do. I mean the born rich. There are always signs. If he were wearing a tie, the knot would be loose, not neat, and his coat would be—how do you say it?—rumpled. And see how the back of his neck is not shaved? That is another sign. I told this all to your Jim before—how I was able to detect them—and at first he did not believe me, either. But, chérie, this beautiful one is rich. Maybe he will buy us a drink."

"You don't think he can hear us, do you?"

"Not unless he is Superman behind those Clark Kent glasses. I wonder if they are real."

"Of course they're real. Why would he wear glasses if he doesn't need them?"

"Do not be naive, Laurie. Men plan that kind of thing more than women do. Like Billy. If he is in the bedroom and one of my friends visits, he comes out in his undershirt and talks to us. He holds his arms like this so that his muscles stick out." She pushed up the sleeve of her black cotton sweater and flexed her arm. "Like this."

I laughed. A cold wind blew in from the open French doors, fluttering the tablecloths at the empty tables.

"Jim isn't like that."

"No, Jim is not like that. So tell me, Laurie, are you coming down to the Quarter tomorrow?"

"Jim doesn't want me to go there, especially after the robbery. Besides, he thinks we'll get into trouble, like his old girlfriend."

"Do you know why he thinks that?"

"He said Stacy and Connie got pretty high, and—"

"Did he tell you about the scuba diving lessons? No? Once when Jim and Billy went offshore, they gave the girls some money to take scuba lessons. But they never took the lessons. They spent the money going out. You have to admire them—at least for that." She drained her glass. "I am going to have another. Do you want one?"

"Not yet. It's still early, and I won't get anything done today if I drink any more."

"What do you have to do?"

"Jim left me a list as long as my arm."

Toni rolled her eyes.

"Oh, but we're finally going to have some money. Jim is selling the car. Pat left today to pick up the Corvette and drive it back here."

"Pat? The oily fellow from upstairs?"

"Yes."

"Excuse me." The blond man was standing by our table. He

was even more handsome than I had thought: straight nose, a beautiful mouth, and a tiny round chicken pox scar near his left eye.

"If you are going to say 'tennis anyone?' don't," Toni said. "We are already playing French tennis. It is much less strenuous."

"I suppose I do look rather foolish. I wanted to change before we came here, but no one else wanted to stop. And now they've abandoned me. I thought I heard you say something about a Corvette."

"You heard correctly," Toni said. "Are you interested in buying one?"

"Maybe. What year is it?"

"I don't know. What year is it?" she asked me.

"Sixty-nine," I said.

He smiled. "Good year, although seventy-eight is beginning to look better all the time. Is it your car?" His hazel eyes were gentle behind the tortoise-shell glasses. I was relieved to see him squint for a moment. He did need the glasses.

"No, it's my husband's."

"Do you know how much he is asking for it?"

"I'm not sure, and I don't want to tell you the wrong price."

"Oh, I'm sorry. My name is Lee. Lee Carraway—as in Nick."

"Nick?" Toni said.

"Yes, Nick Carraway. As in *The Great Gatsby*."

"Well, I'm Antoinette as in Marie, but call me Toni. And this is Laurel as in victory, but call her drunk."

"Toni!"

"I'm only kidding. I'm the one who is drunk. But I'm doing the best I can to help her." Toni leaned closer to him. "What's your middle name?"

"Scott. I know. Don't ask."

Toni scooted an empty chair toward him with her foot and he sat down.

"Well, Lee Scott Carraway, isn't it a little cold to play tennis?"

"Not inside. Would you like to try one of these?"

"What is in it, *mon ami*?"

"The waitress always asks me that, too. She has a bad memory."

"And bad eyesight, too. She never did come to our table."

"That's Amy. She's really quite nice when you get—"

"Her to wait on you," Toni said.

"I guess so." He laughed. "Oh, here she is now. We'll have three more of these, please," he said, handing Amy his glass. She looked at his white shorts for a moment and then down at his long, tanned legs.

"Now, Lee, what's in them again? Tequila?"

"Definitely tequila."

"Oh, yeah. Cuervo Gold."

"Right, Cuervo Gold. And Rose's lime juice and a splash of soda."

"What do you call it, Lee?" Amy asked, still staring at his legs. "Is there a name?"

"Heaven," Lee said. "My very own version of heaven."

Toni laughed. It was the first time I had heard her laugh like that—clear and unrestrained.

The drinks were strong and tart. Toni straightened up in her chair, and I wondered how long it would be before she started talking about Aspen. But I could understand. Sipping my drink, I found myself remembering the weekend Jim and I spent together before we were married—ordering room service from our bed in late afternoon, Jim laying his head in my lap, listening to my stomach and laughing. Both of us laughing. . . .

"So, Laurie, where do you work? Or are you a lady of leisure, cruising around all day in your sports car?"

"Laurie is starting work at Rosario's Tuesday night. Do you know the place? It is not too far from here."

"Rosario's! I go there all the time. From now on, I'll ask for you instead of Molly. Have you met Molly? She's a great girl. You'll like working with her."

"Well, if you know Molly, you should have her wait on you. Sometimes it embarrasses me to wait on people I know."

"She is shy," Toni said.

"I am, too," he said, looking at me.

"Of course you are, *mon cher*. That is why you just happened to come over to our table. Your friends abandoned you, but you wanted to stay and have a few more drinks. Yes? And not by yourself."

"No, really. I am shy. No one knows how much you can suffer from it. It's a terrible thing, and it can be dangerous. Yes, definitely dangerous." He stared down at his drink while he moved a long, slender finger along the rim of his glass. In the dim light, his hair was the color of wet sand.

"So, tell us what you do, Mr. Lee Scott Carraway," Toni said.

"Well, it's hard to say. I was going to be a doctor, but I changed my mind after a couple of years at medical school."

"I know," Toni said. "Your golf game wasn't good enough."

He smiled. "I wasn't good enough."

"You mean your grades?" I asked.

"No, I mean I didn't know if I was *good* enough. Maybe I was afraid that I might turn out to be a pill doctor for women named Gravier and Dumaine. My mother's kind of doctor. I don't know. I told myself I wanted to write, but I don't know about that either. I've had the same sheet of paper in my typewriter for months."

"Like Anton Chekhov," I said. "Doctor to writer."

"Except that he *was* a doctor and a writer. Oh, Amy, could you please bring us another round?"

"No more for me, thanks," I said, standing up. "I really have to go. I should never have left Echo alone this long."

"You put out some food and water," Toni said, sucking on an ice cube. "Yes?"

"Yes."

"Well, then, she will be all right. Why don't you stay and have one more of Mr. Carraway's divine concoctions?"

"No, I can't. Aren't you coming over?"

"Well, I thought I might stay for a while. Not too long, though. I have to go home and let Marie out, too."

"Come on, Laurie. Why don't you stay, and then we'll all leave together?" He gave me a long look.

"No, I really can't. But thank you for the drinks."

"My pleasure," he said, standing up. "Are you sure you wouldn't care for one more?"

"I'm sure," I said, smiling. "I can only stand so much heaven."

FIFTEEN

I was about a block from Rosario's when it began to rain. I ran as quickly as I could, holding my ivory-white knit dress carefully above my knees, but my legs and the hem of my skirt were splattered with muddy water before I reached the door. The water beaded on the champagne-colored Mercedes parked in front of Rosario's reminded me of grapes after my mother had washed them.

There were white candles in the dining room and enormous cut-crystal bowls of calla lilies along the bar. The night waiters were placing silver ashtrays, salt and pepper shakers, and shell-shaped dishes of butter pats on the tables.

Felix, wearing white tie and tails, waved to me from behind the oyster bar. A black top hat rested on a pile of crushed ice beside him. Buddy was standing in front of the bar, looking almost distinguished in a gray flannel suit and maroon tie. The air around him was permeated with the scent of Brut after-shave.

"Oh, Lord, baby doll, you must be freezing cold with that wet hair. Don't tell me you walked all the way over here in this rain. It would break my heart to think you would do that before you would call up old Buddy for a ride." He put his hand on his chest. "It would hurt me right here, darlin', you know that?"

"But I didn't get that wet, Buddy, and it just now started to rain." I unbuttoned my raincoat.

"Well, I'll have Vita give you a towel for your hair. But I want you to promise you'll call me when the weather is bad and you

158

don't have a ride to work, hear? Plenty of times I've given the girls a ride, haven't I, Felix? I believe Miss Molly thinks I'm her own private chauffeur."

Felix smiled at me. "Could be, Buddy. Could be."

"Here, let me take that, darlin'," Buddy said, slipping my raincoat down from my shoulders. "Oh, my, my, my. Just look at you! Like you're made out of snow. That's a beautiful necklace, too."

"Thanks. My husband bought it for me before we were married."

"Well, wasn't that sweet! You know they say red coral will ward off trouble. Ooh, and I love all those little seed pearls on the bodice of that dress. They look just like frost. That is what you call a bodice, isn't it, darlin'?"

"Yes, it is."

"But, baby doll, what's all this on your skirt?"

"I guess I stepped in a puddle, but it'll come out."

"Well, you march right back into that kitchen and have Vita scrub it out for you, and I'll tell Joey you're here. He was afraid you wouldn't come tonight, but I told him he was wrong. 'No, sir,' I said, 'she's as responsible as a new mother.' "

When I came back into the dining room, Buddy was pinning a dark-pink carnation to the lapel of his jacket.

"Here she is, looking fresh as a new spring lamb—just like a little snow queen. Felix, what do you think they'll do when they find out the Queen of Comus is right here at Rosario's?"

"I don't know, Buddy. Guess they'll just have to bring the parade to the queen."

"That's right! They will! You'll see, babycakes. The parade will come to you." Buddy reached on top of his head and pulled a blue iridescent half mask over his eyes. "Isn't this beautiful? It was my father's. My mother made if for him out of butterfly wings. I think this will be the last Mardi Gras for it, though. It's falling apart."

"You say that every year, Buddy," Felix said.

Buddy laughed. "Maybe I do, Felix. Maybe I do." He started to walk away, but Felix nodded toward a table close to the bar and whispered something to him. Half hidden by a ficus tree sat a tiny man who resembled Fred Astaire. His skin was oiled and leathery, as if he had spent too much of his life in the sun.

"Is he clean?" Buddy whispered.

Felix shrugged his shoulders. The tiny man glanced nervously at Buddy, blinking his mascaraed lashes.

"What the hell, it's Mardi Gras night." Buddy walked over to the table. "Mr. Clay, it's nice to see you again. Have you been feeling better?"

Mr. Clay nodded, looking down at his child-sized patent-leather shoes.

Felix offered me a cigarette from his silver case and then tucked the case inside a black leather pouch. He put the pouch underneath the bar.

"Mr. Clay Poole, may I present the Queen of Comus?" Buddy said. "She's skipping the parade and festivities just to be here with us tonight. What do you think of that? Laurie, this is Mr. Clay. He helps out from time to time next door enforcing the dress code."

"It's nice to meet you," I said, shaking his small hand. On his pinky finger he wore a large diamond horseshoe ring with one of the stones missing.

"The pleasure is all mine," Mr. Clay said in a high, effeminate voice.

"I didn't know you had a dress code at the club, Buddy."

"Sure we do, baby. Otherwise people would come in looking like trash. Especially the rich kids. They think they're different from everybody else, but I don't treat them any different, do I, Felix? Felix was here a couple of months ago when I almost got into a fight with one of them. Now, Mr. Clay, are you clean tonight? I don't want anyone working in the club who isn't."

"No, I . . . I'mmmm clean," Mr. Clay stammered, still looking down at his shoes.

"Good. Well, then, let's get you to work. Go on next door and see what you can do to help Brent set up. And tell Brent I want all seven dozen tiger lilies out in the courtyard."

"You're opening the courtyard?"

"Sure, darlin'. It's a little cold, but it *is* Mardi Gras. We always open it up on Mardi Gras night."

"Buddy, what about the orchids for Mr. Rosario?"

"Oh, yeah. Glad you reminded me, Felix. Mr. Clay, you have the orchids and champagne sent upstairs and make sure they rope it off."

"Private?" Mr. Clay asked.

"Private party for the big man himself. Tell Brent I said to have *all* the champagne cold. And, Mr. Clay, remember last time. We don't want—"

"Don't worry, Buddy." Mr. Clay adjusted his bow tie and smoothed the wide lapels of his sky-blue, navy-trimmed tuxedo jacket. He opened the door to the courtyard.

"I think he'll be all right tonight, Felix, but this is the last time. I mean it, so don't you smile at me. If you see Brent, tell him to make sure Mr. Clay pays for his drinks. And none until midnight."

"I doubt Brent had anything else in mind, Buddy."

"Well, Queenie, good luck!" When Buddy bent over to kiss my hand, a bright piece of his mask floated to the floor. "This is the last Mardi Gras for sure." Sighing, he carefully pulled the mask up from his face and walked away.

Joseph came out of the kitchen with a job-application form folded under his arm. He was wearing an expensive black tuxedo.

"Fill it out and find me," he said, turning away. "I'll show you what to do next."

Felix handed me a silver fountain pen. "Sure are a lot of little boys wearing out daddy's shoes tonight," he said, shaking his head.

For the first few hours, most of the customers were silver-haired couples in evening clothes, the women gleaming with diamonds and pearls. The dining room smelled of bread pudding and damp fur coats; a gentle, steady rain fell outside.

By eight o'clock, the room was filled with a younger, louder, costumed crowd. Those who couldn't cram inside had formed a line outside in the rain. Couples from the courtyard next door were demanding tables. And people kept coming: ballerinas, bullfighters, vampires, devils, pirates, and men so delicate and cool it was difficult to believe that they were not women. My feet hurt, and there was a small, crackling pain above my eyes from the incessant clinking of crystal and silverware and the constant murmur of conversation around me.

By midnight, strangers began to kiss each other. When I went to the oyster bar to tell Felix that he had a phone call from a man at the Black Cat Lounge, he kissed my hand before he answered the phone. His mouth was smooth, and his lips were darker than his skin, as if he had stained them eating blackberries.

Buddy suddenly appeared beside me and planted a wet kiss on my cheek.

"Happy Mardi Gras, sugar."

"Thank you. Happy Mardi Gras to you, too. Hey, Buddy, what's the Black Cat Lounge?"

"That's just a little club Felix owns—does pretty well for himself, too."

"I'd like to go there sometime."

"No, you wouldn't, baby. Take old Buddy's word for it." He patted my arm and walked away.

Around two o'clock, there was a loud commotion at the entrance. A red-haired goddess Diana wanted to bring her greyhound into the restaurant. She was accompanied by a black-haired Queen of Hearts and a little man in a wheelchair who was dressed as Pinocchio. Women standing nearby screamed when the greyhound shook water on them. The man in the wheelchair finally told Diana to tie the dog outside, and the Queen of Hearts pushed the wheelchair up to the oyster bar.

Pinocchio ordered Dom Perignon for everyone at the bar and a bottle of red wine for himself. Amid the popping of corks, he announced that Felix was the fastest oyster shucker he had ever seen; then he pulled his mask down and asked the crowd at the bar whether his nose had grown. Everyone laughed.

"How about an iced tea, darlin'?" Felix's soft voice carried uncannily over the din at the bar. "Gerald, fix this lady an iced tea the way I like them."

"Thank you, Felix," I said.

"Laurie, this is Gerald July. Gerald works for me over at the Cat, and sometimes he helps me out behind the bar here."

"It's nice to meet you, Gerald," I said.

Gerald nodded without looking at me. He was about the same age as Felix—in his early thirties—but lighter in color, sullen and handsome, with something wild and hurt and cold in his dark eyes that reminded me of Jim. He was wearing a double-vented tuxedo jacket that was tight at the hips.

"Hey, what is this?" I asked. "It tastes great."

"Long Island iced tea, but there ain't no tea in it," Gerald said, still not looking at me.

"Don't just talk about it. Make the customers a couple," Diana said, pushing money over the bar.

Pinocchio raised both arms above his head to get everyone's attention.

"Now, if you all will please shut up, I have a proposition for Mr. Oyster Shucker here . . . ah . . . Mister——?"

"Felix."

"The Cat," Gerald said. "The Black Cat."

Pinocchio laughed. "Well, Black Cat, I have a proposition for you."

"Go on." Felix lit a cigarette and took off his white tie.

"A pretty good proposition for a pretty good oyster shucker. Are you interested?"

"Curiosity killed the cat."

"Most people are interested in a chance to make two hundred and fifty dollars in fifteen minutes, aren't they, Black Cat?"

"Most people are."

"Most niggers are, wouldn't you say?"

"Most niggers are interested in making two fifty in a month."

"We'll make it an even three hundred, then. And all you have to do is shuck and eat ten dozen oysters in fifteen minutes."

"I'd prefer it was a wager. Three hundred to you if I lose."

"I'll buy the oysters either way. That's more than fair." Pinocchio had to reach high over his head to put the three one-hundred dollar bills on the bar. "Shake," he said.

"You have my word."

Pinocchio jerked his hand back as if he had been burned. His lips tightened and went white. Felix took off his jacket, laid it gently beneath the bar, and rolled up his shirtsleeves.

"I'll get the oysters," he said, walking away.

By the time the oysters were iced and piled high in the sinks, people were packed together at the bar. Buddy stood next to me. Beside him, Mr. Clay tore the filter off a Virginia Slims cigarette and lit it, sucking in his thin cheeks.

"This is going to be something, baby! Ten dozen oysters! That Felix! People are betting thousands!"

"Do you think he'll win, Buddy?"

"I wouldn't bet against him, precious."

"I hope he wins," Mr. Clay said, eyeing my drink.

"Would you like a sip?"

"Thank you. I am thirsty." In the light from the oyster bar, his skin had a greenish glow, like tarnished metal.

"They're going to start," Buddy said, putting his thick arm around my shoulders.

Diana and the Queen of Hearts took confetti out of their raincoat pockets and threw it into the air. The crowd was yelling. Buddy said that he didn't think it was fair—the noise might throw Felix off. I had to stand on tiptoe to see.

Felix grabbed oyster after oyster, shucked them, threw them into a plastic quart container, and tossed the shells on the floor. I saw Brent leaning against the door to the courtyard, his arms folded across his Union Jack apron and a knowing smile on his face. I moved from beneath Buddy's arm.

After filling the container with oysters, Felix raised it to his lips. The crowd gasped and laughed. Pinocchio announced the time every minute, holding a large gold pocket watch in front of him. Felix maintained a fast, steady pace—shucking, tossing the shells, filling the quart container, then relaxing his esophagus and letting the oysters ooze down his throat. Once the Queen of Hearts threw a large handful of confetti on him, but he didn't slow down.

"Stop him! He's cheating!" the Queen of Hearts screamed. "I saw him! He's throwing shells down without even opening them!"

Felix stopped shucking for a moment to fix his cool eyes on the Queen of Hearts. Then he laughed a loud, resonant laugh in the sudden silence, and the crowd began chanting in unison: "Black Cat! Black Cat! Black Cat!"

"Did you hear that? Rich trash! Calling Felix a cheat! You don't do that during a bet! To do something like that would never enter your mind, would it, precious? Just rich trash with no manners. Right, Mr. Clay?"

"Right, Buddy," Mr. Clay said, sniffing.

"But he still might win," I said. "It's not over."

"Don't worry, baby. He'll win."

"He's got to." I asked Mr. Clay to hold my drink, and I crossed my fingers on both hands.

"He's cheating again! Look on the floor! He's not opening all of them!" The Queen of Hearts almost knocked over a bowl of calla lilies with her flailing arms, her eyes searching the crowd for believers.

Pinocchio held one finger in the air to quiet her, but he never took his eyes off Felix. The chanting grew louder.

"Black Cat! Black Cat! Black Cat!"

"Lawrence, call it off! Call it off! I tell you, I saw him—" The Queen of Hearts stopped in mid-sentence, her mouth wide open and her eyes staring at Vita, who was standing in the kitchen doorway. Vita's eyes were closed, and she seemed to be saying something, her body swaying back and forth in a slow rhythm. I closed my eyes, too, mouthing the word "win" several times. When I opened them, I caught a glimpse of Vita's golden hair disappearing through the swinging doors.

From across the room, I recognized the man I had seen in the kitchen a few days earlier. He was wearing a white dinner jacket, and a sequined black mask dangled from his neck. A big blond woman to his left was fingering the orchid in his lapel while he looked over the crowd, his dark eyes darting restlessly. When he smiled at me, I pretended that I had been looking at Brent, who was standing on his other side. Brent opened his mouth and winked. I moved out of his view, closer to Buddy. He put his big hand over mine.

"Excited, precious?"

"I want Felix to win so much. He has to."

"No one has to do anything except die." Mr. Clay finished the last of my drink.

"Mr. Clay! No more morbidity now. Especially not with this little baby standing here."

"I'm sorry, Buddy."

"Well, you should be, Mr. Clay. It's Mardi Gras night. Besides, she asked you to hold her drink, not down it. You have Gerald make her a new one. Go on, now! Gerald won't bite."

"That's all right, Buddy. I don't need another one."

"No, it is not all right. Mr. Clay has had trouble with his manners before. Haven't you, Mr. Clay?"

Mr. Clay bowed his head, smoothing a few copper-colored strands of hair over his bald spot. I closed my eyes and prayed that Felix would win. When everybody gasped and laughed, I knew that he must have swallowed another container of oysters. The crowd pressed closer to the bar.

I felt as if I couldn't breathe. I walked up to an empty table near the front door and rested my hip against it to steady myself.

"Black Cat! Black Cat! Black Cat!"

Mr. Clay's hand shook as he held out my drink. I took a sip, and then I felt a small, cold hand in mine and a warm, wet kiss on the corner of my mouth. A licorice-scented kiss.

"Happy Mardi Gras, chérie."

Toni was wearing her blood-red mask and Billy's burgundy bathrobe. As she moved away, the robe opened slightly, exposing the tattoo on her left shoulder.

"My God, Toni! Is that all you're wearing?"

"It was all I could find. When I was taking a bath, I realized I did not have a costume, so—"

"And you're barefoot! You'll catch pneumonia."

"I lost my slippers. My beautiful Chinese slippers. And I do not know where, chérie." She took a deep drink from her plastic cup of Pernod. "So tell me, *ma douce amie,* what is all the excitement? The crowd is fantastic!"

"Can you see the guy in the wheelchair? Pinocchio? Well, he bet Felix—he's the oyster shucker I told you about—three hundred dollars that he couldn't shuck and eat ten dozen oysters in fifteen minutes," I said.

"Jesus! How is he doing?"

"He just has to win," I said.

"He will, Laurie. Felix is the best I've ever seen." Lee took off his white half mask and put it in the pocket of his black cashmere topcoat.

"Lee! I didn't know you were here, too!"

Toni threw her arms around Lee's neck. "We have been celebrating Mardi Gras with all of Lee's cousins. Before, I was so depressed. Then Monsieur Clean here stopped by my house just as I was sharing the last of my Pernod with Marie."

"It's true," Lee said. "Marie was enjoying a saucer of Pernod."

"Poor Marie."

"What do you mean, poor Marie? She adores Pernod. All dogs do. Please, chérie, we want you to go back to the Quarter with us. We left Lee's cousins at Pat O'Brien's. Or was it Que Sera?"

"No, it was Pat O'Brien's. Remember?" Lee was shifting his weight from one foot to the other, as if he were trying to keep his balance.

"And I lost my beautiful Chinese slippers," Toni said, looking down at her feet. "Do you think they're at Pat O'Brien's?"

"Perhaps you left them at the Dream Palace, Toni."

"The Dream Palace," I said. "You were at the Dream Palace?"

"Yes, Lee knew where it was! *C'est très magnifique.* Like a dream—you never know what is going to happen there. You should have been with us, Laurie."

"Oh, I wish I had."

"You will go sometime, chérie. I promise you." Toni gave me another wet kiss, and then, laughing, swayed and nearly fell against a man wearing a skeleton costume. She finished her drink and handed Lee the plastic cup. "I'll have another one, General."

"General?"

"She's been calling me that all night."

"Well, his great-uncle was a general in the Confederate army. Or was it your great-great-uncle, General?"

"Both," Lee said, laughing. "How about you, Laurie? May I bring you one, too?"

"No, thank you. Not yet."

"*Quel dommage.*" Toni took the glass from my hand and drained it. "Now you must have one. Do you think I came all the way up here barefoot so you could refuse to have a Mardi Gras drink with me?"

"All right," I said.

"I will get the drinks, General. I want to see this oyster shucker Laurie thinks is so special." Toni took the twenty dollar bill Lee held out to her, tightened the belt of her bathrobe, and vanished into the crowd. I realized Mr. Clay had disappeared, too.

"Toni is compelling but not exactly calming."

"No," I said. "Not exactly."

Lee moved closer to me, his coat sleeve brushing my shoulder. "How are you, Laurie?"

"Oh, I'm fine."

"I mean really. You look tired—beautiful but tired."

"I guess I am a little tired." I could smell the candy like sweetness of the gardenia in his lapel.

Lee was saying something to me in a low voice, but people were screaming so loudly that I couldn't hear him, and then I saw Toni, a drink in each hand, weaving her way through the crowd. Her hair was tousled and her eyes glittered black, as if the pupils had finally devoured the irises.

"*Pour madame.*"

"How did you know what I was drinking?"

"I've had Long Island iced teas before, chérie, in Aspen." She raised her glass. *"À le chat noir,"* We touched glasses. The "Black Cat" chant was quieter now.

"They called time when I was up there coaxing your man on, Laurie. It is all over but the counting."

"We didn't know."

"Yes, I could see you didn't know. But win or lose, Laurie, that Felix—" She said a few words in French that I couldn't hear and Lee laughed.

"I want so much to find my slippers, General."

I stared at Toni's feet. They had turned the gray blue of slate. "Your feet must be freezing!"

"What is that all over them? Confetti?" Lee swayed slightly as he bent down.

"Butterflies," I said. "Buddy had a mask made from butterfly wings that's so old it's falling apart."

"You're right! A morpho, and a mighty long way from Brazil." Lee stood up, dusting his hands. "I think we'd better leave, Toni, and find something for your feet."

"I'm not leaving, General—not until we know who won." She stumbled and steadied herself against his arm, biting her lower lip hard. I looked at Lee. He seemed completely sober now.

"Toni," he said. "Toni? Can you hear me?"

"My slippers," she mumbled. "My goddamn slippers."

"Did you take something, Toni? Tell me! It's important."

Toni opened her hand. A bright blue capsule lay in her palm. Lee took the capsule and put it in his topcoat pocket.

"How many, Toni? Did you take more than one?"

"Who the fuck cares, General? Who the fuck cares?" Her robe slipped open, and I saw the butterfly tattoo on her shoulder.

"I care. Laurie cares. Very much." Lee pulled the robe back on her shoulders, tightened the belt, and tied it into a knot.

Toni fell forward onto her knees. She laughed and pressed her hands together as if she were about to pray.

"Oh, chérie, I am high. I am so high."

Lee lifted Toni up from the floor, holding her around the waist. "How many, Toni? I have to know."

"Let's go back to the Quarter. All of us. Order her, General. No, she is ordered around enough."

"I'm ordering you to tell us how many of those you took."

"One."

"Are you sure?"

She didn't answer him.

"Was it just one? Tell me, Toni."

"Two. *Deux bleus*." She smiled, biting back her lower lip again. A thin rivulet of blood trickled down her chin. Lee dabbed at the blood with a paper cocktail napkin.

"God, Laurie, I hate to leave, but this is serious. Even one Amytal with all she's had to drink—"

"But, Lee, driving—"

Lee looked embarrassed. "I have a driver. But please, don't worry about Toni. I'm going to take her to a friend just out of medical school. Have him mix her a mild emetic. You know, something to make her throw up."

"Are you sure she'll be all right?"

"Christ, yes. I will be fine. General, kiss Laurie good-bye for me." She held my left hand, palm up, in front of him and passed out in his arms.

I pulled my hand back, but I knew that it was too late—that he had seen the scar. I slumped into an empty chair and, without thinking, snuffed out the candle. The wax was still warm on my fingers when Lee touched them. He sat down on a chair next to me with Toni on his lap.

"I have to take her out of here, Laurie. But before I go—" He moved his chair closer to mine and Toni stirred. "I wish I had more time to explain—"

"Explain what?" I couldn't meet his eyes.

He put his fingers around my left wrist. "This filigree here. Most people have it all wrong. I know. I did myself at one time—until a friend of mine tried it." He shifted Toni's weight onto his right leg and stretched his other leg out in front of him. "God, this is a bad time to talk."

"I know. You'd better get Toni home. I'm worried about her."

"I will. Very soon." He held my wrist tighter. "What I mean is . . . they think that people who do this kind of thing want to die. But that's not true. Not most of them. They want life more than anyone, and sometimes it's not until they see their own blood that they really believe in their own existence. Do you understand what I'm saying?"

I nodded, staring at a half-eaten piece of bread pudding on the table in front of me.

"I want to live, Lee."

"Of course. I'm sorry. I didn't mean to be presumptuous. I've had too much to drink trying to keep up with Toni. Toni the tiger." Lee stood up, propped Toni upright against his hip, and held her shoulders between the crook of his right arm and chest. Toni awakened while he was trying to put on his gloves.

"Where are my slippers, General? I'm not leaving without my goddamned slippers."

"Yes, you are. We're leaving right now. Happy Mardi Gras, Laurie. I hope we see each other very soon." His lips brushed my cheek. "Don't worry. Nothing will happen to her. I promise."

SIXTEEN

I pushed my way through the crowd at the oyster bar. Gerald was trying to maneuver Pinocchio's wheelchair through the narrow aisle behind the bar.

"Will everyone please shut up!" Pinocchio screamed. "This is the third time we've had to stop the count!"

"Why didn't you make your friend shut up when Felix was shucking?" someone yelled.

"So there you are, baby," Buddy said, hugging me. "What happened to your friends?"

"They had to leave."

"Got too high, huh? Occupational hazard of the rich. Jesus, and her in just her bathrobe. Even for Mardi Gras—"

"Toni isn't rich."

"That's not his name, and he's rich."

"No, Toni is the girl. My friend. It's short for Antoinette."

"Well, don't tell me he isn't rich because I know for a fact he is. I know it, doll. I've had trouble with him before."

"With Lee? When?"

"Couple of months ago. He came in here with some of his high-horse friends. Uppity nigger friends."

"How you doing, lady?" Felix was standing in front of me, smiling.

"Oh, Felix, you were just wonderful! But how could you eat all those oysters? Don't you feel sick?"

"No, I've ate more."

171

"Well, I sure hope you win. I don't think it was fair with that woman yelling and everything."

"Thank you, darlin'." He leaned over the bar and lowered his voice. "Could you do me a little favor? Tell Vita I don't need her anymore. She can go home now and wait for her call from Comus. And could you bring me the lemons she has back in the kitchen? I need them out here for drinks—and other things. You'll do that for me, won't you?"

"Of course."

"She won't give them up easy. She's that way. But tell her I need them. Like to like. Lemon draws gold. I need *all* of them. Will you do that, darlin'?"

When I turned around, I saw Buddy glaring at a short-haired woman in armor surrounded by a loud group of men near the doorway to the courtyard.

"It's a good thing she hasn't crossed over to my courtyard," Buddy said, "because it wouldn't be for long. But he's letting her."

"Who is? What's she doing?"

"That Joan of Arc standing over there. She's showing some tit is what she's doing. Excuse me for being so blunt, precious, but—"

"Why don't you ask her to stop?"

"If it was in the courtyard . . . but he's here. He knows what's going on. If he wants to stop her, he'd tell me. But if it was my—" Buddy made a flat chopping movement with his hand.

"Who is he?"

"Your employer, baby, Mr. Rosario. Standing beside that cheap blonde over there. Now don't tell me nobody ever introduced you to the man himself."

Before I could answer, Brent pushed his way over to us. He shook his platinum hair back from his forehead.

"Boss said to break it up, Buddy! He says to tell her to button it up or get out."

"Christ, it's about time he realized this ain't the Hotsy Totsy Club."

"Want me to take care of it?" Brent's eyes were bright.

"No, it'll be a pleasure. You see if you can scrounge up Mr. Clay. We might need him."

Gospel music blared from Gabriel's radio. Vita had emptied her refrigerator, and the cutting boards were littered with cheeses, sweating fruits, butter, salad vegetables, and quarts of whipping cream. Dirty dishes and glasses were stacked everywhere.

I watched Vita shake three packs of sugar onto her plate of rice and red beans.

"Tired, baby?"

"I am dead."

"You go on home now. We ain't serving no more food."

"I can't leave until I know whether Felix won."

"Don't worry. He'll win. Felix comes from the lucky side of the family. He's got natural luck, baby, and that's the best kind."

"Do you know his family?"

"I am his family. He's my nephew. Comus his cousin." She smiled, showing the golden cap with the white cross. "Felix got me this job here."

"Felix said to tell you to go home and wait for your call."

"Comus already come by, so I'm not going nowhere. Now, are you hungry?"

I glanced at her rice and beans. A new penny was half-buried in the mound of rice. The wet, warm smell made my stomach turn over.

"No, thank you. Oh, Felix needs all the lemons you have for drinks. He said to be sure and get all of them."

"Oh, he did, did he?" She opened the refrigerator door and pulled out a large wooden bowl filled with lemons. "Maybe he's not from the lucky side of the family after all," she said, handing me the bowl.

Felix was leaning against the wine rack, sipping brandy from a snifter. I gave him the bowl of lemons.

"Thank you, darlin'. You sure this is all of them?"

"Yes."

"It's all over!" Pinocchio screamed, waving his scrawny arms. "One hundred and seventeen! Three short! How do you like that, Black Cat?"

Smiling, Felix ran his forefinger around the rim of the brandy snifter: it made a loud, piercing ring. The crowd began chanting, "Black Cat! Black Cat!" Dozens of people were waving money over their heads.

Felix reached under the bar for his leather pouch. He placed three unwrinkled hundred-dollar bills on top of the three on the bar. Pinocchio snatched up the bills and shook his fist at Felix.

"You lost, Black Cat! You'd better come out only at night from now on!"

Gerald pushed the wheelchair from behind the bar. The crowd swirled around Pinocchio, who was flanked by Diana and the Queen of Hearts.

"Buddy, I seen him put something in the seat!" Gerald yelled.

Buddy knelt in front of the wheelchair and felt with his hands beneath the seat. He was breathing hard and his face was shiny with sweat. There was a long red scratch on his right cheek.

"Look under the seat!"

"Liar! Liar!"

"He's cheating!"

"Liar! I won fair!"

"Search him!"

"Search his chair!"

The Queen of Hearts pounded Buddy on the back. He grabbed her wrist and pushed her out of the way.

"Not twice in one night, madam. I already got me a dueling scar from Joan of Arc," Buddy said.

The wheelchair shook as Buddy shifted Pinocchio from one side to the other; then he held a small oyster shell triumphantly over his head.

"Here's one, you cheating son of a bitch!"

"Get him! Get him!" someone yelled. The crowd converged around the chair. Pinocchio tried to move away, but Gerald was holding the wheels of the chair. Buddy held up another oyster shell.

"Here's another one, rich trash!"

"He's hurting me! Make him stop, someone! My legs!"

"He's faking it, Buddy. Keep looking!" a woman shouted.

"I'll sue this second-rate restaurant, and that sleazy club, too! I will! Someone call the police! He's going to kill me! Keep that big nigger away from me! You hear me, Rosario?"

"All right, Brent," Mr. Rosario said behind me. "Tell Buddy to knock it off. All we need is another goddamned lawsuit on our hands. Go on, get Buddy off the guy! And tell him to get back to the club."

"I didn't put them there!" Pinocchio screamed. "Can't you see I'm being set up? My legs!"

Brent tapped Buddy on the back. Buddy swung around as if he were going to hit him. Brent cupped his hands over Buddy's ear. Buddy glared at Mr. Rosario and then walked away, holding the two oyster shells above his head.

"It's all over, folks! Let's break it up!" Brent yelled, tossing back his hair.

"Police! I want a police escort out of here!"

"Not until he gives back the money!" Buddy shouted from the courtyard door. "The money he cheated Felix out of!"

"I didn't cheat anyone! I'm the one who's being cheated! I'm the one who's being set up!"

Gerald snatched the money out of Pinocchio's hand. Diana and the Queen of Hearts reached for it, but Gerald held it over their heads.

Brent was holding a man up by his collar and slamming his head forward over and over against the marble facing of the oyster bar. "This'll fucking teach you to steal tips!"

The man kicked his legs straight out; then suddenly he went limp. Brent pulled him up and onto a bar stool, then he clubbed him on the back with his hands clasped and the man fell to the floor.

Mr. Clay was doing a jerky dance on the oyster bar. He kicked a crystal bowl of calla lilies to the floor. The crowd moved away from the broken glass. In front of me a man was hit on the head by a flying Heineken bottle. He collapsed slowly into the arms of two men wearing identical pink golf shirts.

"Call an ambulance!" a woman in a fur stole bellowed at a jockey.

Someone grabbed my arm. It was Joseph.

"Are you all right, Laurie?"

"I guess so."

"You sure? You look a little shaky."

"No, I'm all right. Really."

"Well, you did a great job tonight. We can start you waitressing on Thursday. You'll have tomorrow to recover from all this." He gestured at the room.

"What time Thursday?"

"Oh, about ten. That'll give you a chance to talk to the other girls. They can show you what to do. Oh, I almost forgot." He held out a crumpled twenty-dollar bill. "Your blond friend with the glasses told me to give this to you for a cab. Don't forget to punch out."

As I walked to the kitchen, I saw three policemen forcing their way through the crowd.

Vita was standing beside the refrigerator, sucking on a maraschino cherry. She popped another cherry into her mouth.

"What's wrong, baby? The police here?"

"Yes. Three of them."

"Did Felix win?"

"No one knows exactly. The man in the wheelchair was cheating. Gerald saw him and told Buddy, and then Buddy searched the wheelchair."

"Gerald?" She scowled,

"Why? What's wrong?"

"Nothing, except his mother was a starch eater."

"What's that?"

"They eat starch, baby. Laundry starch. Makes them crazy—always a half-step in front of a fit."

"Does Gerald eat starch?"

"I don't know about now, but he used to when he was little. The damage already done, you ask me. How many oysters they find?"

"Two, but Buddy was getting rough and the man in the wheelchair threatened to sue. Mr. Rosario made Buddy stop."

"It should never have got this far."

"I didn't realize the man I saw here the other day was Mr. Rosario. I thought he was just a food salesman."

"A salesman? Mr. J.T.? Well, maybe you're not that far off, baby." She opened the refrigerator door and brought out a large lemon. "Look here, sugar. I thought I had one more left. A big fat one. I'll take it in to Felix myself. You go on home now. Ash Wednesday's here already."

"But I hate to leave without knowing if Felix won."

"He'll win. I'm sure of it." She was so close to me that I could see the green flecks moving in her eyes. "Here." She handed me a brown paper bag spotted with grease. "Bones for your little dog."

"Thank you."

Vita turned me in the direction of the door and pushed me lightly on the back.

"Go on now, baby. And don't you worry."

SEVENTEEN

A loud tapping at the front window awakened me. My body felt half numbed, and my mouth tasted dry and bitter. Echo followed me into the living room, whimpering and licking my hand. Jim was standing in the window. He was smiling. I unlocked the window and raised it over my head.

Jim put down his diving helmet and mesh bag and took me in his arms. He kissed my ears, my neck, and finally my lips.

"I missed you, Laurie. I really did. And little Echo. I missed you too." When Jim leaned down to pet Echo, his Saint Erasmus medal swung against the dog's head. He slipped off the medal and laid it carefully on the mantel; then he took my hand and pulled me over to the sofa.

"Two words," he said. *"Tres Puentes."*

"What does that mean?"

"Billy says it means three bridges. *Tres Puentes* is a ship. A Spanish galleon. She went down on July twenty-one, 1733."

"I don't—"

"Laurie, just listen. I read this book, see, when I was at Brownsville. It was written by the guy who ran the diving school I went to out in California. He's a great guy. A fucking brilliant guy!" He thrust a paperback book at me. On the cover was a brightly colored illustration of an open treasure chest with strands of pearls and gold coins spilling out onto the ocean floor.

"Thousands of wrecks, but all you need is one. And I found her! The *Tres Puentes*. It's all here in this book—everything I

177

need to know. At least most of it. Don't you see, honey? Who salvages wrecks? Divers. What am I? A diver. And a goddamn good one. Don't you see now? The *Sheherazade!* We'll use her to raise the son of a bitch! Raise the *Tres Puentes!*"

"But where is this ship?"

"Not far. That's the most beautiful part! Florida. She went down four miles southeast of Islamorada. Just between Upper and lower Matecumbe Key. Twenty fathoms down."

"Is twenty fathoms very deep?"

"Nah. It's a piece of cake. Think of it, baby: two hundred and fifty years just sitting down there, waiting. Waiting for us. Millions in gold and silver bullion. Kane's up for it, and so are Trulock and Kenny Perkins. They definitely want in, and they're both first-rate divers. This isn't just some crazy scheme, Laurie. I looked into it real carefully when I was out in the Gulf. And we have everything it takes: the boat, divers, the location—"

"What about the money? Jesus, Jim, we already owe—"

"We'll get backers. Hell, I know a lot of people who would be real interested in an investment like this. Rich people."

"Like that woman with the debutante daughter?"

"You got a good memory, little girl. You know, Mrs. Beausoleil wouldn't be such a bad idea at that. It's not as much money as you might think, either. I'm making out a list of what we'll need. Soon as I sell the car, I'll have five or six thousand to put into the *Sheherazade*. I've been working all morning on a map at the library."

"*This* morning?"

"Now, before you get mad, honey, I want you to know I'm sorry. I would have come home first, but I didn't think it would take so long. I needed to get more information before I could piece together a map. Hey, maybe you could draw the finished map for us! Yeah, that's a great idea."

"I guess it wouldn't be real buried treasure without a map."

"Don't get smart, Laurie. Just lighten up or we can always change the subject. We could pick up right where we left off when I had to go to Brownsville. Talking about honesty and all that. Or have you forgotten?"

"No, I haven't forgotten."

"Anyway, I'm sorry. I got caught up looking for more maps and stuff, and time just went by. But don't think for a second that I don't want to see you—come back to you. I'm so glad to be home again, honey—with you and Echo."

With a quick movement, he unbuttoned my nightgown and shoved his hand inside. He held my left nipple between his thumb and index finger.

"Like a rosebud. I could just tweak it off and pop it in my mouth like a gumdrop. You got tits just like a little girl."

"I hate it when you say that. You know how much I hate being flat chested."

"I didn't mean anything, honey. I've told you a million times— I like you the way you are. I love these little guys." He pushed my head back onto the arm of the sofa and lifted my nightgown up to my neck. He started kissing my breasts.

"Please don't, Jim."

He didn't stop kissing me. My entire body stiffened.

"Please, I don't want you to."

"Every time you say that and I keep going anyway, you start quivering like a little bunny rabbit and roll those big eyes of yours back in your head. I don't think you know what you want."

"I don't want this! Not now."

"Well, I don't think we ought to leave it up to you, sweetheart. Just relax." He began kissing my stomach.

"But I really don't want you to."

"Sssh. Relax and I'll make you really want to." He pulled my panties down to my knees. His lips were burning the inside of my thighs. My legs unstiffened and I stretched them out and it felt as if they were covered with warm, prickling sunlight. I closed my eyes. I heard him unzip his jeans and suddenly he was inside me.

"I'll be gentle with you, baby. You know that."

"But I don't want you to be gentle."

"You want me to do it hard? Like this?"

"Yes, like that." I wanted him to do it so hard that I would forget who I was and who he was—so hard that it would drive me down through the sofa and the floor, down, down, down until at last I would be in the cool earth underneath the house. Alone. I unbuttoned his shirt and, thrusting my hands inside, dug my fingernails deep into his back.

"This part has always been good, hasn't it, Laurie?"

"Yes."

"I missed you like crazy, little girl. And you missed me, too. I can tell."

I didn't answer him. For the first time there were no dreams.

When I awakened the next morning, Jim was sleeping on his side, fully dressed, his finger still marking the page he had been reading in the book about buried treasure. His eyes quivered slightly beneath their lids, and a stray curl on his forehead rose and fell gently with the rhythm of his breathing.

Beside the book were several crumpled sheets of paper and a list with MATERIALS NEEDED printed in clumsy block letters at the top. There were no crossouts, no corrections, nothing written over. For a moment I was touched by the thought of Jim painfully rewriting his list until it was flawless. It reminded me of the unexpected vulnerability I had seen once in a wild farm boy struggling to pass an algebra exam. But then I remembered the other list—the one Jim had shown my mother and me less than a month ago. He had rewritten that list over and over, too. . . .

I couldn't hear anything except the water in the shower, like the sound that a seashell makes when you cup it against your ear. Shampoo ran into my eyes, and I tilted my head back to rinse them.

The air in the bathroom suddenly became colder. I heard a thudding noise and the shower curtain shuddered momentarily under the spray. The shampoo still burned my eyes, and all I could make out clearly was the yellow curtain, tenting wildly toward me again and again. My mouth was wide open but I couldn't scream. The shadow of an arm kept stabbing. I slipped forward and crashed down on both knees. I felt a sharp burst of pain. The hooks of the shower curtain scraped against the bar.

"Please. Please."

I heard laughter. Jim's face was looming above me in the mist. He was wearing my bathrobe.

"Boy! I really had you going, didn't I?" He turned off the shower. "Hey, look down! You got so scared you pissed all over yourself!"

A thin stream of urine ran beneath me and downward into the drain. Jim tapped me on the shoulder with my largest sable paintbrush.

"Who'd you think it was? Did you think it was *Psycho,* little girl?"

"Why, Jim? Why?"

"Hey, it was just a paintbrush." He laughed again. "You should have seen your face. I've never seen anything like it!"

My knees were turning a deep purple. I knew that my light-beige nylon stockings—the only pair I owned—wouldn't hide the bruises. I hugged my knees and cried.

"I've been waiting for that. Come on, Laurie. It's not my fault you don't have any coordination. Your mother told me you had a good sense of humor. Well, maybe she's right, at that. Peeing on yourself was pretty funny." He left the bathroom whistling.

When I went into the kitchen, Jim was making coffee. He smiled.

"Hey, honey, it was just a joke. How was I to know you'd fall on your knees?"

"Shut up."

"What? What was that, Laurie?"

"I said shut up. Just shut up."

Jim walked slowly toward me. When he was a few feet away, he stopped. He put his right hand on his hip.

"All right, Laurie. You have my attention. Now what in the fuck is your problem?"

"You're the one with the problem!"

"No, you have the problem. You're the one who peed all over yourself. You're the one who doesn't have a sense of humor."

"Oh, you don't think I have a sense of humor? Well, here's a joke for you. I'm married to a sick son of a bitch. You like that one? Here's another—"

He rushed at me and smashed me against the wall, holding my chin with his hand.

"I might be married to a sick son of a bitch, and I might have to do what he says, and I might not be able to leave his sight. But there's no way I'll ever love you again. No way I'll ever stop wishing that you were somebody—anybody—else when we make love! Now, I think that's funny!"

My voice was rasping because of the way he was holding my chin. Pain spread slowly over the back of my head.

"Shut up! Shut up, you cunt! Or—"

"Or what? You'll hit me? Go ahead and get it over with, then, so I can go to work. Unless you want me to lose my job."

He squeezed my face harder. I choked but he didn't loosen his grip. With his other hand, he clamped my wrists together and my hands went numb.

"Go on! You know you're going to eventually. Why not today? More bruises for my first day waitressing."

"You'd like that, wouldn't you? You'd like to see me fuck up and hit you. Well, no way, baby. I wouldn't give you the fucking satisfaction."

He dropped his hands and I slid down the wall to the floor.

"But don't think I'm forgetting about this little outburst, sister, because I'm not. I'm getting the fuck out of here—get some breakfast with Kane." He took his suede jacket from the back of a chair and put it on. The veins in his forehead were pulsing in a V, and his hands were shaking. Suddenly he picked up my rose dish from the table and threw it against the wall.

"I'll see you later, princess." He smiled. "Oh, and good luck today sucking off strangers."

I waited until I was sure that Jim wasn't coming back; then I began picking up the pieces of broken china from the kitchen floor.

EIGHTEEN

As usual, Buddy was hosing down the sidewalk in front of Rosario's. When he saw me, he turned off the water. "Well, good morning to you, little baby. Now I know that spring is really here." Suddenly he stopped smiling. "Jesus, just look at those knees! What happened?"

"I fell down in the bathtub."

"You mean you slipped?"

"Yes. I slipped."

His eyes moved slowly from my face to my knees and then back to my face again.

"Well, you'll have to be more careful, precious. Don't you know that most accidents happen in the bathroom?"

"I know." He was still staring at me. I looked away at the chained camellia shrubs glistening with water.

"You're too petite to be slipping around some old bathtub. You could break a bone. Don't you have a mat?"

"Not yet. We just moved in, and we still need a lot of things."

"Well, you stop off at the K & B drug store after work and pick yourself up a mat, hear? It's at the corner of Louisiana and St. Charles."

"All right."

"There it is! That long-awaited smile. Back by popular demand. And the sun is out today for the first time since I met you. Just look at you in this light. Beautiful!"

"You're embarrassing me, Buddy."

"Beautiful. Bruises and all. Take a deep breath of this air, baby. It is so sweet. Everything has seemed right with the world since Mardi Gras, hasn't it, darlin'?"

"I guess so."

"Oh, you don't know yet, do you, doll? You didn't get to see us find that last oyster. Gerald plucked it right out of Pinocchio's pocket."

"So Felix did win!"

"Believe me, darlin', it was something to see. It's a blessing you left when you did, though. Everybody here was going wild. Take my word for it—it was no place for ladies." He smiled, shaking his head. "Come on, babycakes. I'll walk you to the back."

He led me, his heavy arm encircling my waist, around the oily puddles in the parking lot that glowed gold, blue, and magenta in the dazzling sunlight.

"I can't get over that rich trash thinking he could pull a fast one on us. Still, I guess Gerald did get a little carried away. You figure if anybody was obliged to hit him, it would be Felix. I know a cheat is a cheat, but the man *was* in a wheelchair."

"I can't believe Felix won. It seems like a miracle."

"This is a town for miracles, precious. You just got to believe. Now if you would ever . . . that would be a real miracle. It could happen, though, baby. Everything moves slow down here—even miracles." He bent down and kissed the top of my head.

I could hear gospel music from Gabriel's radio in the kitchen. I moved toward the door, hoping that no one had seen. Buddy leaned against the door.

"Please, Buddy. I have to go to work."

"Don't look at me like that, darlin'. Those eyes of yours will break my heart. But I could never say no to you." He held the door open for me. "See you at lunch, baby."

Gabriel was twirling one of the knobs of his radio. He was wearing a pale yellow silk tie and a pink candy-striped shirt with the sleeves rolled up. His thick forearms reminded me of oiled cherrywood logs.

"Good morning, Gabriel."

He muttered something and turned back to the ham he was frying. Someone chuckled behind me. A pale-skinned black man was sitting on one of the steel tables, drinking a bottle of orange Nehi soda. He studied me from behind dark sunglasses.

"Hey, pretty, " he said.

"I'm Laurie."

"Bigtimer."

Vita appeared suddenly from her corner of the kitchen, wiping chocolate frosting from her hands onto the front of her apron. Bigtimer jumped down from the table and took off his sunglasses. I realized then that he was no more than sixteen years old.

"Suppose you start making some fast time with those dishes."

"I was just taking a break, Vita."

"Well, your break is over. I told you I need little plates."

Bigtimer pulled a huge clattering rack of dishes out of the machine, and the air around him turned milky white with steam. Vita continued to wipe her hands on her apron. She was staring at my knees.

"You come with me, baby. Pay no attention to those two black snakes."

I followed Vita back to her corner. She handed me a piece of toast and a slice of ham from her plate on the marble cutting block.

"Here, girl. You eat that even if you don't want it. You don't need to be collapsing from hunger on those knees during the rush. And always give us your order as soon as you take it. Right when you're getting your soup. Otherwise, it'll get confusing when they pile up. Okay, baby? You're going to do just fine."

The screen door slammed and Vita's smile faded.

"Well, it must be the Queen of England," she said, without looking up.

Molly was wearing a white oxford cloth shirt with the three top buttons undone and boy's tuxedo trousers that made her hips look heart shaped. She wore a ring on every finger.

"Hello, sweetheart," she said to me. "Well, I sure have a royal hangover, Vita."

"I thought you must be the Queen the way you was carrying on last night. Coming back here with that parade of boys."

"Mum, if I were the Queen of England, what would I be doing here serving these sods lunch?" She hugged Vita, and Vita finally smiled.

"Jesus, love, what happened to you?" Molly asked.

"I fell in the shower."

"Ow!" Molly winced, scrunching up her shiny nose. She

opened her compact and studied her face in the mirror. Her eyelids were painted an iridescent lilac shade that made the irises of her eyes appear almost violet. "God," she said, snapping the compact shut, "I look like shit. Come on, Laurie. Let's get a cup of coffee and go in the other room. It's too hot back here."

"Too bad you ain't got your parade with you. Get one of them boys to fan you," Vita said.

Molly picked up a bundle of linen and put it in her lap. Then she lit a menthol Benson and Hedges cigarette and inhaled deeply.

"I really should quit," she said. "Someday."

While Molly and I folded napkins, we talked—or rather Molly did. Molly was from London. She had never been to college. She hated her father, and she loved Mary Quant makeup, Dixieland, and the Arthurian legends. She had come to the United States on a visitor's visa, and now her visa had expired.

"I suppose I shouldn't worry, really," she said, "but sometimes I have a dream of being led away in irons by a man from your Department of Immigration." She laughed. "And the worst part, love, is he has my father's sideburns."

"Good morning," Joseph said, coming over to our table. "Molly, did you fill Laurie in on everything?"

"Of course, Joey." Her voice was almost like singing.

"Good. Molly makes the best tips here."

"I used to—until you put me on lunches," Molly said, pushing out her lower lip in a mock pout.

"But, Molly, you asked to work lunches. You said that you needed your evenings free." When Molly didn't answer, he looked down at his clipboard. "From now on, liquor has to be inventoried at the end of each shift. Rosario's order. There's too much shortage."

Molly smiled when she saw him glance at her cup.

"Don't worry, pet. It's just coffee."

"Good girl." He looked back at his clipboard. "Well, I guess that's it. Good luck, Laurie."

"Thanks."

We watched him walk to the kitchen, the clipboard tucked under his right arm.

"Just coffee with a little Irish whiskey," Molly whispered. "And after last night, I need this. I must have been so bloody high! Can you imagine waking up next to a wide receiver for the bloody New Orleans Saints? I don't remember any of it, pet. Honestly. When I got out of bed this morning, I could scarcely walk."

"You don't remember anything?"

"No. Nothing. Zero. Except the chandelier. I don't know where we were, but I remember being on someone's shoulders and taking down a piece of crystal. I put the wire through my ear for an earring, which was an extremely idiotic thing to do. Look, my ear is infected already." She pulled back the hair over her right ear. The earlobe was red and swollen. "I really must cut back," she said, shaking her head. "No more Quaaludes—at least on week nights."

A tall, pretty blond girl came through the kitchen doors, carrying a glass of chocolate milk. Her skin had a kind of glowing transparency that reminded me of the clear pastel shades of miniature animals blown out of glass. There was a slight adolescent gawkiness in her movements; and when she stopped in front of us, her glasses slipped forward. She shook her bangs from her forehead and pushed the glasses back to the bridge of her upturned nose.

"I'm sorry, Molly. I overslept. I was up so late studying last night that I missed my class."

"Studying? Is that all you ever do? Oh, Laurie, this is Jayne Doe. That's Jayne spelled with a y, if you please."

"It's nice to meet you," I said.

"Hi, Laurie," she said, smiling. Her large, even teeth were very white. "My last name is Carlisle, not Doe, but Molly always says that. I don't know why."

"Jayne goes to Tulane and she belongs to a sorority," Molly said. "Doesn't she look like she is right off the cover of *Seventeen* magazine"

Jayne blushed and pushed up her glasses again.

"What did *you* do last night, Molly?"

"Don't breathe a word, Laurie. She's still a baby, and it's up to us to set an example."

"Oh, Molly, was it that bad?"

"Well, it wasn't exactly *bad*. No, bad wouldn't be the word I would choose to describe it."

"Or maybe you don't remember how it was? That sounds more like it to me."

"In fact, love, you would probably approve," Molly said, standing up.

"Good," Jayne said as we followed Molly into the kitchen. "I'm glad you think I would approve."

Molly poured herself a cup of coffee. Then she pulled out the metal basket from the Bunn machine and dumped the steaming filter and old grounds into the garbage. Bigtimer rinsed the metal basket for her, and she put in a new filter and fresh coffee.

"Well, who is he, Molly?" Jayne asked. "What does he do?"

"He plays football. For the Saints."

"He does! Does he have any friends?"

"I don't know. But the next time I see Forest, I'll ask him."

"Forest! Johnson? The wide receiver? But, Molly—"

She didn't finish the sentence and Molly laughed.

"I don't believe it! How? I mean, Molly, why would you?"

"Hey, Molly," Bigtimer said. "You know once you go black, you never go back."

Molly pulled the oversized plastic comb from Bigtimer's back pocket and smacked him on the behind with it.

"Bigtimer, you quit eavesdropping!"

Laughing, Bigtimer wrestled the comb away from her and went back to the dishwashing machine.

Jayne, Molly, and I sat down at a booth in the dining room. Molly lit a cigarette and Jayne fanned the air and moved away from her. Felix was behind the bar, rolling up his shirtsleeves. He smiled at us, and Molly blew him a kiss.

"Forest Johnson," Jayne said, more to herself than to us.

"And don't you dare tell Buddy," Molly said.

"I won't."

"I mean it, Miss Sunbeam."

I had to smile. The way Jayne's hair was pulled into a bundle of curls on top of her head did resemble little Miss Sunbeam's hairdo on the bread wrappers.

Molly slid from the booth and walked over to the oyster bar with her cup.

"Good morning, darlin'," Felix said. "You look like you have a problem."

"I do. It's my coffee."

"What seems to be the trouble with it?"

"It tastes like coffee," Molly said. "Do you think you could remedy that, love?"

*   *   *

At a quarter to eleven, I was looking out the glass front door when a chauffeur-driven, chocolate-and-cream-colored Bentley pulled up to the curb outside. A rotund, red-faced man got out of the car and stood in front of the glass front door with his hands in the pockets of his opened Burberry raincoat. Joseph unlocked the door for him and then locked it again. The red-faced man waved to Joseph and headed toward the bar, where Felix had already set down a martini.

I rejoined Molly and Jayne at the booth. Molly patted my thigh when I sat down next to her.

"Isn't that Mr. Foster a dear? Every day he comes in here before we open, has a couple of double martinis, and is gone before eleven-thirty."

"He is sweet," Jayne said.

"I should say. He's the only regular customer who doesn't screw you with his eyes."

"Molly!"

"Well, it's true, Jaynie. And you know it."

At eleven o'clock Joseph unlocked the front door. Molly's section immediately filled with businessmen who had requested her to wait on them. Molly greeted most of the men by name and shook hands with the few she didn't already know.

"You just wait," Jayne said. "We'll get all the blue-haired old ladies in fur coats that don't ever tip. But Molly works hard. She's really good."

My first customers were four young women who ordered shrimp remoulades and carafes of house Chablis. One of the women was wearing a bracelet on which the words "Rich Bitch" were spelled out in dozens of small diamonds.

"Texans," Molly whispered in my ear as she passed me.

Buddy sat down in my section. He ate quickly, watching me as I moved around the dining room, and left five dollars and a pink paper bag on the table. Inside the bag was a white rubber bath mat.

By noon the dining room and bar were filled with customers, and more people were lined up by the door to the Cache-Cache Club. As soon as a table was cleared, a new party was seated. I put Jim out of my mind. I had to concentrate on exactly what I was doing every moment. By two o'clock the dining room was nearly empty. My station of six tables had turned over three times, and I had made thirty-nine dollars. I leaned against the wall near a ficus tree and closed my eyes. Suddenly I felt Molly's small hand on my arm.

"Love, you will never believe it!"

"Believe what?"

"I have just found a Lancelot! I don't know where Joseph is, so I'm going to seat him myself. Oh, Laurie this could be it!"

"A Lancelot must be pretty high on your list."

"Only a Galahad is higher, but they're even harder to find. And usually they don't like me or they're gay or something. But this guy is definitely *not* gay. Wait until you see his eyes. One of them says bed and the other says room."

"Where is he?"

She pointed to the left of the ficus tree. "Do you see him? The guy in the blue jeans."

First I saw his long legs and then his hands.

"Molly, that's my husband!"

"What! You mean you're married to a doll like that, and you didn't even mention it? Not that I blame you. He's bloody gorgeous. A real-life Lancelot!"

"More like Mordred," I whispered.

"Well, Mordred is coming over here."

"Hey, there you are, baby."

"Jim, this is Molly. I'm sorry but I don't know your last name."

"Duffy. Hi. Has anyone ever told you they would give five years off their life to sleep with you?"

"No," Jim said, smiling and raising his eyebrows.

"Don't worry, love. You're both altogether too darling for me to do anything more than dream."

"Molly, table seven wants coffee." Jayne was breathing hard, as if she had been running, but there was no perspiration on her face. "Do you want me to take it out to them?"

"No, thank you, pet. That table can smell innocence a block away. They would tear you to shreds. Well, it was super to meet you, Jim."

Jim reached down and shook her hand. "My pleasure, Molly."

"Definitely a Lancelot," Molly whispered, leaning close to me. As she walked away with Jayne, she moved her heart-shaped hips even more than usual.

"You'd better watch that one, Laurie. That little girl looks like she could be real trouble."

"What are you doing here, Jim? I'm still working."

"Honey, I finally figured it out! Kane and me were over at Acy's Pool Hall, see. You remember Acy's—that place I took you to where we got those great muffulettas. Anyway, we were sitting there having lunch and suddenly it hit me—bang!—just like that. And, Laurie, it's so simple, it's beautiful! Old Jimbo's a fucking genius!"

"What are you talking about?"

"How to raise the *Tres Puentes*! We tie a few thousand plastic garbage bags to her, see; then we blow them up with an air hose and just wait for the son of a bitch to surface! I know it sounds crazy, but that's because it's so simple."

"It does sound a little crazy."

"I'm telling you, Laurie, it'll work! The smart asses in the world always want to make everything so fucking hard. They thought Ben Franklin was crazy for that kite shit. He was crazy like a fox."

"Jim, please lower your voice. People are staring at us."

"Fuck them. Well, what do you think?"

Joseph walked over to us, a menu under his arms, and stopped in front of Jim.

"Sir, are you waiting to be served for luncheon? We will only be serving for a few more minutes before we close the kitchen."

Jim gave him his warmest smile, the one he reserved for other men.

"No, thanks, I'm Laurie's husband, and I needed to talk to her before I go offshore. I'm a diver, and I'm going to be leaving from here." He turned to me. "Guess it's going to be up to you to sell the car, honey. I put an ad in the *Times Picayune* just before I got beeped to go back to the Gulf. Oh, the name's Jim. Jim Wellman."

"It's a pleasure to meet you. Joseph Salerno." He stood up even straighter as he shook Jim's hand. "What kind of car are you selling?"

"Sixty-nine Corvette."

"Fast car. I have a Trans Am."

I held my breath. Jim thought Trans Ams were grease-ball cars.

"Hey, T.A.'s aren't exactly slow."

Joseph smiled gratefully. I almost hated him—and Molly, too. "Well, it was nice meeting you, Jim." He shook Jim's hand again. "You should come in for lunch sometime. We have a new menu."

"I'd like that. Thanks. But only if I can have your best waitress." Jim put his arms around my neck and pulled me closer to him. "So I'd better not come on Molly's day off."

They both laughed.

"I'll give her back to you in just a few minutes."

"No problem." Joseph winked and walked away. Jim looked at me.

"Nice moustache," he said.

I didn't say anything.

"What's the matter? Still hot about the shower? Or is it that cheap fucking dish?"

"No, I just didn't know you were leaving again so soon."

"I would have been here sooner, but Kane had to stop in every fucking bar in his neighborhood looking for the champ tramp herself. I hope you're making some tips because I had to take all the money at home." He lit a cigarette and looked around the dining room. "Hey, who is that jerk-off studying you?"

"Where?"

"The guy over there. At that shady table."

It was Lee. He was staring down at the white rose in a small silver vase in the center of the table.

"Well, do you know him?"

"No," I said.

Then Jim was kissing me hard on the lips, crushing my body against his. My teeth clenched and I didn't move. Finally he pulled away, and I walked out of Lee's view without looking over.

"What's the matter? You're white as a sheet. Does kissing me make you sick, little girl?" He gripped my arm tightly. "Well, you better get well real soon. I want that car sold before I get back. The ad is written out beside the phone. Show the car, but don't let anyone drive it. If a guy is interested, get his name, and I'll let him drive it when I come back."

"When will you be back?"

"A few days. Could be one, could be seven. I don't know for sure, but if I did, I wouldn't tell you. Now, have you got everything straight?"

I nodded.

"I better not find out you fucked up. Even a mental case

could sell a car." He took a long drag from his cigarette. "Come on outside for a minute. Kane wants to ask you something."

The truck was parked across the street from Rosario's. Above the telephone wires, budding trees spread out their branches against a sky of Titian blue.

"Hey, Laurie." Billy put his head through the open window on the driver's side of the truck. "Could you do me a favor and call Toni sometime today? I left her a note but I'm not sure she'll see it. She wasn't home when I got beeped."

"Sure. I'll be glad to."

"Thanks. I really appreciate it. God, what happened to your legs"

"It's a good story, Kane," Jim said. "I'll tell you on the way."

"Yeah, we better hit it soon, Jimbo," Billy said, glancing at his wristwatch.

"Just give me a few more minutes with the princess here." Jim took my arm and pulled me away from the truck. "The same thing goes this time, understand? You want to see Toni, you have her come up to the house. I don't want you down in the Quarter. Christ, I'll have enough to worry about now with that English tart you work with. Are you listening to me, or are you in outer space?"

"I'm listening."

He squeezed my arm hard. "I know you think my idea about the *Tres Puentes* is crazy, but you wouldn't know a good idea if it smacked you in the fucking head. I can't wait to see your face when I raise her." He let go my arm and ran to the truck. "I'll see you when I see you."

Billy honked the horn as he roared toward the stop sign at the intersection. Jim turned around in his seat.

"Garbage bags!" My voice echoed in the empty street.

NINETEEN

In the kitchen, a skinny black boy of about ten was helping Bigtimer load the dishwashing machine. Bigtimer told me that the boy was his cousin Maurice. Behind his small sunglasses, Maurice's eyes were the same almond shape as Bigtimer's; and like his cousin, he had a nickel in his right ear. I leaned against one of the steel tables and sipped my Coke.

"You guys look almost like brothers."

Bigtimer thumped Maurice on top of the head.

"Don't worry, ma'am. It don't hurt me none."

"He likes it," Bigtimer said.

They stopped laughing when they saw Vita.

"Don't you pay no attention to him, Maurice. If he knew what hurt and what don't, he wouldn't be in jail."

"I ain't in jail," Bigtimer said softly.

"No, you ain't in jail, but you ain't free, neither. Living out at the Phoenix House on that work-release." She continued to stare at Bigtimer as he walked slowly back to the dishwashing machine.

"That Bigtimer been here longer than any of them, but he still got to behave. It don't take much to go back, and he gets excited too easy. He's good if he don't get excited."

"Go back where?"

"To jail, baby. All our boys is here on the work-release."

"Oh, there you are, love. I've been looking everywhere for you." Molly's eyes were brighter than I had ever seen them.

194

"Why? What's the matter?"

"Nothing's the matter. We're having a little celebration! Lee Carraway is leaving for Mexico."

"Mexico? Lee?" I felt numb.

"He asked about you, Laurie. I didn't know you knew him."

"I don't really—I mean not very well. He seems nice."

"Well, I'd say that's the understatement of the year. He's a doll—a perfect example of a Galahad. Pure of heart. Grab four glasses, love, and I'll get the champagne."

"*Four* glasses?"

"Yes. Your friend Toni is joining us. She's lovely."

"*Bon voyage,* General," Toni said, raising her glass of champagne. She closed her eyes and sipped. "Come quickly. I am tasting stars."

"What was that, love?" Molly asked.

"It's what the man who first made champagne said to his wife." Lee took the white rose from the vase on the table and twirled the stem slowly between his thumb and forefinger. "I am tasting stars."

"Lee, do you know everything in the world?" Molly asked.

Lee laughed, shaking his head.

"He does! Ask him about anything, Laurie."

"All right," I said. "What about roses?"

"Come on, love. Say something smart about roses or they'll think I'm exaggerating."

"Something smart?" Lee put the rose back in the vase and leaned his forehead against his hand, mimicking deep thought. "Well, roses played a prominent part in the ancient Roman games. The winners were garlanded with roses and thousands of them were festooned on the spectators' boxes. And at a feast that Cleopatra gave for Mark Antony, the floor of the great hall was covered with roses eighteen inches deep. Then there was the Emperor Heliogabalus."

"Heliogabalus," Molly said, laughing. "You made that up."

"Word of honor. Emperor Heliogabalus. He was an extravagant and frivolous fellow who made a dancer his commander in chief and a hairdresser his minister of supply. Anyhow, old Emperor Heliogabalus inadvertently killed several of his guests at a banquet by showering them with rose petals until they suffocated."

Molly jumped up from her chair and stood behind Lee with her arms around his neck.

"See! What did I tell you? I always say that's the sexiest thing about a man—his brains. Next to a great body, of course. And you have both."

"I'm sorry for going on like this," Lee said, looking at me. "I'm just not used to anyone really caring about flowers. Oh, maybe a few of my gay friends. But they're more interested in knowing how to arrange flowers for the brunch table than anything else. And my straight friends think I'm gay if I talk about flowers too much. So *voilà*! I bore pretty girls to tears."

"Go ahead, General," Toni said. "You aren't boring us."

"Are roses your favorite flowers, Laurie?"

"Yes. I love them."

"All right, then. I'll go on. Where was I?"

"The Romans," Molly said. "And Helio-what's-his name."

"Oh, yes. Well, with the coming of Christianity, roses fell into disrepute. The early Christians disapproved of roses because they associated them with pagan rites and Roman excesses. But then someone decided that the petals represented the five wounds of Christ. And red roses became the symbol for the blood of the martyrs."

Toni poured herself another glass of champagne. "Why five wounds? I read that they tied Jesus's feet when they crucified him. There would only be three wounds, including the one from the spear."

"I remember reading that, too. But the church always claims five."

"They would claim five hundred if they could," Toni said.

"Why are you going to Mexico, love? Mosquitoes and poison water. You may as well stay here."

"I can answer that," Toni said. "There is a girl, of course, and it is springtime, and it would be unthinkable without her. Unbearable. Every little thing reminds him of her, et cetera, et cetera." She drained her glass of champagne and glanced around the deserted dining room. "We're the only people here, General. Let's order another bottle and go somewhere else."

Bigtimer came up to the table. He was carrying a plate piled high with French bread, sausage, red beans, and rice.

"Vita wants to see you," he said, tapping me on the shoulder.

* * *

Vita was closing the door of the microwave oven. Mingled with the odors of garlic, butter, and shrimp was an indefinable but somehow familiar aroma.

"Bigtimer said you wanted to see me. What are you baking? It sure smells good."

"It is good, sugar. You'll see." The buzzer went off in the microwave and Vita opened the door. "Girl," she said, "you got a look you could pour on pancakes. Do you know that?"

I laughed. "Aren't you going to wear a mitt?"

"It ain't hot. I only cook it for a second or two. Just enough to take the damp out so it don't rot in the mail." She set the cookie sheet covered with brown, steaming crumbs on the counter.

"What is it?"

"What it look like." With a single sweep of her hand, Vita brushed all the crumbs into a shoe box lined with tinfoil.

"It's dirt?"

"Earth. And I got some for you."

"What for? I mean—"

"To eat. Haven't you never eaten it?"

"No, I don't think so."

"You sure, girl? Not even when you was small? I bet you did. Children do. This batch is for my sister up north. She's been craving it. The earth there ain't the same. Get that funny look off your face, girl. It's good red earth from Mississippi."

"But isn't it bad for you?"

"You think I would give you something that's bad? There's nothing better for you. Good for the blood. It ain't like eating starch. Try it, girl."

I scooped a small handful of the steaming soil from the shoe box, tilted my head back, and sprinkled it on my tongue. A half-forgotten taste a little like iron filled my mouth.

"I remember now," I said. "My father told me that when I was a baby, he had to force dirt and rocks out of my mouth all the time."

"Told you so. Children crave earth, and it don't hurt them none. The Chinese know. They don't hold back the children."

"The Chinese are smart people."

"Believe it!" She handed me a small white box tied with string. "Now you eat a handful a day, baby. Just put a little vinegar on it. You'll start feeling better. And give some to the little dog on her food. Help her, too."

"I will. Thank you, Vita."

"Go on now, girl. And don't let Gabe see it. He gets excited and starts going on about the Board of Health Department."

I put the box in my purse as I walked back to the table.

"Don't get upset, Molly," Lee was saying. "All I did was ask."

"Well, for your information, love, yes, I still go out with him once in a while. Mr. Foster is a friend. Besides, he's rather cut up right now, the poor dear. They found his girlfriend dead in the pool at the Hilton last week."

The air in the cemetery smelled of rotting vegetation, and in the early twilight the tombs glowed as if they were lamp-lit from within. Lee sat, legs outstretched, on the top step of a pale vault. Echo was licking his hand. On a gray granite step nearby, Molly was hugging her knees and holding her breath to get rid of the hiccups. Toni lay on a low pink marble vault on which the name *Poirell* was inscribed in Roman capitals, sipping champagne and watching Lee and Echo. I leaned against the same vault and looked up at the milky sky tinted with streaks of delicate aqua, rose, and yellow.

"It's almost opalescent, isn't it, Laurie?" Lee said.

Echo turned her head toward Lee; then she jumped onto his lap, her paws smearing the front of his shirt as she strained to lick his face.

I clapped my hands. "Echo! Get down! I'm so sorry. She got mud on your shirt."

"It's all right, Laurie. She's a wonderful little dog." He rubbed her ears. "Yes, you are. You are a little beauty."

"Oh, God," Molly said. "See what I mean? He knows everything in the world, and all the animals love him." She hiccuped loudly.

"Hold your breath, Molly," Lee said, smiling.

"Just like a movie by Disney," Toni said. "The General gets up in the morning and the darling little birds and mice dress him. And he sings with them as the morning light star-bursts on his glasses." She sat down next to Lee, and they stroked the dog's ears and the smooth, short fur under her muzzle. In the distance, a woman knelt in front of a grave with a sheaf of red gladioli in her arms.

"Come here, chérie, and share the last of it," Toni said, holding out her glass of champagne. "How long do you think the old buccaneers will be gone this time?"

"Buccaneers?" Lee asked.

"Hasn't Laurie mentioned Jim's gold fever to you?"

"No."

"Well, Jim and Billy are going to dive for sunken treasure in Florida. A Spanish galleon or something. Billions in bullion under the poop deck. Christ!"

"When are they going to do this?"

"Who knows, General? Who cares? It's getting cold."

Lee put his arm around Toni and hugged her shoulders. She smiled up at him.

I looked at Molly. "How are the hiccups?"

"Gone," she said, walking over to Lee. "Treasure or not, at least you two are married."

"Consider yourself lucky. Right, Laurie?" Toni said, standing up. She took the champagne glass out of my hand and emptied it.

"It's just a piece of paper if you marry the wrong person," I said.

"That's easy for you to say, love. You *have* the piece of paper. And you have that blue-eyed hunk to curl up with night after night. I'm not married and I'm nearly twenty-seven. I don't even have a bloody visa." She stood behind Lee with her arms around his neck, leaning her body against his back. "Why don't you marry me, you lovely man?" She put her cheek against his face. "I could force you to, you know."

"And how do you propose to do that, Miss Duffy?"

"It's a secret. I promised Vita that I would never divulge it to anyone."

"That's never stopped you before, Molly. Come on, 'fess up."

"Well, I really shouldn't, but since you insist. She told me that to make a man yours forever, you must mix a few drops of your menstrual blood with some food you've prepared for him."

"Sounds interesting," Lee said. "I don't believe I've ever heard of that particular practice before."

"So that's all there is to it?" Toni asked. "The blood business?"

"No, actually there are some words you're supposed to pronounce as you mix in the blood, but I've forgotten them." She stood up straight and tousled Lee's hair. "Not that it would make a particle of difference to Sir Galahad here."

"What is it, Moll?" Lee said, patting her hand. "What's really on your mind? Thinking of giving it up?"

"Giving up what, dearie?"

"All of it. Late nights. Drinking."

"Damn it, you do know everything! Well, for your information, I was considering it." She sat down next to Lee and studied her fingernails.

"I don't know. Last night was a touch embarrassing. I hate to admit it—especially to you—but it really was. Just look at my ear. Maybe I have to cut down—or quit. When you really start to embarrass yourself, perhaps it's time to quit."

Tiny copper-colored sparks flew into the air as Toni's cigarette glanced off the side of a nearby tomb. "You know what I think? I think that when you begin to embarrass yourself, it isn't time to give up drinking at all."

"It's not?"

"No. It's just time to drink alone." Toni put her empty glass upside down on the vault step and began snapping her blue jean jacket. "Let's get the hell out of here. The champagne is gone, and this place is beginning to give me the creeps."

I left the three of them at the cemetery while I took Echo home.

Lee was standing in front of the house, staring up at the branches of the oak tree. A sudden gust of wind rustled the branches, blowing his hair across his forehead. He brushed it back with his hand.

"God, Laurie, listen to that wind! Isn't it wonderful?"

"Yes." We stood facing each other under the oak tree, our hands almost touching. I realized suddenly that this was the first time we had been alone together—really alone. "What happened to Toni and Molly?"

"Well, Molly had a dinner date, and Toni remembered that she had to meet her boss for drinks." At that moment the streetlights came on, and a nimbus of light encircled his head. "I couldn't leave without saying goody-bye to you."

"I'm glad you did."

"Laurie." He moved toward me and the nimbus disappeared. "Would you like to come to my place for some of my famous coffee? The best in the world. Actually, Molly is the only person who thinks that, but it isn't bad. And I have a little book of Redouté's work I think you would like. It's beautiful. The Rembrandt of the rose."

"I'd like to, Lee, but I really can't."

"I understand. You probably have plans."

"No, it's not that. I'm just a little tired."

"Well, maybe when I get back this summer, all three of you can come over. Molly and Toni have already taken rain checks on it." He leaned forward and kissed me near my right temple, so close to my ear that I could hear him breathe. "Take care of yourself, Laurie."

In the fading light, his silhouette was a paler blue than the air. He walked about ten yards, then he turned around suddenly and came back.

"All right, I didn't want to have to do this. But do you suppose I could change your mind if I were to perform my deathless imitation of Wayne Newton singing 'Dixie'? I promise you, Laurie, it's a rare treat that few people have been privileged to witness. Actually, only my brother."

"Wayne Newton?" I laughed. "Can you really do him?"

"Word of honor. It has taken me hundreds of showers to perfect it. Well, what do you say?"

"What *can* I say to that? I'll come."

"You will? Splendid!" he said, offering me his arm.

Lee cleared his throat as we approached Commander's Palace; then he took off his glasses, cocked his head at a silly angle, and broke into syrupy, adenoidal song.

I was laughing so hard that I let go of his arm and walked into a man wearing a winter suit who was laughing, too.

"I'm a little rusty, but what do you think?"

"Perfect," I gasped. "Probably the best in the world."

TWENTY

S tanding in the tiled porte cochere, I could see the silhouette of a tall palm some distance away through a large
rusted wrought-iron gate.

"That's the courtyard. We go this way," Lee said, taking my
arm in the darkness. "I'm sorry the light's burned out."

We walked up two flights of wide stone stairs, then along a
colonnade that overlooked the courtyard.

"It's beautiful, Lee."

"It's falling apart. I think you'll like Aleister." Coins jingled in
his pockets as he felt for his keys.

"Oh, is he your roommate?"

"Yes. It's definite now. He's staying."

I pursed my lips together to redden them and ran my fingers
through my hair.

When Lee opened the door, I saw a folded sheet of paper on
the floor. He picked the paper up and stuffed it into the pocket
of his black corduroy jacket. The air inside the apartment
smelled like coffee. Coffee and chocolate.

Lee flipped on a light. We were standing in a narrow foyer a
few feet from a black iron stairway that spiraled up to another
floor. Violet ribbons with golden chrysanthemums attached to
them were taped around the banister. In a few places the tape
had given way, and some of the flowers almost touched the floor.

"Those flowers have about had it. I should take them down,
but Aleister likes them."

"They're very pretty. Did you put them up for Mardi Gras?"

"Yes. Well, a friend of mine did. Let me take your coat."

I heard a thud upstairs and Lee smiled. A very fat, white cat bounded down the stairs and rubbed his head against Lee's legs. Then the cat spun four times in tight, frantic circles in the middle of the small oriental rug.

"The end of his dance is really very exciting. Now watch."

The cat crouched down on his haunches and then sprang several feet in the air, right paw extended, as if he were swatting a bug. He jumped two more times and ran over to Lee.

"It's spectacular," I said, laughing. "But what does it mean?"

"I have no idea, but he does that every time I come home. You're quite a dancer, aren't you?" he said, stooping down and patting the cat's head. "I think he definitely hears a different drummer. Actually, he doesn't hear anything. He's deaf."

"He is?"

"Totally. Aren't you?" he said to the cat. "Aleister, this is Laurie."

"Aleister! Well, Aleister, you sure are beautiful," I said, bending over. Before I could pet him, his head was against my open hand.

"I knew he would like you. He's not usually that affectionate with strangers."

Aleister looked up at Lee and then ran over to the stairway and batted a loose ribbon, hitting it so hard that chrysanthemum petals flew into the air. He batted the ribbon again.

"Okay, pal." Lee walked across the room to a window and opened it. Aleister brushed against him a couple of times and then leapt onto the sill and out the window.

"Whenever he wants out, he hits at something. As of late, it's been my poor, bedraggled Mardi Gras decoration. So if I'm not in the room and you hear him banging at the window, please let him in. Usually, he uses his paws, but if I don't hear him, he has been known to use his fat, empty head."

I laughed. "That must be a long climb to the ground."

"He's a great climber. That's how I found him, or, I should say, that's how he found me. One night last summer I was sitting here reading when he jumped through the open window. He was considerably skinnier then."

"Well, he sure isn't skinny now."

"I know," he said almost gleefully. "I spoil him. Unfortunately, he has to swear off marshmallows. Except on special occasions, of course."

The loud ring of the telephone startled me. Lee walked over to the small black marble mantel and picked up the receiver.

"Carraway Buick and Opel," he said, smiling at me as he listened. Suddenly he stopped smiling and turned away. "No," he said in a much softer voice. "I haven't read it yet. I just walked in the door." Cradling the phone between his shoulder and chin, he walked back to the kitchen, stretching the cord taut beind him.

I looked around the living room: faded flesh-pink wallpaper printed with blue forget-me-nots; a black velvet painting of Jesus, His face streaming with blood under the thorns; a framed display of arrowheads on white cotton; sugar skulls from Mexico; a photograph of F. Scott Fitzgerald inscribed "For Vic and Dorothy— Happy fêtes, Scott"; jade-colored lamps with fringed black silk shades; rows of bright butterflies mounted under glass; an antique love seat draped with a silk screen on nylon velvet of a bloated, rhinestoned Elvis; a mahogany Victrola; and a white marble bust of Lord Byron, the face half-hidden by a blood-red mask like Toni's. . . .

There was a scratching noise at the window. I opened it and Aleister fell into my arms. His fur was cold and smelled of rain. I held him against my face and closed my eyes. When I opened them, Lee was staring at me from the kitchen doorway.

"That cat really loves you."

"And I love him," I said, kissing the top of Aleister's head.

"Bring him in here, and we'll give him a marshmallow. The coffee's almost ready."

I put Aleister down on the floor. He ran into the kitchen and jumped onto a small round table.

"Well, what do you think of my clock?" Lee asked, pointing to the wall above the stove.

The clock was constructed of a cheap alloy. Long rays fashioned to resemble sunbeams radiated from its golden face; the ends of the rays were decorated with alternate metal cutouts of ballerinas and grape clusters sprinkled with glitter. Beneath the clock was an unframed photograph of Nijinsky wearing shredded roses.

"It's wonderful!"

"Allah be praised!" he said, handing me a cup of coffee. "At last someone else likes it. I bought it in New York when I was at Columbia—from an old Puerto Rican man near Times Square. How's the coffee?"

"Delicious." The sweet, rich aroma of coffee and chocolate made the cluttered kitchen seem even cosier.

"I'm glad you came, Laurie."

"So am I."

Aleister stretched out between a glass half filled with red wine and a couple of paperback books lying face down on the table.

"I'm teaching him sign language. I tell you, Laurie, this cat is a genius. Watch." Lee formed a circle with his thumb and forefinger. Aleister jumped down from the table, sprang to the edge of the sink, and then to the top of a small refrigerator. He batted at the knob of a closed cabinet.

"He *is* a genius!"

"What did I tell you?" Lee opened the cabinet door and brought out a large bag of Campfire marshmallows.

The phone rang again.

"Damn! I hate phones. Here. Go ahead and give him one. I'll just be a minute."

I walked into the living room, carrying the bag of marshmallows. Aleister followed me.

"No," I heard Lee say into the phone, "it's not a good idea." He lowered his voice. "Because there's someone here."

Like the rest of the apartment I had seen, the bathroom was clean but disheveled. I picked up a twisted tube of Crest from the basin and smiled. Lee squeezed toothpaste the same way I did—from the middle. Jim always started from the bottom, rolling up the tube carefully after each squeeze.

I washed my hands and face in cold water. As I reached for a towel, I saw the small pen-and-ink drawing in an ivory frame above the toilet: an unsmiling, naked young woman was standing by the sea, her arms folded across her breasts. The drawing was signed "Picasso, 1915." I dried my face, put the towel back on the rack, and flipped off the light.

A fire was burning in the fireplace in the living room. I could hear Lee opening and closing drawers in the kitchen.

"I'm making soup for us," he called. "I know you must be hungry."

"I am. Thank you." I sat down beside Aleister in front of the fire and rubbed his ears. "I love your Picasso drawing. It's beautiful."

"You're beautiful, Laurie."

"Oh, right."

"Toni told me you had a lot of art history courses in college."

"Yes, I did."

"Then you know too much about art not to know that you're beautiful." Lee appeared in the kitchen doorway, carrying a tray. "I hope you don't mind alphabet soup. It's embarrassing to admit, but I've never lost my fondness for it."

"Neither have I. I like the tomato soup, too. Campbell's."

"Absolutely." He set the tray down on a low black-laquered table. "Sit down and make yourself comfortable." He scooted a green wing chair closer to the fireplace.

I sat back in the chair and smoothed the nap on its velvet arms. "It's so soft. Like moss."

"It is nice, isn't it? It belonged to my grandfather."

I picked up a fist-sized yellow mass of quartz crystals from the top of the little table and held it to the light.

"I love your apartment, Lee. You have so many things."

"A lot of junk, flotsam of the ages," he said, laughing. "But I'm very glad you like it." He glanced at the window. "Listen. It's raining."

"Yes."

"When is your birthday?"

"October fifteenth. When's yours?"

"April eighteenth."

"Were you born in New Orleans?"

"No, Biloxi. Actually, I was born in an airplane flying over Biloxi, but I was immediately taken to a hospital there. Upon landing, that is. It's a nice town, but slow. Have you ever been there?"

"No, but I've been to Jackson."

He laughed. "Well, Jackson's a nice town, too, but not so nice as Biloxi."

"If you were born in an airplane," I said, "that means you weren't exactly born on earth. That must make you pretty close to being an angel, right?"

"Right, an angel."

"You know too much about religion not to have considered

it," I said. We both laughed. The fire popped and sparked but Aleister continued to doze.

"It's almost like *Beauty and the Beast*," I said. "I mean, the way the fire is burning."

"It really is! What a great film. Josette Day. You know, you look like her."

"I wish I did," I said. "But she was blond and French."

"All right, I'll prove it!" As he stood up, he bumped against the table. His soup bowl tumbled off the tray and broke on the floor.

I automatically got up.

"No, no, Laurie, I'll get it. Just sit down. Please. God, I can't believe I did that. And it's your fault, Beauty."

"My fault? Why is it my fault?"

"Because I'm nervous. Because I can't believe that you're really here with me. You know, I've thought about it ever since that day I met you at Que Sera's."

"You have?"

"Yes. Too much." He put the broken pieces of china on the tray and stood up. "I'll be right back." His footsteps made a deep, chimelike sound on the narrow iron stairs.

"Hey, Laurie! Come up here!"

Lee was pulling a white chenille bedspread over an unmade twin bed.

"I believe I have found the proof."

"Proof of what?"

"That you look like Josette Day." He patted the bed beside him. "Please have a seat."

I sat down on the bed next to a folded quilt made of squares of dark velvets and tapestries. A thick manila envelope was on top of it. Lee picked up the envelope and emptied its contents on the bed.

"As I recall, it's in here somewhere, but who knows? I just throw things into envelopes—it's my way of appearing organized."

I glanced around the small room: unevenly stacked books and a dusty manual typewriter on top of an oak desk; a cinnabar vase filled with pussy willows; a green-tiled fireplace in the far wall; a large blue bowl containing a speckled banana and an overripe peach; a worn alligator suitcase and a Sunday *New York Times* on the floor beside the bed.

"I'm sorry my room's such a mess."

"I love it."

"Messy?"

"Yes." I picked up three agate marbles from the heap of folded papers and small curios on the bed. "These are beautiful. They must be very old."

"You can have them."

"Oh, no, I couldn't take them. You've probably had them a long time."

"I have, but so what? People give me things, I give things away. Please take them." He put his hand over mine and curled my fingers around the marbles. "You know," he said, "you really have an exceptional smile."

"Thank you," I said.

Aleister came into the room, scaled the desk, and stretched out on it to sleep. The smell of the river came in through the open window, mingling with the sweetish odor of the fruit. Lee continued to unfold scraps of paper, glance at them, and put them aside.

"Where—" I cleared my throat. "Where are you going in Mexico?"

"Copal. Palenque," he said without looking up.

I could see how his face would look as he slept in the heat, surrounded by a thousand shades of green.

"How long will you be gone?"

"I really don't know. I had planned on staying until summer. Aha! Here it is!"

The photograph had been taken in Beauty's bedroom at the Beast's castle. Beauty, her face suffused with a soft, dreamy light, was turned toward the camera; behind her, sheer curtains billowed into the room, and in the distance beyond the window stood misty trees. Beauty was wearing the magic glove that transported her between the castle and her home.

"See! She *does* resemble you. Don't shake your head, Laurie—it's true. You had that exact expression today at Rosario's."

"What expression?" I said, laughing.

"Kind, intelligent. Almost ethereal. I want you to keep this picture. And I have something else for you if I can find it." He stood up and faced a tall bookcase, tapping his forefinger against his lower lip. "Well, it must be downstairs. I'll be right back."

I waited until the sound of his footsteps had died away before I picked up his bathrobe from the back of the desk chair. It was an Indian blanket robe, coffee colored, with gray and black diamond shapes. Like everything I'd seen him wear, it was old but in perfect condition. I held the robe close to my face. It smelled like him. Chocolate.

When I looked up, Lee was standing in front of me. He held a small black book in his hand.

"Hey," he said, setting the book down on the desk near Aleister. "Have you ever read *The Big Sleep*?"

"Yes."

He put his left foot up on the desk and pulled back his gray flannel trousers, revealing blue nylon socks embroidered with clocks.

"Remember? Before Marlowe went to see the old man?"

"Yes! And he was wearing a blue suit."

"Right!" He laughed. "I've wanted a pair of socks with clocks ever since. These are my lucky socks."

"Are they really lucky?"

"Without a doubt—you're here," he said, taking his foot down from the desk. He picked up the black book and handed it to me. *Redouté* was printed in faded gold letters on the cover.

"Come on, Beauty. Open it."

The roses bloomed before my eyes, page after page of them, in all shades of white, yellow, red, and pink—Noisette's Rose, Perfumer's White Rose, Rose of Orleans, Royal French Rose, Apothecary's Rose, the Blood Rose of China—perfect, dewy, and inviolate. I turned to the last page—the Thornless Rose.

"That's my favorite. I used to have a certain fascination for the thorns with the flower, but not anymore. Not since I met you, Laurie." He looked down at the suitcase on the floor, pushing it slightly with his right foot. "You really don't understand, do you? About my going away?"

"No."

He sat down beside me on the bed. "Laurie, we have to talk—about Jim and you and me. I realize that we haven't known each other long, but—"

"Please. I don't want to talk about him."

"We have to, Laurie. I saw your face when he kissed you. And

I know that things can't be perfect between you two—or you wouldn't be here with me now."

"Lee, I—I don't love him."

"You don't?" He laughed. "You don't?"

"No."

"Oh, Laurie!" His mouth was near my ear. I turned my face toward him and put my arms around his neck and we lay back on the bed. He kissed my throat, my mouth, my hair, and then he moved his body on top of mine. I was grateful for his weight; it seemed to crush Jim's presence from the bed.

"Am I too heavy?"

"No." I lowered my hands to the small of his back. I could smell the river.

"I've never felt like this before, Laurie. Never."

"Neither have I." I unbuttoned my blouse and slipped off my skirt. "You know I've never been unfaithful to him."

"I know."

I kissed the tiny chicken-pox scar near his left eye. "Please," I said.

My forehead was hot as he brushed the hair back from my face. His hand smoothed my damp hair.

"Are you sure?"

"Yes. I'm sure."

He kissed my shoulder. I could hear his heart. I thought it must be the sound of both our hearts because it was so loud. It seemed to grow louder with every kiss, every breath. Suddenly it changed. Heavy and wooden. A cold sensation started in my shoulders and raced down to my feet.

"What is it?" I shivered. "Did you hear that?"

"It's the door. Someone's at the damned door."

"It's Jim!"

"No, it can't be Jim. He doesn't know me. He doesn't know where I live. But whoever it is, we're not here."

The pounding continued, even louder. I closed my eyes, trying not to hear, not to let my body stiffen, but it did. Lee raised himself off me and lay on his side. He kissed the tip of my nose.

"Damn it, I'd better go down and see who it is. But I swear to you, Laurie, it isn't Jim."

"No, don't answer it. Please, Lee."

"I don't want you to be frightened. I won't let him come between us tonight, even if it's only in your imagination. Besides, it's probably my peripatetic friend, Hammond—he has a terrible habit of showing up at the worst possible time. But whoever it is, I'll get rid of him."

He kissed me quickly and left the room, still buttoning his white shirt. I listened for his footsteps on the stairs, but I couldn't hear them. The pounding was too loud.

I got up and closed the window; then, standing in the doorway, I put on my skirt and wrinkled blouse. They were colder than my skin. Aleister stretched and jumped down from the desk. He ran through my legs and out the door.

"It's about time, General! Where is Laurie? I have to see her now! Chérie? Chérie!"

"What's wrong, Toni? Jesus, what happened to you?" I heard Lee ask.

"Chérie! Please come down!"

Lee was holding Toni in his arms, his back to me. When she saw me on the stairs, she rushed over and hugged me. Her hair was damp and wild, and her mascara was smeared into dark crescents under her eyes. As usual, she smelled of licorice.

"I have been fired! The bitch!"

"Oh, Toni, I'm so sorry."

Toni flopped down in the green wing chair and closed her eyes. "Do you have anything to drink, General?"

"Only beer."

"I guess that will have to do."

I sat down on the arm of Toni's chair after Lee had left the room. I didn't look at her. The fire had died down to thin blue flames.

"I knew you would be here with him."

"What happened? Why did she fire you?"

"I don't know and I don't give a fuck." Her eyes glistened, hard and feline, through her tears.

"You poor thing," Lee said, handing her a glass and a can of Dixie beer.

"I don't really care. They didn't sell art. Remember those stupid lamps, General?"

Lee smiled at me. "I liked those lamps. They had shades made from sea anemones."

"They were garbage." Toni tilted her head back and drank from the beer can. "Molly believes she has your car sold, Laurie—to Forest Johnson. She's still at the Chart Room. You are supposed to meet them at your house in half an hour."

"That's great," Lee said. "Isn't it, Laurie?"

"Yes."

"I'll drive you home. You too, Toni. You look as if you could use ten years' sleep."

"Thanks a lot," she said.

The sky had cleared, and black raindrops glistened on the tree branches along Toulouse Street. Toni stopped to use a pay phone, and Lee and I waited for her in front of a florist's shop. Fluorescent lights cast a vibrant lavender on the double rows of potted Easter lilies inside. The streetlight behind us reflected our images on the window. We seemed to be standing together in another world, beneath an unfamiliar sky, among the lilies beyond the glass.

"I'll write to you," Lee said.

"No."

"At Rosario's."

"All right."

Toni was jubilant when she rejoined us.

"At least now she's drunk enough to talk it over logically. Could you please drop me off at the Pontchartrain?"

"Of course," Lee said. "I hope it works out for you."

He unlocked the door of an old dark green Mercedes.

"It will work out," Toni said. "She is very drunk. I'll sit in back because you're letting me out first."

I sat in front beside Lee. Strands of Mardi Gras beads hung in loops around the rearview mirror. A pale magnetic figurine of Mary stood on the dashboard, her raw heart exposed, on fire and wrapped in pink roses.

"Have you ever heard of Saint Erasmus?" I asked.

"Sure, Old Saint Elmo, patron saint of sailors. I'm not positive, but I think the Church revoked him when they revoked Saint Christopher and all the rest. Sorry, ladies. I know the car sounds bad, but I promise it'll get us there."

"Who else was revoked, General?"

"Well, let's see. I know Saint Nicholas and Saint Valentine were, and I'm fairly certain about Barbara."

"Barbara! Are you sure?" Toni asked.

"Pretty sure."

"Christ!"

"You must be Catholic," I said to Lee.

"No, I was raised Episcopalian."

"So was Laurie," Toni said, sitting back in her seat.

Lee switched on the radio. He held my hand beneath my folded raincoat.

"Do you like Fauré?" I asked.

"Very much—especially this elegy."

"Merde," Toni said.

I looked over my shoulder at her. Dragging hard on her cigarette, she was staring out at the opulent antique shop windows up Royal Street.

"Stupid, romantic *merde,*" she said.

" *'Le coeur a ses raisons que la raison ne connâit point,'* " Lee said softly.

Toni touched the back of my neck.

"Chérie, maybe we had better take you home first after all. I am *sure* Jim wouldn't want you to miss Forest or Molly."

"You're right."

"Whatever is best for you," Lee said. The pressure of his fingers against mine made me want him to kiss my hand—kiss it even with Toni here in the car, even if Jim would somehow find out, and a warm, exhilarating calmness came over me.

When we crossed Canal Street, I could no longer smell the river. No one said anything else until we turned off St. Charles onto Washington.

As we passed the dark cemetery, Toni leaned forward and whispered, "Chérie, I just thought of something! What if the boys didn't leave town at all? I would not put it past them."

"Oh, God, don't say that!"

Lee turned down Prytania. I held my breath. The truck wasn't there.

"Good night, chérie," Toni said, kissing me. "I will call you tomorrow."

Lee walked around the car and opened the door on my side.

"Lee, I hope you have a safe trip. A wonderful trip. And thank you for everything."

"It was my pleasure," he said, kissing me on the cheek. "We'll all get together when I come back." He moved closer, his lips against my ear. "I promise you," he whispered.

* * *

After Molly and Forest Johnson left, I didn't fall asleep for a long time. Finally, it came—a deep, black, dreamless sleep, my mouth wide open, the pillow wet beneath my cheek.

I awakened when I heard a sound at the window in the living room. It was still dark.

"Jim?"

There was no answer.

I listened hard, heart pounding, but there was only silence. Echo followed me into the living room. When I turned on the light, I saw a brown paper bag on the floor beneath the window. I picked up the bag and looked inside: *Redouté.*

I wrapped the book in a plastic garbage bag; then, carrying Jim's flashlight and spade, I went outside. The beam of light cut the dark into sudden angles of black and silver. I followed Echo through the opening beneath the house.

Everything was quiet except for the sound of the spade as I scooped out the damp earth. I smelled something dead.

PART III

TWENTY-ONE

"Forest Johnson! What do you know?" Billy said, grinning. "Yeah," Jim said, "I told him a lot of other people were interested in the Vette and he better make up his mind fast—fish or cut bait."

"So he's giving you what you're asking for it, then?"

"Yeah, eight big ones, and I'm putting them right into the *Sheherazade*. But this little doll here is the one who actually sold it."

"Hey, good work, kid," Billy said, clinking his glass against mine.

"Here's to you, baby." Jim downed his shot of Wild Turkey and signaled to Sheila. "Doesn't Laurie look hot tonight, Kane?"

"Man, you got that right. Satin always did turn me on—especially pink."

"It's not pink," I said. "It's mauve."

Jim laughed. "Hear that, Kane? It's mauve. Laurie was wearing that dress the first time we went out together. It's my favorite so I made her wear it tonight."

He put his arm around my shoulders and hugged me. "Getting hungry, little girl? Well, as soon as we're done with the meeting, we're really going to celebrate. You guys want to go to Antoine's with us?"

"Sure," Billy said. "Sounds good to me."

Jim started kissing my neck.

"Are you going to tell him the car was hit?" Billy asked.

217

"What do you think?"

They both laughed. His head on mine, Jim brushed the hair back from my forehead, and for a moment an old, lost happiness returned. The trick of touch. The tender weight of his stroking hand, a promise broken made again, like the list he had shown my mother . . .

The taste and smell and expectant silence of snow all around us. Snowflakes on his eyelashes and our breaths in clouds when he fell back softly and still, arms outstretched, and rose into my arms again and again until across my mother's front yard I saw snow angels wing to wing over his shoulder, his cool, stroking hand along my hair, and all his promises on a folded paper in his overcoat pocket. The trick of touch. Perfect touch.

The amber light inside Dauphine's was dim, and the room seemed to fade back into the brown shadows. Along the bar, people huddled together among the empty stools. Toni was standing near the entrance to the women's room, talking to a young man wearing a beige windbreaker.

"Hey," Jim said. "Who's that guy rapping down to Toni?"

"Friend of hers. Kid who hangs around the Jade Moon. Guess he's got a crush on her or something."

"Oh, man! Look at that, Kane. They're going into the toilet together. Probably do a little blow."

"So what?"

"So what? I'll tell you what—if it was Laurie back there with some kid, I'd break her fucking—"

"Fuck you!" I said, standing up.

"I'm ready if you are, baby."

As I walked to the restroom, I heard them laughing.

Toni was sitting on top of the basin, sniffing.

"Hi, Laurie. This is Andy."

The short, stocky boy standing beside her looked about seventeen. His fair skin was lightly pocked with acne.

"Hi," he said softly.

"Why don't you do a line? You'll feel better. Andy, give her a little."

Andy unzipped a pocket of his windbreaker and pulled out a small vial.

"No, thanks," I said.

Toni took a sip of her drink. "Andy, let me speak to Laurie alone."

"Sure. Do you need a ride tomorrow? Because I'd be glad—"

"No, I want to walk."

"Then I'll stop by the Moon, if that's okay."

Toni lowered her eyes, he smiled, and then he was gone.

"Here," she said, holding out her drink. "Have some. You'll need it. Jim is in a nasty mood."

"How do you know? You haven't even been sitting with us."

"But I do know, chérie. I saw Billy give him Quaaludes back at the house."

"Jimbo will be right back," Billy said. "He went out to the truck."

Sheila raised her eyebrows at Billy and he nodded to her. She poured out four shots of Wild Turkey.

"So, Toni, what happened to your little friend?" Billy asked. "Have to get home before curfew?"

"What the hell do you care?"

"You know I care, babe." He picked up her left hand and kissed it.

She pulled her hand away. "Is that what you do to Connie?"

"Come on, now. I don't do that."

"No, you kiss her feet, don't you? Don't you, Billy?"

"No, ma'am."

"Then what do you do with her?"

Billy leaned his head close to Toni's and whispered into her ear. She laughed.

Jim came into the bar, pushing the door closed against the wind. He took a roll of papers from inside his suede jacket.

"Can you believe it? It's fucking raining again!" He unfurled the papers and examined them carefully for water spots. Satisfied, he flattened a nautical chart on a table, weighting the corners down with empty beer mugs. He glanced at his wristwatch.

"You think they're coming, Kane? I said nine. It's almost ten now."

"They'll be here."

"Yes, give them time," Toni said. "They can only drive their sports cars eighty in this weather. Oh, here's one of your little friends now."

Ray was standing at the end of the bar, his lank hair blown over his eyes. His glasses and brown leather coat were beaded with rain.

"It ought to be a successful venture now, if Ray's in on it," Toni said. "He in charge of entertainment?"

"We didn't invite *him*," Billy whispered. "Just Kenny and Ted and Dean."

"Hey, Sheila," Ray called. "Janelle been in tonight?"

"Haven't seen her, Ray."

Jim looked up from the papers on the table. "Ray, how you doing, man? Come over here a minute. I want to show you something—a project you'll be interested in—salvaging a treasure ship."

Billy ordered a pitcher of Dixie beer and joined Jim and Ray at the table. I closed my eyes and listened to the Bee Gees' "Stayin' Alive" on the jukebox. Toni touched my arm, but she didn't say anything and I didn't open my eyes—not until I heard a loud smack.

I turned around to see Ray crashing over in his chair. Jim reached down, pulled Ray up by the shirt, and hit him in the mouth, knocking him back to the floor. Billy grabbed Jim's arms before he could hit Ray again. A trickle of blood ran down Ray's chin. His glasses were lying next to him on the floor.

Jim shook Billy loose.

"Fuck you doing, man?" Billy said. "You letting a couple of 'ludes push your buttons? Come on, man."

"Stay out of it, Kane! He's got it coming to him. Stupid shit. He almost killed me once and you know it!"

"It was a fucking accident!" Ray yelled.

Jim lifted him up with both hands and pinned him against the wall.

"Let him go, Jimbo!"

"You'd have fucked everything up, anyway! You're going to get somebody killed someday. And it ain't going to be me or Kane! You hear me, Ray? You hear me?"

"I hear you," Ray choked.

"Good."

Jim let him go and threw his coat after him. Then he carefully rerolled his papers. He sat down next to me at the bar and stared at his cut knuckles.

"What are you shaking for?"

"I'm sorry," I said.

Sheila came over and stood in front of him. He looked up at her through half-closed eyes.

"I'll get you some ice," she said.

Jim watched her as she turned around, bent over and took a bar towel from a wooden cabinet, filled the towel with ice cubes, and folded it gently around his hand.

"That should help. It's cold."

"I know what would help, and it sure wouldn't be cold, either."

"You divers," Sheila said, laughing.

Toni elbowed me in the ribs, her eyes narrowed, lips wet. "Do something," she said.

"Yeah, why don't you do *some* fucking thing. Like something right for a change."

"I sold the car, Jim. I thought we were going to have a nice—"

"Look at you. You're still shaking! You'd think I cold-cocked you instead of that little popcorn-fart." Jim turned back around to face Sheila. "Doesn't Sheila have the nicest tits? You know, I'd forgotten what real tits look like."

He stood up and put one hand on Sheila's neck and pulled her toward him over the bar and kissed her on the lips. She closed her eyes. With his other hand, he held Sheila's tiny cross in the light for a moment; then he pressed it against her left breast.

"Jim!"

Billy was studying the quarters in his open palm. I turned to Toni, who was staring wide eyed at Jim and Sheila over the rim of her glass. I grabbed my purse. The room seemed full of smoke.

"I'm getting out of here!"

Billy stood up, too. "We're all going. Come on, Jimbo, let's split. Sheila, how about a bottle of Turkey to go?"

Sheila took the bottle down from behind the bar and gave it to Jim.

"Come on, Jimbo. They ain't going to show."

"You go on. I got to make a call."

"Make it at my house."

"No, man. Go on." He handed Billy the bottle.

Toni slid down from her bar stool. She reached inside her glass with her fingers and brought out an ice cube. As she passed Sheila, she threw the ice cube at her.

"Ow!" Sheila rubbed her chest near her cross. Toni walked over to me without looking back.

I was sitting next to Billy on the sofa. Toni stood near the fireplace, smoking a cigarette and petting Marie. The front door slammed. Unzipping his pants, Jim staggered past us toward the back of the house.

"Don't worry," Billy said. He held his head in both hands, as if it were too heavy for his neck.

"You gave him Quaaludes, didn't you?" Toni asked.

"No, ma'am."

"I saw you. Where did you get them? From Connie?"

"No, ma'am."

"Is that all you can say?"

"I'm leaving," I said.

"Hey, Jimbo didn't mean anything back there. We're celebrating. Yes, ma'am, we're celebrating."

As Billy filled my glass, it overflowed onto the coffee table and he laughed. I stood up, but Billy took my hand and pulled me back down.

"It's true, Laurie. He did almost kill Jim once out in the Persian Gulf. Ray was Jim's tender then, and he locked him in the decompression chamber and just went away and forgot him. I like Ray okay, but I can see Jimbo's point. Guy like that's dangerous."

"He's a weasel-dick," Jim said, coming back into the living room. He went over to where Toni was standing and lit a cigarette.

At first, I couldn't believe the expression on Toni's face. She was looking at Jim the same way she had looked at Lee when he was sitting beside her in the cemetery. She was smiling and he was speaking low. Billy raised his glass to mine. Jim moved closer to Toni, and then he was kissing her.

Billy put down his glass and took my hand. "Maybe me and you should get together, too."

I pulled my hand back. "Oh, come on!"

Jim laughed. Marie started barking so loudly that I had to yell in Billy's ear: "Give me five dollars!"

"What for?" He pulled a wad of bills from the back pocket of his jeans.

"So I can call a cab and get the hell out of here!"

"Yeah," Jim said, without looking over at me. "Go on and get out of here, you old party pooper. Why don't you go cut your wrists again?"

Back lit by the moon, Jim stood over me at the side of the bed, swaying. He crouched, grabbed my arm, and jerked me to my feet.

"Don't!"

Jim had one arm around my shoulders, his fingers gripping one of the straps of my mauve dress. I twisted free and ran into the living room, but he caught me from behind before I could open the door. He turned me hard and squeezed my face against his chest; I closed my eyes tight, listening to the heartbeat wild behind his ribs, and pushed. He let go and I looked up, panting, into his eyes.

"Fine fucking friend you got!" He slapped me twice fast; then he backhanded me down and across the floor, and for a moment it was quiet and Echo was licking my ear. When Jim moved for me again, I balled up like a baby on my back and drew my elbows in tight against my ribs, and he kicked me once in the side.

I watched him walk slowly away, a paler gray than the moonlight, arms relaxed, fingers curled slightly, thumbs extended, like a statue. I waited until he shut the bedroom door before I pulled myself up on the sofa. Echo stretched herself beside me.

When I was sure that Jim was asleep, I crawled to the closet. I leaned against the door frame, hugging my knees. After the chills had passed, I opened my little chest of drawers and took out the necklace Jim had bought me before we were married from my jewelry box.

Five minutes later I was walking in the dark to Rosario's. I stopped at the phone booth near the cemetery and called my mother collect. I didn't have anything to tell her. I didn't want to talk about Jim. I didn't want to go back home. I guess I just wanted to hear the sound of her voice, to hear her talk about

Grace or her job or the neighbors or somebody she'd run into who had asked about me.

As the phone rang, I stared through the sweating glass at Saint Michael rising blurred and white in the mist. After six rings the operator's voice cut in: "I'm sorry, ma'am, you're party doesn't answer. Would you like to try again?"

I looked at my wristwatch: eleven twenty-five. Mother and Grace were probably in Indianapolis visiting my Uncle Leland.

"No. Thank you. I don't have time."

TWENTY-TWO

Bigtimer was alone in the dining room, mopping the marble floor. I tapped on the door and he unlocked it.

"Is Buddy still here?"

"Nah, you just missed him." He smiled, his mouth stained bright orange from Nehi soda. "You don't look too good."

"I know."

"I mean, you look tired. I sure like that dress, though. I like that pink color."

"Thanks. I've had it a long time." I looked up at the tall ficus trees, their branches almost touching the ceiling. "It seems bigger in here at night."

"Yeah, 'specially if you're mopping. But I sure do like that pink."

The white telephone cord stretched from behind the bar through the open service door into the kitchen, and Felix was saying into the phone; "Not now, baby. I've got to go." He held the receiver against his chest as he walked through the service door back to the bar; then he hung up.

"Why, hello, darlin'. Cordon Bleu?"

"Please."

He took down two brandy snifters, from the shelf behind him.

"I left my husband, Felix."

Felix stopped pouring and looked up at me.

"I'm never going back to him. I can't understand why I ever stayed with him this long."

He put the drink and a cocktail napkin on the bar in front of me. "Honeybee."

"Honeybee?"

"Sure, darlin'. Can be just plain the way someone smells. Like bread and butter. Like honey. Don't matter what they drink, they stay sweet. It's their breath draws you to them."

"I know." Jim always smelled warm and sugary when he would whisper low after we fought, his arms around me, drawing me closer, his lips brushing against my ear. It was his breath, never his words, that promised the sweetness to come.

"I saw him kiss you in here the other day—like you was his, like it or not. They fool you with that sweet breath, baby. It promises you good, just like a child's. So sweet you think it's got to be their soul coming through." He laughed. "But someday it stops. Always does someday. Sometimes sooner than later, and that's when the spell is broken."

Gerald came in from the kitchen and leaned against the service door. "How come you're in here? I know you wasn't working dinner tonight 'cause I could have used you, hostessing, you know, help with the seating."

"I came down to see Buddy."

"Buddy's not here."

Felix poured a little more cognac into my glass. "Gerald, I need you at the Black Cat later on."

Gerald scratched the top of his ear and frowned. He yanked off his bow tie, pulled the collar away from his neck, and blew lightly down his white, starched shirt.

"Guess so," he said, looking at me. "Let me have a Crown and Coke." He took the drink and pushed through the doors to the kitchen.

"Felix, I was going to ask Buddy, but I may as well ask you. Do you know anyone who would be interested in buying this?" I held my palm open in front of me, realizing as I did that I had been squeezing the necklace hard in my fist ever since I'd left the apartment.

"He give it to you?"

I nodded.

"Why don't you put that away? You might end up wishing you had it back later on. If you want, I could let you have a hundred till you get yourself sorted."

"No, Felix. I've been thinking about it. I want to sell it. I'm sure. I hardly ever wore it to begin with, and this way I can make a clean start, on my own. That's what I want."

Bigtimer sat down next to me at the bar. "What you got, Laurie?"

"It's just a necklace. I'm selling it." I picked up the necklace and folded it in a fresh napkin.

"You ought to keep it. It's pretty. Could I get a cold drink, Felix?"

"A person can't always keep a thing just because it's pretty, even if they want to, as I believe a certain gentleman may be learning right about now," he said, smiling at me. He turned toward Bigtimer. "What kind of a cold drink did you have in mind?"

"Orange. Guess you wouldn't put some vodka in there, huh?"

"You guessed right. I'm out of orange, too."

"Then give me what Vita drinks."

Felix filled a tall glass with grenadine and 7-Up. "Now how about drinking that in the kitchen, help Gerald finish up."

"Okay." Bigtimer stood and put on his sunglasses. "Hey, Gerald!" He kicked open the kitchen door and walked through. "Where you at?"

"How you feeling now, lady? Would you like a cigarette?" Felix brought up his pack, a lighter, and an ashtray from beneath the bar.

"Thanks." I pulled out a cigarette from the pack in his hand and he lit it for me.

"Tell you what. I could hold on to that, like security, and let you have the hundred. A couple days from now, you still want to sell it, you take it downtown to a jeweler and pay me back."

Gerald came in from the kitchen. "Bigtimer says you're selling your necklace."

"She was thinking about it, that's all."

"No, I'm selling it." I began to unfold the napkin. "It's white gold with—"

"I saw it on you Mardi Gras night, remember? Pieces of red coral and that teardrop pearl. That's good looking. What do you want for it?"

"Well, it's worth a few hundred dollars at least. I was going to ask two hundred."

"Give you one-fifty. I need to keep a little cash reserve for later." He laid three crisp, folded fifty-dollar bills edgewise on the bar.

"Gerald, it's worth two easy," Felix said. "If you're short, I'll front you fifty, take it out your wages at the Cat."

Gerald stared at him for a moment without expression. "No need, man. I got it." He pulled a fourth folded fifty from his shirt pocket. "We got a deal?"

"We've got a deal." I slipped the money into the pocket of my coat and Gerald picked up the napkin. The phone rang in the kitchen.

"Stay off it, Bigtimer! It's for me."

Gerald and Bigtimer passed each other at the service doors. "And go tell Wally to wait up. Tell him I want to return a favor. You go up too if you want, Laurie. We'll have a little toast. Seal the deal." The door shut behind him.

"You don't got to jump every time he says, Bigtimer," Felix said.

"I know it, but he's giving me a ride back to the home."

"Who's Wally?" I whispered to Felix.

"He's a maitre d' at night. He won't bite you." Felix smiled. "I've got to wait a little bit for a phone call myself, but you go on up. Buddy ever show you the place?"

"Just the first-floor bar and the little courtyard outside."

"Hey, Laurie. You going to like this. It's wild, brass every place and one wall is all tropical fish just like they was in the ocean somewhere." Bigtimer spread his arms wide apart. "The whole wall."

"You tell 'em, Junior. Laurie'll come up in a minute. Skedaddle and find Wally like Gerald says."

When Bigtimer was gone, Felix leaned close to me over the bar. "You're set now, lady," he said softly. "You don't have to worry about a thing. Just go relax up at the club and then we'll see about you getting a room for tonight. Will you do that for me?"

"All right, but I just want to say, I mean about Gerald and the other fifty, and earlier, talking—"

Felix put his finger to his lips. "Hush, now. You'll make me blush, only I can't."

Except for the light coming from the aquarium set in the length of the far wall, the Cache-Cache Club was dark upstairs. Turquoise ribbons of reflected light trembled across the ceiling and a few of the tables. An overweight man with ginger-colored hair and a handlebar mustache sat talking with Bigtimer at a table across from the aquarium.

"Hey, Wally, this is Laurie."

"Wallace," the man said, standing up. "Wallace Beacham." He made a sweeping gesture with his hand. "Please sit down. I understand from Joseph you're an excellent waitress."

"I'm happy to hear he thinks so."

"Like you're the boss, right?" Bigtimer said, smiling.

"I like to know who's working. It makes a difference, Bigtimer, in how smoothly dinner goes. I realize that your concern for the welfare of Rosario's doesn't extend beyond an interest in whether or not you get a plate of rice and pinto beans."

"So?"

"So you could benefit from my expertise."

"I worked a fourteen-hour day. That's concern. Right, Laurie?"

"Sure," I said.

"Wally knows a lot about wines. He wants to teach me."

"The offer still stands."

"I keep asking you, what do I got to know wines for? I don't even like wines."

"Haven't you ever thought of promotion? You've lasted longer than any of your unfortunate predecessors. Besides, I heard that Felix wants more time off for the Black Cat, and if he doesn't get it, he's quitting. You could be next in line, but you have to have the knowledge, Bigtimer."

"Who told you that about Felix?" Bigtimer asked.

"Gerald told me." Wally set his glass of red wine down carefully. "Where is Gerald, anyway? I don't have all night."

Across from me, an angelfish pressed its blue and gold flank in a slow turn against the glass, and I remembered another angelfish. We had been married a month. One night a steak in the *Brigand*'s tiny refrigerator leaked blood through its paper wrapper, and in the morning I saw blood pooled on the opened lid of the Magnolia milk can below it. Jim told me to use the milk anyway. The coffee curdled as soon as I stirred it in. He threw his black Bic lighter at me, and then he slapped my face three times, very fast. That was the first time he ever hit me. Later, after we had made up, after he promised it would never happen again, he took me snorkeling off the boat yard by a tiny coral reef.

Under the shallow water, his hair feathered greenish black in front of his face, he gently cupped his hands around an angelfish. He rose to the surface, arms upraised, the water running through his fingers, the fish gleaming like a shimmering conflux of precious metals in the sunlight. The fish didn't swim away when Jim let it slip out of his hands into the water, and he cupped his hands around it again and held it up, and it was flipping in his hands, and his eyes and the cloudless sky were the same color in the bright white light. And when he let his palms fill with water at last, the angelfish drifted on its side, bobbing and glinting in the white light, and Jim kissed me over and over, his tanned arms around my neck, and said he was sorry for everything.

"You really think that can come true?" Bigtimer asked. "What you was saying about taking over for Felix?"

"It's possible," Wally said. "I can't make any promises . . . You can open an oyster can't you? Once you become a shucker, you can move up to mixing drinks. But I'm not putting in a good word with Joseph unless I can say that you know your wines."

"Felix know his wines?"

"Of course he does."

"Yeah, but it's still ten bucks a lesson."

"Bigtimer, that doesn't even cover half the cost of the wine. You've got to taste them to know what you're talking about."

'Well, I'll think it over." When Bigtimer tilted up his glass, the remainder of the rosy ice slid into his mouth.

Wally straightened his red bow tie and smoothed his dark plaid vest. "And another thing, Bigtimer. You ought to take that apron off."

"Nah." He ran his hands down the front of his apron. "I got stuff in the pockets and I got a hole in my pants. Covers it up." He looked over at the aquarium. "That's a fine tank, isn't it, Laurie? Someday I'm going to get me one."

Gerald had changed into a silk shirt the color of dead irises. He set a bottle of Dom Perignon on the table and sat down in the chair across from me. The bright blue of the aquarium radiated out from behind him. He popped open the cork, took a drink, and put the bottle on the table in front of me.

Wally rolled his eyes and jumped up. He brought back three champagne glasses from the chrome rack that hung over the bar.

"The DP is from Felix to me," Gerald said. "I got to go to the Cat afterwhile. Pour y'all out some, Wally. Good times, everybody."

"Good times," I said, clinking glasses with Wally and Gerald.

"Hey, man, you aren't sorry you waited around for me now, are you? This makes us even for last week."

"As you wish, Gerald." Wally swished a little champagne around in his mouth and swallowed. "Delectable."

"Is it good?" Bigtimer asked.

"What do you think? The best." Gerald drained his glass and poured himself another.

To my right, up two black-carpeted steps and about forty feet away in the shadows, Brent was moving among the empty cocktail tables. He switched on a light over a pool table that was covered in marine-blue felt a slightly deeper shade than the water behind Gerald. Then he drew the black velvet drapes over two white French doors with fanlight windows and turned off the light above the pool table.

Bigtimer pulled out an unopened package of Kools from his apron pocket and laid it on the table. He tore open the bottom of the cigarette pack.

"I can't believe you still do that," Wally said.

"It's a habit, I guess."

"Well, it's one you ought to break. You're just advertising that you have a job where you get your hands dirty."

"What do you mean?" I asked. "I don't understand."

"It's quite simple, really," Wally said. "When you work a job where your hands get dirty, you can soil the filter end of your cigarette if you take it out from the top. Therefore, you open the pack from the bottom and take out your cigarette by the smoking end. That way, only the part that burns gets soiled— the filter end always stays clean. Understand?"

"Yes, I think I do."

"Tell you what's worse. If a guy who had a dirty job pretended he didn't, he'd go around smoking cigarettes with dirt on the filters," Gerald said, looking at Wally.

"I suppose that would be worse."

"Believe it," Bigtimer said.

I ran into Felix as I came out of the ladies' room. He was carrying what I guessed was a pool cue in a narrow morocco leather case.

"Darlin', it looks like I'm going to be here late. Mr. J.T.'s got me in a game upstairs at the club. But here's what you do. Take a cab out to the Belclair Motel. It's plenty clean, and the driver will know how to get you there."

When I returned upstairs to say good night, everyone was standing. Bigtimer had taken off his apron before Brent reached the table.

"Party's over, you guys," Brent said. "Clear out. Boss is having a little private party of his own."

Bigtimer started folding his apron into a small bundle "Gerald, maybe we'd better—"

"I said I was giving you a ride, didn't I? You act like you can't wait to get back to that Phoenix House."

Wally finished his last sip of champagne and carried the empty glasses back to the bar.

Brent turned on the light over the pool table and racked the balls, alternating stripes and solids, his fingers tight and pale against the triangular wood frame.

"Give you a ride too, Laurie. Where you going?"

"Belclair. Belclair Motel."

He studied my face for a moment. "I know it. White frame place out by the bridge. Hey, Wally, we got to book." He turned to Bigtimer. "Okay, Junior, grab your rags and hoist your bags. This train's pulling out the station." He pushed the cork into the bottle of champagne and put it under his arm.

"Sweet dreams everybody. Have fun," Brent said. He was smiling at me.

TWENTY-THREE

"You first, Junior." Gerald held open the passenger door of a midnight blue Cutlass Salon. "Milady."

Bigtimer slid over to the middle of the seat. As I got in, he was opening a box of powdered doughnuts. Gerald closed the car door and walked over to the driver's side.

"It smells good in here, right, Laurie?" Bigtimer said, his mouth filled with doughnut. "Like flowers. Wait till it heats up. Gerald fixed it to smell that way."

"Joy perfume," Gerald said, sucking in his cheeks. "You want a doughnut? Bigtimer, offer the lady a doughnut." He thumped Bigtimer on the head.

"Hey, what's that for?"

"That's from Maurice. Payback." He laughed. Bigtimer laughed, too, wiping the powdered sugar from his lips. "Have one," he said.

I was so hungry that I ate three doughnuts as we drove up St. Charles, past block after block of massive gray houses set back and fenced off from the street. From the cut-glass doors, sudden glittering light sprayed across the damp grass toward the car and then vanished in a sharp tangent behind us. The radio was tuned unintelligibly low to a soul station. We passed the Audubon Zoo, turned off at Carrolton, and drove to the highway.

"I love riding in cars," I said. "When I was in high school, that's what we did for fun. Cruised around in cars or on motorcycles. It was great. But God, I'm the worst driver in the world."

"You can't be. Wally's the worst," Gerald said.

"Wally the Walrus," Bigtimer said.

"Is he English?"

"Nah, he just talks that way. Joseph knew him from before when he worked at the Beer & Steer in Fat City."

I laughed. "Is there really such a place?"

"Fat City's a real place. It's over by the lake. They got a lot of discos there. New bars, like the Ski Lodge. I been there once. They got skis on the ceiling. Turn off here," Bigtimer said. "A right."

"I know where I'm going, brother."

We turned off the highway onto a two-lane road and drove about half a mile in complete darkness before we came to a two-story tar-paper house. Large floodlights above the porch made the grass in the yard appear flat and yellow. A high gray-white cyclone fence enclosed both the house and yard. Gerald pulled to a stop.

"You're home, Junior."

"Thanks, Gerald. Hey, the gate's still open."

Bigtimer followed me out of the car. The sky was peppered with stars.

"That's about as clear as it ever gets in New Orleans, Laurie," he said, looking up at the stars.

"I believe you. Good night, Bigtimer."

"Good night." He went through the open gate and up the shining white gravel driveway. The muffler started rattling as I got back into the car.

"I'm going to get that fixed."

"Well, the inside sure is nice and clean."

"Thanks."

"You know, I think spring has finally come."

"Spring here comes in the night. A lot of nights it's warmer than the day."

We didn't talk again until we were back on St. Charles.

"I heard you tell Felix you left your old man," Gerald said, glancing over at me.

"Yes, I did."

"You going to stay in New Orleans?"

"Probably for a while. I'd really like to move to New York."

"Rosario has a place in New York. Felix says he's got one in Miami, too."

"I didn't know that. Oh, Gerald, I'm so glad you bought the
necklace. I left the house so fast I didn't have a cent on me."

"Well, you got some money now. Two hundred bucks can take
you places."

"You're right, and thanks. Thanks a lot."

"No need of thanking me. Price you asked was fair. I knew
that piece was heirloom quality the minute I laid eyes on it."

He turned left at Canal Street. We were in an unfamiliar part
of the city, passing dark shotgun houses where black people sat
on top of their cars, coatless and drinking.

"They're just out there looking at the stars," Gerald said. "And
howling at the moon."

Gerald drove fast, and soon the little dilapidated houses were
gone, and we were moving down a deserted street past old,
broken-windowed warehouses. There was an immense peeling
billboard of a tuxedoed black man holding out an icy glass of
Champale at the end of the street.

I yawned. "God, I didn't realize how tired I am. Is it much
farther to the motel?"

"No."

We drove into a narrow alley filled with steam that led to a
side street of small, steel-gated storefronts. Gerald parked in an
empty lot and turned off the engine. He yawned and stretched
his arms over his head; then he looked at me.

"Why don't you come over here?"

"I'm all right." I stared out the car window. There was no one
around. The only sounds outside were the faint strains of jazz
coming from a squat black brick building. The door and windows
were covered with flat black paint. Above the door, a purple
neon sign sputtered: *Black Cat.*

"Why are we stopping?"

"To have a nightcap."

"In the Black Cat?"

"Nah, in here. This is as good a place as any." He reached past
me and took two plastic glasses from the glove compartment.

"You know, it's late, Gerald, and I'm pretty tired."

"Come on." He brought up the bottle of Dom Perignon from
under his seat. "Just one."

"All right. Only one. So that's the Black Cat?" The champagne
was warm and slightly flat and its gassy, sour odor filled the car.
A long blue marabou roach clip hung down from the rearview

mirror. Paper garbage blew across the parking lot in the warm wind. I set my empty glass on the dash.

"That's the Cat." A black limousine with its lights on was parked in front of the building. Gerald watched the limousine until it pulled away, then he turned up the radio.

Suddenly he was next to me, on top of me, unbuttoning my coat with one hand and kissing me on the neck.

"Gerald! Gerald, don't! What are you doing?" His arm was around me now.

"Don't what, doll? You know what I'm doing. You want to as much as me."

"No, I don't, Gerald. I don't! Please!"

"Just relax and come here." He pulled his arm away.

"Please, Gerald, please stop!"

"Why, you have sweet little tits. You shouldn't be shy."

He put his hands on my breasts and looked down at me. "Don't be shy—it feels good. See, you're breathing fast."

I pushed him as hard as I could, but he didn't move. Then he raised up on his elbow to take a drink from the bottle and I grabbed the door handle, but he took my hand and pulled me back to him.

"You don't want to go out there, baby. You're safer in here." He reached up under my coat and started unzipping my dress, his face against mine. I started to cry.

"Please, please, don't, Gerald. Please, I thought you were my friend."

He couldn't get the zipper down completely, so he pulled me up, took off my coat, and threw it in the backseat.

"I thought you were my friend! I did. I thought you were just being nice to me—giving me a ride." My lips were right by his ear. "Please, Gerald, please," I whispered. "I thought you were my friend." He held me tight against his chest and I didn't move or make a sound—and then he let go of me. When I opened my eyes, he was back in his seat, his forehead pearled with sweat. I smoothed out my dress and zipped it up slowly. My hands were shaking.

"I'm sorry. I'm sorry if I gave you the wrong impression."

"Forget it, babe. I'll take you where you want to go. I'll take you to the Belclair."

He started the car. I found a wadded Kleenex in my coat pocket and tried to wipe off the eye makeup that had run down my cheeks. I thought about being alone in the motel. I looked over at Gerald.

"If it's okay, I'd rather just go on to my house. Up on Prytania."

"I thought you wasn't going home. Said you'd never go back."

"I know. I know I said that."

"Going to make it up with your old man?"

"Yes, I want to make up with him."

"Just a little misunderstanding, huh? You know, I had you figured right, baby doll, but you almost had me fooled. For a while there I thought you wanted to win."

TWENTY-FOUR

I fell asleep on the sofa without taking off my dress. Warm sunlight on my face awakened me. Just before I opened my eyes, I smelled the wild, sweet fragrance of raspberries. On the floor near my purse were a dozen long-stemmed red roses in a plastic florist's vase molded to simulate cut glass. Echo sniffed the air. She jumped from the sofa when I reached down to pick up the note next to the vase.

I got beeped. Remember I saved your life—now you can save mine. Please, please don't leave until I get back! I love you more than anything!
Jim

I ran to get dressed for work.

"Hey, Laurie," Bigtimer said. "Vita's got a letter for you."

She was sitting on top of the marble counter, her thin ankles crossed above peeling pink patent leather house slippers trimmed in white rabbit.

"Do you really have a letter for me, Vita?"

"Surely do, baby." She reached inside her apron pocket and brought out an old, tinted postcard.

"Thank you." I started to walk away, but then I stopped. "Vita, I hate to ask you, but I was wondering if I could have a little more of that earth you gave me."

"Ssssh," she whispered, putting her finger against her lips. She glanced over at Gabriel asleep at his station and smiled. "I'll have you some before you go home."

I walked into the dining room and sat down in a corner booth.

Lafayette Cemetery   Copyright 1917   Vu-Art Co.
This Space for Message:
Strange and familiar, no? You pick up these things when you've been here too long. Anyhow, I remember everything.
Forever, Lee

I turned the card over. Behind a lime-white wall smeared with bright red flowers, Saint Michael, inexplicably green-gray, raised his sword against a purple-and-yellow sunset.

When I looked up, Gerald was standing in front of me. I felt suddenly as if someone were standing on my chest.

"How'd it go last night? Get back with your old man?"

"Yes," I said, staring down at the postcard. "We made up."

"That's good. Makes sense. Hey, I hope you're not thinking about getting that necklace back, 'cause it's long gone."

"Gerald!"

"Just a minute, Felix," Gerald said, but he was already walking toward the bar.

I hurried past the bar to the kitchen. Molly was standing next to Bigtimer near the dish-washing machine. Squinting her eyes, she blew on a cup of coffee.

"Morning, love. Forest wants Jim to call him about the car."

"I'll tell him."

Felix came into the kitchen, his black bow tie in his hand. He looked at me. "Sometimes Gerald thinks 'no' is a three-letter word. Bigtimer, call Maurice and see if he can come in. I need you out there at the bar."

"You do? Opening oysters?"

"Making drinks. Gerald's not working here anymore—I'm keeping him at the Cat. He has some extra clothes around here. Ask Vita for them."

When Bigtimer walked back into the kitchen, he was wearing a white shirt, tuxedo pants, black bow tie, and sunglasses.

"You look gorgeous!" Molly said.

"You do look good, Bigtimer."

"Well, I feel good."

He strutted over to Vita's corner. From the edge of the walk-in refrigerator door, I saw Vita's powerful disembodied arms holding out a saucer of bread pudding to Bigtimer. I thought of the magic arms holding out the candelabra in the Beast's castle, and of Lee's arms holding me. Vita's arms disappeared and Bigtimer walked past me.

"I'm starving, Bigtimer."

"So am I, Laurie," he said, laughing. He took a big bite of the pudding and then held the saucer out to me: the blended aroma of bourbon, butter, vanilla, and sugar filled the air.

"This is so delicious. God, Vita's a good cook."

"Uh-huh," he said, his mouth full of pudding. "You can have the rest. I got to get out there."

I closed my eyes to savor the last bite and licked my fingers one by one.

When I turned around, Buddy was behind me, leaning against the counter, his arms folded across his chest. He was wearing white canvas gardening gloves.

"Hi, Buddy."

He answered with a sigh, shaking his head.

"What's wrong?"

"I'm surprised at you, that's all." He poured a cup of coffee and went into the dining room. I followed him and sat down beside him at the bar.

'What's wrong, Buddy?"

"Brent says you were upstairs last night drinking with Gerald and Bigtimer until he broke it up. Then he says you rode off in a car with them. Is that true? You riding around at night with a car full of niggers?"

"Yes, it's true, but Buddy, I—"

"And this—in the kitchen just now," he said, standing up. "What're you thinking of?"

"Wait, Buddy. You're being—"

He walked out into the courtyard, carrying his cup of coffee. I didn't see him for the rest of the day.

As I unlocked the front door, I heard a light scratching sound from the bedroom. At first, I thought it was Echo; then Toni called out to me: "Don't come in here!"

Toni was on her hands and knees, scrubbing the bedroom floor. Beside her were an opened bottle of K&B Chablis and a bucket of soapy water. She was wearing a powder-blue sweater that made her look softer than I had ever seen her.

"Toni, what are you doing? How did you get in the house?"

"You didn't lock your window. Don't walk in here. I am almost finished. It looks good, I think."

"But why are you doing this?"

"Because, Laurie, I am so sorry."

I slipped off my shoes and walked across the wet floor and knelt down in front of her.

"I asked Jim if he would go to bed with me last night. I didn't think of you—I don't know that I was doing. I didn't give a fuck for anything except to hurt Billy. I am so sorry." She put her hand on my cheek.

"I don't care, Toni. I really don't. I already knew."

Toni turned my face toward hers and kissed me in the space between my nose and upper lip. She kept her face near mine, her eyes closed, until I stood up.

"So he told you?"

"More or less. I didn't see him this morning, but I understand." I offered her my hand, but she didn't take it. "Please, Toni, why don't you get up?"

She put her arms around me, her face against my stomach. "Laurie," she said. Her voice seemed to vibrate inside me. "I am so glad you understand. It was terrible! We went back to Dauphine's and Connie was there. Billy stayed and I went home. Jim went home, too, but then he came back to our place, looking for you. He was in bad shape—crying. Where were you, anyway? I was worried."

"Christ, please don't ask."

She held out her hands to me, and I helped her up from the floor.

"I saw the flowers," she said. "What a bastard."

She stroked my face gently with her hand. "You know I love you, don't you?"

"Well, I love you, too," I said.

"No, I *love* you."

"And I love you. You're my best friend, Toni. You know that."

She laughed and pulled me to her, clasping her hands around my back. I turned my head away, her sweater soft against my face.

"You don't know what I mean, Laurie. Love is rare; hate is

everywhere." She kissed me once on the side of the neck before I moved away.

"You know," I said, glancing behind her, "it really is turning green outside."

"Is it?" she said, putting her hand on my breast; she lowered her head and kissed me through my blouse.

"Toni, you're pretty drunk, aren't you?"

"Are you?" she asked, smiling.

"No."

"Well, then, we need a glass. We're celebrating." She walked into the kitchen.

"What's there to celebrate?"

"That I did not lose you."

After she had poured the wine, she looked out the dirty window at the silvery-green light of late afternoon.

"Too bad the General went away—things seem worse ever since."

"I know."

She opened her mouth to say something, but at that moment the hall door slammed. We went into the living room and listened.

"Oh, that wasn't him. The truck isn't here." Toni sat on the arm of the sofa, staring through the lace curtains at the street.

"You know," I said, "I've never been kissed by a girl before."

"Not ever?"

"No. Well, I kissed Carlene Bowen, but we were only ten or eleven, and we were both in love with Paul McCartney. I used to stay Friday nights with her sometimes, and she would lend me one of the flannel nightgowns her grandmother made for her. We'd stay up late and listen to her little transistor radio, waiting in the dark for 'Michelle' to come on."

Toni laughed.

"We did. And when it finally came on, we would cry."

"But why would you cry?"

"Because we loved Paul so much. Because we wanted to be older. And then we'd kiss each other. Long kisses, on the lips. We took turns showing each other how we would kiss Paul."

Toni smiled and poured the remainder of the wine into our glasses.

"She was such a beautiful girl, Toni. Black hair and violet-blue eyes."

"What happened to her?"

"In sixth grade she moved from Catalpa to Indianapolis, but it might as well have been the moon. She was so sweet."

Toni seemed lost in thought as she gazed into the blood-red roses.

"They smell like raspberries," I said.

"They do." She got up and put on her raincoat.

"God, Toni, I don't know what I'm doing. I feel like I'm going crazy."

"Don't do that." She lifted the window high and stood beneath it, looking at me. The smell of new leaves and grass wafted through the open window.

"Don't do it," she said. "Don't go crazy."

"I'll try not to."

"When you leave the bastard, we'll get an apartment together."

She pulled me under the window. Her eyes were closed and her mouth opened before she kissed me. I turned my face away. She was smiling at me.

"That is how *I* would kiss Paul, chérie."

"Who is it?"

"Sarah from upstairs."

I opened the door. Sarah was wearing faded striped overalls and carrying a newspaper.

"Hi. Come on in."

"I'm sorry if I got you out of the shower—but it's Echo."

"She's in here with me."

"Well, she escaped somehow. I tried to get her, but she wouldn't come to me."

"Oh, shit! Do you know where she is now?"

"She's under the house. Laurie, she has a cat head in her mouth!"

"A cat head! Oh, my God! She killed a cat?"

"She must have found it. It's been dead for a while, and I'm afraid it'll make her sick."

"Is it a skull?"

"Mostly, but there's still some black fur on it. It looks kind of like it's petrified." Sarah glanced down at the roses. "I remember a long time ago, I think it was in *Life* magazine, where they showed pictures of these soldiers' heads they found petrified in a desert somewhere like Egypt or Israel. It looks like that. I thought we could wrap it up in some newspaper, but there's no way I can squeeze in there and get her." She leaned over and gently stroked one of the rose petals with her index finger. "These are so beautiful. You're really lucky, Laurie. I wish Pat was romantic."

Echo sat between two floor joists, her eyes glinting purple in the semidarkness. A dusty green corner of the garbage bag containing my Redouté book protruded from the earth beneath her right haunch. She wagged her tail, the cat head sideways in her mouth. Leaning into the dank coolness under the house, I could feel the sun warm on my back. Echo let the head drop and the dust fumed around it. When she jumped up to greet me, her breath was miraculously sweet.

The dry air in the hallway reeked of scorched eggs and coffee.

"I know Sonny will want it," Sarah said. "It's better for him to take it than let Echo get it back out of the trash. Maybe he'll trade us a couple of joints for it. That would cheer Pat up." She stopped in front of number 12 and knocked on the door. "Sonny's an artist. He draws the cutest little pictures of penguins, and he makes a ton of money. He works all night, so he sleeps during the day."

Sarah knocked on the door again, louder this time. "He should be up by now, though. Sonny's a little strange till you get to know him, but he's really pretty nice."

The door opened and a thin man in his late twenties stood before us. His shoulder-length, dyed-black hair gave his skin a grayish cast. He was wearing a long black velour robe covered with lint.

"You can't stay long, Sarah. Somebody's coming over." He smiled, showing small, dull teeth.

"Oh, we won't stay, Sonny. We just brought you something."

The walls inside were painted deep red; on the wall facing the door, a red neon lightning bolt blinked on and off. Dozens of glass jars filled with formaldehyde were arranged in rows along the tops of dark wooden bookcases. They contained a coiled snake, a lizard with its slender limbs drawn tight against its body, a large, folded bat, and other putty-fleshed, indistinguishable creatures. Through the grimy windows, the bright greens of the budding branches outside appeared murky, like the cloudy, yellowish solution in the jars.

Sarah and I sat down on a lumpy black sofa. A low-slung slab of redwood stood in front of us, so thickly varnished that it looked as if it had been dipped in Karo syrup. Sonny perched on the edge of the redwood table and lit a joint.

"So how's Pat?"

"All right, I guess. He started working at the zoo. He doesn't like it much."

"Doing what?"

"Making fake rocks."

"Fake rocks, huh?"

"Yeah. They use chicken wire and concrete. They're renovating."

"I heard. What you got for me?"

Sarah handed him the newspaper bundle. "Laurie's dog found this under the house. We thought maybe we could trade you for a couple of joints."

"Done." Sonny opened a tarnished silver cigarette case on the table and took out two joints rolled in black paper.

"I've never seen black papers before," Sarah said.

"Well, maybe you never looked hard enough." A broad smile twitched on his mouth when he held the cat's head out in front of him. "It's fucking great!" he said.

I got up and walked into a pale blue hallway. Six chrome-framed pictures of penguins hung in pairs at eye level along its length: penguins in parkas, penguins at the beach, penguins flying shiny little airplanes, all meticulously rendered in bright inks and watercolor. I waited until Sonny had rewrapped the cat's head before I came back to the sofa.

"I told you he was pretty nice," Sarah said. "Just about everyone I've met in New Orleans is pretty nice. Don't you think so?"

"Yeah, I guess. I really haven't met that many people."

Sonny shook his head and smiled, his gray eyes suddenly bright. He took a hit on his joint, chuckling.

"What's so funny?" Sarah asked.

He laughed out loud.

"Tell us," she said.

"Well, this gay guy I knew—I kind of knew—was always whining about how he didn't have any friends. Seriously, every time you would see him he'd be pissing and moaning about it. It got to be a real drag." He looked at Sarah. "Have you ever met Martin?"

"I don't think so."

"Well, Martin lives in the same building in the Quarter as this guy did. He says that one day there was this terrible stench in the hall, and when the police broke the door down, the guy had hanged himself." Sonny laughed and took another hit on his joint.

"What's so funny about that?" I asked.

"Well, here's this guy who kills himself because he doesn't think anybody cares about him—and they don't even find the bastard for *two* fucking weeks. Nobody called. Nobody came by. Don't you see? It's fucking great!"

"We better get going," Sarah said.

Sonny walked us to the door, and the slapping of his bare feet on the floor reminded me of the sound of Jim's feet on the deck of the *Brigand*.

"Hey," he said to me. "Does that rough-trade hunk in the first apartment belong to you? The one with the old Corvette?"

"That's Laurie's husband."

"He's perfect. I've seen him through the window, washing his car. You really should buy him some engineer's boots."

"Well, thanks for the swap," Sarah said.

"No, thank *you*, honey, for my new kitty."

TWENTY-FIVE

It had happened the way Gerald said it would—spring had come in the night. The buds on the branches had turned into leaves, and azaleas bloomed fuchsia and lavender in gardens and on the meridians up St. Charles. The air hung warm and humid, as filmy as a bridal veil, blanching the colors everywhere, even the deep leathery green of the magnolia leaves. In the mossy cracks between the bricks of the sidewalk, ants struggled to build their hills higher, a sure sign, according to Vita, that it would rain.

Maurice was back in Vita's corner, an untouched piece of pecan pie in one hand, his face tear streaked.

"And he just got promoted," Maurice said.

"I know, baby. I know. Let me think. . . ." Vita picked him up and set him on top of her counter.

"What's wrong, Maurice?"

"It's Bigtimer," Vita answered. "He got sent back to jail."

"Oh, no! what happened?"

"Seems Mr. Vonn E. White's wallet got stole—he's the man in charge of the Phoenix House. Anyway, Mr. Vonn E. White dreams up a way to find out who did it: he lines up all the boys and numbers them one through twenty-four."

"Bigtimer was seven," Maurice said.

"I don't understand."

"He lines them up, baby. Lines them up, numbers them, and then he starts calling out numbers, and he keeps calling them

247

out till someone 'fesses up. If he calls your number, you get sent back to jail. The next boy confessed—number eight, but Mr. Vonn E. White sent them all back just the same, all the ones he called."

Maurice started sobbing, and Vita held him close to her. Looking over at me, she said, "Baby, go behind the bar and get him a cold drink." She kissed Maurice on top of the head and eased him down to the floor. "Now I hope you don't plan on deserting us, Maurice. We're going to be needing you around here more than ever."

"No, ma'am," Maurice said. "I'll be available."

The phone was ringing when I opened the apartment door. It was Toni.

"What are you doing?" she asked.

"I just now got in. What're you doing?"

"Well . . ." She paused, and I could tell that she was smoking a cigarette. "I have had it, chérie."

"Had it with what? Billy?"

"Yes, Billy. I have had it with him, and I have had it with that bitch Connie, too. I'm moving out."

"You are? You're sure that—"

"Of course I am sure. That is why I called you. I want you to move out with me. I have already found us a place up on Carondolet."

I felt the pulse quicken in my temples. "This is pretty sudden, Toni."

"The boys going offshore—that was sudden, too. And we should move before they get back. You know—"

"I know, I want to, it's just—"

"Just what?"

"It's just that it's so sudden, and I don't know what Jim will do when he finds out."

"When he finds out, so what? We won't let him near. We'll call the police if he tries to see you. I told the landlord we would speak to him today. Andy and I will be by in half an hour, so be ready."

"Who?"

"The kid. You met him in Dauphine's. Why don't you wear a skirt? And oh, bring all of your money. We can always borrow the rest of whatever we need from Andy."

As I hung up the phone, I saw Jim's diver manual lying next to it on a cardboard box. I picked up the manual and opened it to a dog-eared page. Suddenly two words, hard-edged and clear, lifted up from the page, suspended: "Air Embolism." I sat down on the floor and began reading.

Bloody, foaming sputum at the mouth resulting from rupture of lung tissue, disorientation, paralysis, unconsciousness, seizure, cessation of breathing. . . .

I turned the page.

Body Squeeze: bleeding from the eyes, nose or lungs, swelling of the tissues of head, neck, and shoulders; bleeding through the skin and mucous membranes, loss of consciousness . . . condition can force upper body into the helmet space. . . .

I closed the manual. I could see the gold Saint Erasmus medal around Jim's neck glinting in the jerky orb of light around a welding station, somewhere under millions of tons of dark water, somewhere far away. I stretched my bare legs out from under my skirt. The bruises on my knees were almost gone.

Andy parked the van on a sloping street in front of a white, vaguely Italianate bungalow.

"Wait in the car," Toni said. "If we take the place, we'll all go out and celebrate." Andy nodded and turned up the radio.

Behind the house, against the heavy green sky, poplar and pine trees swayed in the wind. It started to rain as we climbed the steps to the porch.

"Why don't you let me have the money now?" Toni said. I gave it to her. She put both her hands on my shoulders.

"You know you are shaking. Try and stop it—I hate it, cheríe."

"I hate it too."

"If you are that afraid, couldn't you instead go back to your mother's house to live?"

"I'm not going to. I can't. I think I'd rather die than let her know how bad this all turned out. I've worried my mother sick, Toni. I really have. She didn't want me to come down here in the first place, but Jim convinced her that if we moved to New

Orleans and tried again, he would keep his promises. He even made out a list of things that he was going to change in himself. My mother believed him, finally—she wanted to believe him. I believed him, too. Was I ever stupid!"

"He's the one who's stupid, and you don't have to see him anymore," Toni said, ringing the doorbell. "You shouldn't be shaking—you should be dancing."

A stocky man, fiftyish, with a crew cut rinsed rosy-auburn opened the door. He was wearing a black turtleneck sweater and a greasy black blazer with brass buttons.

"Mr. Kouro? I'm Antoinette Kane. We spoke on the phone. This is my friend, Laurel Wellman."

"Hi," I said. "It's nice to meet you."

"Very well, then—let's go right up." He spoke in a low monotone with a foreign accent I couldn't place.

Toni and I followed Mr. Kouro up the winding stairs. The walls were papered with black-and-white caricatures of film stars, but the features of Jean Harlow, Clark Gable, Laurel and Hardy, Greta Garbo, Rudolph Valentino, and James Dean were so crudely distorted and their head sizes so different from one another that they looked like posed corpses in various stages of decay.

Above the second-floor landing was a large leaded window depicting either Saint Roch or Saint Lazarus, an old, lesion-covered man surrounded by skinny dogs. One of the dogs, which must have been gray, to judge from the lone remaining foreleg, had fallen out, and the resulting hole had been covered with contact paper meant to resemble stained glass. I could hear Mr. Kouro drawing the musty, damp air through his large nose.

On the third floor, he unlocked the door to number 10. The linoleum floor inside was pale green, shot with gold glitter and overpainted with streaks of gray enamel to give the appearance of marble. In the far corner, a queen-sized mattress splotched rusty brown lay askew its box springs; and on the wall next to it, dried brick-red splatters spread fanlike toward the ceiling. A fissured onyx-and-marble fireplace stood along the wall to my right. The blackened hearth was heaped with hundreds of cigarette butts.

"No cooking in the rooms and the bathroom is down the hall," Mr. Kouro said.

Toni walked quickly over to the mattress and squatted down. "What is this red stuff all over the wall, Mr. Kouro?"

"The last tenant was a painter. He just moved out yesterday— that's why the place is still like this."

"Good. I thought maybe someone was murdered here."

"No, no one was murdered here. I'll let you girls look it over. Remember, I need first and last month's rent in cash. That's two hundred dollars. Come down and tell me what you decide." He closed the door.

I sat down on the mattress. "Well, what do you think?"

"It's shit," Toni said. "It's small, it's dreary, and of course the light is bad. But it is cheap." She stared unblinking into my eyes. "I think we should take it. We can decorate it and make it decent—and remember, the boys will be back soon."

"But don't you think Mr. Kouro is pretty strange?"

"Landlords are all scum, Laurie, one way or the other."

"Yeah, I guess so."

"You know, Laurie, if we threw away these disgusting blinds, the light in here would not be that bad. If we take this place— think of it—you will be painting pictures again. And I will, too. I used to paint before I left France—at the Sorbonne."

"You never told me that."

"It's true." Toni sat down next to me on the mattress and began rubbing my shoulders. "So we will both paint again. There will be canvases everywhere—and music and fruit and flowers."

Smiling, I turned to face her. She was very close to me.

"I know how miserable you have been," she whispered. "It is in your eyes and your face all the time. Tell me, have you painted anything since you married?"

"No. I can't believe it, Toni. I haven't done a single drawing since I married Jim."

"Of course not, chérie. Who could? An artist needs tranquil hours—days and days to dream—and you cannot dream if you live with fear. Men like Jim are born to keep a dreamer from her work. They keep you off-balance all the time. Do you see what I mean?"

"Yes."

"You do not paint because you make your own survival the piece of art—your very life—and you work on that masterpiece moment to moment, second by second, until at last you are finished—until you leave him or you are dead. Do you understand?"

I nodded.

"Good. Don't worry. With a little peace and the grace of God, you will paint again. Maybe better than before. And if the boys try to see us here, we will call the police. Right?"

"Right!"

"That's what I want to hear, chérie. So now we go down and give him your money."

On the porch Toni and I stood close together, shielding the match from the wind as we lighted our cigarettes. Heavy metal music blared from the van. Andy waved to us and I waved back. The rain had stopped, and in the greenish yellow light Toni's face looked waxen.

"So how long were you at the Sorbonne?" I asked.

"Not long—a few months."

"Why did you leave? Didn't you like it there?"

"Yes, I liked it, chérie. But that damn professor's wife . . ." She blew a short gray stream of smoke into the wind. "Let's get out of here and find someplace to celebrate. Where would you like to go?"

"How about Que Sera's?" I said.

"No, we always go there."

I thought for a moment. "How about the Dream Palace? I've never been."

"I know, chérie! I will take you to the Emerald Isle. It's up near Tulane. Andy won't mind. I want you to meet Chris. He is the bartender there. Don't shake your head, Laurie. He is beautiful, and I think he likes me. Wait until you see him. I showed him to Molly once, and she said he was a Perceval."

The man behind the bar at the Emerald Isle was tall and muscular, with symmetrically waved blond hair. He was wearing a dark green softball uniform.

"Hey, Toni!" he called. "You didn't bring your dog with you."

"Not this time."

We sat down at the empty bar and Toni introduced us to Chris. Andy bought the first round. He and I had bottles of Guinness stout and Toni ordered blackberry brandy and a shot of vodka.

"Molly was meeting Jayne at Delacroix's and wanted us to join them. But I didn't feel like it, Laurie."

"Jayne? Are you sure? I don't even think she drinks."

"I am sure that Molly said Jayne. I met her once at Rosario's, remember?"

I didn't remember, but I nodded anyway.

"Molly says Rosario owns Delacroix's, too," Toni said.

"A regular whore hangout," Chris said, pouring Guinness into my glass. "It's pretty fancy, though. They serve breakfast all night."

Toni drank three blackberry brandies and three shots of vodka within fifteen minutes. After that, a bleary somberness seemed to overtake her, and she turned around on her stool, her back to me. Andy began nuzzling and kissing her hair. I moved to the end of the bar and ordered another Guinness. From the adjoining room, I could hear the light, cheerful bells of pinball machines. Chris pushed a bowl of pretzels in front of me.

"You seem lonely," he said, smiling. Toni was right; he was handsome—but with the blank, flawless features of male models in fashion magazines.

"Not really. I was just thinking."

"Yeah, I could tell. What're you thinking about?"

"Oh, I'm just trying to figure out some things."

"Well, I wouldn't try too hard. Nothing ever gets figured out. Take me—I thought I had that electric baseball game all figured out, and then I got three strikes, one after the other. Boom, boom, boom. just like that." He leaned over the bar. "Hey, my softball team is throwing a party tonight. It's already started. I'm cutting out of here in another hour. You girls should come and party down with the Green Machine."

"Where is it?"

"My house." He took out a ball point pen and started drawing a map on a cocktail napkin. "You guys really should come. Five kegs of Dixie and a ton of food. You name it, we got it."

"Well, it sure sounds good, but I'm pretty tired, so I kind of doubt I'll make it. But thanks. Could you give me some change for the cigarette machine, Chris?"

"You shouldn't smoke." He even scowled like a male model— as if he were angry at nothing.

"I know. I'm going to quit sometime."

"I quit three years ago," he said, handing me my change. "Better watch out, darlin'. You might get the black pack."

"What's that?"

He laughed. "You mean you never heard of the black pack of cigarettes before? Well, I guess I first heard of it when I was about thirteen—whenever it was I started smoking. The black pack was supposed to be so poisonous that if you smoked even one cigarette, you'd die. Us kids were always scared of getting the black pack. My brother said sometimes you didn't even have to smoke one to die—just getting the pack would kill you."

"You know something, Chris?" I said, standing up. "I think I've already had the black pack."

Chris leaned over the bar. "Hey, Laurie," he said in a low voice. "I want to ask you something. You're good friends with Toni, right?"

"Right."

"Well, tell me, then, what's she doing with that kid? He isn't her boyfriend, is he?"

"No, they're just friends."

"Sure don't look like they're just friends to me." He walked away, shaking his blond head.

When I came back from the ladies' room, Chris was serving four new customers, two men and two women. Toni had turned around on her stool as if she were waiting for me, her eyes wide open and glazed. She stood up before I could sit down.

"You whore! You little whore!"

"Toni, what are—"

"You whore!" she said again, even louder.

"Toni! What the hell are you doing?" I whispered, hoping that she would lower her voice.

"You are! You are a whore, Laurie!"

I could feel everyone staring at me. My face was burning hot.

"I can't believe this! You're drunk, Toni. I'm leaving." I walked over to the pay phone near the front door, but Toni ran after me and jerked my arm to keep me from putting any money in the slot.

"Who are you calling?"

"I'm calling a cab! I'm not staying here!"

"Oh, yes, you are! You are staying!"

Tears were streaming down my face.

"You bitch," she screamed.

"Come on. Let's talk outside," I said.

She grabbed my hand and pulled me out the door. A mist hung over the street, obliterating the cars and houses. It was as if we were the only two people in the world.

"You are a whore, Laurie! Do you have to have Chris, too? Of course you do, you slut!"

"Shut up! Shut up and listen to me! What in the hell is the matter with you? I don't want him! Besides, he's as dumb as a stick."

"Yes, you do! I heard him inviting you to a party!"

"All of us! He invited all of us! What did you want him to do, with Andy hanging all over you? Don't you know I would never want anyone you wanted—especially not Chris. I would never do that."

"Liar! You have! You already have!" She slapped me hard across the face. "He would have loved me! You could see that and you still had to have him!"

"Stop it! What are you talking about?"

"The General loved me, you fucking bitch!"

This time I turned when she slapped me and her open hand hit the side of my head. It was as if someone had cupped a flaming seashell against my ear. Toni was crying now, her hair swinging in her face. A long thread of saliva hung from her lower lip.

"I hate you! I hate you, you lying bitch!" She slapped me again. I slapped her back as hard as I could, harder than she had hit me. She lost her balance for a moment but she didn't fall. Then she slapped me again. I made a fist, and when I hit her, she fell down on the sidewalk and stayed there.

"Don't!" Andy rushed up to me.

"You'd better take her home," I said, but it didn't sound like my voice.

Andy helped Toni to her feet and she buried her face against his neck. "Come on," he said as he lurched past me.

"No, I'll get a cab. And you tell Toni I want my deposit back! You tell her to drop it off at Rosario's!"

I was shivering, and I couldn't seem to move. Andy pulled the van up in front of me. He rolled down the window.

"Last chance," he said.

I looked back at the Emerald Isle. Chris's blurred face was

framed in the bar window. A "Guinness" sign was glowing green on and off over his head.

"I can't. I don't want to talk to her. I don't even want to look at her."

He turned up the car radio.

"Come on. Hop in. She's out cold."

TWENTY-SIX

I stood on the porch calling Echo. The sound of the traffic on
Prytania was muted, broken occasionally by the melancholy
cooing of a mourning dove. From the porch roof, dead
brown vines and new yellowish green tendrils swayed in the
warm wind; through the shifting spaces between the vines I
could see curvilinear fragments of clear colors: the bright blue-
green of Commander's Palace, the powder blue of the almost
cloudless sky, the translucent emerald shade of the tree leaves,
and the lime-white wall of Lafayette Cemetery.

I couldn't see Saint Michael—Commander's Palace hid him
from my view—but I knew that he was there, just beyond the
cemetery wall. The sun slipped behind a cloud, and the shadow
across my face made me feel as if Saint Michael were standing
in front of me without his sword or scales, his stone flesh washed
with dew and sparkling, his white-veined arms outstretched.

The sun flickered once more on my face, and the front door
opened. Pat came out on the porch, tucking his orange T-shirt
into his jeans; Sarah followed, combing her wet hair.

"Isn't this a beautiful day?"

"It really is. The prettiest day in ages," Sarah said, putting the
comb into the front pocket of her striped overalls. "The humidity
has finally dropped."

"Come on, Sarah. We don't have time to shoot the shit." Pat
slapped her on the behind and started down the steps. "Dumbo
here forgot to set the alarm."

"I'm sorry, Laurie, but we're running late. Are you looking for Echo?"

"Yes. I can't leave for work until I find her."

"She's probably upstairs crapping in the hall," Pat said. "Come on, Dumbo. Let's go!"

"We do have to get going, Laurie. Why don't you check around in back? Echo seems to like it there."

She was lying near the opening that led beneath the house. Purple stars of nightshade blossomed beside her. A bare human foot, gray with encrusted dirt, emerged from the opening. It was followed by a head of long, greasy black hair. Sonny rose to his full height. He was wearing his black robe.

"Hello, Sonny."

"Hey there, Laurie. How you doing?" He smiled, squinting in the sunlight. "You'll never guess what I found under there. Take a look." He held out my Redouté book, the cover splotched with powdery white fans of mildew.

"After I got that cat head from you, I started thinking maybe there were some other goodies under the house, so I dug around a while and found this. It was in a garbage bag. Can you believe it? It's not as good as the head, but it's not exactly shit, either."

The book felt cold and damp in my hands. "Was there anything else in the bag?"

"Nah, just a picture of some blond babe in bed wearing a big glove. I threw it away."

"Sonny, do you think I could have this book? I mean, can I buy it from you? I'm kind of broke right now, but I could pay you later. " Echo was licking my hand.

Sonny knitted his thick eyebrows. "Nah, I want to keep it. But I'll tell you what I'll do." He took the book, opened it, and ripped out the last page. His long fingernails were caked with fresh earth. "Here, you can have this. After all, you did turn me on to the place. It's a fucking gold mine under there."

"Thank you," I said, staring down at the Thornless Rose.

After Sonny had gone, I went through the opening, crouching to keep from soiling my white blouse. After a few moments, I made out a crumpled ball of paper in the half-darkness, and I knew that it was my picture of Beauty. I took it out into the sunlight.

She was ruined. Tiny fissures marbled her face, one deep crack cutting through her eyes where the white paper had separated

from the glossy surface of the print. I put the Thornless Rose
and the photograph of Beauty in my purse.

Before I left for work, I carefully placed the two pictures, with
Beauty on top, on the living room floor and covered them with
the heavy diver's manual.

A bush of white lilacs overhung the fence that ran along the
back of Rosario's parking lot. I broke off a twig from a drooping
branch; and when I held the flowers to my face, I remembered
bringing lilacs to my mother one evening in late spring when I
was a child, the tap water frothing up to the mouth of the glass
vase in her hands, the lamplight glinting softly off her wedding
ring as she set the vase on top of the piano.

Sometimes, after my father had left for his evening walk, she
would sit staring down at the piano keys, her thin legs crossed
and tanned beneath her, her white cotton crew socks baggy
around her perfect ankles, her eyes unblinking, beautiful and
dark. When she played, the notes rolled out into the cooling air
in a melancholy, slow cascade, and I would press my cheek
against the window in the delicate blue twilight—the leaves
trembling on their branches outside, the dried shocks of long
grass by the walk, the dying light like fire at their tips, and the
notes a gentle bath of sorrow all around me, over and over again,
until it was dark.

Whenever I thought of those long evenings, I could never
recall my mother's made-up melody, I could only feel it, and
when I asked her to play it for me a few days before Jim and I
left for New Orleans, she looked away and said she'd forgotten
it, too.

Molly was alone in the kitchen. She wasn't wearing any makeup,
and her eyes looked small and puffed and red. Even though the
back door was propped open, the kitchen was sweltering.

"They're lovely," Molly said, looking at the lilacs I had picked.

"They're for Vita. What's wrong?"

"You didn't show up at Delacroix's last night, did you?"

"No, I was too tired."

"I didn't make it, either." Her lower lip was trembling. "But
Toni said you two were definitely coming."

"I'm sorry," I said. "I guess I didn't know it was that definite."

Her eyes filled with tears. "They beat her up, Laurie! They beat Jaynie up."

"They what! Who did? Who would beat her up?"

"Bloody whores beat her up. I still can't believe it."

"Is she all right?"

"She's in hospital. They hurt her quite badly—I just spoke with her roommate. She says Jaynie has two black eyes and cracked ribs, and they broke her nose, Laurie, her pretty nose. Can you believe they broke her pretty nose?" She started sobbing.

I put the lilacs down on the steel counter between two stacks of dirty dishes and took Molly in my arms. She felt like a child. When I kissed her cheek, I saw that her right earlobe was still raw and inflamed.

"She had such a pretty nose, Laurie." Her shoulders shook under my hands.

"I know. I know she did. But why would they do that to her?"

"Jaynie was all dressed up. I—I told her to wear something sexy," Molly said, moving away from me. "She had on lots of makeup, and you know she doesn't even use it. She was wearing her new contacts, too. They thought she was trying to take over—move in."

"You mean they thought she was a prostitute? *Jayne?*"

"I know; it's so sick it's almost funny. We should have met her, Laurie. We fucked up."

"Oh, God, Molly. Where is she?"

"St. Charles General. Her parents drove down from Baton Rouge this morning."

"Well, that's good."

"Yes—but she's not coming back to Rosario's."

I didn't expect it to happen, but after I had given Vita the lilacs, I started to cry. She wiped the tears from my cheeks with the side of her hand and smiled.

"Why, thank you, baby. Just what we need in here—pure white flowers." She leaned her face, eyes closed, into the lilacs and sniffed. "Heavenly—nothing like white flowers to take away the dark. And I got something for you, girl. Something sweet that come clear from Mexico." With her free hand, she reached deep into her apron pocket and brought out a letter. "Here,

baby. You can read it right here in private. I'm going to see if
I can't locate me a vase."

As soon as Vita walked away, I tore open the thin airmail
envelope.

Perla Preciosa (bonita muy estimada)
Hot food, hot nights, cold in the secret heart-cave, then
I remember us, the burning kiss and impossible fire. Our
love is the piercing ray, the strong sword through all imped-
iments—when I return (as soon I shall) let's leap, hands
tight together, off the terrible wheel of the world we know.
Whatever might get broken, let's keep the perfect promise
of our love.
Somebody trashed my nonchalance and now I'm prattling
on under my new sombrero like a cheap romance. I'll say
it plain: I love you, only you, and somehow we belong.
Meanwhile, watch the skies; and keep all this mushy clap-
trap sub rosa.

Forever,
Lee

I leaned against Vita's steel refrigerator, so cool against my
back that it made me shiver. I imagined a pink ribbon, suspended and undulating; slowly it formed itself into a word—
Forever—shimmering behind my eyes, and then suddenly collapsed upon itself and disappeared.

"Nothing is forever," I said aloud. Vita was standing in front
of me, but she turned away as if she hadn't heard. She set a
cylindrical silver vase on the counter, lifted the dusty silk orange
blossoms from it, and dropped them into the garbage can beside her.

"I've wanted to get rid of these for a long time, but Buddy
didn't want me to. He still ain't talking to you is he, girl?"

"No. I don't care, though."

"I can see something's bothering you, baby. You want to tell
me about it?"

"Oh, Vita, I was thinking about Jim. I loved him so much
once, and now—"

"Jim your husband?"

"Yes. I fell in love with him the first time I saw him, when I

was fifteen, and I knew someday we'd be together. I just knew
it."

"That's the way it was with my first one, too, sugar. Sometimes
you just know them things."

She opened the door of the walk-in refrigerator and took out
an enormous jar of maraschino cherries, unscrewed the lid, and
tossed three cherries into her mouth.

"I used to walk by his house every day, praying that I'd see
him—even just for a second. I remember standing in front of
his house one day—it was such a beautiful day, so sunny and
warm—and suddenly it started to rain, great big drops of rain,
and—"

Vita frowned. "Was there any clouds in the sky?"

"I don't remember any. It was so weird, Vita. The rain only
lasted a couple of seconds, and then everything was sunny again.
Anyway, I was standing by this square of fresh cement in the
sidewalk, and the rain made little marks—little pockmarks—all
over it. It was like the rain was frozen there forever. And as I
looked down at that cement, this feeling came over me—a
strange, kind of wild feeling that I'd never had before—and I
knew at that moment someday Jim would marry me."

"We got a saying: 'If it rain and the sun is bright, that's when
the devil beats his wife.' "

"I never heard that before." The silk orange blossoms, their
petals blighted with dried coffee grounds, lay at the top of the
garbage can where Vita had dropped them. "Oh, Vita, I want to
be free again! I think I want that more than anything else in
the world."

"Now, baby, I didn't say this to you before 'cause I was scared
I might hurt your feelings, but I know you ain't been like this
always. Since the first time I saw you in this kitchen, I thought,
what a beautiful little thing she is, but it was like a shell of a
beautiful thing. Like a seashell you find in the sand you think
to yourself it's beautiful—and it is—but what you can't know is
how beautiful that seashell was when it had something alive inside it. Something living in it and moving it through this world.
You can't know that. And I can't know you before, but I have a
strong feeling, baby, that you was different."

"I was, Vita. I was different before I knew Jim—knew what
he was really like."

She moved closer to me, holding the lilacs down by her side.

"You got to leave him." She put her other hand spread-fingered over my heart. "That something is still there, baby, and you got to find it again—find it and let it lead you away."

"But I'll never get away from Jim, Vita. If I left he'd chase me down and beg me to come back like a little boy and beat me or anybody in his way if I wouldn't come back. He told me he would rather see me dead than be without me. He said, 'Don't test me, Laurie. Don't make me famous.' "

There was a faint smile in the corners of Vita's mouth.

"Well, then," she said, "you *do* got a problem." She put the lilacs in the vase and wiped her hands on her apron. "Now on that day you was just talking about, was there a rainbow?"

"No, I didn't see one."

"You sure?"

"Yes."

"All right, girl, you go on in the other room now and get busy with your sidework. But first I want you to write your husband's name on a piece of paper. You got a little piece of paper in your purse?"

"I don't know. I'll see." I felt inside my purse and pulled out two lipsticks, a ballpoint pen, and a book of matches. I held the matches out to her. "I could write it on these."

"No, it's got to be clean. Your own paper. Got to be *your own* paper."

At the very bottom of my purse, I felt a small triangle of paper; as I handed it to Vita, I noticed that two of the edges were yellowed.

"That'll do fine. Just write his name on it—print it real clear. His whole name. Then give it to me and go help the Queen of England out front."

While Molly folded napkins, I collected the salt shakers from all the tables. I had refilled only six of them when the salt ran out. I went into the kitchen for another box.

Vita had her back to me. She was wearing her leather-patch jacket with the white rabbit collar.

"What do you want?" She didn't turn around.

"I ran out of salt, and there wasn't any at the waitress station."

She jerked her head toward the shelves above her.

"God, right in front of my eyes. I guess I'm not exactly thinking straight."

She didn't answer me.

"It's so hot back here, Vita. How can you be cold?"

"Sometimes I get deep-down cold, like a stone on the bottom of the lake. This is just one of them sometimes." Even her voice was cold. She reached up for the box of Red Cross salt, and I saw a fish covered with black pepper on the counter beside her. The fish was lying on a sheet of tinfoil: it had been slit lengthwise and then sewn together with thick black thread.

"What's that for?" I asked.

Vita moved sideways, blocking my view of the fish. When she turned around, she looked old, her face unsmiling and drawn, lips slightly blue.

"Girl," she said, handing me the box of salt, "don't you got nothing better to do than hang around back here?"

As I walked to the dining room, I saw Gabriel standing in the parking lot. A gentle breeze stirred the branches of white lilacs behind him, ruffling his lavender shirt. When he saw me, he smiled and waved. I waved back. And then suddenly I remembered it—the melody my mother had played, her beautiful eyes dark in the blue twilight and I smiled.

TWENTY-SEVEN

The porch window was open, the curtains flapping softly. Through the lace, I could see flickering gleams of color—pink, white, and deep red. I stepped into the living room and closed the window.

There were roses everywhere: on the mantel, the floor, in loose bunches on the sofa, even on top of the cardboard boxes. Their fragrance permeated the room—heady, pristine, ineffably delicious.

"Lee," I whispered. "Is it you?"

Jim appeared in the bedroom door, holding Echo in his arms. He was wearing his dark-blue suit and a blue knit tie. His shirt was the same blue-white as his eyes. Everything about him was different. His eyes seemed larger and softer, and his lips were curved slightly in a sad, sweet smile. I knew before he spoke that his voice would be different, too.

"Look who's here, Echo—Mom's home. I told you she hadn't left us." He kissed Echo on top of the head and put her down on the floor. "Now you play for a while. Mommie and I want to talk."

Holding his hand near my face, he hesitated for a moment and then gently stroked my cheek with his thumb.

"Don't touch me!" I said, moving away.

His eyes filled with tears. "Oh, baby. I'm so sorry. I just want to talk to you—about what happened the other night."

"I don't want to talk about it. There's nothing to say."

"Don't say that, Laurie. Please."

"It's over between us, Jim. Completely over."

"Oh, no. Please don't say that, little girl."

"And don't call me little girl. I hate it."

With the window closed, the odor in the room was overpowering, dizzying. I felt as if I were being smothered under a blanket of roses, like the guests of Emperor Heliogabalus. I pushed aside a bouquet of white sweetheart buds and sat down on the sofa. Jim knelt in front of me and took my hand; his hands were trembling.

"You like the roses, though, don't you, honey? From now on, I'm sending you roses every day." Over his shoulder, I saw the diver's manual between two vases filled with blood-red roses.

"Where are my pictures? You threw them away! You threw them away, didn't you?"

"No, no, I didn't, Laurie. I put them in the other room. But honey, you can't leave things on the floor like that. The dog will pee on them."

I pulled my hand away from him.

"Laurie, I love you so much—more than anything in this world. I've done a lot of thinking on this last dive, and I want to tell you that you've been right all along. I mean, about me having a problem. It's real hard to admit you got a problem you can't take care of yourself, but I'm admitting it now. And I know I can't tackle it alone. I need you, honey, to help put me back on the right track. I've even been making out a new list. I got it here in my pocket. Let me show—"

"I don't want to see it, Jim. I don't care. I just want you to let me go."

"You don't mean that, baby."

"Yes, I do. I do mean it. I'm not afraid of you anymore."

"Jesus, Laurie, I know I've made you scared to death of me, and I would do anything to take all that away—just wipe it clean out of your mind. It breaks my heart, honey—it really does."

"Jim, we've been through this so many times before. God, I can't breathe in here!"

After Jim had opened the window, he came back to the sofa and stood over me. Echo lifted her head and sniffed the late-afternoon air. Jim put out his hand to smooth my hair and then quickly brought it back to his side.

"Jesus, just looking at you—you're so beautiful. I know I don't

tell you that enough, but you are. The most beautiful girl I've
ever seen—like this rose." He picked up one of the white roses
from the sofa and put it in the lapel of his jacket.

"Why are you so dressed up, anyway?"

"Because you and the kid here are going out on the town
tonight. I told Billy that he and Toni could come with us. I said
that we'd probably go to the Dream Palace. I remembered you
always wanted to go there."

"I don't want to go anywhere with the Kanes."

"God, I was hoping you'd say that—that you would just want
to be with me. And we don't have to go to the Dream Palace
either if you don't want to. I'll take you anywhere you say—
Pascal Manale's, Brennan's, Antoine's—we could even go to
Commander's Palace. Anywhere you like—you name it. I just
want it to be a perfect night—the way things were before we
were married. Remember?"

"They can never be like that again, Jim. Never. Too much
has happened."

"I know I've treated you bad, honey. I had no business taking
those Quaaludes the other night, but I guess I let the pressure
get to me. Honest, Laurie, I didn't know what I was doing. But
you'll see. Things will be different from now on. I'm not even
asking you to forgive me. I'm just asking you to go out tonight
and forget all the bad shit for a little while. Even if you hate
me right now, don't you think you deserve to have a perfect
night? God, yes, you do, and I'm not asking you to believe me
when I tell you I've changed. I know it's something I have to
prove to you."

"You don't have to prove anything to me, Jim. I just want you
to let me go. You promised me that if things didn't work out
down here, you wouldn't stand in my way—that you'd let me
leave. All I want in the world is for you to keep that promise.
Don't you understand?"

"I understand, Laurie. I really do. I'm not going to rush anything. I realize I have my work cut out for me proving to you
that I've changed. But I know I can do it. And you were right
about that garbage-bag idea, too. I met this diver, Cal Yates, on
the barge, and I asked him what he thought about it, and he
said you were right—it wouldn't work. Turns out it's physics.
Honey, this guy really knows his shit. Hell, he was down in Key
West working side by side with Mel Fisher for three years. And

he told me how to raise the *Tres Puentes*! He knows fucking everything about diving for treasure. Everything! He even knows how to go about getting backers. Big-money people. Forget that bitch, Mrs. Beausoleil. I called her up when I got back to town, and the butler said she was in Europe—the lying limey bastard. I drove by her house, and sure enough, there was her car in the driveway—that big purple Rolls, bigger than life. Hell, Cal knows people that can buy and sell her. Anyway, I just wanted you to know you were right, honey: the garbage-bag thing won't work. I'll explain it all to you at dinner." His hand trembled as he lighted a cigarette.

"I couldn't sleep at night on the barge, Laurie. All I could think about was you. I thought about how it was before things got bad—when we first met in Catalpa, I thought about making love to you. Remember how I used to kiss you? I'd start down at your toes and kiss every inch of you—for hours—and you'd be smiling. If you'd let me, I'd make love to you that way right now. You wouldn't have to do a thing—just lie there and relax—and try to smile. I could make you feel so good, baby." He leaned forward to kiss me, but I turned my face away.

"I know how you feel, Laurie. Believe me, I really do. I lost my temper again after I promised you that I never would. And I'm not going to ask anything of you until I prove myself to you." Suddenly he smiled. "I can't believe it! I almost forgot. I bought you some presents! Come on back to the bedroom. Come on, honey."

A wooden drawing table stood in the middle of the bedroom; on top of the table were Redouté's Thornless Rose and the photograph of Beauty.

"This table is top of the line," Jim said. "Isn't it something? I know you've had a lot of trouble getting back to your artwork, and I wanted to do something to show you I'm behind you a hundred percent. I never said it before, but I think you paint real good. Oh, I bought you some oil paints, too. Every color I could find."

About fifty silver tubes of paint were lined up in a straight row on the bed; carefully laid out above the row of paints was a black cocktail dress adorned with a black velvet rose at the waist.

"Not too shabby, huh? I didn't know what kind of dress you liked, but the salesgirl said I should play it safe and buy you a black dress. She said every girl should have a little black dress.

I had her try it on, and it fit her fine, so I thought it would be okay. She was about your size. Maybe you could wear that necklace I bought you with it."

"No, it would be too much."

I walked over to the table and picked up the Thornless Rose; the lower right hand corner was missing.

"You tore my picture! Why did you tear it?"

"I didn't tear it, baby. All I did was pick it up off the floor. It was already like that. I looked for the corner, thinking maybe I could glue it on for you. I tell you, though, I can't figure out why you'd want those pictures. They're in pretty bad shape."

"Because they're beautiful—that's why."

He smiled, shaking his head. "I swear, you're the strangest little girl—I mean, young lady. God, Laurie, I love you so much. You'll see. Oh, that reminds me. Your mother called this afternoon. She said she'd called a couple of times before, but we weren't home."

"What did she say?"

"Not much. She just wanted to know how we were getting along. I said we were fine and that you loved New Orleans— and I told her about Echo. I said we were going out for dinner, but we'd call her as soon as we got back."

"Is that all you said?"

"Well, I said we'd had a few little problems, but that everything was okay now. And it will be, Laurie. I promise you." He held up his hand, palm toward me his fingers together. "Now you go ahead and change into your new dress, and I'll call Kane and tell him that we want to be alone tonight." He glanced at his wristwatch. "We'll have to hurry, though. I rented a limo, and it should be here in about twenty minutes. So where's it going to be, honey? It's up to you."

"The Dream Palace."

"Then the Dream Palace it is." He flicked his cigarette through the open bedroom window.

TWENTY-EIGHT

"Just drop us off at the corner," Jim told the driver. "We'll walk the rest of the way."

"Sir, I have an umbrella for you. If you'd like—"

"That's okay, man. I don't think we'll need it. Thanks, anyway."

I shivered and Jim put his arm around my shoulders.

"Cold, baby? Don't worry. I'll keep you warm."

As we turned the corner, I caught our reflections in the glass door of a phone booth, and I moved out from under Jim's arm.

Set back about fifty feet from the street, the narrow three-story house was flanked by two giant weeping-willow trees. A black wrought-iron fence with gilded spear-shaped tips ran along the perimeter of the yard to the walk and up either side of a flight of steep pink marble stairs. Both the stairs and the fence ended at the front door. Above the door glowed a peach-and-blue neon sign: *DREAM PALACE*. The last three letters of *PALACE* were burned out, and the bright lilac paint of the house had chipped away in places, leaving livid bluish scars. A line of people extended about halfway down the stairs.

"Are you sure you want to go there, honey? It doesn't look that nice, and there's a lot of people waiting."

"Yes, I do. I still want to go."

We got into the line behind a middle-aged, platinum blond woman wearing a pale-green dress.

"Well, sweetheart, it's your night. Besides, you can never tell

270

how good the food is just by how a place looks—not in New Orleans." He pulled out his pack of Winstons and held it out to me. I shook my head.

"Are you quitting?"

"I'm quitting a lot of things, Jim."

He took the unlighted cigarette from his mouth and put it back in the pack.

"You're right. I have to quit. They'll kill you."

The line moved up a few steps. Most of the people were drinking out of translucent plastic to-go-cups, resting them on the wide railing bolted to the fence.

"I would have made reservations, but they don't take reservations at the Dream Palace," Jim said. He stared up at the lavender-gray sky. "God, it sure was a beautiful day, wasn't it, honey?"

"It was a lovely day," the platinum blond woman said, smiling down at Jim from the step above us. "A perfect day."

Jim squeezed my arm. "It'll be a perfect night, too."

"Well, aren't you an optimist?" the woman said. "I hate optimistic men." She took a long drink from her plastic cup. "Deep down they're always bastards."

"I'm sorry," a silver-haired man standing beside her said. "We've been in line for a long time, and Fay is a little—"

The line moved again, and the silver-haired man grasped the woman's elbow and pushed her up to the next step, spilling her drink. As Jim moved away, the white rose from his lapel fell onto the step near the splattered red wine.

"Hey, don't do that! Not when I'm talking to an optimist." The woman leaned down and picked up the rose, her fingers glittering with diamonds. She pressed the bud to her nose. "May I have it?"

"Sure," Jim said, shrugging.

"Maybe you'd better slow down a little bit, Fay," the silver-haired man said. "Can't you see that they want to be left alone?" He whispered something to her, and she turned abruptly and faced the door.

"I had to give it to her, Laurie," Jim said in a low voice. "What else could I do? Besides, she stepped on it before she picked it up."

"I don't care, Jim."

"Well, I didn't want you to get any wrong ideas." He took out his pack of cigarettes again, looked at it, and put it back in his shirt pocket. "You know, honey, I've been thinking a lot about the *Sheherazade*."

"I don't want to talk about that."

"No, wait, baby. Listen. I know it was stupid buying the boat when we owed so much money, but you're going to be happy when you hear this. Cal Yates wants to buy her! He's been looking for a pleasure cruiser and he's interested—I mean, *real* interested. I may have to come down a little in price, but here's the beauty of it, Laurie: Cal says he might use her for the *Tres Puentes*! Don't you see, honey? This way I'll have the cash to take you on a real vacation and still raise the *Tres Puentes*! We could leave in a couple of days. How does Jamaica sound to you? Negril. You'll love it there—the water's so blue and the sand is like sugar. We never did have a honeymoon. Hell, we never had a real wedding—in a church, I mean. We could get married again! God, you'd look like an angel in a white wedding dress."

"Jim—"

"Okay, okay, honey. You don't have to decide anything tonight. It's just something to think about. What do you say you and the kid here have a drink while we're waiting? What'll you have?"

"I don't really want a drink."

"Come on, Laurie. You have to have a drink. We're celebrating. Besides, it'll warm you up, and you're shivering."

"All right. I'd like a tequila—Cuervo Gold—with Rose's lime juice and a splash of soda."

"I never heard of it. Does it have a name?"

"It's called Heaven."

"Heaven. I like that. You wait, baby. I'll show you some real heaven later tonight. I'll be back in a flash."

Jim went up the marble stairs, his back militarily erect under the dark-blue suit, his legs moving with the effortless grace of a cat; people in the line, both men and women, watched him as he passed. He stood in the foyer and lit a cigarette before going into the restaurant.

The sky was turning a deeper shade of lavender, and the branches of the weeping willows threshed wildly in the wind, the undersides of their leaves gleaming silver. In front of me, the golden spear tips of the fence glinted in the lights from the Dream Palace, their brightness gradually fading the farther away they were from the building.

A light-haired man wearing glasses was climbing the steps. It was Lee, his face very tanned now, a pink ribbon of sunburn running across his cheeks and the bridge of his nose.

For a moment everything around me seemed absolutely still—and then I was in his arms, my head pressed against his rumpled white linen jacket. He was kissing my hair.

I moved away from him. "When did you get back?"

"About an hour ago. I drove straight here from the airport."

"But how did you know I was at the Dream Palace?"

"Toni told me."

"*Toni* told you?"

"Yes. I phoned her to find out where you were. Let me look at you. You're even more beautiful than I remembered—a vision in black. My Dark Lady."

"You're looking pretty well yourself, Lee. Mexico seems to have agreed with you."

He looked down at the steps. "I hope you understand, darling. I just had to go away for a while and sort things out—for both of us. And then the other morning in Palenque something happened to me. I was reading Lorca—*Ansia de Estatua*, I think—when I suddenly realized that my heart was filling up with smashed wings and silk flowers, too. It was a real epiphany, Laurie. The moment I read that poem I knew I had to be with you." He tilted my chin up and began kissing my face. "Oh, Laurie, I've missed you so much—so very much."

"Don't. Please,"

"Why? What's the matter?"

"I don't want you to stay, Lee. Jim will be back any minute. He just went to get us some drinks."

"Are you saying that you're going to stay with him?"

"No, that's not what I'm saying. It's over between Jim and me."

The platinum blond woman tapped Lee on the shoulder.

"You have a light?" The cigarette in her mouth moved up and down as she spoke.

"I'm sorry. I don't smoke."

"No, I can see that you wouldn't. Where'd that optimist go? He'd have one."

"Come on, honey," the silver-haired man said. "Turn around. I have one right here."

Lee took my hands in his.

"I don't understand, Laurie. If it's really over, what are you doing here at the Dream Palace with him?"

"I'm not sure I understand it myself. I guess maybe because it's the last thing I have to do."

"I don't—"

"Please, Lee, you really have to leave now. A lot of things have happened since you left for Mexico—a lot of bad things."

"But I had no way of knowing. You never told me anything about your marriage, and I didn't feel as if I should ask you. You said you didn't love him—and I guess now it seems idiotic, but at the time I thought that was all I needed to know. I had no idea how things really were until tonight when I spoke to Toni. You could have talked to me, darling. I thought you knew that."

"But you weren't even here!"

"I'm here now, and I'm very serious about you, Laurie—about us. It's the first time I've been really serious about anything in my entire life. I love you, and I believe you love me, too."

"I don't know. I thought I did. But it's hard to believe in this white-knight stuff anymore—all of the old whirlwind Harlequin romance bullshit. It hurts too much. Ever since my father died, I've always looked for someone to save me. But maybe no one in the world can save you except yourself."

"Let me try, Laurie, let me try. We can go as slowly as you want, however long it takes."

Jim was pushing his way through the crowd in the foyer, holding the drinks above his head.

"Oh, God. Lee, you've got to go *right* now."

"But when am I going to see you again?"

"Soon. I'll call you."

"Well, the optimist is back," the platinum blond woman said. "Did you bring me a drink, Mr. Optimist?"

"Not this time. Here you go, honey." Jim handed me my drink. "I tasted this Heaven stuff and it's not bad. Did Toni turn you on to this?"

"I don't want to stay, Jim. I'd like to go home."

"Go? But I just slipped the hostess a little something to call us next. Why? What's wrong? This guy isn't bothering you, is he?"

"Oh, no! No, he's not bothering me. I just don't want to stay. I don't feel well."

Jim set his drink down on the railing. "Hey, wait a minute.

I know you. You're the jerk-off who was eyeballing my wife at Rosario's."

"Excuse me," Lee said. "But I'd like to have a word with Laurie."

"Well, pal, the only word you get to say to Laurie is good-bye! So say it now and then get the fuck out of here!"

"Please, Jim!"

"No, goddamn it! I mean it, buddy—get the fuck out of here!" He pushed Lee hard on the chest.

"Stop it, Jim!"

"Then you tell him to get lost!"

"No, I won't. I'm through taking your orders. I'm leaving with him." I took Lee's arm and started down the steps.

"You're not going anywhere, little girl."

"Oh, really? Well, just watch me."

"You can't leave me! I saved your life—*twice*—that time with your mom and once when you tried—"

"So what if you did save my life? You've been taking it ever since!"

"Well, you owe me. Remember what I said about owing—"

"I don't owe you a goddamned thing!"

"You tell him, sister!" the platinum blond woman said. "They're all a bunch of bastards."

"Keep out of this, Fay," the silver-haired man said. "I'm going to get us some drinks, and I want you to behave yourself while I'm gone. I mean it now, hear?"

Jim was staring at me, his eyes mirrored and silver-blue in the waning light, his hair whipping in the wind.

"I'm not forgetting this, Laurie. All right, pal, I gave you your chance!"

"Fine. That's what I've been waiting for." As Lee started to take off his glasses, Jim hit him in the face.

Lee's head jerked back but he remained standing, his glasses askew. Blood dripped onto the front of his white jacket from a cut on his cheek.

Fay grasped Jim's arm and shook it. "Hey, handsome, play fair!"

Jim jerked his arm free. "Get the hell away from me!"

"Are you all right, Lee?" I asked.

"Yes, I'm all right."

"Then let's leave. Right now."

"You're not going anywhere, Laurie! And neither are you, rich boy!"

"Don't, Jim!" I yelled, but it was already too late. Before I could move, Lee was lying on the step, his smashed glasses beside him. I picked up the glasses and clutched them tightly in my hand. "Goddamn you, Jim!" I knelt down beside Lee. "Did he hurt you? Do you think you can get up now?"

"You're not leaving me, little girl!"

"Oh, I just love strong, handsome men!" Fay said, throwing her arms around Jim's neck and pushing herself against him.

"You old whore! I said get the hell away from me!" He tried to tear the woman's arms from his neck but she held on tightly. "Goddamn you, let go! Fucking let go!"

And then for a long moment it seemed that she was flying, her arms flailing up and down, her dress a pale fluttering blur above Jim's dark back. Then the pale blur disappeared and a woman in front of me started screaming.

Fay was lying outstretched on top of the fence. Blood bubbled from both sides of her open mouth, streaming down her chin and neck and over the front of her dress. She arched her back, her hands slowly beating the air; then a long shudder ran through her body.

The voices around me seemed to be coming from an immense distance.

"Jesus! Call an ambulance!"

"Is she dead?"

"Is she dead? Look at her eyes!"

"Somebody call the cops!"

"Take her off the fence! Please, please, will someone please take her off the fence!"

"Don't move her. You're not supposed to move her!"

Stray raindrops fell on my arms and face. I sat down beside Lee on the step. Jim was standing above us, head bowed, arms held stiffly at his sides, his fingers flexing slowly in and out of his palms. The crowd formed a half-circle behind him. It started raining harder. I could smell the earth, dark and pungent, and the candy-sweet fragrance of wisteria. Blood was trickling down my arm and I opened my hand. In the lavender glow of the neon lights the shards of broken glass glittered like tiny stars.